Call of the Lion

He went over what he'd heard on the news again, about Iraqi troops massing on Kuwait's border – and realised that he was onto something important. After all, he, Mkhulu and Sonny had broken into a house and killed several men, yet there'd not been a single report of it on the news. By chance he'd also stumbled on the blueprint for a weapon that could alter the balance of power in the Middle East. He sensed that the Iraqi wanted the development of the Supergun kept very quiet. And that could hardly be because he was using it to launch satellites.

Paul contemplated his drink – and then looked up into the eyes of Dr Torr. The doctor was sitting opposite him with his girlfriend, Dr Fassbinder, drinking a Guinness. Paul shifted his eyes away and felt his pulse racing. He couldn't believe his luck.

He felt the engery coming back and the excitement. He was going to follow this thing right through to the end.

Christopher Sherlock is the author of three bestselling novels, *Hyena Dawn*, *Night of the Predator* and *Eye of the Cobra*. A former advertising copywriter, he lives in Johannesburg.

CHRISTOPHER SHERLOCK

Call of the Lion

Mandarin

A Mandarin Paperback
CALL OF THE LION

First published in Great Britain 1993
by William Heinemann Ltd
This edition published 1994
by Mandarin Paperbacks
an imprint of Reed Consumer Books Ltd
Michelin House, 81 Fulham Road, London SW3 6RB
and Auckland, Melbourne, Singapore and Toronto

Copyright © Christopher Sherlock 1993
The author has asserted his moral rights

*The characters, organisations and situations
in this book are entirely imaginary
and bear no relation to any real person,
organisation or actual happening.*

A CIP catalogue record for this title
is available from the British Library

ISBN 0 7493 1324 2

Printed and bound in Great Britain
by Cox & Wyman Ltd, Reading, Berkshire

*To anyone who ever had a dream
and had the guts to make it come true.*

But great men tremble when the lion roars.

William Shakespeare,
Henry VI, Part II

Prologue

The wind blew softly up the valley. Paul readjusted the rucksack on his back and scanned the tops of the hills. Then he felt the new beard on his face. He lifted up the battered video camera and viewed the valley through the lens.

There was an uneasy stillness about the place. It had taken him many weeks and an incalculable number of risks to get there. The excitement mounted as he stumbled quickly down the mountainside till he reached one of the many paths that ran into the valley. He never took the roads, of course; the roads were too dangerous.

The woman was still on his mind – a memory from months before. No, she was more than that. Far more than just a memory. At first her dark eyes had avoided his, as was the custom in a society which regarded women as inferior to men. It was her eyes that had first attracted him, for her face was hidden beneath the yashmak, the black veil that covered her mouth and nose. He had felt the sexual electricity, indefinable and inexplicable, a magnetic attraction that drew them irresistibly together. In that one first fleeting glance, he knew she understood how he felt.

Later, the veil had been removed, and their bodies had melted together. He had always been attracted by Nomadic peoples, who lived for the day, and she had been hardened by a life of war. She made love with an intensity and a passion that took him by surprise. She exhausted and excited him. Being close to her was a constant process of discovery. She was wild, and knew how to trigger responses in him that most women, including his wife, Helen, had never even imagined.

His father had always hated Helen – told him from the very beginning that the marriage would never work. Goddamnit, his father had been right. The old man had a way of seeing through things that was almost terrifying. Paul realised that was the gift he'd inherited from him – the ability to expose, to cut deep into the heart of people's consciousness.

He thought about Helen again. Yes, he was still married to her – but he needed passion in his life, and Helen didn't fulfil that need. He was coming back for this woman. There could be no more compromise, he had filled too many years with compromise. Not in his reporting, of course, but in his private life – and that was what mattered most in the end. He had compromised his relationship with his father to try to appease Helen – he hadn't seen the old man as much as he should.

His thoughts returned to the Kurdish woman. Her husband, one of the leaders of the Kurdish Peshmurga guerrillas, had been killed in action the year before. Widowed, she was alone with her child. Paul was all too aware of her bitterness. She had loved her husband. God – now she loved him.

At first he'd told himself he had to come back to Halabje because he needed more background material. For . . . ? Well, he'd convinced himself that he needed more footage of the Kurdish guerrillas and their women, for his documentary. Of course, he'd been lying to himself. In his heart he knew the real reason why he was coming back.

He wrapped a scarf around his head, which, with the battered leggings and scuffed shoes, made him look like a typical villager. He spoke the language. That was how he had survived for so long.

In a way, he supposed, languages were his curse. At first, younger and more naive, he had been proud of his command of words and his ability to speak more languages than he had fingers. That ability had come from the old man, too. It was what had got Paul where he was now. God, it had been such a long, long journey.

His mind was made up. He was going to take this woman. His daughter Charlotte would have to understand. He and Helen were finished. He only had one life, and Helen had already taken enough of it.

He knew he'd also had enough of making documentaries about wars – just as, years before, he'd known he'd had enough of being a soldier. He knew in his gut that this Kurdish woman was the right choice – it was love without compromise.

He should have smelt the fires by now, maybe heard the occasional cry of a child. But instead there was nothing except that soft breeze. Again he wished he was armed, an old wish. He never carried a gun – his weapon now was his camera, he was a film-maker, not a soldier.

He slowed down, something about the place was bothering him. Survival was a matter of responding to instinct, and a sixth sense told him to beware. He breathed heavily – the video camera and the pack weighed over forty kilograms, one hell of a load. He looked out across the valley and realised what it was that was bothering him. There was a strange smell in the air. He couldn't quite define it.

He moved on cautiously, working his way down into the valley. Further down, he realised that things were just too quiet. He dropped his pack, and took out a couple of extra videocassettes. A little further on, he came across the bodies of sheep and cows. Detached, he started filming. When he'd got enough footage, he pressed on.

The body on the path caught him by surprise – a shepherd, lying dead, face-down.

Jesus Christ – this can't be happening.

He filmed the corpse and then walked on, moving towards the outlying streets of the town.

He saw more bodies. They were lying in the street – they had died as they ran to escape. Their faces looked wax-like, a peculiar detachment in their eyes.

He was moving more slowly now, hyper-aware, keyed up with adrenalin, the buildings unfolding before his eyes as he explored the dusty confines of the heart of Halabje.

A sound made him swing round – the squeak of a bucket hanging above a well, swaying backwards and forwards in the breeze. What the hell had done this? Nerve gas? Cyanide? Mustard gas?

He moved past the grey walls of the concrete building that was the mosque. He peered inside to see where the shell had struck into the heart of it, blowing a gigantic hole in the centre of the first floor. Bodies were lying everywhere.

He wished he had never returned to Halabje.

The bundle was lying in the centre of the road, unmoving. It looked vaguely familiar. He dropped the video camera and staggered on. He coughed as the breath burst from his lungs and he sprinted forward.

No. Jesus Christ. No!

He dropped over her, looking at the still open mouth and the wide, dark eyes. The child was wrapped in the folds of her gown, pressed next to her.

'No. Oh God. For God's sake, *no*!'

His words lashed out against the dull walls of the houses and were lost in the stillness. He lay on the road, in the dirt, hugging her to him, sobbing uncontrollably.

'Bastards. Bastards.'

He staggered back and picked up his camera. He filmed the scene, determined to produce the most damning documentary he had ever compiled.

Slowly the reality of it crept over him. All over the town were bodies. Nothing was left alive. A strange smell lingered inside the houses.

He came back to her and the child. He thought of the good times they'd had, the child's body convulsed with laughter, the innocent little face filled with joy. He couldn't remain detached from this; he was involved, through the death of this woman and her child; he had loved them, and they had been taken away. Now they were just memories that would torment him till he died.

In the distance he heard the noise of motorised vehicles, and the instinct that had kept him alive for so many years persuaded him to grab his camera and rucksack and melt inside the closest house.

He lay down by the front window facing the street, and felt something next to him. Another body. He retched uncontrollably, and then gathered his nerves as he focused his camera and checked the videotape was running.

It seemed to take an eternity for the vehicle to come closer. He hardly breathed. He thought of lying in the grass at Klaw, watching the lions on the sand next to the waterhole. Another time, another world; it was so long since he had been back there.

6

The noise of the vehicle was louder – he searched for it in the distance through the camera lens. Then he caught sight of the armoured car as it moved into view. Soldiers in the back, at least sixteen of them. Shit!

Now the whole procession of vehicles in convoy swung into view. Iraqi soldiers. Slowly they passed the mosque, Paul willing them on. But the lead vehicle pulled up in front of the body of the woman and child lying in the centre of the road, and a lean man, dressed in a perfectly cut uniform, jumped in one swift movement from the passenger seat. There was a two-day stubble on his handsomely chiselled face, and his lips, though refined, had a certain sensuality about them. His eyes were dark and restless.

Paul kept the camera rolling; the noise of the motor winding the tape on seemed unnaturally loud in the stillness of the house.

The lean man had a swagger-stick which he occasionally beat against his left thigh. From this, and from the Piaget on his right wrist, Paul noted that he was left-handed. His nails were perfectly manicured and his hands had clearly never been used for manual labour.

Paul kept filming. One cassette finished. Automatically he loaded in another.

'Search the huts!' the Iraqi commander ordered in Arabic.

The troops disgorged from the vehicles behind and disappeared into the buildings on either side of the dusty road. Paul felt his pulse beating. It would only be a matter of time before they found him. He looked around the room and saw a wooden trunk. A possible hiding-place . . . the only hiding-place.

He heard a scream in the distance, and one of the soldiers dragged a young boy by his hair from one of the huts. Paul kept the camera rolling.

The boy was thrown at the feet of the commander, who rubbed the top of his lip with the forefinger of his left hand.

'Take off your clothes,' he ordered.

The boy stripped, and the commander walked around him, striking his buttocks hard with the swagger-stick.

'Kneel.'

The boy obeyed, and the commander drew out his pistol. He pointed the weapon at the lad's head and pulled the trigger. The boy pitched forwards with the impact of the shot, then lay at the commander's feet, begging for life. Paul saw that the shot had merely creased the lad's skull.

'Get in the back!' the commander shouted, then turned to his men – who were still laughing. 'Continue the search. If you find anyone else who has survived the cyanide . . . kill them.'

Paul reeled back into the room. Cyanide! The bastards were using cyanide! The smell of almonds . . . the silence. Suddenly it all made sense.

There was a noise behind him. He should have been in the trunk. Paul's eyes met those of the soldier who had burst through the door, and his nose took in the smell of rancid sweat. If there was a shot, the others would come. He had to stop the soldier from getting off a shot.

His eyes noted the rifle barrel being raised, and he swung his boot upwards, deflecting it, then smashed the camera lens into the soldier's face and heard the man sob. He gripped the soldier's lapels and dragged him forward, head-butting him and throwing him to the floor. But as the soldier fell, his leg shot upwards, catching Paul hard in the scrotum.

As Paul doubled up with pain, the soldier was on him, digging his thumbs into his windpipe. Paul gripped the soldier's little fingers and wrenched them back, hearing the bones snap. The soldier's grip slackened, and Paul shifted, toppling him and throwing him to the floor. Then he grabbed the man's assault-rifle and smashed the butt hard between his nose and his teeth. The soldier rolled over, dead.

The assault-rifle felt good in Paul's hands, very good. He worked the selector by instinct, and moved back towards the window.

The scene unfolded quickly before him. The commander got back into the passenger seat of the jeep, unaware of the fight that had just taken place in the nearby house, and the jeep moved forward, its wheels crushing the legs of the dead woman in the road, but missing the child. Paul lifted the assault-rifle to his shoulder, levelled the sight at the commander's head and curled his finger fondly around the trigger . . .

The memories came back. Angola. The atrocities, the killing. Then Vietnam . . . And the vow he'd made . . .

The tears ran from his eyes, the weapon shook in his hands. The commander moved out of the bead of the sight and Paul threw the weapon hard onto the sandy floor of the hut. And was bitterly ashamed.

The chill of the night air awoke him. The town was silent. He raised himself and looked out of the window. The scene had not altered. She was still lying out in the middle of the road.

Slowly he slithered out across the dusty ground, crawling towards the body. Instinct told him to be cautious. He moved up close to her and lay next to her like a lover.

His hands searched the folds of her robe and found the necklace he had given her, clasped tightly in her left hand. He carefully lifted it away. Then he removed her rings: no Iraqi soldier would add these to his collection of booty.

Then he dragged himself away, out of the moonlight and into the shadows. He quickly returned to the house, picked up his camera and rucksack, and then moved outside again.

He climbed soundlessly up the rocky mountainside and left the valley of death behind him.

As the sun rose, he placed the last rock on the grave where he had buried her precious things, and wept. It was all so useless. He could show his film on every television channel in the world, but it wouldn't bring her back. The valley and its people would be forgotten.

He took the videocassette from his camera. He placed it between the rocks, picked up his rucksack and walked away.

It was over.

Paul arrived home late in the evening to find the Johannesburg house in silence. He padded soundlessly across the floor and went to the main bedroom. He looked across at the large double bed, perfectly made-up. Where was Helen?

He walked into the living-room and looked at the photograph of Charlotte which was standing on a side-table – his only child. He hated himself for the lost years, boarding school, then university – he hadn't even attended her graduation ceremony. The passion with which she painted must have something to do with the love and attention he'd denied her as a child. He hadn't had time for her then, he'd been committed to his work, he still was. And Helen hadn't wanted her around the house. Strange, that a mother could feel that about her daughter.

Where was Helen?

He spun round as he heard a faint noise, and looked down the hall, seeing one of the other bedroom doors open. It was Charlotte. Dark hair, olive skin, and those fierce dark eyes.

'Oh, Dad. It's you . . .'

He held her close, loving her more intensely than he'd loved anything in his life.

'Charlotte, where's your mother?'

Charlotte remained close to him, silent. Eventually she spoke.

'She said to tell you she can't stand it any longer. She can't take waiting and waiting, wondering if you're going to come back alive. She wants a divorce, Dad. She's not coming back.'

Almost 10,000 kilometres away, in the MacLeod Group headquarters in London, Wayne MacLeod growled quietly, and scanned the sheaf of computer print-outs again. It was bad enough being left off the Queen's New Year's honours list, but this was a far harder blow.

He ran his long fingers through the mane of white hair that sprang low on his forehead and was always swept dramatically back. On the left of his forehead the white hair was shot through with a streak of black, giving him a distinctive, almost startling appearance. A tall, well-built man, he had been married four times; he was now unattached, and was often seen in the company of society beauties. His name was well-known – he was the daring and talented Scottish entrepreneur who had made his money in Africa. Of course, he was still involved in Africa, in fact he planned to develop the biggest private game park on the continent, straddling Botswana and South Africa.

He had thought his entry into the newspaper business, ten years before, would bring him respectability – that this and his conservation work would finally assure him a place in the British establishment. True, it had made him a public figure, but that was all.

He was a hardened Africa hand, on first-name terms with just about every black leader south of the equator. As his wealth and ambition expanded, he'd moved to London and become one of the major financial players in the city.

Money – that he had plenty of, but status, well, that was another thing. He'd discovered that the British aristocracy didn't easily admit outsiders to its ranks, especially not a crofter's son who'd spoken Gaelic before he could speak English. Wayne MacLeod wanted a title desperately, and he'd spent a vast amount of money entertaining people of influence in the hope of winning approval. They had accepted his hospitality graciously, but he'd rapidly found that they could not be bought.

Naturally, over the years there'd been attempts to cut through the web of mystery that surrounded his business dealings. A government enquiry had found him unfit for stewardship of a public company many years before – another direct slap in the face.

And now there was this . . .

He'd started buying shares in the House of Napier a year ago. By the end of May he'd almost wrested control from the major shareholders. Naturally, he'd sensed that the senior executives of the group were getting worried about the possibility of a takeover – but it wasn't so much the House of Napier he wanted, it was their flagship store, that epitome of British culture, Fentons.

Now the directors of the House of Napier had done a deal with a Kuwaiti oil magnate, Al-Jabir, and blocked Wayne's takeover strategy.

MacLeod ran his eyes over the computer print-out again. The whole deal with Al-Jabir had been done at lightning speed, out-manoeuvring Wayne at the last minute. Now he sat with a huge shareholding in the House of Napier, and no control. Already, after the takeover, the share price had dropped significantly. If he sold out, he would make a huge loss.

His left eyebrow began to twitch. Why had he allowed himself to be drawn into the takeover battle? Emotion, of course. He'd been a fool – chasing an elusive dream. Now he must concentrate on what he did best, the kind of behind-the-scenes dealing that carried big rewards.

Yes, he would continue to appear to be chasing a title, but in reality he was through with all that. From now on he would concentrate on expanding his assets and his power-base. The only common denominator in this equation would be the ruthlessness with which he pursued his interests.

Part I

Paul folded the telegram slowly in his hands and looked out of the window. He watched the dust blowing off a mine dump in the distance. The moisture welled up in his eyes.

Life could be a bastard.

The divorce had been tortuous. It had taken a whole year to negotiate, and he'd finally had to accept Helen's terms. She'd got the beach house in Cape Town and half his money.

His mind wandered back to the present, to reality – the telegram in his hand, the mine dump in the distance.

First the divorce, and now this . . .

He felt a dullness inside. He read the telegram again. His father was dead.

He was overcome with a terrible feeling of guilt. All the years with Helen, years spent away from his father . . . And now, just as he'd planned to go back to Klaw to spend time with him, his father was dead.

All his life Paul had been a fighter, but against this he couldn't win.

His father had been murdered.

A week before, Channel 4, the British TV station, had offered him the opportunity of shooting *Living Dangerously* for them, a new documentary series. He'd accepted the assignment immediately – he needed to get away from Johannesburg and the memories of the divorce. He'd been looking forward to it – but now he knew he'd turn it down. He would return to Klaw, to bury his father and to recapture something he'd lost years before.

Charlotte came in off the verandah. Her eyes were red with crying. She'd been very fond of her grandfather, the old eccentric with his love of the wild. Paul came up behind her and folded his arms around her.

15

'I'm not taking the Channel 4 job, I'm going up to Klaw. I want you to come later – to paint. No, that's not true. I want you to come because I want to make up to you for the years I never gave you – the years when I was always away. It wasn't your mother who was at fault, it was me. I can't make it up to her, but I want to make it up to you.'

She pulled away and looked him straight in the eyes. 'Do you know, that's what I've wanted all along. Of course I'll come – I'll help you make it work. I love you, Dad. I'll always love you.'

Dr Vance Torr looked across the water at the silver shafts of light radiating down through the long cloudbank, and held Maria's hand tightly. He would be sixty this year.

Perhaps, at last, he might achieve his life's ambition.

The surface of Loch Leosavay was perfectly still, and he could smell the smoke of peat fires in the air. Across the rocks to his left, the golden waters of the burn cascaded into the loch.

Here was isolation, an opportunity to work again on his designs. And he had the promise of major funding.

'What are you thinking of, my dear?'

Her accent was barely noticeable, but it was that precision of speech that had first attracted him to her the year before. Until then, women had always played an insignificant part in his life; his work had been everything.

'I'm thinking that at last I can achieve my dream. Everything is in place.'

Dr Maria Fassbinder looked closely at the face of the man she loved. He was twenty years older than she was, a man not in the least concerned with his own appearance, exceptionally tall, with a bulldog look about him. He was blunt to the point of rudeness, his formidable intelligence totally unforgiving. Had he been capable of a little more diplomacy, he might have been one of the United States' top military scientists; instead, he was a fugitive, shunned by those whose approbation he secretly longed for.

She had come here under orders, to get close to this man and know his thoughts. This she had done.

She held the sleeve of his overcoat tightly. 'Oh yes, you will do it,' she said. 'But on your own terms, Vance.'

16

He turned and looked up at the walls of Amhuinnsuidhe Castle behind them. 'With you, everything is possible. You are right. It will be a success, and on my terms.'

They walked back across the manicured lawn towards the castle, holding hands. Huge black clouds scudded across the sky and a faint wind blew up across the loch.

Paul stepped out of the Land Rover and looked beyond the trees, across the vast expanse of shattered land. He looked up at Bush Camp, the spacious wooden retreat with its thatched roofs, built on stalwart wooden stilts that lifted it high above the river bed. The lion-proof fence had gone. He studied the holes the staples had made in the wood and realised the fence had been down for a long time. That explained a few things.

The memories came flooding back. He'd grown up here. He remembered playing in the sand below the main deck. The smell of the bush brought back memories of his father – the love, the closeness, the intensity. Again, a wetness in his eyes. What the hell had he been doing with his life?

The conversation with the police in Francistown hadn't yielded much. They'd told him that his father had been murdered, along with two of his camp staff, by poachers who'd come down from the north. He understood the lack of emotion in the policemen: the Tuli Block was enormous, and although the area was policed, poachers could easily evade surveillance. His father had never avoided danger – he'd always confronted it. Paul was certain the old man had died as courageously as he'd lived.

In the early days at Klaw there'd been many guests, though they had stayed chiefly at the reserve's magnificent main lodge – Rock Lodge – built high on a rocky outcrop ten minutes' drive from here, with spectacular views over the bush. Then, as the old man pursued his research on the lion, he'd neglected the business side of Klaw and retired here, to Bush Camp, and there'd been fewer visitors. Then he had found a lion cub in the wild that had lost its mother to a hunter's bullet. He had reared the cub successfully and returned it to the wild. Since that time he'd rehabilitated many lions bred in captivity – an activity that had drawn a lot of flack from conservationists. Latterly the old man had been working on a film, to share his knowledge of the lion with a wider audience.

His father had lived for the lion, developing an almost telepathic understanding with the big cats.

Paul sat down in the hot sand and stared up at the main deck of Bush Camp. He had the gift, he knew it: an intuitive ability to communicate with lions, something his father had passed on to him. And now he knew he could no longer walk away from it.

He looked into the sand and the memories ebbed and flowed. Why had he chosen to remain with Helen for so long? Why had he never defied Helen's directive that Charlotte was not to visit Klaw? He'd been too caught up in his own career. He hadn't had time for anyone except himself. He'd neglected his father and his family. But at least he'd have a chance to put things right with Charlotte.

Paul got up, walked onto the deck and went into his father's study. He stared at the battered typewriter. Then his eyes moved up and took in the long line of lever-arch files. Next to them were round silver containers that held rolls of film. He'd forgotten about those.

He prized the lid off one of the containers and unwound the spool of 16mm film, staring at the black-and-white images. It was all documented on film – his father's work. He'd inherited the love of film reportage from his father, growing up with a 16mm movie camera in his hands. Now he realised the richness of this legacy.

His hand moved to one of the lever-arch files, and he pulled it out and opened it carefully. Inside were hundreds of foolscap pages of neat handwriting and drawings. He felt his hands beginning to shake. This was a distillation of the old man's knowledge, detailed observations of lion behaviour – everything that he had learned, perfectly recorded.

Paul moved back to the desk top, resting his hand on the carefully stacked pile of typed pages next to the typewriter. He looked up at the rear wall of the study, which was covered with photographs. He started to take them down. No point in drawing out the agony.

A black-and-white photograph caught his attention. An emaciated young man in his early twenties stared out at him – his father, just after he'd been liberated from the prisoner-of-war camp in Singapore at the end of the Second World War. The old man rarely talked about that; he'd written a book about it, though. The experience had given him a quiet fortitude and determination, an inner core of spiritual strength. That was what the old man had always said, that experience either made you or broke you.

There was another photograph of his father in England, just after the war. That was where he'd made his money, directing feature films.

Paul sat down in his father's chair and picked up one of the pipes from the rack to the left of the typewriter. The old man had been just sixty-five – he could probably have lived another twenty years. Paul squeezed the bowl of the pipe hard. Damn. He should have seen more of the old man. And now it was too late. Far too late.

There was a roar outside, and Paul felt his flesh tingle. He looked out of the window to see a lion looking up at him. Paul dropped the pipe.

Judah. So many memories . . .

It was over seven years ago, on a visit to his father, that he'd been introduced to Judah, the sole survivor of a litter of four abandoned cubs. Judah was one of the biggest lions his father had ever reared. Now, at over nine years old, he was in his prime.

Paul went out of the study and walked down the ramp to the sand. He fought back the momentary fear . . . It was a long, long time since had had been close to Judah.

The big cat leapt up, his giant paws resting on Paul's shoulders. Paul smelt the lion's breath – the smell of sweet hay. Judah moved back, and his front paws touched the ground. He nuzzled up against Paul's leg. Paul noticed that Judah walked with difficulty, probably because of an old wound sustained in a territorial fight. He sat down on the sand and the big cat moved around him, looking up at the main deck.

'He's dead, Judah. He's not coming back.'

The lion growled.

Other memories came back to Paul. Of Helen and his father having a row at the wedding. Of holidays spent in Cape Town

19

because Helen refused to see his father. Of wars, of people dying. Of suffering. He started sobbing. At forty-four years old, after witnessing innumerable wars and deaths, he still couldn't accept the cruelty of everyday life.

Judah lay down next to him, and in the fading light of day Paul's spirit hardened. He looked into the setting sun and realised he'd been living a lie – trying to deny a part of himself.

Paul felt no urge to move now, and remained in the sand, next to Judah. And somewhere in the darkness of the night, his spirit and the lion's became one.

He awoke in the first light of dawn, his clothes damp from the dew, the smell of Judah still in his nostrils. He caught sight of the lion moving slowly through the bush on the perimeter of the camp.

The early morning light had an almost surreal quality to it. The air smelt fresh, and Paul felt the vitality that had been lost for so long, returning to his body. He staggered across to the outbuildings, turned on one of the showers and stood under it, the cold water soaking his clothes, waking him up. Then he walked across to the tree where his father used to sit in the afternoon – the place where they'd buried him.

It was the distinctive, dull mechanical action of a rifle bolt being worked backwards and forwards that brought him to his senses. In seconds his mind put together the jig-saw of observations he had made since his arrival – the fact that his father's men had abandoned their huts, the uneasy quietness about the place.

He looked up – to see a man levelling a bolt-action rifle at him. It was a big-calibre gun, a .416 Rigby, an elephant gun. Then Paul put two and two together, his eyes running over the other two men in the distance, armed with AK-47s. These were poachers. Perhaps they were the men who had killed his father.

Everything was very still. Paul spoke softly, trying the Matabele dialect, guessing they were from across the border. He saw the poacher's eyes flicker, no doubt in surprise at the white man's command of the black man's language. The rifle barrel remained rock-steady.

20

'Why you sleep next to the lion?' The harsh voice was full of menace.

'He is my friend.'

The other men laughed. Dry laughter; chilly, and full of foreboding.

'Get a spade and dig yourself a grave, white man.'

Paul's eyes flitted across the scene, taking in the men, knowing that he couldn't level the odds. These men were fighters, too experienced to make mistakes. He moved slowly towards the huts, picked up a spade and returned, trying to buy time.

'Dig.'

He started half-heartedly – till the butt of an AK-47 crashed down against his neck. Paul stumbled across the earth, pain exploding in his head.

'Dig faster.'

The process of digging the grave seemed to last for an eternity.

'Into your grave, whitey.'

The rage was building in him now. These must be the bastards who'd killed his father. With a sick feeling in his gut, Paul jumped down into the grave, his feet sinking into the loose earth.

'Kneel.'

Close by, the deep-throated roar of a lion broke the stillness. Judah bounded forwards out of the bush and mauled the poacher closest to Paul.

'Aieee!'

There was the deafening noise of an elephant gun being fired. Judah rolled over dead.

Paul staggered out of the grave, knowing he was about to die but wanting to get close to Judah. Then another shot rang out, this time from further away.

The poacher holding the elephant gun sagged forward, clutching at his stomach, a red patch spreading across his dirty white shirt.

Paul was up and moving forwards. He saw Izak, his father's tracker, burst from the bush, a smoking 30–06 bolt-action rifle in his hands, aiming at the other poacher. But Izak was too slow, and as his old hands feverishly worked the bolt he was cut down, screaming, by a burst of fire from the man's AK-47.

21

Paul's feet bit into the earth as he sprinted forward, wrenching the AK-47 from the dead man's hands. Then he flew forward, finger flat on the trigger, tracing an arc of fire across the poacher. The man fell dead in his tracks, but Paul continued firing till the magazine was spent.

The air was redolent with the smell of death – warm blood coagulating in the hot sand. Paul instinctively dropped down, rolled towards the body, snatched the AK-47 rifle from it and levelled the sight across the horizon. There could be more of them.

The breath burst from his mouth as he prepared to fire again, but nothing happened. In the distance he heard death moans, and realised it was Izak – the man who had saved his life.

Paul dragged himself across the burning sand, still wary, till he was level was Izak's closely cropped grey hair. The dark, lean hand clutched at his own.

'Paul, you came back. I knew you'd come back,' the old man managed, blood dribbling from between his lips.

Paul raised himself up. Again he heard the roar of a lion in the distance.

'Oh Paul, that is Shiva, she is so beautiful. Shiva was with your father when he died. Now she has lost Judah, her mate, and must fend for her cubs herself. You must help her.'

Izak coughed, and Paul realised he was fading fast.

'You fought like a man,' he said.

Izak's hand tightened its grip on Paul's. 'Don't abandon what your father worked for, Paul . . . I have been protecting Shiva and Judah. They have cubs. The poachers tried to kill them – your father died this way, also trying to protect them.'

Paul felt cold. Why had his father not told him of the danger? The poaching must have got worse, far worse.

Paul looked down at the line of holes across Izak's stomach. It was just a matter of time.

'I knew you would come back, Paul. He longed for you.' The old hand would not release his own. 'I ask you two things.'

Paul looked into Izak's dark eyes. There was nothing he could refuse this man who had stood by his father to the end.

'You must protect Shiva and her cubs – there are more and more poachers. And, of course, there are the MacLeods.' The grip of his hand intensified. 'And you must find Mkhulu. He will help you.'

Paul recognised the name. His father had written to him often of Mkhulu.

'Mkhulu is a good man.'

Then the grip slackened and the old man rolled back, his mottled eyes closed forever.

Paul began to dig again, and the physical activity restored his determination to survive. He worked on without a break, and by the time the sun was high in the sky – so that the shadows lay directly beneath the tree – he was finished. One small hole and one large. First he buried Izak, next to his father's grave, then he turned to Judah. But there was no way he could lift or drag the lion's body by himself. Paul guessed Judah must weigh over four hundred pounds.

He took a length of rope from the Land Rover and wrapped it tightly around Judah's torso, then drove the vehicle up and wound the remaining end of the rope round the front bumper. He slipped the gearbox into low-ratio reverse and carefully backed up, dragging the body towards the tree. In a matter of minutes he had the lion's body in the grave he'd dug.

He worked slowly, covering Judah's body with soil. Suddenly he felt very tired – energy loss made him doubly aware of the fact that he had not eaten since the previous day. In the distance he heard the sound of a vehicle. The police must have finally responded to his call.

Sure enough, after another ten minutes a police Land Rover drew up behind Bush Camp.

Paul looked across at the bodies as the police officer walked around them. He had had to call in the police – there would have been problems if he hadn't. He didn't want to get on the wrong side of the Botswanan government because, after all, they had been reasonably sympathetic to his father's interests all his life.

'Mr Norton, you will have to remain in Botswana till we complete our questioning.'

The man was tall, with a huge beer-gut and a dullness in his watery dark eyes. Paul sensed corruption. Perhaps this man had been taking kick-backs from the poachers.

'Who are you going to question?' Paul replied quickly.

'All the witnesses are dead.'

The police officer looked irritated. Paul knew there was nothing much the policeman could do about the situation. Anyone could see what had happened.

'Izak opened fire on them. After that it was every man for himself.'

The police officer picked up the Rigby and carried it over to his car. No doubt to give it back to some other poachers, thought Paul.

'Going to kill some more elephant, Lithuli?' a voice enquired sarcastically.

Paul turned, to see a huge black man with an artificial leg attached below his right knee. The man had a hard expansive face.

Lithuli's face darkened. 'Stay out of this, Mkhulu.'

'No. You go away and leave this man alone. Otherwise there might be a few enquiries from the capital about how you managed to buy that Mercedes last year.'

Lithuli drew his pistol and levelled it at Mkhulu. Paul didn't see the slightest trace of fear in the black man's eyes.

'Pull the trigger, bastard,' Mkhulu said. 'Go on. No questions asked.'

Paul watched Lithuli's lips twitch. 'You're a madman, Mkhulu.' The pistol was returned to its holster. Lithuli moved away, speaking to Paul as he made for his car.

'Go, Mr Norton, if you want to . . . But remember, I have the right to call you back to Botswana for questioning.'

Paul watched the car drive away, leaving a dust trail as it sped down the long, winding dirt road.

Mkhulu hobbled over to him.

'You must be careful. If you stay here, the poachers may try to kill you again.'

Paul extended his hand. 'Paul Norton.'

'My name is Mkhulu. I have heard much about you. Your father talked about you all the time.'

Paul felt himself trembling. He had been a bastard. He should have come here more often.

'I'm sorry, Mr Norton.'

'Call me Paul, dammit. Izak was your grandfather?'

'No. I have no family. But I must bury him, along with these vermin.'

'What about the police.'

Mkhulu laughed dryly. 'Lithuli will not be coming back here in a hurry. He has the Rigby and the AK-47s. That was all he really came for.'

Paul gestured for Mkhulu to come up with him onto the deck. He poured them each a whisky, and they sat on the deck surveying the bodies below, flies buzzing around them in the heat.

'I want to protect Shiva and her cubs . . .' Paul said softly.

Mkhulu sipped at his whisky. A frown crossed his face. 'It's a noble idea. With Judah dead, they are vulnerable. But do you have the time to be with them?'

Paul looked the black man directly in the eyes. He saw power and suffering in those eyes. There was something about this man that he liked very much, perhaps the feeling that he could be trusted – a rare quality.

'All the time in the world,' he said.

The silence lingered. Paul remembered his promise to Izak that he would look after Mkhulu. But he knew that the last thing a man like Mkhulu would want was charity.

'How did you lose your leg?' he asked.

Mkhulu chuckled. 'Most white men like to avoid things – you confront them head-on. My leg? Well, I was close to your father and that meant being close to his lions. We were trying to help an old lion we'd found – he was starving to death. I suppose I got overconfident. He attacked and mauled me before your father could get off a shot.'

Paul weighed his next question carefully.

'So how do you feel about lions now? Are you afraid?'

As if in answer to his question, Shiva walked out of the bush and across the open ground. She sniffed at the corpses and went across to her mate's grave. Then she looked up and saw Mkhulu, and roared with pleasure.

Mkhulu hobbled down from the deck and she bounded up to him, resting her massive paws on his shoulders. Then they rolled together in the dirt.

Paul saw Shiva's cubs moving out tentatively from the bush. There was no doubt in his mind now about Mkhulu; the man was without fear. He would need Mkhulu if he was to protect Shiva and her cubs successfully.

Paul walked down and joined him, playing with Shiva and her cubs in the fading light of the day. Eventually the lioness and her young left them, and they returned to the deck, the air refreshingly cool with the coming night.

He and Mkhulu drank whisky steadily, talking of nothing in particular, taking in the atmosphere. Paul felt the alcohol gradually numbing him. It was a good feeling – letting the tension go, experiencing the sadness again at the death of his father.

'What are you going to do?' Paul asked Mkhulu softly.

'One-legged game rangers aren't in demand. I play the saxophone passably. I'll get work at a club in Gaborone.'

Paul nodded. 'I need a manager for Klaw,' he said. 'I haven't had any luck in finding one. I need a man who understands lions.'

'Such men are hard to find.'

Fahad ran his tongue across his upper lip. He stared at the naked white buttocks that were exposed to him. Her sobbing, her begging for mercy, spurred him on. He grasped the lariat tightly and brought it hard down against her flanks.

Again she screamed, and this time he lost control, his arm swinging backwards and forwards as he hit her again and again, her screams driving him to a frenzy of sexual excitement. Then he untethered her, grabbing her by her hair, turning her round and bringing the whip sharply down across her breasts. Then he was on her, extracting pleasure from her pain, her screams driving him on and on.

His body was covered in sweat by the time she passed out and he drew back, sated.

Fahad went back to his desk, rolled himself a cigarette using Turkish tobacco, and held it between his trembling lips as he lit up. He inhaled deeply, feeling the effect of the tobacco in his lungs, and breathed out slowly, watching the smoke fill the air of the darkened room.

It felt so good, so very good.

Weakness. Every man had a weakness. At least, as head of the Mukhabarat, Iraq's dreaded secret service, he had the opportunity to indulge his. His President had once held this position, and Fahad knew he had also enjoyed its unlimited power to abuse.

He settled into the chair behind his desk and lay back, letting his mind wander. He thought about the long, bloody war with Iran that had emptied Iraq's coffers – a war the United States had not discouraged them from fighting. What had they gained from this war? They had annexed very little new territory, but what they did have was an awesome military machine and a strong president.

The Baath Arab Socialist Party to which Fahad belonged had taken power in Iraq in 1968, ending the succession of coups that had followed the assassination of the king in 1958. Fahad thought about how they had purged the army, eliminating all political opposition. Then it had been the Kurds, always a problem; but they too had been suppressed.

Working with President Saddam Hussein, he'd established peace through terror. All opposition had been silenced. The country had become successful – medical facilities and new housing projects were developed. The Iraqi people had enjoyed a wave of new prosperity. And the rest of the Arab world hero-worshipped Saddam for rejecting the Egyptian peace treaty with the Israelis. Giving aid to the poorer Arab states had also drawn favourable support.

Now, with the fourth largest army in the world, comprising over a million men, five thousand tanks and some six hundred combat aircraft, they were in a position of power.

There was a low moan, and Fahad looked down at the bitch on the floor. She was groaning, crawling around in her own blood. He studied her with distaste and pushed the intercom button.

'Take the prisoner away.'

He lay back in his chair again as the guards dragged her out of

27

his office and took her back to the cell. He would get the doctor to clean her up, then let her get a bit better. She would talk, it was just a matter of time. She was a British nurse who'd been having an affair with a senior government official – he was sure she was a spy. He hadn't had her arrested, of course; that wouldn't have been diplomatic. Instead she'd just 'disappeared'. It was less embarrassing that way.

Fahad returned to his earlier thoughts. Who cared about a few Kurds? But he hadn't liked the US reaction to his suppression of them. It irritated him. Why didn't their neighbours, Jordan and Saudi Arabia, stand up against the US? The problem in the Arab world was the lack of unity. He and President Hussein had discussed this on many occasions. Now the time was right to change that situation. From a military standpoint, Iraq had never been stronger.

At heart, Fahad was a strategist – what President Hussein lacked in military knowledge, he made up for. Already certain projects, instigated at Fahad's suggestion and carried out with Saddam's blessing, were close to fruition. The men and the weaponry were in place and it would soon be time for a display of power.

Fahad cast his mind back across the events of the previous few decades to the Russian invasion of Czechoslovakia. Yes, you could do what you liked territorially – it just took power, nerve and timing.

The US had always favoured Israel. Well, Iraq would disguise her warlike intentions towards Israel for the moment – she would become an apologist for US policy. Then it was a matter of timing – they would strike Israel when the US least expected it. First they would use their massive army to embark on an expansion programme into the countries surrounding Iraq; the first, perhaps would be Kuwait, and then possibly Saudi Arabia. And by that time they would be so strong that they could ignore the US threat, and launch an attack on Israel that would gain the support of the entire Arab world.

But in case the US tried to interfere, he needed something that could level the odds. That something was already close to fruition.

*

Dr Anne Madison waited somewhat nervously in the sumptuous reception area of the inner sanctum of the MacLeod Group, while MacLeod's personal secretary, a very businesslike woman in her late forties, worked without emotion at her computer and handled phone calls with robotic finesse.

Anne looked at the paintings on the walls, all originals. She noted a Turner, an early Picasso, a Pollock and some others she could not put a name to, but knew to be of equal value. One way and another the reception area did look very like a modern art gallery – high, plain white walls suffused with natural light from a number of skylights.

Perhaps she shouldn't have arrived so early – she hadn't wanted to take the risk of being late for her appointment. MacLeod had paid for her flight in from America, so she felt under an obligation to fit in exactly with his hectic schedule. The meeting, the secretary had told her, would last for one hour exactly, and then Mr MacLeod would take her to lunch – for one hour precisely, no doubt, thought Anne.

She put down the fourth *National Geographic* she had paged through, glanced at her watch and then stared up at the skylight above her. Still another fifteen minutes to go. She'd felt intimidated even outside the MacLeod Group headquarters, a black monolith standing across the road from Hyde Park. The building was a landmark, particularly arresting because of the absence of any exterior windows. It appeared unmarked and impenetrable, apart from the small brass plate and the intercom. Anne knew that secrecy and confidentiality were hallmarks of Wayne MacLeod's operation.

MacLeod had an excellent reputation, both as a businessman and a conservationist. Anne was excited about the project he had outlined to her over the phone. Only a handful of people were being interviewed, he had said, all recommended by top people in the conservation movement.

'Dr Madison.' The voice made her jump and she looked across into the grey, steely eyes of MacLeod's personal secretary. 'Mr MacLeod would like you to come through.'

A black marble plinth set in the white wall slid back to reveal an open lift. Anne stepped inside, and stared at herself in the mirrors that covered the interior. The door closed and she felt herself rising. She looked at her face, checking the line of lipstick across her lips, and making sure that her long blonde hair was still neatly plaited and the black bow securely in place. She had chosen a formal, dark suit for the interview and a blouse with a high collar. She felt that this, with the dark stockings and court shoes, would make her look businesslike.

The mirror she was looking at herself in slid back, and she found herself staring at Wayne MacLeod.

'Dr Madison, a hearty welcome to you,' he boomed.

She blushed, and he took her outstretched hand and kissed it softly.

He was a big man, not fat but broadly built, with an expansive face. She had the feeling that nothing would ruffle him, that he was totally in control. The long mane of white hair, with its dramatic black streak, lay across his broad shoulders. She knew when he was younger he must have been totally irresistible to most women. His presence both intimidated and excited her.

She could feel him watching her as her eyes moved round his office. High glass windows surrounded the entire area, giving a three-hundred-and-sixty-degree view of the London skyline. There was no desk, just an informal lounge area in the centre of the room, and one phone.

'Please sit down. You'd like tea, coffee, or something else . . . ? Perhaps a Perrier?'

'Coffee, thank you.'

He lifted the phone and requested two coffees. His eyes dwelt on her. She sensed that he found her attractive, though not fully realising how the severity of the suit highlighted her voluptuous breasts, her exquisite face with its full lips, and her long, firmly muscled legs.

MacLeod put the phone down and smiled across at her. 'Relax, Dr Madison. This is probably the wrong place for our first meeting – far too formal. This is where I conduct my business meetings, but perhaps in another place you might have felt more at ease?'

She liked the faint Scots accent. 'No, don't worry,' she said. 'I like it here. I think your office is fantastic. I thought it would be quite cut off from the outside world, but in fact I see it's quite the opposite.' Her eyes dwelt on the greenness of Hyde Park stretching off into the distance.

A black plinth on the wall slid back and a secretary in a tartan suit came in with their coffee. Anne thanked her, but MacLeod did not utter a word until she had gone. 'You don't need to thank her,' he said. 'It is her duty to serve, and she gets paid handsomely for it.'

Anne suddenly felt apprehensive. If she worked for this man, how much would he demand of her? She had definite ideas about conservation, and had no plans to tailor them to suit the demands of big business.

She sipped at her coffee. It was delicious.

'Ah, you like the coffee, I see. I am fastidious about coffee. That is my favourite blend.'

Without warning, she felt the sexual electricity he generated – there was an aura of power about him she found irresistible.

'I'm sure you didn't fly me over the Atlantic to talk about coffee,' she said.

MacLeod laughed softly. 'Aye, Dr Madison, I see you like to get to the point. You know, in Africa as in the Hebrides, there is always time. It is not good to rush into a discussion there, you must take the time to learn about a man and how he's feeling.'

'I am a woman.'

'Of that, Dr Madison, I am only too aware. A very beautiful woman, I might add.'

Anne blushed crimson and smoothed her skirt over her knees.

'You will be working at my Botswana farm,' MacLeod said quietly, 'for my son Hyde. You are the only woman I have approached . . . You are also the most highly qualified applicant and have the best reputation. Your work on the lion makes you the leading authority in the field.'

Anne recovered herself. She knew what MacLeod was getting at: how would she cope in an all-male environment?

'Mr MacLeod, I was an only child. My father taught me to hunt, shoot and fish as soon as I could walk. He tried to turn me into the son he never had. I think I can say that I cope better in an all-male environment than most men. And I am used to chauvinism of the kind you are now displaying.'

Wayne MacLeod lay back on the couch and stared at her. 'I'd

expected a shrewish woman in spectacles,' he said. 'Instead, I find myself confronted by a beauty of formidable intellect . . . You have convinced me that I need not be afraid of your ability to cope with the position. I'll show you what I have in mind – your decision, and my decision, will be based on the fact that this must be a long-term association.'

Anne followed him to the lift. As the doors closed and the lift glided downwards, she was even more aware of his attractiveness, and she decided then and there that she would like him to make love to her. The sexual chemistry between them was very exciting.

The doors opened to reveal a completely different environment, an operations centre that looked like the foreign dealing room of a big bank, with people working in front of computer monitors and talking rapid-fire over the phone.

'This is the nerve-centre of the MacLeod Group,' MacLeod said proudly. 'From here, I keep in constant touch with my operations around the world. I believe in fiscal vigilance – all the companies in my group deliver twenty-four-hour statements.'

Anne suddenly wondered if her interests and MacLeod's might conflict. MacLeod clearly demanded performance from all his minions, and was obsessed with value for money, whereas her values were rather different . . . But perhaps his son might be different? MacLeod gestured to her to follow him into a boardroom area, and led her into a small theatre.

'Please, Anne, take a seat. I have something I'd like to show you.'

He went to the front and stood beside a small podium. The lights dimmed and a map of southern Africa was projected across the screen.

'I have a dream, he said softly.

He actuated another projector and the area of the Kruger National Park was highlighted in green.

'The Kruger is the great game park of South Africa,' MacLeod said. 'But it's north-south axis only allows game migration up and down the reserve – not across.'

Anne knew exactly what he was talking about, because part of her work had been on the impact of fences on the American west and other wilderness environments. Fences prevented game migration, and so interfered with the natural order. In the past, when game was thirsty or hungry it moved to a new location, but with the advent of fences, game was trapped. MacLeod's dream was a magnificent one – one she would like to be a part of.

'I want to create a reserve greater than the Kruger,' he went on. 'A huge reserve that offers the opportunity for east-west game migration – that is, a natural environment for predators.'

He illuminated another section of the map in red. 'This is Vembe, part of a vision conceived by Jan Smuts, the Prime Minister of South Africa during the Second World War. A vision I want to continue.'

Anne stared up at the map, and at the Vembe reserve flanked by the Limpopo river which formed the border between South Africa and Zimbabwe.

'He wanted to incorporate all this land . . .' MacLeod said. Now he illuminated vast tracts to the east, west and south of the Vembe reserve. 'And now I am acquiring it,' he continued. 'I own most of the Tuli Block in north-eastern Botswana – only a few private reserves are holding out against the offers I have made for them. In South Africa I have bought the farms along the banks of the Limpopo right up to Vembe, and then to the south as far as the town of Alldays.'

Anne sucked in her breath as she saw what he intended. It would be an incredible reserve, and would give her the opportunity to do work on lion that no one else could match.

'This is exciting,' she said. 'I assume you intend to introduce lion in large numbers into this new reserve?'

'Exactly. I have a particular fondness for predators.'

He faded up the lights and walked back to where she was sitting.

'I will fund you to run a project introducing lions into this new reserve from the Tuli Block and the Kruger – genetically balanced stock that will roam vast tracts of land as their forefathers did. I believe you are the right person for the project. I want your answer now, yes or no.'

Anne felt her pulse racing. It was the opportunity of a lifetime.

'Yes,' she said.

*

33

Paul looked out across the skyline to the south. The glass windows in the tall buildings of Johannesburg's central business district caught the sunlight, flashing it across to him. In the distance he could see the mine dumps and a long stretch of motorway, the cars crawling along it like a fast procession of ants.

He had returned to Johannesburg to pack his things before moving permanently up to Klaw. Johannesburg, a place where people lived hard under the almost perpetual sunshine; a city built on the wealth created by the gold that lay in the ground beneath it. There was a newness and a volatility about it. It was a place he was always trying to get away from, but almost inevitably kept coming back to.

He turned back into the house, and his thoughts returned to Klaw. Now his life was to revolve around protecting Shiva and her cubs. He looked forward to the isolation – a chance to forget about the divorce, and to distance himself from the horrors of war he'd been filming for over fifteen years.

His books, neatly packed into carboard boxes, lay in the hall. These he transferred carefully into the back of his Range Rover. He would have liked to take his whole library, but then he would need a Dakota to fly it up. Anyway, he remembered something his father had told him about the importance of travelling light . . .

His camera gear was already packed, over one hundred kilograms of it in special aluminium suitcases. He never went anywhere without his cameras – it was a discipline that had rewarded him again and again, allowing him to capture footage that no one else was prepared for.

By nine that evening he was finished. He made himself a light dinner and then collapsed into bed, exhausted.

He woke early the next morning and packed as much stuff as he could into the Range Rover. Then he went back into the house for a final cup of coffee and to say goodbye to Charlotte.

She was still in bed. He leaned forward, kissed her cheek. Her eyes opened. 'Don't try to sneak off, Dad.'

He laughed nervously. 'I want you to come up to Klaw as soon as possible. I want you to see Shiva and the cubs.'

'Just stay out of the way of the MacLeods, Dad. You've been in enough trouble already.'

'They know I won't sell to them, so I don't think we'll be seeing much of each other.'

He kissed her softly on the cheek once more.

An hour later he was on the road, heading out to Lanseria. He felt much better by the time he made the airport, and his King Air was waiting on the tarmac, the mechanics having already completed the pre-flight inspection. The plane was his one indulgence – a million-and-a-half rands-worth of machinery. He'd always liked airports. They filled him with excitement because they seemed so full of possibility, offering the chance to fly away to somewhere else, to do something different. To Paul, airports represented freedom.

The porters helped him load his baggage into the plane, then he sealed the door and walked forward to the pilot's seat. It was good to be alone.

He made contact with the control tower, then fired up the two turbo-props and moved out onto the runway. Permission to take off came through and he eased the plane forward, feeling the thrust pushing him back in his seat. Then came the exhilaration of taking off, and the steady climb to the clear sky above the clouds.

Visibility was exceptional, and around him was a world of blue with a white carpet of clouds beneath. He switched on the satellite navigation system and kicked in the auto-pilot. Now he had time to think.

He thought first of his childhood at Klaw, how his father used to take him out alone, after dark, to move amongst the lions. Then other memories flooded his consciousness, memories of the world's most successful combat cameraman. Angola. Vietnam. Northern Ireland. The Middle East. Violence and conflict, and through it all, human suffering.

What the hell was he going to make of his life? His father had left Klaw to him in his will, and because of this he would give up his work as a combat cameraman and turn Klaw into the exclusive game lodge his father had wanted to develop. Klaw was ideal for this purpose, an exceptional reserve in every way. But it would take hard work to establish the anti-poaching patrols that would make it a place of safety for Shiva and her cubs.

The sky cleared and he looked down onto the rolling landscape beneath him. He was now north of Pretoria. To his right, about fifty kilometres away, he saw the town of Potgietersrus, named after Piet Potgieter, a Voortrekker killed at a siege of the nearby Makapansgat Caves in 1854. Slightly further off was Pietersburg where, if he was travelling by road, he would turn north-west, heading for the border post with Botswana at Pont Drift. Ownership of the land below him had always been hard. If it wasn't war that threatened the Boers, then it was drought.

He crossed over the small town of Alldays and saw the banks of the Limpopo river coming up, the border between South Africa and Botswana. The Northern Tuli Block, in which Klaw lay, was an area of land to the north of the Limpopo, with the Shashe river defining the uppermost border with Zimbabwe, and the Motloutse river to the south.

One of Paul's ancestors had owned a trading store on the western side of the Limpopo, known as Bryce's store. It lay on the famous Great North Road, the route Cecil Rhodes' Pioneer Column took. The Column had established a community at Fort Tuli, which was to become the first town of the newly formed country of Rhodesia, and Bryce Norton had built his own stronghold on a rocky outcrop, naming it Fort Klaw. An adept negotiator, Bryce Norton had side-stepped much of the conflict that troubled the region, and over the years had made good profit from the ever increasing traffic.

Paul looked down along the Limpopo. The point at which Rhodes had first crossed this broad river was named Rhodes Drift, and later another fording point was established slightly above it – Pont Drift, the access point by road to Klaw from the South African border.

Bryce Norton's store had flourished as one of the staging points for the Zeederberg Coach, which took four days to make the journey from Pretoria to Fort Tuli. Now that journey had taken Paul just over an hour. Already well into his descent for landing, he looked across to his lands – the Klaw reserve. He felt his skin tingle as the rocky outcrop came into view, standing up majestically from the surrounding veld.

He dropped the undercarriage and backed off the engines, then made one low pass over the kilometre-long strip to make sure the runway was clear. His eyes searched the sand but found nothing. He banked round and came in to land, the sandy strip rising slightly and disappearing on the horizon, out of view. The wheels touched down gently and he backed off the power as the plane bumped along the runway.

He parked the plane at the side of the sandy airstrip and turned off the engines. Then he walked through the cabin and opened the side-door at the back, which formed a staircase down to the sand. As he stepped onto the dry earth he breathed in deeply, taking in the smell of the bush. It felt very good. Already he could feel his spirits lifting.

He found the Land Rover where he'd left it, hidden in the bush, a month before. Then he went back to the King Air, took out the battery he'd brought with him from the hold, and fitted it to the Landy. Having checked the oil level, he turned the ignition key. The engine spluttered and fired, blowing a cloud of dark smoke from the exhaust. Paul engaged first and drove across to the side of the King Air.

It took him about fifteen minutes to unload the plane, fit the chocks under the wheels and cover the air-intakes, then he was bumping along the sandy double-track road through the bush. His eyes rapidly adjusted to the topography. In the city you kept your eyes on the area immediately in front of you; in the bush it was different, you had to learn to see through the scrub far into the distance – open your eyes up. This openness was natural to Paul; the city closed him in, stifled his soul.

He reached the edge of the rock outcrop, and the sand road turned into a concrete one that banked steeply upwards. He brought the Landy to a halt and pulled the red lever next to the gear-stick back, to engage low-ratio four-wheel drive. Then the Landy chugged slowly up the slope with no apparent effort. The road twisted and turned amongst the rocks as he went higher and higher.

The top took him by surprise as it always did. The round stone parking area, and the main building, Rock Lodge, constructed of stone and slate, looked majestically out over the bush. Paul pulled on the handbrake and killed the engine.

The silence was almost unnerving, the heat intense. He felt the sweat drip from his brow as he walked across to the front stoep – and suddenly the memories hit him hard, like a punch in the gut. He sat down on one of the wicker chairs and remembered his childhood. His father had spent a lot of time with him, teaching him about survival. Everything had a reason, a purpose. With every experience they shared, Paul had learned something more. Then, as Paul turned twenty-one, out of the blue his father gave him a million rands, to spend, as he expressed it, on living.

Paul had been determined not to let the money control him, not to let it influence his career. Yet in a way, he realised, it was the money that had brought him to Helen – he could have whatever he wanted, and a beautiful wife seemed the ultimate possession. At the time he'd ignored the fact that Helen hadn't the remotest interest in the bush, in Klaw, in his father and his lions or Paul's own passion for the outdoors. Now, over twenty years later, he had come full circle and returned to the place where he'd begun – an older, wiser man.

The main lodge on Klaw was the finest in Africa. His father had imported stonemasons from Italy to build the imposing structure that clung to the edge of the rock and looked out over the veld. It was a bush palace in the classic tradition, and Paul knew he could turn it into the most exclusive retreat in Africa.

He went through to the main living-area, with its rough floorboards as solid as ever, the giant table made from old railway sleepers still standing in its centre. He looked back through the wooden double doors that gave onto the stoep and the breathtaking view beyond. His father had never lived up here after his mother died. The old man said it reminded him too much of the woman he had loved with such passion, and who had been cruelly taken from him by cancer. Paul had vague early memories of his mother; after that there was an emptiness that even his father with all his love had failed to fill.

In the large kitchen with the terracotta tile floor he tentatively turned on a tap. At first there was just a trickle, then the water came out muddy brown and began to clear. In the rock above Paul knew there were special rainwater tanks, taking the run-off from the gigantic slate roof that covered the lodge. He cupped his hand and tasted the water – pure and fresh.

He went back to the Landy, took out a bottle of whisky and a glass. In the kitchen he mixed himself a whisky and water, then sat on the stoep, staring into the vastness beyond. Finally the tiredness hit him and he drifted into a deep sleep.

He awoke with a start in darkness, and glanced at his watch to see that it was after eight. He groaned, and got to his feet. There was no way he would spend the night at Rock Lodge – he never had. Like his father, he felt uncomfortable in the place; he preferred to be closer to the bush.

Paul staggered out to the Land Rover, fired the engine and edged it slowly down the precipitous drive. Then it was ten minutes along a sand road, and he was at Bush Camp. The headlights of the Land-Rover ran over the wooden poles that supported the long thatched lodge standing at giraffe height above the dry river bed below.

This was where his father had died. This was where he'd buried him.

He thought back to how he'd nearly been killed by the poachers a month before. He hadn't heard anything more from the police on that score, so he would be cautious. There could be more poachers in the area, planning to ambush him when he returned. He got out of the Land Rover, leaving the headlights on and the engine running. Then he cursed silently, realising he'd forgotten the keys.

The walkway creaked as he made his way up to the main deck, the headlights of the Landy casting shadows everywhere. He noticed that one of the windows of the main building was broken, and he swore again as he cut himself on the glass, letting himself in. Then he was inside, scratching around for a paraffin lantern. He couldn't see a bloody thing.

He lit a match that revealed total chaos. Someone had obviously been through the place – all too easy, as it was completely deserted. He'd been a fool. What if the thieves had taken his father's films? He found the spare set of keys, unlocked the front door and went through to the study. He relaxed. The room was as he'd left it, everything in its place.

He went outside again, drew a sleeping-bag from the back of the Landy and switched off the engine. The stillness was refreshing. In the distance he heard a hyena bark. He pulled out another bottle of whisky and went back through the front door. He tidied up the kitchen and managed to find a glass that wasn't chipped. He took it outside and sat in the moonlight on the deck, wrapped in his sleeping-bag, listening to the sounds of the night and drinking steadily.

The hours passed slowly. He thought about Helen, the wasted years of their relationship. Perhaps he just wasn't cut out for marriage – but it was a pity it had taken him twenty years to find that out, he muttered mirthlessly to himself, staring at the now empty bottle. Then he lay back and fell into an uneasy sleep.

The morning sun woke him. He didn't want to open his eyes and he felt his head spinning as he lurched forward. He stared hard at the empty bottle of whisky.

'Norton, you bloody fool,' he said quietly.

The first sunlight shone through the trees, casting dabbled colours across the thatched wooden rooms whose doors opened out onto the main sun-deck. He staggered off the deck and across the bush to the creaking windmill beyond the mopani trees, and threw himself into the dank waters of the metal reservoir beneath it. Green slime covered his face, but he felt himself recovering.

He staggered back to the Landy, pulled out an axe and moved over to a pile of tree trunks. The axe moved steadily up and down as he built up a pile of firewood. He stripped off his shirt and felt better as the sweat poured from his body. Then he carried the logs into the kitchen, and opened the door to the old stove. Soon he had a blaze going and a coffee pot on the boil on the hob above.

An hour later he had poured himself a hot bath in the zinc tub that stood in the washroom next to the kitchen. After that, feeling clean and a lot more sober, he started to tidy up the sprawling bush house, pulling out the broken panes and sweeping out the rooms. By the time the sun was about to set, he had prepared the main bedroom and organised the lounge to a passable level of comfort.

He stood on the sun-deck and stared across at a sky filled with clouds painted a vivid red by the setting sun. It was indescribably beautiful, impossible to capture on film – the reason why Africa always drew him back like a magnet. And in the ending of the day he again felt sadness at the loss of his father.

Later he made himself some pan bread on the stove, then cooked a passable beef stew. A bottle of 1972 Cabernet that he'd found completed the meal.

Afterwards he lay in bed, reading a book of poetry by a paraffin light. He tried not to think. Whenever he gave himself time to think, his mind went into overdrive, analysing the past. Why had he allowed Helen to distance him from his father?

He needed time to relax, to reorganise the chaos into which his life had fallen. The book fell against his chest, he rolled over and collapsed into a deep sleep.

The next morning he was up early, made himself a quick breakfast, drew up a list of the things he needed to fix the place up, and drove off to get supplies. He arrived at the Botswanan border post at Pont Drift just after it opened at eight thirty, and informed the customs officer of his arrival by plane two days before. Then he drove the Landy over the sandy bed of the Limpopo – the border between Botswana and South Africa.

He drove to Messina, just over an hour away, and bought what he needed to straighten the lodge out. He also ordered bales of game fencing to rebuild the lion-proof enclosure under Bush Camp that his father had taken down. He arrived back at Pont Drift late and found the border closed. Bugger it.

He drove south for half an hour, and came to the four-way stop that marked the town of Alldays. In the distance he saw the *koppie* that lay just beyond the town. He turned right, taking the road to the local hotel. He booked a room and went down to the bar. This was hard farming country. The people were conservative, but not in the British political sense – they were ultra right-wing. Some of them he respected, others he hated. The nature of his profession made him curious to find out why people believed in and fought for what they did.

In the tiny bar the atmosphere was warm and convivial. Some people were playing darts in the narrow space between the counter and the rear wall. Pushing in amongst the row of big men who pressed against the counter, Paul ordered a double whisky and soda, and fell into conversation. The man's English was pretty basic, so Paul switched to Afrikaans and the conversation picked up speed. It turned out that the man was an English teacher at the local school. The irony of this was not lost on Paul.

The farmers all around them talked of the changes occurring in the South African government – changes they did not agree with. Paul sensed their fear that they might lose the farms their forefathers had established in the previous century: the new black government would have no sympathy for them, the tables had finally turned. Paul wondered how these men would cope, and he knew that somehow they would, because they were survivors.

Later he retired to his room and slept soundly. He checked out of the hotel in the first light of dawn and drove the Landy flat out with the canvas top down, the cool wind buffeting his hair. The energy and the enthusiasm were coming back to him. He began to get excited about his plans for Klaw.

It took him only half an hour to clear customs at the border, and then he was free to drive back to the reserve. But as he drove the Landy into Bush Camp, he had the uneasy feeling that something was wrong. A smart new Land Cruiser was parked outside. Paul felt the hair on his head rising. Who the hell had dared to invade his territory?

He ran up the ramp and found Hyde MacLeod leaning against the edge of the balcony. Hyde turned and smoothed back his dark hair as Paul approached him, then folded his arms across his chest.

'Norton, we have a few matters to discuss,' he said gruffly in his Scots accent.

Paul nodded, staring at Hyde, thirty-five years old, with thick black wavy hair parted in the middle, and dark eyes that moved away from his own a little too often. His father had had continuous hassle from the MacLeods over the last few years, mostly because he'd refused to sell Klaw to them. Paul had a suspicion that they might even have paid the poachers to kill his father.

'Yeah, Hyde, we do. Like what the fuck are you doing on my property?' Paul put his hands on his hips, blocking the way.

'Your property?' Hyde laughed dryly. 'Not for much longer, I think.'

Paul raised his right hand, moved to one side and pointed to the ramp. 'Get out now!'

He saw Hyde's eyes flicker. He had guessed right, Hyde did not want a physical confrontation – he seemed to be scared of a fight.

Hyde moved away from the main deck. 'Enjoy it while it lasts, Norton,' he said.

'Just who do you think you are, arsehole?'

Paul wanted a fight. He'd had enough of this arrogant bastard and he reckoned he could take him.

'I'm the biggest landowner in the Tuli Block, Norton. I've bought up just about every reserve in this area, you're the only person who resisted my offer. Anyway, your time is up. My attorneys have done a little investigation into the title deeds of this property, and it turns out that I have a right to it. Think about that before you threaten me again.'

Paul's blood went cold as he watched Hyde MacLeod drive off into the bush. Later, he walked up the ramp to the deck, went into his father's study and spent some time rearranging the books and files above the big desk, gathering his thoughts. Finally he positioned his own battered Olivetti in the centre of the desk.

In the afternoon he pulled the riot pump out of the back of the Landy, stripped off his shoes and shirt, and walked into the bush. Africa, he mused, thinking back to Hyde MacLeod's visit, was always full of surprises.

He moved quietly across the desolate landscape to the north of the camp, becoming more and more angry as he went. Vehicle tracks criss-crossed the sand – new roads had been created, on *his* land. The reserve had obviously become a thoroughfare. He'd been a fool to stay away from Klaw for over a month, leaving it unattended. The surrounding reserves, owned by Hyde and Wayne MacLeod, operated as an exclusive game lodge, and the MacLeods did have traversing rights over Klaw for game viewing. But there were strict rules governing the number of vehicles allowed in any one area at a particular time, and the number that could converge on an animal sighting. Looking at the tracks, it was clear to Paul that the MacLeods' rangers had been using Klaw as the main area for their game drives – Klaw had the highest concentration of game in the area. Paul deeply resented this invasion of his territory.

The noise of an engine quickened his senses, and he melted into the bush at his side. He waited patiently, keeping still by instinct, for the ultimate act of camouflage is to remain unmoving.

The vehicle drew closer, heading onto his land. He raised the nose of the shotgun, drawing the bead across the bush. Damn. What was he doing? He lowered the gun. He'd been drinking too much, he was living in his imagination again.

The Land Cruiser burst through the bushes, narrowly missing a tree, and drew to a halt quite near to him. He remained hidden. He heard the smooth voice of a professional game ranger: 'From here we'll cross to the south-eastern border of the reserve – the Limpopo. You'll probably see quite a few eland in this area, and we might be lucky – a leopard was sighted near here this morning.'

Paul stepped out of the bushes, and two pairs of eyes rested on him. But he was conscious of only one pair, green. Their owner was pretty, very pretty. The neatly starched khaki bush-shirt did nothing to disguise the firm breasts, and she had a strong face, well-defined cheekbones, and natural blonde hair.

The silence was getting longer. Paul didn't say anything, and began to feel he was making a bit of a fool of himself.

'Don't move,' the ranger said quietly.

'Are you a poacher?' the woman asked imperiously, the green eyes never flickering. He noted she had an American accent.

'That's rich,' Paul said, the sarcasm in his voice thinly veiled. It was they who were trespassing.

The ranger had the rifle out of its holder on the dashboard and was pointing it at him. 'Move, and I'll shoot.'

Paul smiled, and dropped the shotgun. He could have reacted, but he knew it wasn't necessary. Anyway, he loved drama. He held the green eyes.

The ranger picked up the microphone and switched on the

two-way radio. 'Vehicle Five in the south-eastern block on Klaw Drive. I have suspected poacher. Please assist.'

More silence. The ranger raised the rifle again and aimed it at Paul, who bared his teeth. The woman giggled. So, she had a sense of humour. He turned his gaze back to her and took in the long legs inside the khaki pants. It was almost, he thought, as if she had purposely disguised her sex.

He heard the noise of another Land Cruiser coming up fast. This was becoming rather amusing. The woman lifted her nose slightly and he thought he caught the flicker of a smile.

The Land Cruiser came up behind him, and he turned to see the stocky, dark-haired form of Hyde MacLeod, now wearing a bush-hat. Arsehole, Paul said to himself.

'Are you OK, Anne?' Hyde asked the woman.

'Fine, thanks.'

'Do you want to handle this, Hyde?' the runtish-looking game ranger asked deferentially.

'My pleasure, Charles. Take Anne down to the river, I'll sort this out.'

The ranger put down the rifle, and he and the woman got back into the Land Cruiser. It drove off across Paul's farm, leaving a trail of dust.

'You're in serious trouble, Norton. Threatening a guest with a loaded gun . . .'

Paul felt the tension-level rising. Hyde drew out a flamboyant, stainless steel, .357 Magnum and levelled it at him.

'I'm arresting you. Lean over the bonnet so I can tie your hands. One false move and I'll blow your brains out.'

Paul didn't budge. He whistled, and stared nonchalantly at the MacLeod crest on the side of the Land Cruiser. Hyde MacLeod, son of the legendary Africa hand and multimillionaire media tycoon, Wayne MacLeod. His father's enemy. Out of the corner of his eye he saw Hyde raising a buffalo whip.

'You're going to regret you ever set foot on my land,' he said.

The whip curled, and caught Paul across the shoulder blades, sending him flying into the sand. He dropped, rolled, and whipped out his right foot, toppling Hyde, who was trying to whip him again. He was angry; he could smell the blood seeping

45

from his back. He drove his fist into Hyde's face, then into his stomach, smashing the wind out of him.

Hyde staggered up, his face bloody. 'You'll die for this!'

Paul restrained himself and dragged Hyde to the Land Cruiser. He used the leather thongs of the whip to tie Hyde's hands to the dashboard grab-handle. Then he emptied the chamber of Hyde's Magnum and tossed the gun into the bushes.

'You're making a serious mistake,' Hyde snarled.

Paul got into the driving-seat and gunned the vehicle forwards, following the tracks that he knew led to main camp of Cayzer, the MacLeods' reserve. He was spitting with anger.

The main camp at Cayzer contrasted vividly with the rustic simplicity of Bush Camp. Fountains played at the entrance, and superbly kitted black rangers strutted around the reception area; in the distance, wooden chalets looked down onto the Bojale river below.

Paul snatched his shotgun and stormed up to the main reception. The prettily made-up receptionist in her tight-fitting T-shirt took one look at him and reached for the phone.

'I hope you're calling Wayne MacLeod,' Paul said angrily.

She looked at him nervously. 'Mr MacLeod Senior is at the London headquarters of the MacLeod Group. Can I help you?'

'Cut the bullshit. I know he's out here for the week.' He had seen the announcement of Wayne MacLeod's visit in the paper before he left – rumour had it that he was about to pull off a major coup on the Johannesburg stock exchange.

'Tell Mr MacLeod senior that if he isn't here in a minute, I'll ram this shotgun up his spoilt son's fat arse!'

Before he could say any more, he was grabbed from behind and dragged outside. Hyde MacLeod was standing in front of him, rubbing his wrists, with a couple of ugly-looking customers beside him.

The first blow caught Paul in the teeth, the next struck his left ear, and then came a hard kick to his groin that lifted him upwards. He let out a sob and rolled over. He caught sight of Hyde raising the whip with which he had been tied to the grab-handle.

'That's enough, lad!' a voice barked.

Paul rolled over in relief. An immaculately buffed pair of

bush-boots appeared before his eyes. He stared up to see the cool grey eyes of Wayne MacLeod looking down at him dispassionately.

Paul staggered to his feet, glad to see Hyde and his cronies retreating. Wayne MacLeod stood facing him, leonine good-looks and long, dramatically streaked silver hair above crisp khaki fatigues.

'Let me warn you now,' MacLeod said. 'If you threaten one of Hyde's guests again, it'll be worse, laddie. Far worse.'

Paul felt the anger coursing through his veins. 'I didn't threaten anyone, MacLeod. Your son's a weak-willed bastard.'

'Watch your language, Norton . . . You've ignored Hyde's letters, refused to answer his calls. He's tried to be reasonable . . .'

'I'll never sell Klaw.'

'Listen to me, Norton. Hyde's bought up all the reserves surrounding your farm. He's also acquired most of the farms across the Limpopo . . .'

'No doubt ripping off local farmers who're battling to make ends meet.'

MacLeod ignored Paul's jibe. 'Your reserve is worthless if you don't have access,' he said calmly.

Paul was suddenly nervous. He couldn't get to Klaw without crossing MacLeod property. But there was no way they could deny him access. Or was there?'

'What do you mean?' he said.

'We're not allowing you over MacLeod land again. You'll be shot on sight.'

Paul knew in a flash exactly what MacLeod's objective was. Klaw was the best reserve in the whole block; add it to Cayzer, Hyde's game farm, and the MacLeods would have one of the finest game parks in Africa.

'I have a legal right to access,' Paul grated.

'Not any longer.' MacLeod drew a sheaf of legal-looking papers out of his pocket and threw them on the sand in front of Paul. 'Read through those, and the situation will be abundantly clear to you. Now, get off my land.'

MacLeod laughed, revealing a perfect set of teeth. 'If you go to court, Hyde'll kill you with costs.'

Of course, money would be largely irrelevant to Hyde Mac-Leod, it was power that mattered to him. 'We'll see about that, you bastards,' Paul said.

He picked up the papers and staggered off down the road.

Mkhulu arrived at Bush Camp late in the afternoon, and immediately felt his spirits rise. The Land Rover was parked outside, so Paul Norton must have returned. Then he saw the bales of lion-proof fencing lying next to the edge of the camp – Paul was no doubt going to replace the fence that Lionel Norton had pulled down. This would also act as a protective enclosure for Shiva's cubs if there were further threats from poachers.

Of course there were other risks as well, with Judah dead. There could be another pride in the area, and if that was the case, the dominant male would kill Shiva's cubs so that she would come into season and sire his own. It was vital, therefore, that during the next six months Shiva and her cubs should be protected. After that, the cubs would be stronger and could begin to fend for themselves.

Mkhulu went up onto the deck. The place was the same as ever – most of the rooms in chaos. Now he saw more similarities between father and son. Recently he'd found himself comparing the two Nortons – Lionel, the father and Paul, the son. Paul had a fire burning within him, an anger that blazed in his blue eyes.

Mkhulu went to the refrigerator and found that Paul had stocked it with venison, ready for Shiva and the three cubs should they come into the camp. He looked over the disorder in the kitchen with disgust, and then he cleaned out the sink and placed the pots back in the cupboards. He remembered first coming to work for Paul's father. He'd heard about 'Lion' Norton from the trackers who worked for the MacLeods on Cayzer, and had been fascinated by the stories they told about the man who lived with the lions. So Izak had asked Lion Norton to take him on – and at last Mkhulu had found a man who understood him, who believed in him. That was why he had remained loyal to him. A bond of blood with a man of strength – a white man devoid of the racial prejudice that characterised so many of his kind in Africa.

Now Lion Norton was dead, buried beneath the soil of the land he loved. But his spirit lived on, indestructible, breathed into Mkhulu's blood through long association and shared suffering.

The son, Paul, had not been what Mkhulu had expected – standing over six foot tall, with a ravaged, sunburnt face. Paul's body was thin, though big-boned, and he moved with a strange grace. The lines on his face spoke of suffering, of an inner turmoil and a great sensitivity. He was different from the father, but with the same affinity for the lions they both loved. For Norton senior the lions had almost come to replace his real family.

Mkhulu did not think about his own family. That was beyond pain. It was only through enormous effort that he could hide the bitterness.

Late afternoon turned quickly into night. Mkhulu lit the paraffin lamps on the deck and stared out into the darkness for a few moments, wondering what Paul was doing. Then he opened his travelling-bag and took out his old leather shaving-box. He slid out the first drawer, and removed from it the thin knife with the blackened blade in its soft leather sheath. He looked at the knife, remembering, then he fastened it inside the structure of the ugly plastic and metal device attached to the base of his right knee. Then he lay down on the deck, staring at the stars and listening to the sounds of the night, thinking.

He was half-asleep when he picked up an alien noise in the bush outside. He rose like a cat, hobbled noiselessly off the deck, and melted into the darkness, waiting. He had always been a survivor. In the African wild you could never become complacent, you lived on your guard or you died young.

A figure staggered into the light of the paraffin lamps on the deck. It was Paul, looking tired and worn. Mkhulu moved out of the darkness and greeted him with the three-handed shake. Then they went back up to the deck together, and sat down on the rattan chairs.

'Sir, I need work,' Mkhulu feigned crisply in English. 'I have little money.'

'I came here to be alone. Besides, I cannot afford to employ someone like you,' Paul replied, continuing the banter.

'You have this reserve – you have plenty of money. You're making an excuse because of my leg.'

49

Even in this light-hearted exchange, Mkhulu could tell Paul found him unnerving. He knew men found the candour in his eyes disturbing – but he never shifted his eyes from Paul's.

'What do you call yourself?'

'Mkhulu.'

'Mkhulu, you look like a good kaffir,' Paul said, mimicking the language of a born racist. 'You can have a job.'

Mkhulu burst out laughing and, the banter finished, he leaned over and slapped Paul on the back. Paul wheezed with pain – and it was then Mkhulu noted that his shirt was soaked in blood.

'God, Paul, what happened?'

'Later. It's nothing time won't heal. I'm going to draw myself a hot bath.'

After Paul had bathed, Mkhulu tended to the cuts across his back. 'Hyde MacLeod is a bully, Paul. But his father, that's the one we have to watch. The son is merely his puppet.'

Paul winced as Mkhulu applied the liniment where the whip had caught his back. 'It's going to be difficult, Mkhulu. They own all the land surrounding Klaw – they've got us walled in.'

Mkhulu laughed, a hollow, bitter laugh. 'I have a roof and food, and for that I should be grateful. But as for Shiva and her cubs, they have no such security. I do not trust the MacLeods. Do they know Judah is dead?'

'Not unless that policeman told them.'

'Your father was constantly fighting with them. They don't like me, they tried to get me deported back to Zimbabwe but your father organised Botswanan citizenship for me. I lay low while you were gone. I knew the moment you were away they would try to force me off Klaw.'

Paul gripped Mkhulu's hand and stared into his eyes. 'You can stay here for ever. I'm not going.'

Mkhulu lay back in the armchair and gazed round the lounge of Bush Camp. Everything looked warm and yellow in the light from the paraffin lanterns – the huge thatched roof, the *riempie* chairs, and the old Cape dresser in the corner.

'I came here for peace,' Paul said softly, 'And it has eluded me.'

'Perhaps it is for the best.'

Paul took in Mkhulu's reply and stared into the darkness. 'The

50

keys for the Landy are in the study. You'll find a 30-06 in the back and a Browning Hi-Power.'

Mkhulu nodded grimly.

'If it isn't poachers . . . it's the MacLeods. Paul, I'll see you later. I want to drive around and look for foreign lion spoor – I'm not taking any chances with Shiva and the cubs.'

'Fine. I'm sorry not to offer to come with you, but I'm exhausted. I don't think there are any lion in this area, but I might have missed the spoor. Look, I'm sorry the lion-proof fence isn't up but it won't take long – we can just enclose the area under here. We can start putting it up early tomorrow morning.'

Mkhulu stood up and laid his massive right hand on Paul's shoulder. 'I'll look after Shiva and her cubs, you fight for your land.'

Paul heard the door of Landy opening. He hoped Mkhulu would take the guns, there was no telling what stunt Hyde MacLeod might pull next. He would contact his attorneys in Johannesburg next morning and check out the situation. He was quite sure that Hyde MacLeod was bluffing. They couldn't cut off his access, could they?

In the darkness, Mkhulu worked the action of the rifle. Not bad. It was a Musgrave, a South African hunting-rifle that served as an excellent multi-purpose weapon. He slid a bullet into the breech and worked the action backwards and forwards.

The Browning Hi-Power he was used to. He tightened the webbing belt and holster round his waist, and thought back to the last time he'd carried a Browning. It was a long time ago, over ten years. A time best forgotten.

He spent the next hour listening for Shiva and the cubs in the darkness. It would be a long time before Shiva could assimilate with another pride. At this moment, the arrival of a dominant male would be a disaster: he would kill the cubs so that Shiva came into season for him. That was the way of lions – it was all a case of genetic dominance. A lion would never support and protect cubs sired by another male, he would kill them. Once a female's cubs were dead she would automatically come into season, and the male would cover her, siring cubs of his own. So for the moment, with Judah dead, it was vital that he and Paul assume the role of Shiva's protector – the males of the pride. Later, Mkhulu knew, that could cause problems – nomad males might challenge Paul or himself to a fight for possession. It would also be natural, once the cubs were fully grown, for Shiva to try and mate with him or Paul, for in her eyes too they would be the males of the pride.

For the moment, however, he and Paul would kill game to help Shiva feed herself and the cubs. Gradually, as the cubs grew, they could help Shiva to make a kill, and in that way the cubs would learn the art of hunting in order to survive.

After an hour Mkhulu started up the Landy and headed to the west. He tightened the strap that held the artificial leg to his right knee – it was difficult working the brake and the accelerator. He moved along the dirt roads slowly, killing the engine occasionally and listening in the darkness for the distinctive grunts of the lion.

He knew this area so well that he could disappear into it without being found. Already a survival plan was forming in his mind: over the next week he would familiarise himself with the layout of the MacLeods' camp. He sensed that Paul was heading for trouble, and he wanted to be able to help him.

Paul woke at first light and began the work of putting up the lion-proof fencing. It was a simple enough process, unrolling the big bales and then driving metal staples to hold the wire into the poles that supported the wooden building above him. First a lower section of fencing, then an upper one, rising to a total height of four metres.

The work proceeded slowly, and he was glad when Mkhulu joined him at just after eleven. The process speeded up then, and by the end of the afternoon they were finished; there were two enclosures, one for the cubs if they ever needed protecting, and the other surrounding Bush Camp, protecting Paul and Mkhulu. Bush Camp was Shiva's core area, and she would return to it often – and it was vital that she did not come upon either of them asleep or under the influence of alcohol. That was when accidents happened. That was why, for men who worked with lions, a lion-proof fence was a necessity.

That evening Mkhulu took first watch. He slept outside

on a stretcher underneath the house – he had absolutely refused Paul's offer of a room. Later, Paul would relieve him, waiting for Shiva and the cubs to return. If they were hungry they would provide them with meat.

Very early the next morning Paul started off in the Landy and eased her onto the dirt road that led off the reserve towards the border post at Pont Drift. The sun was just peeping over the horizon, the air smelt clean and fresh. He engaged third gear, settled back in his seat, swept round the next bend – and slammed his brakes on hard. The Landy drifted across the track and ploughed into the side of a Baobab tree.

'Bugger it!'

Paul leaped down onto the cold, red earth and stared at the blockade across the road. Poles had been driven deep into the sand at an angle, ready to impale the radiator of any vehicle that tried to cross them.

So it had begun. Hyde MacLeod would not allow him the right to traverse MacLeod land, which completely encircled his own. This was not like civilised territory where the government owned the roads that ran between and through properties – here the landowner was king. True, traversing rights were supposed to be guaranteed, but Hyde MacLeod had obviously done his legal homework and found a loophole in the law that was supposed to allow Paul access to his own land across Hyde's.

Bastards. Paul walked over to the MacLeod's barricade and started to pull it apart.

He heard the shot as the bullet creased his right shoulder. He dropped down and fell backwards.

'The next one will be terminal,' a voice bellowed eerily through a loud-hailer. 'You are trespassing on private property.'

'Well, fuck you,' Paul shouted back.

Mkhulu woke as Paul returned in the Landy – he'd expected him to be gone for the day. As soon as he saw the huge dent in the side of the vehicle and Paul's torn shirt, he knew what had happened, Paul didn't need to explain anything.

When he'd dressed the wound, Mkhulu poured them both a steaming mug of coffee.

'We're trapped,' Paul confided, as they sat staring out into the bush. 'If either of us tries to make it to the border, we're dead. I'll have to fly out.'

Mkhulu shook his head. 'We'll go tonight. I'll find a way.'

The darkness was both an enemy and a friend. It could hide predators, but at the same time, if you were skilled in bushcraft, it could make you invisible. Paul imagined he was back in Angola, twenty years before. He'd been in the army then, looking for action and adventure. In the end he'd found bitterness and death.

There was a full moon, so once his eyes were accustomed to the darkness, he could see his way quite easily.

Mkhulu surprised him – for a man with an artificial leg, he was very agile. They followed a game path to the west of the road, crawling in the lighter, more exposed areas to avoid detection, then running in the shadows. They made good progress and soon they were past the blockade.

A few minutes later they came to a tiny clump of trees and Paul spotted a Land Cruiser hidden in the bush. He guessed that this was where the man with the rifle must be placed, maintaining a constant vigil to make sure they didn't try to drive out by night. Mkhulu gestured for Paul to be quiet, and moved closer. In the moonlight he could see the man in the distance, resting over his rifle, staring in the direction of the blockade. Nearer to them, a small table was laid out with a thermos, mugs, biscuits and coffee. Paul spotted a bag of sugar, and whipped it off the table. He went over to the Land Cruiser, and to his relief found that the keys were in the ignition. He carefully removed them and unlocked the cap on the fuel tank. Then he poured the sugar slowly down the filler spout and replaced the cap when he'd finished.

Mkhulu waited in the shadows. 'What are you doing?'

'Making sure he won't be travelling far in the morning.'

Mkhulu's pearl-white teeth flashed in the darkness. Then they both moved on, heading towards the Limpopo.

The sun was rising by the time they made it to the border post at Pont Drift. They moved quietly past the administrative offices of Cayzer. Paul felt uneasy when he thought of how much power

Hyde MacLeod wielded – he must now be the biggest employer in the Tuli block.

After crossing the border, they walked on a tarmac road that led from Pont Drift to Alldays. Paul then took a turn-off that led to the small store at Palma, where they bought some bread and milk for breakfast. Then they trudged back to the main road, passing the dirt turn-off to Den Staadt on the left, and two huge baobabs, one of which had been riven apart by a bolt of lightning. Along the sides of the road lay a cream-coloured dust which added to the ethereal quality of the place. Paul's eye followed the line of telephone poles stretching off to the horizon. After a kilometre, they turned left onto the Dongola road to Messina.

Paul stood in the heat, staring at the sandstone outcrops in the distance, part of the old Limpopo valley. A faint wind blew across the veld, and the game farms on either side of him seemed empty, a feeling of foreboding in the air.

Eventually they hitched a lift with a black lorry driver who was returning from making a delivery to the border post. As they drove on, Paul saw the signs on the fences, the distinctive MacLeod crest. The MacLeods owned most of the land round here, and Paul had already sensed Hyde MacLeod's insatiable need to acquire and control. Well, there was no way Hyde MacLeod was going to take Klaw. Paul became more and more enraged as they drove on. He was almost certain that Hyde was bluffing – that he had no right to deny him access, and was just trying to unnerve him. And if that was the case, Paul would lay charges against him and make sure Hyde was liable for his costs.

Soon, to the right, Paul stared up at an impressive massif of sandstone cliffs. Then, with the swaying motion of the cab he drifted off to sleep, waking up as they passed Groot Billai, a solid lump of rock that stood out dramatically from the surrounding land. As they approached Messina he was aware that many of the vehicles on the road were land-mine-proofed, a stark reminder that South Africa had been at war until very recently. Now the threat of land mines was gone, but the proofed vehicles would be used until they wore out. Nothing was ever certain, and there were probably many among the rural community who suspected that the situation might worsen again.

They passed the De Beers headquarters on their left, and crossed the narrow-gauge railway that ran over the road. The lorry driver dropped them off outside the station. Messina was a pretty, bustling town, with green trees and dramatic splashes of red bougainvillea.

As they got down at the side of the road, the train from Johannesburg pulled up and disgorged a stream of black passengers who passed their belongings down from the carriage side-windows to their waiting friends. In the distance Paul saw two steam trains, no doubt booked by enthusiasts for a special excursion to the north. In the distance he saw the grey, concrete radio mast that dominated the town.

Mkhulu went off to buy groceries, and Paul walked through the station to look at the Zeederberg coach. This was the wagon that had made the journey every week along the Great North Road, past Bryce Norton's trading store. Paul looked at the scarred coach, its doors restored with plywood that had already been kicked in by vandals. Everything in Africa was transitory, but somehow Klaw had remained in his family for a century. Nothing, decided Paul, was going to wrest it from him.

He walked down to the smart brick buildings of the new municipal offices, passed through the front entrance and turned left past the small museum to the library. There he sat, collating his story in preparation for his legal battle with Hyde MacLeod. He wrote out exactly what had happened in his neat script. Then he went to the bank and faxed the statement to his attorneys in Johannesburg.

He met Mkhulu outside the general dealers. Mkhulu looked at ease; the town was progressive and reflected the changes sweeping South Africa.

'I get the feeling that things are a little different here,' Mkhulu said.

'Today, it's the colour of your money that counts. I'd better organise us some transport.'

Paul bought a Toyota diesel pick-up from the local dealership at the south end of the town, arranging finance through his bank. He wanted another vehicle besides the Landy on Klaw. MacLeod would take some time to realise he had another means of transport besides the King Air and the Landy, and this would limit Hyde MacLeod's ability to track his movements.

In the afternoon he telephoned his attorney, Leo Steyn, from his bank. On his divorce and other matters, Leo had always been very professional. Paul listened carefully to his advice. 'As you have no doubt realised, it's basically a very simple strategy . . . What Hyde MacLeod's doing,' Leo advised, 'is treading the thin edge of the law, a tactic probably suggested by his father.'

Paul let out a groan, and mentioned MacLeod's threat to kill him with costs.

'Relax, Paul. I've made contact with Hyde MacLeod's local attorneys. Unfortunately their key man is in the Regional Court today, in Johannesburg.'

'So I sit a prisoner on my own land?'

'I'm starting proceedings immediately to put a stop to this. We just have to get a court date in Botswana. I'm briefing counsel in the next hour.'

'What about costs . . . ?'

'The court will give you temporary right of access till the matter's decided. Hold on . . . I think that's MacLeod's attorney on the other line. I'll phone you back.'

Paul waited patiently. He looked round the bank, studying the faces of the staff and the customers. Nine-to-five people, he thought; caught in the trap. But perhaps it was better living here in Messina than in the pressure-cooker environment of Johannesburg.

Five minutes later the phone rang and Leo was back on the line.

'Klaw was acquired by Bryce Norton with Leander Cayzer. They later split the property in two, and the title deeds are quite complex. Hyde MacLeod has bought all Leander Cayzer's land, so he's acquired Leander Cayzer's rights from the Cayzer family. As you no doubt realise, your grandfather and the Cayzers had an excellent relationship; there was never any legal disagreement between them. What your grandfather could never have imagined was that the Cayzers would eventually be forced to sell their lands, but they made big losses in an Australian mining venture, and Hyde MacLeod bought them out. Now what's given Hyde his opening, Paul, is simply that you've neglected to observe an old stipulation in the deeds which states that the owner must be resident on the property for at least two weeks of the year – otherwise the right to access can be denied, and would then have to be re-negotiated. Obviously, the Cayzers would never have enforced this stipulation – but Hyde MacLeod is a different animal altogether.'

Paul cursed silently. He'd had a sneaking suspicion that Hyde MacLeod might have taken advantage of some loose agreement made between the Cayzers and the Nortons years before. All his life he'd been a victim of small print. He preferred action, doing things, he couldn't be bothered with the pathetic minutiae of everyday life. Now his inability to focus on detail had caught him out yet again. He wondered how much it was going to cost him to contest Hyde MacLeod in court. The bastard must have been waiting for him to slip up; he should have moved into Bush Camp straight after his father's murder, instead of returning to Johannesburg for a month.

'There's more,' Leo Steyn was saying. 'You see, this could affect your right to the land. Hyde Macleod could try to force the trust to sell Klaw, on the grounds that the reserve is useless without access. And according to this document, he has first option.'

'Damn it!'

'His attorney also told me that he'll fight you all the way. But they'll make an immediate settlement if you agree to sell Klaw to him at a market-related price.'

'Well, I'm buggered if I'm going to be screwed by Hyde MacLeod,' Paul snorted.

'Paul, relax. These are typical opening tactics . . .'

'So what are the potential legal costs at this stage?'

'I'd say about a hundred and fifty thousand rand, but of course he could draw it out. Then it could be as much as half a million,' Leo said dryly. 'Look, I came on hard. They've agreed to give you access for the moment, but they want the hearing in three months' time.'

'Very generous of them.'

'There's more. Hyde MacLeod has negotiated to buy back the land the Cayzers owned in Smuts' time, to which he has first option, from the South African government – the Vembe Nature

Reserve. Which means that on top of owning almost all the land surrounding your reserve, he owns most of the land over the South African border as well. Now he could approach the Botswanan and South African governments with a plan for a mega-reserve. If the Botswanans approved, they could also force you to sell to him.'

Paul told Leo to continue with the action, whatever the costs. He thought about the MacLeods' plan: to build the reserve that Smuts had originally planned – an area almost the size of the Kruger National Park – and to use Rock Lodge at Klaw, with its perfect location, as the main camp. Well, he wasn't going to give in. He'd even sell the house in Johannesburg and the King Air to raise money, if that was necessary. He'd learned enough about life to know that if you didn't fight for what you wanted, you never got it. Hyde MacLeod would have to kill him before he got Klaw. Anyway, he had no choice: the reserve was home for Mkhulu, and for Shiva and her cubs.

Paul and Mkhulu drove back to the border post at Pont Drift just before four. Paul made an arrangement with the owner of the store at Palma to leave his Toyota bakkie there.

As they walked through the Botswanan border post they saw some wealthy American tourists, who had flown into Hyde MacLeod's reserve earlier in the day, going through customs. Paul eyed the woman's hands, dripping with diamonds. He could imagine what sort of rates Hyde MacLeod charged for a week on his game farm – probably more than most people earned in a year. Then and there, Paul decided he was going to make Klaw work as a paying proposition – to spite Hyde MacLeod by offering guests a better bush experience than he ever could.

Now moving on foot, they made it to the border of Klaw towards the end of the day. Paul saw that all the poles of the MacLeods' barricade had been removed from the road, except one with a typed legal notice nailed to it. He tore it off and read it in the half-light. It was notification of the pending case and the time and location of the hearing. The bastards had been waiting to get him all along.

They walked as quickly as they could along the sand track, getting back to Bush Camp just as the sun was beginning to fade. Later, Shiva and her cubs came to see them. Paul got the meat he'd taken from the freezer that morning and tossed it to them. He watched them feast on it. In six months time they'd be able to fend for themselves, but now they were vulnerable, dependent on man for their survival – a situation Paul did not want to persist for any longer than was necessary.

As the sun set over the horizon, angry and red, Paul sat with Mkhulu on the main deck. Long white clouds, tinged with yellow, lay suspended in the blue. Paul got up and went inside, fetching a bottle of whisky and two glasses. 'Join me?'

Mkhulu laid his hand on Paul's arm. 'Have a drink, I'll be back later. I want to take a look around. I don't trust that Hyde MacLeod at all.'

The big man disappeared below, hobbling on his artificial leg. There was the sound of the Landy starting, then driving away. Paul looked ruefully at the whisky bottle. Now was not the time for drinking. He needed his wits about him.

He took the bottle back inside, poured himself a glass of water and went back onto the deck. He laughed quietly to himself – then started coughing. There were tears running from his eyes by the time he got it under control. God, he'd been smoking and drinking himself to death since the divorce. And he knew his last documentary hadn't been up to standard. Fortunately he'd managed to sell it, but he knew the station wasn't exactly happy with it. He'd been a fool to think they wouldn't notice the drop in quality. He'd fought hard to earn his reputation, but it wouldn't take him long to lose it. He had to get his act together. He'd allowed himself to become complacent.

He sat down on one of the old *riempie* chairs and stared up at the darkening sky.

In the distance there was the crack of a rifle shot. He felt uneasy. It might be poachers, or it might be hunters in the Zimbabwean reserve. It could even be Hyde MacLeod indulging his guests in some unauthorised hunting. How safe were Shiva and her cubs? In Africa the last thing one ever felt was a sense of security.

Far away he heard a lion's roar. He felt drained; things seemed to be mounting up against him; he should have gone with Mkhulu, but he was exhausted. He didn't want to think about losing the reserve, there was no way he was going to give in to Hyde MacLeod, even if the legal battle cost him everything he owned.

He went into the study and started reading through the first of his father's files. Time passed, but he was oblivious.

Just after ten, he heard the noise of an approaching vehicle. He hunched forwards. Not more trouble from Hyde MacLeod? Then he recognised the sound of the Landy's engine, and moments later Mkhulu hobbled onto the deck.

'Did you hear the shot?' Paul said.

'Yes, but it was far to the north – hunters.' Mkhulu sat down next to Paul.

'Something bothering you, Mkhulu?'

'You'll have to speak to Hyde MacLeod about Shiva and the cubs, Paul. I spoke to one of his black trackers – he told me MacLeod's farms across the South African border are used for hunting.'

Paul stared out into the blackness. 'No,' he said. 'I don't want the bastard to know about Shiva and her cubs. Anyway, it's illegal to shoot lion here and in the Zimbabwean reserve. Shiva and her cubs will be fine, there's no reason for concern. There's an electric fence across the South African border, and I can't see Shiva crossing that.'

Mkhulu nodded. 'I suppose you're right.' He put his rifle down against Paul's chair. 'That old upright piano inside – can you play it?'

'Yes, but I'm a bit rusty.'

'Wait a moment.'

Mkhulu disappeared for a few moments and returned carrying a large black case. Paul moved to help him, but Mkhulu gestured him away. He put the case down on the deck, undid the two chrome latches and raised the lid to reveal a tarnished saxophone. He lifted the instrument out of its case, then attached the reed to the mouthpiece.

As he rose and lifted the instrument to his lips, he staggered forwards, off balance. Paul caught a look of desperation on the black man's face.

'Here,' Paul said, grabbing a high stool, 'use this.'

Mkhulu shifted onto the edge of the stool, drew in his breath and started to play. A long, agonised opening note, followed by

61

a series of short stabs. Then he moved into a short piece, intense in its agony – so much held in the air, so much that could never be put into words, now expressed in the lyrical, haunting notes of the saxophone.

As he finished, Mkhulu looked up. 'Your father told me that when you lived here as a young boy, you used to play the piano at night.'

'I still play . . . not very well. Helen, my wife, didn't like jazz.'

'I never stop playing. When I first lost my leg, I thought of suicide. I'd wanted to go to Soweto, to play in the clubs. But I went on playing all the same; music is a language that takes no account of the colour of a man's skin; it eases my soul. If you have the talent to express yourself through music, don't cut yourself off from it.'

Paul went silently into the lounge. He touched the old upright piano, and then he pushed it outside onto the deck. He drew up the stool and opened the lid. His fingers caressed the keys and he was transported back thirty years, his father sitting next to him. You must feel, his father had said. And in order to play well, you must practice till you want to scream. Only then will you obtain the skill, the technique, to reveal your innermost feelings.

He hit the first note, and Mkhulu's sax joined with him. They began to play, each communicating with the other, and Paul felt free for the first time in months. As the tension worked its way out of his body, his playing became frenzied and intense, the sax rising higher and higher in accompaniment. Paul did not want the experience to end, but it was Mkhulu who brought him down, took him through to the sadness and the hardship that were such an essential part of life, of Africa.

As they finished Paul heard a soft clapping in the distance. He rose from the piano and peered out into the bush which was brushed with silver in the moonlight. His eyes searched the shadows, till he caught sight of the long blonde hair. She was standing in the shadow of a tree with one of Hyde MacLeod's trackers.

Paul didn't say a word. He walked down off the deck, crossed under the wooden stilts, opened the gate in the lion-proof fence and walked towards her. As he drew closer, he recognised her – the woman in the Land Cruiser.

A cool anger suffused him. The moment had belonged to him and Mkhulu, and she had desecrated it. She and her tracker were on his land, spying on him. How dare they trespass on his land.

She came forward, and he fought back the temptation to strike her.

'Get off my land!'

'I'm sorry, Mr Norton, I thought we could walk here,' she said softly.

He gripped her wrist hard, but she did not cry out. He intensified his grip, wanting to hear her whimper, but she held his gaze defiantly, refusing to capitulate.

'Don't you ever, ever come onto my land again.'

She pulled away, and he caught a fleeting look of sadness in her eyes. Then she and the tracker were gone, disappearing into the bush.

Paul walked slowly back to the deck to see Mkhulu putting away his sax. Mkhulu looked him steadily in the eye.

'You should not have done that. She was watching me with Shiva the other night. She's called Dr Madison and she knows a lot about lions.'

Paul went up to the piano again and began to play. He hit the keys hard, aggressively, trying to drive the image of the blonde American from his mind. He had wanted to hurt her but she hadn't let him, and now Mkhulu was angry with him too.

Wayne MacLeod leaned back in his chair, away from the computer screen, and stared hard across at Dr Anne Madison. He could see she was upset, clutching her bruised wrist. He pulled a cigar out of his humidor, clipped it with a silver cutter and then placed it slowly in his mouth, moistening the tobacco leaf between his lips. He savoured the pleasure of sucking on the cigar, flicking on his lighter, toasting the end and inhaling the first smoke.

'I need you to press charges,' he said. 'It was a clear case of assault, Anne. He had no right to hurt you. Besides, Johannes was witness to the incident.'

He gave the Reuters screen a quick glance and then turned

back to the matter in hand. He desired this woman. He wasn't interested in her qualifications, her reputation, or her big cat project funded by the United States Fish and Wildlife Service and the Cat Specialist Group of the World Conservation Union.

He scrutinised her carefully; the dark green eyes, the long blonde hair, the firm jaw and wide, expressive lips. Her body was tall, perfectly proportioned and very strong; he knew she excelled at sports – she'd given Hyde a hard match on the tennis court. And yet Dr Anne Madison still remained largely a mystery to him – she wasn't forthcoming on the subject of her background or her beliefs.

'I think Mr Norton had the right to be annoyed,' she said. 'I was under the mistaken impression that we were free to walk on his land.'

Another taste of the cigar. 'We are.'

'But Hyde denied Mr Norton access to his farm up till yesterday. He was justifiably angry.'

He would have her soon – pull off her clothes, feel those firm nipples with his lips.

'Hallo, Wayne.'

Damn. It was Charles Fox, Hyde's best friend and chief ranger. Charles sat himself down in an easy-chair and leered across at Anne. 'Did you enjoy your evening out with Johannes? Nothing like a black man in the sack, eh?'

Anne gave him an icy glance.

Wayne MacLeod frowned, concentrating his mind on Norton. He had to nail him once and for all. He was becoming a menace. He sucked on his cigar again, and said: 'I want you to make a statement to the Botswanan police, Anne.'

She turned away and he noted her stubborn jawline. She gave the impression of being immovable, but underneath he knew she was very vulnerable.

'Listen, I've given you a lot of support on your project, haven't I? Now all I'm asking from you is a little co-operation.'

He watched the swing of her hair, felt her green eyes locking onto his. 'Wayne, I can understand how you feel about Paul Norton,' she said. 'Look, I'm against his treating his lions as glorified pets. It could cause serious and lasting problems with the local lion population.'

'Ah, so that's what he's up to . . .' MacLeod stared up at the ceiling. 'Looking after old Lionel's lioness and her cubs, eh? I heard that the male had been shot.'

Anne wondered if she should have let on that Shiva and her cubs were on Klaw.

'Look, Anne, I'm not asking you to do anything except tell the truth. Norton ordered you off his property, and that's expressly against the terms of the traversing rights that govern his property and ours. Even that I can forgive. But as for hurting you, that's another matter. I'd like you to file a charge of assault. Look . . . He's not going to go to jail for it. It will just be a warning.'

Anne thought about the look in Paul Norton's eyes as he hurt her. He'd wanted to see her cry.

'All right, I'll make a statement.'

His eyes caught a flicker on the screen, and he turned away. 'Ah, excuse me, another flurry of activity in Tokyo. Got to concentrate now.'

As he stared at the screen he heard the sound of Anne's low-heeled shoes on the tiled floor. Good, he'd finally got full control over her. He would use her to put another nail in Paul Norton's coffin.

Sure that Dr Anne Madison was gone, he leaned back from the screen and stared at Charles Fox. 'Have you and Hyde devised a scheme to get Norton out of the way? The man's irritating me.'

'No, sir.'

'I don't like you, Fox. If you want to keep your job, I suggest you find a way to nail Norton, fast.'

'All right sir, I'll try.'

'No, don't try. Do it. And another thing. Keep your hands off Dr Madison – she's out of bounds. Get it?'

'Yes, sir.'

Anne Madison walked across the hot sand, back to her room. She supposed Wayne MacLeod was right. Anyway, it was her project that was of primary importance. She went up to the portable computer and started to work, analysing the information she'd collated. But she gave up after a few minutes, because Paul Norton's face appeared in her mind and wouldn't go away. She couldn't believe the attraction she'd felt when he came close.

She focused again on the screen and typed in another observation. The theory had been that the lions in Tuli were isolated from other prides, but she had accumulated evidence that there was a movement of lions in and out of Tuli. For the past month she'd gone out day and night with Johannes, tracking lions.

It was the day before last that they'd spied the giant of a black man with the artificial leg. He was striding through the bush with a rifle.

Johannes had touched Anne's arm. 'He was a hero in the Zimbabwean bush war. He says he lost his leg to a lion, but I know he lost it trying to save a man's life. His foot got blown off by a mortar. He's protecting Shiva, Lionel Norton's lioness, and her cubs.'

Anne was immediately intrigued. She had been involved in the controversy surrounding 'Lion' Norton, the charismatic figure who had reared lion cubs and eventually reintroduced them into the wild. She and other conservationists had criticised 'Lion' Norton on the grounds that he was interfering with nature and turning his lions into glorified pets.

The following day she and Johannes had walked close to Bush Camp, and with her binoculars she had seen the big black man playing with a fully grown lioness in the sand. Suddenly she'd realised how removed she was from what she was studying. She sensed the danger of the situation and admired the courage of the man. She had wanted to get closer, but Johannes had touched her arm.

'No, leave them.'

That evening she'd insisted Johannes take her onto Klaw again. They'd been skirting the edge of Bush Camp when she was drawn by the music. Johannes suggested they move away, she was the one who'd insisted they go closer. She wanted to learn more about Lion Norton's son, Paul – the man who owned Klaw.

Now she felt compromised. She needed Wayne MacLeod's support to continue her work, but she felt uneasy about the way he was using her.

Her mind drifted back to her father, Joe Colson, head of the Central Intelligence Agency. He was a bit like Wayne MacLeod – a driver. Her father had pushed her hard, trying to turn her into the son he'd never had. He'd put her through the agent training course and she'd excelled. Except that she hated the thought of becoming an agent. Well, he'd never forgiven her after she dropped out, just before the end of the course, and since that time she'd never been allowed in his home. They hardly ever talked. God, why had he tried to push her so hard, and why hadn't she resisted before he put her on the course?

Just as she was about to begin working again, she smelt burning. Looking out of the open window, she saw a plume of smoke rising above the compound next to the camp. Something was wrong.

She ran outside, her feet flattening the sand as she sprinted towards the village of thatched huts where the workers lived. Now she knew which hut the smoke was coming from, and she forced herself to move even faster.

The scene unfolded before her. Hyde, holding the jerrycan; Johannes held firmly by two of the camp's security guards. In front of them, Johannes' belongings were going up in flames.

Charles Fox's Land Cruiser was parked slightly to one side and she veered towards it, snatching up the custom-made pump-shotgun Charles always took with him. She pumped a round into the magazine and aimed the barrel at Charles' back.

'What are you doing, you bastard?' she cried.

'Put the gun down, you silly bitch,' he replied coldly, turning round.

'Stop it!'

She pulled the trigger. The shot exploded, ripping through the side of Charles' bush-pants.

'Put it out!' she ordered.

The guards let go of Johannes, looked at the mad American woman in terror, and tried to stamp out the flames. Charles remained staring at her, blood running down his leg where the shot had grazed it.

'You bastard!' She threw down the weapon and wrenched the fire-extinguisher from the front of the Land Cruiser. But despite her efforts and those of the guards, the fire refused to go out. Soon Johannes' possessions were a charred pile.

Charles limped across to the Land Cruiser, hatred burning in his eyes. 'Stay out of this. Johannes was caught stealing. He's not setting foot on MacLeod property again.'

She felt the anger coursing through her veins. She hated Charles for what he had done.

'You can't turn him out!'

'Leave the compound this instant, Dr Madison. This is none of your business.'

She held his gaze for a few moments, then turned on her heel and stormed back to her room. She lay on her bed and stared at the large ceiling fan that whispered above her. She lost all sense of time, and at last drifted into an uneasy sleep.

Knocking woke her. She opened her eyes and stared out of the door into the darkness. Was someone there?

'Dr Madison . . .'

She recognised Johannes' voice. 'Come in,' she said quickly, drawing the curtain and closing the door softly.

She switched on the light and saw Johannes staring at her, a hardened expression on his face.

'So, have the MacLeods bent your will to their ways?'

Anne blushed beetroot-red. 'What do you mean?' she stammered.

'I refused to make a statement that Norton hurt you. That is why they burned my hut down. They planted Hyde's Rolex watch in my hut and said that I stole it. Now I shall have a criminal record, but at least my conscience is clear.'

Johannes melted out of the door into the darkness, leaving Anne alone in her room, unable to reply. She stared for a long time at the wall. She knew that if she didn't make her statement, Wayne MacLeod would fire her. She couldn't back out.

Paul watched the big cat walk off into the fading light, and in his heart felt a tremor of anxiety. She had come to visit him for a short while without the cubs. Now she would return to them, and in the darkness he could do little to protect them.

Mkhulu picked up the rifle and moved off into the darkness

after her. How he managed to track in the blackness was beyond Paul, but the black man worked from instinct.

'Take care . . .'

'Sleep well, Paul. I think she's heading towards the Limpopo. You can take over at first light.'

Hyde laid down his binoculars and snarled, watching the lioness heading off towards the east. He could imagine the publicity that would accrue to Paul Norton and Klaw – people would come from all over the world to see Shiva, Lion Norton's lioness. Hyde had thought that with Lion's death his work would end. He had thought that the war-cameraman son would sell the reserve to them. But he had miscalculated.

Now Hyde sensed that his own work would be overshadowed. He wanted fame, but it eluded him; he lived in his father's shadow. Worse, his own fear of lions had increased. It was almost as if the lions sensed the weakness within him.

As he watched the big black man play with the lioness over the previous few days, jealousy had grown in him like a cancer. He wished he could enjoy the same rapport. He hated Paul Norton and Mkhulu. And now he sensed that Dr Madison, employed to heighten his own and Cayzer's stature, was also developing an interest in Norton's lioness.

Well, that was all about to end.

Thoko made her way carefully through the darkness. She had not been able to leave Messina early, and the sun was setting when the man who always gave her a lift dropped her near the Pont Drift border post. There was a long-standing arrangement that she could walk through Hyde MacLeod's farm on the South African side and then cross the border much further north, through a gate in the electric fence.

Darkness fell quickly as she continued on her way along the track that ran to the east of the Limpopo, parallel with the electric border fence. Just an hour's walk and she would be with her father, Johannes. A whole month of working for a weekend of living . . . She was determined to pass her exams, then she would qualify for a loan from the bank, and she could buy a house for them in Messina. Later would come a car – then she and her father could live like human beings.

Only the week before, the regional manager of the bank had visited the branch where she worked and taken her aside. He said that he had been impressed with the manager's reports on her progress and with her diligence in studying part-time. Her efforts would be rewarded, he promised her. But these things she kept from her father. She would only tell him about it all when it actually happened. She would never stop dreaming of a better life. She saw how Hyde MacLeod exploited Johannes; her father was more knowledgeable than any of the white rangers, yet as a lowly tracker he earned even less than the pittance they received.

Now, in the dark, she stripped off her town clothes and changed into a simple shawl that she wrapped tightly around herself. Then she put her city clothes into the big shopping bag and put it up on top of her head. She wasn't scared of the dark. She had spent a lifetime in the reserve and knew the paths well. Risk was something a black person lived with, night and day. Life was a matter of survival.

But after half an hour she had the uneasy feeling she was being watched. Then suddenly there was a click, and a beam of intense white light blinded her. She backed away.

'Thoko. What a pleasant surprise.'

The voice made her shiver. Hyde MacLeod. What did he want now, the bastard? She decided not to say anything, just to keep moving.

'Whoa. Another step, my dear, and I'll shoot.'

She heard him work the action of his shotgun. She stumbled, and her bag crashed from her head to the ground. She made to pick it up.

'Leave it there.'

'Mr MacLeod, I want to go home.'

'You're trespassing.'

'I'm Johannes' daughter – you know that.'

'Charles Fox dismissed Johannes earlier today for stealing. I thought Johannes would have told you not to come back on my land.'

She went very cold. 'I have not seen my father.'

Hyde MacLeod moved forwards, gesturing towards her bag with the barrel of his shotgun. 'Let's see what you've got there. Maybe you've been selling stolen goods for him?'

She held the bag close to her, pushing it against her breasts. 'What do you want?'

'I want to see what you're carrying.'

She knew it was useless to object. She felt sick with fear. How could Hyde MacLeod dismiss her father? He would never, never steal. She knelt down and started to unpack her bag. Then the butt of the shotgun came down hard against the back of her head and she blacked out.

When she came round, her shawl was gone and except for her panties she was naked. Her hands were tied behind her and she was lying on the dirt in front of the Land Cruiser. Hyde MacLeod was sitting on the front bull-bar, staring at her as he smoked a cigarette.

'I'll see that you are punished for this!' she cried.

'Oh, really. I was thinking that you'd be grateful for your life. Accidents can happen to people walking through the bush. You know what I mean, Thoko?'

She got up with difficulty, and in a flash he was over, kicking her feet from under her so that she fell heavily to the ground.

'Leave me alone, you animal!'

Then he was on her. With her hands free, she could have fought to resist him, but now she was powerless. She'd always been aware that Hyde MacLeod desired black women; he watched the young girls washing by the river. Many of the other girls had slept with him, afraid of what might happen if they didn't comply with his wishes – he had the power of a feudal landlord over them. But she had never allowed him to take advantage of her. She despised him. He was totally dominated by his father.

Now his hands were exploring her breasts and she smelt whisky on his breath.

'Leave me alone!'

He dragged her up to the Land Cruiser and bent her, face down, over the bonnet. Then he took the belt from his trousers and brought it down hard across her buttocks.

He was hysterical, out of control, and her screams merely

excited him further. He ripped down her panties and forced himself between her legs. She was in agony from the weals across her buttocks, but he was oblivious to her pain, thrusting deep inside her, his fingers digging into her breasts.

'Now let's hear you scream, you stuck-up, fat black bitch.'

She felt his sap rise within her. Eventually, to her immense relief, he pulled away. When he spun her round she could see that his eyes still had a glazed expression. He buttoned up his pants with a sickly grin on his face, then pushed her hard so that she sprawled on the ground. 'Better than doing it with your father?' he sneered.

Thoko rose to her feet. She would get him for this, she would make him pay. 'You are not half the size of any of the men who have had me before,' she spat. 'That is why you have to rape me.'

As he grabbed the long black torch from the seat of his Land Cruiser, she ran for the bush. The thorns tore at her skin, but she pressed on, terrified. For a moment her spirits soared as the silence told her he was not following, but her relief was short-lived. She heard the roar of the Land Cruiser engine and the crash of gears being engaged. She let out a pitiful sigh and pushed herself on, but as she heard the tyres crunching down the bush behind her, she knew she could not get away.

The bull-bar hit her hard behind the legs and knocked her flying to the ground. Hyde MacLeod leapt down and was on her, driving the shaft of the torch up hard between her legs. Quite suddenly the pain was too much, and she blacked out.

Hyde staggered back from the bloody body and stood looking at it. The black bitch. She'd deserved all she'd got.

After a moment or two he picked her up in a fireman's lift and dumped her down in the open area just east of the gate in the electric fence. He stared out across the sands of the Limpopo, eerie in the moonlight.

Somewhere out there was Norton's lioness. She'd be hungry – desperate to feed her three cubs. Hunting alone, she'd be looking for easy prey. All he needed to do was draw her across the Limpopo and let her find Thoko's body. After that, well, nature would take its course.

Hyde inserted the cassette he'd specially prepared for the occasion into the tape-deck in the Land Cruiser and turned up the volume. Immediately the air was filled with the sound of hyenas barking as if at a kill.

'It works every time,' he mused aloud.

He lay back, his 30-06 rifle on the gun-rack above the dashboard, a bullet ready in the breech.

Paul rose before first light, and taking his rifle, made his way quietly towards the Limpopo to take over the watch on Shiva. When he found Mkhulu, an hour later, he could hear hyenas in the distance.

'I think she's about to follow those calls,' whispered Mkhulu.

'No harm in that . . . I'll keep close behind her. It'll be good for her if it's a hyena kill.'

He bade farewell to Mkhulu, took the rifle, then moved closer to Shiva.

It was a long time before she responded to the hyena calls, but at last, as the sun began to rise, she moved, and Paul set off silently through the bush, breathing out with each footfall, his eyes following Shiva's spoor.

He heard the hyenas barking across the river and crouched down low. Something was not quite right, but he couldn't fathom what. Then Shiva broke cover and moved across the sands, over the Limpopo and through the open gate in the electric fence, and onto Hyde MacLeod's South African farm. Paul wondered who had been so careless as to leave the gate open. Still, he was pleased for Shiva.

He smelt the water in the distance, and then the smell of death. This was what he enjoyed – the danger was real, the excitement of it hypnotised him. He tried to see the hyenas through the undergrowth in the distance. He knew he was close to the kill.

A red sun lifted over the horizon in a fiery dawn. Paul had always been superstitious, and now he had a sudden sharp sense of foreboding.

An ear-shattering scream filled the air. Paul felt the adrenalin surge as he moved forwards. Shiva was poised over something on the ground in the middle distance. Further away stood two hyenas, clearly frightened off the kill by Shiva. Paul sprinted forward, covering the ground between them quickly, and Shiva looked up and growled quietly.

'Easy, my darling,' Paul said softly. Then he saw the bloody body of the black woman.

'Oh, my God . . .'

The dark eyes moved dully. Then her hand gripped his arm, 'You have kind eyes . . .'

Her voice was soft, weak from the loss of blood and the pain. What had she been doing down here by the river? Where were her clothes?

He eased the thin tube from his pocket, pulled off the lid and sent the flare soaring up into the air – a plume of purple smoke across the dawn. God, someone had to respond to the signal!

With a surprising burst of energy the woman lifted herself up, her head level with his own, and Paul gripped her hand tightly. 'Hold on,' he whispered, 'it's not over. Fight it.'

She moaned in pain, and he held her in his arms, her blood soaking through his shirt. The two hyenas moved in closer, sensing weakness, but Shiva roared and they drew back.

The black woman sagged back in Paul's arms. But the blood on her wounds was coagulating, perhaps she still had a chance. . . He marvelled at her strength. Then, with a wave of relief, in the distance he heard the noise of a vehicle. It must be Mkhulu.

Again one of the hyenas moved closer, and Paul smelt its fetid breath. Again Shiva bounded forward, and it backed away. Then, as the noise of the vehicle got louder, both hyenas bolted. . . cowards that they were.

The crack of a rifle-shot burst out, Paul felt the bullet sing above his head. Then the vehicle burst out of the bush and pulled up beside him. As Shiva growled and backed away, Paul looked up to see a man standing rifle-in-hand. The smell of expensive aftershave momentarily overpowered the stink of blood and raw flesh.

'A man-eater,' the man said, looking across from the bloody body in Paul's arms to Shiva.

Paul had only time to shake his head before another vehicle pulled up. It was Hyde MacLeod. Paul wondered what Hyde

74

was doing on the South African side. He heard him talking rapid-fire on the radio. 'Charles, call Dr Madison, urgently. Someone's been badly mauled by a lion at the gate on the border fence.'

Paul held the dying woman close to him. Time seemed to stand still.

Later he was aware of Dr Anne Madison pulling up on the sands of the Limpopo below, leaping from the Land Cruiser and hurrying through the gate in the electric fence with her doctor's bag. He hadn't thought of her as being a medical doctor.

'Anne,' Hyde said quickly, 'the woman's been taken by Norton's lioness.'

Paul looked up into the green eyes that briefly sought his own. Dr Madison's delicate hands explored the black woman's wounds, then she was running back to the Land Cruiser and ripping open the first-aid box. She hurried back with a drip and bandages, and expertly inserted the needle into the woman's arm. Then she connected the drip to the feed bottle and allowed the maximum amount to flow.

'Hold it for me,' she whispered to Paul, and began to wrap bandages over the bloody flesh the hyena had savaged. That was when she recognised her patient.

'It's Thoko, Johannes' daughter!' She looked up at Paul. 'Your lioness took her?'

He shook his head. 'Hyena, just before dawn. I came across the Limpopo, following Shiva. She was investigating the hyena calls.'

Anne took the woman from Paul. 'Thoko . . .' she said softly.

At her name, Thoko's eyes opened, and as they locked on Anne there was a new energy in them.

'Will I be all right?'

Dr Madison forced her eyes down. The wounds were hideous. 'You'll be fine,' she said softly.

Paul was watching Hyde and the man with the rifle, whom he guessed to be the farm manager. They were looking at Shiva, who was still waiting in the distance, and he knew what they were thinking. He handed Anne the drip and rose.

'All right, Ryan, put her down,' Hyde said quietly.

Ryan raised his rifle, moved the bolt and slid the cartridge into the firing-chamber. Paul raised his own rifle and sighted it on the farm manager. 'Shiva did not touch Thoko,' he said. 'You kill Shiva, and I'll pull the trigger.'

Ryan looked across to Hyde, who nodded his head.

Looking on, Anne felt a chill in her bones. The lioness must be put down, surely Paul Norton realised that? She felt Thoko's hand grip her arm, and the woman began to speak very softly, and in her native Tswana, which Anne could not understand. She felt empty, powerless against what was happening. She looked up at Paul Norton, his rifle still trained on the farm manager.

She felt Thoko's hand go limp and then her head flopped to one side.

'Hyde, she's dead,' Anne said quietly.

Then she saw the inner turmoil in Paul Norton's blue eyes. He lowered his rifle and moved towards her, and she breathed a sigh of relief.

The shot exploded across the silence without warning. The lioness pitched forward.

'No!' screamed Paul.

Anne saw him lift the rifle, pivot, aim and pull the trigger. The shot hit the farm manager in the chest, killing him instantly. Then Paul threw down his still-smoking rifle and ran across to the lioness. He buried his face in her fur, sobbing.

No one moved. It was some minutes before Paul rose and walked back towards the gate in the electric fence.

'Stay put, Norton,' Hyde bellowed, levelling his rifle.

'I'm coming back, you bastard. Shoot me if you want to.'

Paul trudged across the sands, and Hyde lowered his rifle without firing. 'I'm calling the police at Alldays, now, on the Marnet System!' Paul kept on walking. The wind blew softly through the bush and silence fell over the killing ground.

Paul returned to Bush Camp sick in the knowledge of what he had to tell Mkhulu. He could hear him in the kitchen, whistling as he cleaned up. He moved across the floorboards of the deck, saw Mkhulu turn and smile, then saw the expression change as the black man read the torture in his eyes. Paul broke down, and fell to his knees. It was no good, he had taken in too much pain.

He had always been the witness, the reporter. Now he was a murderer.

Mkhulu helped him to his feet. 'Is it Shiva?'

'Oh my God, I'm sorry.'

'I must see her.'

'She's dead, damnit.'

'I want to see her.'

Paul saw Mkhulu age in front of him, the laughter-lines fading, the last twinkle going from his eyes. The face became a study in bitterness and pain. Then Mkhulu hobbled out towards the Landy and Paul followed with heavy feet. As they drove, he told Mkhulu what had happened, and Mkhulu gripped the steering-wheel of the Landy with both hands, leaning forward, suffering silently.

'So, you killed the bastard who shot her?' He turned and gripped Paul's shoulder hard with his left hand. 'Whatever happens, my friend, I will stand by you.'

Mkhulu drove quickly, his artificial leg expertly dabbing at the accelerator as he changed gear. Paul lay back in the passenger seat, feeling the first heat of the day against his face, looking across the timeless landscape. If only he could reverse time, rearrange events, change the course of his life over the last few hours . . .

Mkhulu engaged low-ratio and they edged their way through the bush towards the Limpopo. They crossed the sands, then pulled up the bank and came upon the killing ground.

Thoko's body and the farm manager's were now hidden beneath tarpaulins. Beyond, Shiva lay in a pool of blood, flies buzzing around her. High above, vultures were circling.

A yellow police Land Cruiser was parked in the distance. Paul caught sight of Wayne and Hyde MacLeod talking to a South African police officer.

Paul got down and walked across to them, leaving Mkhulu alone with Shiva's body. As he drew closer, the officer turned to him, his face serious.

'Paul Norton?'

Paul nodded.

'I am arresting you for the murder of Ryan Cilliers. You have the right to remain silent. Anything you say may be held in prejudice against you.'

Two black constables appeared from behind him and gripped his arms. As the officer put a set of handcuffs on his wrists, Paul stared across at Wayne and Hyde MacLeod. Wayne pulled a cigar from the top pocket of his immaculately pressed bush-jacket and lit up.

'We don't need your type here, Norton. Bastards like you should be behind bars.'

Paul felt events closing in on him – the enormity of what he had done. His throat went dry.

'I told Cilliers if he shot my lion, I'd kill him,' he said. 'If it had been you, I'd have shot you as well.'

The officer wrote this down and Paul realised he'd already taken statements from Dr Madison and Hyde MacLeod.

'Does this belong to you?' The officer lifted up the rifle Paul had shot Cilliers with, now sealed in plastic.

'Yes.'

Another yellow police vehicle pulled up. The officer and his two men drew themselves to attention as a man in plain clothes got out and talked to them at some length. He then spoke to Hyde MacLeod, nodding his head occasionally. Finally he walked over to Paul.

'Lieutenant Visser, sir. You are the one who shot Cilliers?'

Paul nodded.

'I am the investigating officer on this case. You will now be taken to Alldays police station where a murder docket will be opened. There is no prison facility there, so you will be taken to Louis Trichardt and held there, if bail is not granted, till Monday morning, when you will be charged in court. You have the right to consult an attorney. You realise the seriousness of the charge against you?'

Paul nodded grimly. He felt alone and very cold.

'Take him away.'

He was put into the back of the Land Cruiser, and the door was locked behind him. He pitched around as the officer from Alldays drove back along the track to the dirt road.

What the bloody hell had he done, he kept asking himself. This couldn't be happening to him . . .

*

Mkhulu stared at Shiva's body and felt himself grow hollow. There was no room left inside him for suffering, he had been through too much already.

Wayne MacLeod came over, and his shadow fell over the dead lioness. Mkhulu inhaled the tobacco stink from MacLeod's cigar. He felt his skin itching, he sensed deceit and treachery.

'Well, that's your master finished.' MacLeod paused. 'Look, Charles Fox had to let one of our trackers go – you can work for him, he'll take over the lioness's cubs. Dr Madison will assist you in reintroducing them to the wild at a later stage.'

As he listened to Wayne MacLeod, Mkhulu knew that something had been covered up. He wondered what had really happened to the woman. He couldn't believe that Shiva would have pulled her down – though maybe if she was already in trouble . . . No, there was more to this incident than met the eye, but would he ever discover the truth?

Mkhulu rose and looked MacLeod directly in the eyes. 'I would rather eat my own shit than take your charity,' he said.

Wayne MacLeod smiled, inhaled, then blew smoke into Mkhulu's face.

'You think you've got a safe little haven on Klaw, don't you? You believe that failure of a man, Paul Norton, will take care of you? Well, let me tell you, Norton's going to lose Klaw and he's going to hang – or at the very least, spend the next fifteen years of his life in jail.'

Mkhulu simply walked away from Wayne MacLeod and waited for him to leave. Eventually the Scotsman got into his Range Rover and drove off. Mkhulu breathed a sigh of relief, and went across to Shiva's body.

Lieutenant Visser, who had been observing the exchange from a distance, came over to him. 'I'm sorry, but we have to keep the lioness's body as evidence.'

Mkhulu looked into the man's eyes and found compassion. He said nothing.

'Sir. I suggest you cross back over the border. We could charge you with crossing illegally, but I know you'll co-operate.'

Wordlessly, Mkhulu moved towards the gate.

'Wait.'

He turned. The detective looked across at him. 'Mr Norton's

in serious trouble,' he said. 'It's almost Friday afternoon; if you can, organise him a lawyer, I'll consider bail . . . But it'll have to be at least sixty thousand rand.'

Dr Anne Madison lay on the bed in her room, staring at the fan rotating on the ceiling. She'd witnessed death many times – as a doctor it was all too real to her – but murder, that was something different. This was what she'd always tried to avoid, a confrontation with the uglier side of life; it was part of the reason why she'd refused to join the CIA as her father wanted her to.

She had made a detailed statement to the police officer – and as she recounted the incident she could scarcely credit that it had happened before her eyes. She just remembered the expression on Paul Norton's face as he pulled the trigger. She had never seen a man so filled with hatred. She felt both repelled and fascinated by this man whom she had just seen kill another in cold blood.

There was a knock on her door and Wayne MacLeod came in. He sat down on the bed next to her and laid his hand on hers.

'Anne. I'm sorry you had to be a witness to what happened this morning. I had hoped your time on Cayzer would be a pleasant one.'

She was deeply touched that he had come to see her – that he understood her turmoil. He was so different from his weak-willed son. She half-rose, her lips touched his and he folded her in his arms.

The police video unit arrived from Pietersburg an hour later, and under Lieutenant Visser's watchful eye recorded the position of the two bodies as well as the dead lioness. Detailed photographs of the wounds were also taken, and a careful search was made for spent shells and any other relevant material. The bodies were then loaded into a waiting ambulance to be taken to Louis Trichardt for identification, and then examination by the district surgeon. It took four labourers to lift Shiva's body into the police Land Cruiser, also to be taken to Louis Trichardt.

Paul sat in the back of the speeding Land Cruiser and focused on the passing scenery. They passed the sandstone cliffs of the

Limpopo valley, then crossed green irrigated fields and moved onto the long, bullet-straight road that led to Alldays. Far in the distance Paul could see the De Beers Venetia diamond mine.

He looked down at his wrists and the handcuffs that held them together. Why had he shot the man?

They were nearly there. All too soon. Ahead he saw the helmet-shaped rock that marked the town of Alldays, and then the 'Welcome' sign, followed by another sign enforcing the local speed limit. As the vehicle drew up at the four-way stop at Alldays, he looked back at the local church and the taxidermist's shop. He wondered cynically whether Hyde MacLeod would have Shiva stuffed and mounted. Then the police station, appearing on the right, brought him firmly back to the present.

He was taken into the charge office under the watchful eye of one of the constables. A docket was opened, and the officer in charge again advised him of his rights. Paul decided it was better not to answer any questions till he'd spoken to his attorney. Then he was taken to another office for finger-printing.

The officer rolled black ink onto a board, pressed each of Paul's finger's against it, then rolled them onto the finger-print record. This was done twice, including prints of all four fingers together, and thumb prints. Paul felt degraded by the process, though he knew it was part of the routine.

'I'd like to phone my attorney,' he said quietly.

He made the call to Johannesburg under the eye of the station commander.

'Listen, Mkhulu's already spoken to me,' Leo Steyn's voice said on the other end of the line. 'You're in serious trouble, Paul. They'll be taking you to Louis Trichardt now, and I'm going to try to arrange bail, but whether you're offered it depends on the investigating officer – you may have to spend the weekend inside. I'm flying up now from Lanseria.'

Paul put the phone down dully. He waited in the charge office while rest of the docket was filled out, then half an hour later was escorted outside and again put in the back of the Land Cruiser.

Now the fear sat in the pit of his stomach and started to corrode the rest of his body. He felt himself shaking. This wasn't something he was going to walk away from: at best a lifetime in prison, at worst the death sentence. Suddenly, he thought of Charlotte.

The vehicle sped along the road from Alldays to Vivo, on one side telephone wires, on the other power pylons, in the distance a giant massif. Little details impacted themselves on his consciousness. He passed the Vivo church spire that looked like a rocket taking off, then the vehicle swung off to the left, heading towards the mountains and Louis Trichardt. Now the country became lusher as the road wove its way towards the mountains. A township passed him on the right, the surrounding landscape denuded by over-grazing. Then – it seemed almost before the journey had properly started – there was Louis Trichardt nestling in the valley, its high chimneys pouring light and dark smoke into the atmosphere. They passed a sign for the aerodrome, and Paul wondered what time Leo Steyn would arrive.

The town came up quickly. He saw a big, flat park of sunburned grass and kids playing on swings in the distance. An ordinary life ahead for them, a dark future for him. Then they turned left up Krogh Street, past the municipal offices, and on through a street of shops, and finally pulled up outside the police station. He didn't want the journey to end.

Again he had to wait in the charge office, and sat looking up at the high, vaulted ceiling, listening to the policemen's voices echoing around the room. He felt distant from it all, removed from reality.

Lieutenant Visser came in through the door, looking grim.

'Mr Norton, I'm sorry, but there's no way I can arrange bail on this. I have reason to believe you might interfere with the witnesses, and I haven't completed my investigations yet. There's evidence that the murdered woman was raped. Also, you crossed the border illegally. I've spoken to your attorney, however, and he'd like to see you for a few minutes in private – and that I will allow you.'

Paul was marched to the side of the charge counter and then round to one of the offices behind, where Leo was waiting for him.

'Paul, come in.'

He sat down. He couldn't think.

'I could have got bail, even with the rape charge. But

82

Lieutenant Visser believes you might interfere with two of the witnesses and that's a valid reason for refusing bail.'

'My God, Leo, do you think I raped her!' Paul shouted.

'You were witnessed committing murder. I don't know what your motive might have been, Paul, but the facts speak for themselves.'

'That bastard Cilliers shot Shiva.'

'Paul, I want you to try and calm down. I want you to write everything down over the weekend, every single second of what happened.'

Paul breathed in deeply, pulling himself together, drawing on the strength that had made him a successful combat cameraman.

'That rape aspect,' he said. 'That's bizarre.'

'I know. What you have to understand is that murder with rape is a dead cert for the death penalty. And you're white and she's black, and this is the new South Africa. You're not going to get any mercy.'

Paul gripped the side of the chair. 'So what happens on Monday?'

'You'll appear before the magistrate. The investigating officer will ask for the case to be remanded and we'll push for bail.'

Paul was taken to the cells of the Messina police station. He had expected bail to be granted, he hadn't contemplated spending the weekend inside. The full impact of what was happening finally began to hit him.

He sat alone in the cell and looked at the bars. He would probably spend a lifetime looking at bars. He held his head in his hands.

The next twenty-four hours passed with agonising slowness. He didn't sleep but lay staring at the ceiling, half-awake, trying to maintain a grip on reality. Late the next afternoon the warder ordered him to get up, because his attorney had been granted permission to see him.

He was marched to a small room where Leo was waiting for him. His lawyer got up as he came in, and the warder remained standing at the side of the room. Leo remonstrated with him, and eventually he agreed to leave them alone.

'Paul, on Monday morning you'll be asked to plead to the

charge of murdering Cilliers and committing rape and assault on Thoko Sebi.'

Paul stared hard at Leo. 'Well, it's obvious isn't it,' he said at last. 'I'm guilty of murder, but not of rape.'

'You must plead not guilty to both charges.'

Paul got up and paced round the table. 'That's ridiculous. there were two witnesess: Hyde MacLeod and Dr Madison.'

'Paul, sit down.'

Reluctantly, Paul returned to his chair. 'Do you know what all this feels like, Leo?' he said.

'I don't do a lot of criminal work, but I can guess. Look, I'm trying to find you the best possible advocate. Yours is a very, very serious case, Paul. And it'll be in all the Sunday papers tomorrow, there was nothing I could do to hush it up.'

Paul shook his head. 'Did you get hold of Charlotte?'

'No, unfortunately she's away painting in the Cedarberg mountains.'

It could not have been worse. That Charlotte should learn of his arrest secondhand, via the newspapers, was the last thing he wanted to happen.

'Paul, I haven't stopped trying to get hold of her.'

'Leo, I'm not pleading "not guilty" to the murder charge. That's farcical. I killed the bastard. I wanted to.'

Leo's face hardened. 'Don't be a bloody fool, man, you're in serious trouble. You could get the death penalty.'

'Leo, I'm guilty. There are witnesses.'

'So you won't take my advice?'

'No.'

'Then I can no longer represent you.' Leo got up stiffly. Paul remained sitting.

'You're making a serious mistake, Paul. I want to help you.'

'Go, Leo.' In the few moments before the warder came back, Paul felt his sanity returning. He wasn't going to play legal games. To plead 'not guilty' to a crime he had actually committed would be a form of craziness.

On Monday morning Paul shaved carefully, ready for his appearance in the magistrate's court. He'd had another two nights and a day to think over what was happening, and he knew that his only hope was to stick to the facts and not get emotional. He knew what he had to plead – but that didn't make it any easier.

Eventually he was called from the cells and marched up the stairs into the dock. The courtroom seemed big and airy after the close confinement of the cells. He noticed that the visitors' gallery was packed, and that Leo was standing below the magistrate. He'd thought Leo wouldn't be there after their confrontation on Saturday.

'Are you Paul Norton, resident of . . . ?'

The magistrate's voice ebbed and flowed in his mind. It was all a nightmare. It couldn't really be happening . . .

'Do you plead guilty to the charge of first-degree murder, that you shot Mr Cilliers?'

'Yes.'

'Do you plead guilty?'

'Yes.'

'And how do you plead to the charge of raping and assaulting Thoko Sebi?'

'Not guilty.'

The magistrate looked at him, shaking his head.

The public prosecutor stood up and faced the magistrate. 'The state opposes the granting of bail in this instance on the grounds that the accused may interfere with the witnesses.'

'Bail is refused.'

'The case is remanded for three week's time.'

Paul felt himself swaying on his feet. This was something he'd never imagined having to face. The incident itself was etched forever on his memory in its most intimate detail, and the evidence against him was damning. He had threatened a man, and then killed him in cold blood.

Back in his cell, the grim reality of potential lifetime imprisonment began to settle in. He wondered if he might go berserk. Apart from during his three years in the army, no one had ever controlled him. He had always been a free agent – and each assignment he took on as a combat cameraman was a new challenge. The only pressure on him professionally had been for good footage. Now, suddenly, he was hemmed in by four walls, trapped.

He held his head in his hands as he sat on the bunk. This time he was cornered.

There was a noise in the corridor, and he looked up. What now? He'd read stories about prison life, he didn't want to find out if they were true.

The warder unlocked the door to his cell. 'Your attorney wants to see you.'

'I don't want to see him.'

'Don't be a bloody fool, man. You can hang for what you've done.'

The warder's voice brought him back to reality. He got up and walked ahead of him down the corridor.

'First on the left. I'll leave you alone.'

Leo was staring at the wall when Paul entered. 'I thought you were dropping my case. What were you doing in court this morning?'

Leo turned to Paul, his face ashen. 'I have known you for twenty years, Paul. I realise that you're under great strain, and I don't think you're behaving normally. I want to help you.'

Paul sat down and stared at Leo. 'You still want me to say I wasn't guilty?'

'Yes. It's the only way you have a chance.'

There was an agonising silence between them.

'I'm sorry, Leo, but no,' Paul said at last.

'Then our relationship is at an end.' Leo stretched out his hand and Paul shook it firmly.

'Thank you, Leo.'

'My God, Paul, I hope you know what you're doing.'

The next week was a week in hell. Charlotte came to see him every day. As he feared, she'd first learned about his arrest in the Sunday papers. Evidently he'd made the front page, as well as the international headlines across the print and electronic media. But none of this meant anything to Paul in his new, isolated world; he retreated within himself and refused to appoint another attorney. If the state insisted he have one, then the state would have to provide one.

Seeing Charlotte only made things worse. How could he have subjected her to this humiliating experience? Just when he thought they could spend some time together, he was almost totally cut off from her. He realised how much he loved her, how much he regretted that he'd seen so little of her when she was growing up. He was glad she was passionate about her painting – it was something he could relate to, like his own obsession with combat camera work.

He finally persuaded her to return to Cape Town, promising that when he finally got bail they could spend time together. Her visits only seemed to highlight the seriousness of his position.

When the warder told him he was to appear in court again, he wasn't sure what day it was – he'd lost all idea of time. He regarded the whole legal procedure as a farce. Anyway, as far as he was concerned: he was guilty of killing Cilliers, but he'd been perfectly justified in doing it. After all, hadn't he warned Cilliers sufficiently about what would happen if he shot Shiva?

Paul felt disorientated as he staggered up the steps and once again found himself in the courtroom. He had little idea of the huge storm that had blown up around the case, and the wave of public support that his defence of the lioness had generated. Unknown to him, the pressure on the court was now immense, and his continuing refusal to accept legal help wasn't making matters any easier for the State.

Now he stared into the eyes of the magistrate.

'Mr Norton. Lieutenant Visser has now completed his examination of the witnesses. Your application for bail is accepted and the amount is set at sixty thousand rand, failing payment of which, you will remain in custody. Should you be released on bail, you will be required to surrender your passport and report your exact whereabouts to the closest police station every Friday. The case is remanded till January fifteenth, when the Attorney General will make his decision as to whether you are to be prosecuted for murder or manslaughter as well as rape.'

Paul remained silent.

'You understand the position as I have described it to you?'

'I do.'

As he was led down to the cell again, he actually found himself questioning the wisdom of his rejection of Leo. Who the hell was going to organise the bail money for him? Charlotte didn't have access to his money, and he was too proud to ask Helen to help him. He would have to appoint another attorney – but who?

His thoughts were disturbed by the sound of the warder coming down the passage. He heard the man unlocking the door to his cell.

'You're free to go.'

Paul was taken to the charge office and handed back his watch and his money but not his passport.

'My bail's been paid?'

'You must contact us every Friday to report your whereabouts. You must not leave the country.'

He walked slowly out of the charge office, measuring each step in his mind. He was determined that he was never going to set foot in a jail again.

Outside the police station the warm sunlight felt good on his skin. He sensed someone come up behind him. Then he felt something hard pressed into the small of his back.

'Keep walking, Norton,' a hard voice said in Tswana.

Paul went cold. Who the hell was this? He kept walking, moving north along the street from the police station.

'Turn left, into the park.'

The park was deserted, no one was in sight.

'Put your hands behind your back.'

Paul did as he was ordered and felt a stiff lariat bite into his wrists.

'Turn round.'

Paul shivered as he set eyes on the old black man who had abducted him. It was Thoko's father, Johannes, the tracker from Cayzer who had been fired for stealing.

Johannes' right boot shot up and struck Paul hard between the legs. He dropped to his knees, gasping for breath, his body in agony.

'You white bastard. I am not going to watch you get off with a light jail sentence for raping and killing my daughter. You are going to die, and die painfully.'

The old man put down his gun and pulled out a knife. 'I shall enjoy killing you, you bastard – you took away the only thing I had in the world.'

Paul stared into the yellow eyes. 'For God's sake. You're wrong.'

The knife slashed across his chest and a line of blood erupted across his shirt.

'All my life I've eaten the white man's shit. I was loyal, but I lost my job, accused of stealing when I have never stolen in my life. I brought my daughter up to worship the white man's world. She worked in a bank, became respectable. Then she is raped and murdered by a white man who I know will not die for his crime.'

Paul stepped forward and held his head up, dizzy from the blood loss.

'All right. Kill me. Then you too will hang. But I swear by God that I never laid a hand on your daughter, save to try and keep her from dying.'

Johannes spat in Paul's face. 'You lie. There were witnesses.'

'Witnesses to what? My murdering the man who shot my lioness? My holding your daughter in my arms as Shiva fought off the hyenas who were savaging her?' Paul held Johannes' eyes. 'You paid sixty-thousand rand for the pleasure of killing me? That's logical. But why should I lie in wait for your daughter and then beat and rape her? How could I know she walked that way? Why should I fire a flare to summon assistance after I'd raped her? Surely it would have been better to leave the body to be found by someone else?'

Johannes stared at him.

'Then you tell me who did rape her?'

Paul shook his head. 'I don't know. But ask yourself why I should plead guilty to murder and then not to the rape?'

'These are the sorts of question that will let you walk off the charge even though you violently assaulted my daughter.'

Paul felt himself close to losing consciousness. 'You're the court,' he said. 'You've got the evidence. You choose – do I live or do I die?'

Then he pitched forwards and blacked out.

Paul came round in darkness to the sound of sobbing. His hands were still tied behind his back. In the distance he could see Johannes kneeling, his hands covering his face.

'Johannes,' he croaked. 'Return me to the jail. Get your money back. If you kill me you'll achieve nothing, you'll just be signing your own death warrant.'

Johannes did not appear to hear him, instead he seemed to be staring up at the moon. Paul heard him groan, 'Why?'

He rolled over and staggered across to the old man.

'My friend, we spend our lives fighting for the things we believe in, and in the end we realise nothing is permanent but our own integrity. Do not lose faith in yourself.'

'I have no job,' Johannes muttered, 'and I can't get a reference – I'm accused of stealing. My daughter is dead. There is no future for me.'

Paul sat down next to him. 'You're good, Mkhulu's told me that. I promise you a place to live for the rest of your days and work whenever you want it. You'll probably see me only briefly – I may hang, and if I don't, I'll spend most of my life behind bars. But if the truth about what really happened can be discovered, then you will have your revenge and the man who assaulted your daughter can be brought to trial.'

Johannes pulled out his knife, and Paul closed his eyes. Then he felt the cord binding his wrists loosen.

'Mr Norton, I believe you.'

Paul opened his eyes slowly. 'Let's go back to the jail. I'll go in, you get your money back tomorrow.'

'No. We go to Klaw.'

Mkhulu saw Paul and another man waiting on the pavement in the afternoon sun. At first he hadn't recognised the other man, but as he moved closer he realised it was Johannes. He slipped out of the cab, and Paul pumped his hand warmly.

'Who paid the bail?'

'I did,' Johannes said.

Sixty thousand rand was an enormous amount of money, Mkhulu thought; how the hell had Johannes obtained it? And anyway, why had he done it? Paul was charged with raping his daughter . . . 'Let's get something to eat,' he said quickly. 'I'm sure you're starving.'

'No. I just want to get away from here.'

Later, in the cab of the Toyota bakkie, leaving town with

Mkhulu driving, Paul stared across at Johannes sitting between them. 'I'll pay you back in a few days time,' he said.

Johannes waved his hand dismissively. 'It's not my money, it's Thoko's. She had a huge life assurance policy. The bank agreed to lend me money against it.'

'I can't believe you did this, Johannes.' Mkhulu said softly.

'Relax, my friend. I wanted to kill him with my bare hands for what he had done.'

Mkhulu studied their haggard faces. He wouldn't ask any more questions, he was sure he'd find out what had happened later.

They got back to Pont Drift late in the afternoon. Mkhulu glanced at Paul, then started to get out of the cab to walk across to the control office on the South African side. Paul would imagine he couldn't cross the border because the police had his passport.

'Don't bother,' Paul called out, as Mkhulu had expected. 'I can't come. I haven't got a passport.'

Mkhulu grinned, and took a passport out of his pocket. 'I found this at Klaw amongst your things.'

Paul stared dumbly as Mkhulu handed him his Irish passport – the one he always used on assignment because his South African passport wouldn't let him into many of the countries he operated in.

'Your father taught me the importance of planning ahead, Paul. I haven't forgotten the lesson.'

They passed through the border post without a problem, and drove into Bush Camp late in the afternoon.

'The cubs are in the enclosure, Paul. It took me a few days to find them. They're still waiting for Shiva,' Mkhulu said softly.

Paul spent an hour with the cubs, who still clearly could not accept that their mother had gone. The memories of Shiva came back to him, especially of Cilliers shooting her. In the bush death came quickly, he thought, but in the courts, society's vengeance was agonisingly slow.

The next morning Mkhulu woke to hear the sound of furniture being overturned, and Paul swearing. He made coffee and brought it into the lounge – and Paul burst in, wearing only his shorts, red-faced and sweating.

'Just ignore me, I've lost something.'

'Paul, relax, have some coffee with me, sit down.'

Somewhat reluctantly Paul settled down into an easy-chair, and Mkhulu sat opposite, his metal leg resting on the coffee table. He was about to speak, but Paul gestured to him to remain silent.

'I want you to move permanently into one of the rooms,' he said. 'Johannes can as well, or he can go up to Rock Lodge if he wants to. No, don't argue. I'm contacting my attorney this morning and I'm going to make sure that you're both given a permanent right to live here.'

'It would not be fitting.'

'Who gives a damn about fitting? You're moving in here, whether you like it or not.'

Mkhulu sipped at his coffee. 'I have one question.'

'As long as it's not a refusal.'

'No. My question is, what are you looking for?'

'My typewriter.'

Mkhulu got up and went through to Paul's bedroom. A few minutes later he came back with the typewriter in its black case.

'How did you know where it was?' Paul asked incredulously.

'Charlotte told me you had another passport, but it took me a few hours to find it, and when you search a room you get to know what's in it.'

Late that evening, after Mkhulu had retired to bed in the main house, he heard the clatter of typewriter keys coming from Paul's room. What, he wondered, was he writing?

Fahad, his face sporting its customary two-day stubble, stepped out of the dark blue Mercedes. He buttoned up his double-breasted suit and strode across the busy Knightsbridge street. As he went into Harrods he glanced left and right, looking through the shoppers as if for some acquaintance. He was being followed, at a discreet distance, by two muscle-men, dressed like himself – his praetorian guards.

A slightly-built man walked into one of them by accident, and was shoved roughly aside. He staggered to his feet and, catching sight of a policeman, was about to call him over – but realised that his assailant had already vanished into Harrods.

Fahad walked into the lingerie department and acted as if he was looking for a present for a lady-friend. He asked one of the assistants a few questions, and she laughed and touched her hair – Fahad was an attractive man with a seductive flash in his dark eyes. At the other end of the department another man appeared – well over six foot, with a heavily jowled face and huge gangling hands. He was dressed in a black suit with a white shirt and silver tie, and had rather the appearance of an American evangelist.

Fahad approached Dr Vance Torr cautiously. This was the man to whom his country had already advanced millions of dollars, the man who had helped them obtain the G5 and G6 cannons, the most advanced artillery pieces in the world. But Fahad's government was now after far more deadly weaponry.

Fahad thought about the contents of the dossier he had compiled on the sixty-year-old Canadian. An evangelist, not of religion but of ballistics – perhaps the most brilliant ballistics expert in the world. A man who had only one desire – to obtain enough money to develop and perfect his ultimate artillery piece, a Supergun that could fire satellites into space.

Dr Torr had started a company on the Canadian border, half on American ground and half on Canadian, in the 1960s – the Torr Foundation. Development work had proceeded rapidly, if not expensively, on a sixty-metre-long gun with a forty-centimetre calibre, capable of firing weather satellites into space. It was a brilliantly conceived project, designed to cut down the enormous costs of satellite launching. And as the development work progressed, Dr Torr had talked confidently of being able to fire shells horizontally, as far as two hundred kilometres.

The American military had been fascinated by the weapon and its potential. It would be much, much cheaper than the equivalent conventional warheads fired by missiles.

Then, without warning, funding for the project had been stopped. Soon Dr Torr was encountering serious financial problems – bankruptcy had seemed inevitable. However, Dr Torr's difficulties were mysteriously sorted out after just a few months, by a massive injection of funds from an undisclosed source. Research and development continued at the Torr Foundation, and no one asked any questions. In fact, when over-zealous

93

customs officials tried to investigate the premises for supposed infringement of export regulations, they were told to back off by their superiors. Rumour had it that Dr Torr had received secret funding from the CIA and, indirectly, the Pentagon.

In the 1970s South Africa unveiled the G5 155-mm gun, and astonished the world. The South Africans had successfully fought against the arms boycott and produced their own high-tech artillery equipment. World military experts had quickly agreed that the G5 was amongst the most sophisticated weaponry of its type in the world. Disquiet followed when it was realised that the cannon could be used for firing small-scale nuclear warheads. Further research, conducted over a number of years, had established a link between the Torr Foundation and the design of the G5. There was even a rumour of covert funding by the US government.

The Americans had been put in an awkward situation – accused of funding Dr Torr and leaking his technology to the South Africans. Clearly, an embarrassing situation. To Dr Torr's horror, his premises were seized and he was arrested. Sentence followed quickly – six months in a Canadian low-security jail.

There, bitterness had grown like a cancer. After his release in 1980, Dr Torr left Canada and obtained a British passport, moving to a large property on the island of Harris on the west coast of Scotland. He announced his decision to retire. That was years ago – and Fahad knew that for the past decade retirement had been the last thing on the brilliant doctor's mind.

Fahad pressed against a rack of nighties and came up to face Dr Torr. The haunted grey eyes locked on his own, the grip of the huge hand was formidable.

'Ah, my good friend Fahad. I am glad to see you. Let's have . . . a cappuccino.'

They walked to the elevator and went up to the top floor. Fahad was relieved to see that it was crowded: it was hard to be inconspicuous when one was with Dr Torr, the man's height, his bulldog face and odd style of dress made him stand out wherever he was.

Torr stirred his cappuccino reflectively. He seemed in no hurry to begin the conversation, and Fahad felt intimidated. At first he had thought it would be simple; after all, he had been supplying the funds that Dr Torr needed – he'd heard the ballistics expert was in desperate need of more finance, and to supply that need was obviously a good political move. But lately, to his growing consternation, Fahad knew that Dr Torr had another source of funding.

'Doctor, we are very, very interested in your latest development.'

Torr smiled, lifted the cup to his lips and sipped at his cappuccino. He put the cup down slowly, then laid his big hand on Fahad's.

'Fahad, my good friend, we have done excellent business in the past. But I feel I was short-changed on the G5 deal.'

Fahad flushed. He'd thought Torr was naive, only interested in money for developmental work and not for profit. Now, from the reports submitted to him by his plant, Dr Fassbinder, Fahad knew he had miscalculated badly. He watched the Canadian's grey eyes nervously. 'Short-changed?' he said.

'Don't play games with me – you obtained the G5 very cheaply from me, and then you cut me out and dealt directly with the South Africans. So you see, I'm not in a hurry to see history repeat itself . . . And there are other parties interested in my latest project, who have also provided me with money, as you have – but this time my demands are very specific.'

Fahad looked around the restaurant. No one was watching them. The sweat dripped down his face. Did Dr Torr realise that he held the ace, that Fahad's government *had* to have what Torr had to offer? In reality, the price could be whatever the man demanded.

Fahad's first desire was to torture Dr Torr, to kill him very slowly. But he was powerless to do that, because what he needed most still had to be conceived in Dr Torr's brilliant mind, and funding was the key that would unlock it.

'How much do you need to continue development?' Fahad managed.

'Fifty million dollars. Up front.'

Fahad went pale. 'No. Never.'

Dr Torr rose, dabbed his lips with the paper napkin and smiled. 'Thank you, that was an excellent cappuccino. I wish you a pleasant stay in London.'

He could not let him go. Fahad knew that if he lost him his own career would be finished. He rose, and gestured for Dr Torr to remain seated. 'Another cappuccino?'

'You know my price. If you want to continue this conversation, meet it.'

'I cannot negotiate for such a sum.'

'I thought I was dealing with the front man. I see you are just a minion.'

Fahad screamed a curse at him, and a few people in the restaurant looked around. He sat down, embarrassed at his loss of control.

Dr Torr moved his chair closer into the table. 'I do not appreciate your temper,' he said. 'You told me you had total authority – but you have just proved otherwise to me.'

'Sit. Please.'

'You agree to the amount?'

There was an unmistakable steel in Dr Torr's voice now. He had no more time for negotiation.

'I agree.'

Dr Torr sat down and smiled again. 'Yes, another cappuccino would be most pleasant.'

They talked some more. Then Dr Torr scribbled a number down on a piece of paper and slid it across to Fahad.

'In my Swiss account by the end of the week,' he said. 'I want the payment in American dollars. If the amount is not deposited, I shall consider our contract void.'

'Trust me. But we need a little more time.'

'I trusted once before. I spent six months in jail for that. I will not trust again.'

The next twenty-four hours were possibly the worst of Fahad's life. His initial phone call to President Saddam Hussein was as he had expected it – short and fiery. The President had gone berserk and refused to listen to reason. He told Fahad he must return home immediately and consider himself demoted.

Fahad spent two hours waiting in silence in the opulent, wood-panelled study of his London house in Rutland Gate, till the phone eventually rang again. There was more screaming.

'We must eliminate him, he can no longer be trusted. I thought he was loyal to our cause, now I consider him a traitor to the Iraqi people,' the President shouted. 'Execute Dr Torr.'

'And then we have nothing!' Fahad responded. 'I have it on good authority from my plant that no one else can produce what he can. Without Dr Torr's co-operation, we are powerless to achieve our goal.'

He slammed the phone down in a fury, then broke into a cold sweat. Would the President phone him back? He knew that Hussein trusted no one, and that the slightest hint of insubordination could prove fatal. Besides, Fahad had come up through the military, and he knew that President Saddam – who earlier in his career had failed to achieve a military appointment – had a deep dislike of army men.

The silence that followed was unnerving, but Fahad knew he must be patient. Probably it would be only a matter of time before the President agreed, but the question was, would he make the decision in time? The funds were certainly available, but the amount was significant, by any standards.

He remained in his study for the whole day, intermittently dozing, and reading through routine intelligence reports from his operatives in London. Day passed into night. Fahad had to get clearance by Wednesday morning if he was to transfer such a large sum into Dr Torr's Swiss account by Friday of that week.

The hands of his desk clock pointed to twelve. He felt a cold sweat running down his face. Damn it, they needed Dr Torr's Supergun, there was no other weapon they could buy to match it. But he knew that to phone the President again would be an act of career suicide, and there was no way he was going to make that mistake. But that didn't lessen the frustration he felt at losing the deal.

The phone rang five minutes later. Fahad snatched it up, and felt his spirits soar as he heard the President's voice.

'I must honour my responsibility to the cause, I will pay, Fahad. But this business is now your responsibility. If you fail, if he lets us down, you will pay the ultimate price.'

'He will not fail. The Supergun is his dream.'

Dr Vance Torr folded his hands and looked from the northern-most turret of Amhuinnsuidhe Castle into the sheets of pouring rain. He had not expected such a fast reply from Fahad, nor that the money would be deposited so speedily. But then he was playing by new rules – rules he had learned through bitter experience.

He returned to the computer screen and continued working. Apart from sleep, all he did was work. At over sixty years old, he felt there was no time to be lost.

He liked the isolation and bleakness of the Isle of Harris, and he especially liked the remoteness of Amhuinnsuidhe Castle, overlooking Loch Leosavay. It had been built in 1868 as a hunting lodge by the Earl of Dunmore, and Torr had been offered residence by the entrepreneur Wayne MacLeod, who now owned it. It was a mutually beneficial arrangement: Torr was able to operate here in secrecy, and in return he used MacLeod's network of companies to manufacture his designs. MacLeod, who'd been born on the island and held considerable sway over the local population, had led the islanders to believe that Vance was an eccentric evangelist – Amhuinnsuidhe Castle would be a spiritual retreat for Dr Torr and his converts.

What had first attracted Vance to Amhuinnsuidhe was the beauty of its unique location, overlooking the deserted loch, yet close to the hydro-electric dam on Loch Cleostair, which provided a constant source of electrical power for his computers.

Torr had gutted and refurbished much of the castle's interior. Now the main dining-hall was converted into a small machine-shop where miniature prototypes of his latest designs could be made, tested and developed. He had a team of fifteen experts working for him, all carefully chosen for their unique skills. He looked for the same passionate commitment that marked his own career – and the same dedication. Every day he would eat with his team at the long refectory table in the high, vaulted lounge that he'd had converted into a dining-room – the food a special diet carefully prepared by the resident chef. No cigarettes, alcohol or drugs were permitted – Dr Torr prided himself on the asceticism of his team.

Now he picked up the phone and dialled a number known only to himself – the direct line to his Swiss bank.

'This is Doctor Torr speaking. I hear the deposit has been made . . .'

He smiled with satisfaction at the reply, and rang off.

The money had been deposited in the currency he requested. He was only interested in money as a means of achieving his ends, and the fifty million dollars would go entirely into funding the Supergun project. It gave him a quiet satisfaction to know that the people in the Pentagon would be on their hands and knees to him to obtain the weapon once it was perfected. But he had already decided that he wouldn't sell to them. They had betrayed him.

He went down the circular steps that took him from the turret into the quadrangle. Outside, the wind and rain heightened the feeling of isolation, but inside the castle the atmosphere was warm and hospitable. He had had the interior walls lined with an insulation material, and had then installed a huge central-heating system that created an almost tropical interior environment – nothing must be allowed to distract his team from their goal.

He walked into the refectory, and all conversation ceased. He stood at the head of the table and gave them all a warm smile.

'Again, I must remind you of our common goal, to develop the most sophisticated gun the world has ever seen. A gun able to launch satellites into space.'

They began their meal with wholewheat bread and vegetable broth. Dr Torr took a remote controller from his jacket pocket and activated the music system. Gregorian chant filled the room and echoed up and down its stone walls. His team discussed their projects as they ate. Dr Torr was proud of every one of his scientists, but it was the Aryan beauty to his left, Dr Maria Fassbinder, who held a special place in his heart. He had studied her for a long time from a distance, watching her career develop – had seen her subjected to the same frustrations he himself had encountered. Then, when the time was right, he had moved in and captivated her. However, what he had been unprepared for at their first meeting was his desire for her.

Up to that time he had had the physical side of himself totally under control. He had regarded women as necessary in the scheme of things, for the survival of the human race, but he had had no sexual awakening and had never felt the urge to marry. With Dr Fassbinder his life had changed – an electricity had developed between them over which he had no control. He was infatuated with her looks as well as her mind – her pale, almost translucent skin, her long black hair and her dark blue eyes.

Now he sensed those quick, dark eyes resting on his. Already she had guessed he had good news for them – it was as if she could read his mind.

At the end of the meal, Dr Torr rose, and everyone at the table fell silent in anticipation.

'As you know,' Dr Torr said, 'the biggest problem we face is funding. To take our designs from the development stage to final completion requires huge amounts of capital – especially with the Supergun project. Now, this morning I had confirmation of a backer – a source willing to fund the development of our design to completion and, even better, to use the finished weapon to launch a satellite into space.'

There was muffled applause. He smiled confidently, and continued: 'As a result of this, all our other projects will be shelved for the moment. The Supergun will be a cannon of a type the world has never seen – the main purpose will be to launch surveillance satellites into space for our client. We will develop the design and the prototype, and then, in a facility whose location I cannot yet reveal, we will begin production. Delivery must be achieved by the end of 1990.'

Later Vance stood outside on the turret, its flagstones still wet from the heavy rainfall. The moonlight cast eerie shadows across the castle, and he could see the waves of Loch Leosavay crashing against the shoreline far below.

He remained there a long time, thinking about the Supergun and the sensation it would cause. His vision of projecting a shell into space would be realised. And when the Supergun launched its first satellite, his name would become immortal as history's greatest designer of artillery. It would be the proof of his genius, a triumph over those who had not believed in him.

He sensed someone behind him, and turned. It was Maria Fassbinder – he didn't know how long she had been watching him. He felt no complusion to speak. Then her lips parted slightly, and he smelt the exotic fragrance she wore. He was drawn towards her and their lips caressed, then his mouth closed over hers and he held her in a long, delicious kiss.

Eventually she parted from him. He felt an emptiness, and a longing growing inside him as she disappeared through the doorway into the spacious bedroom that filled the upper level of the turret.

She awakened fantasies in his mind even more exciting and fulfilling than those he had experienced in scientific discovery. She was the first woman with whom he felt sexually fulfilled. It was as if the development of the Supergun marked a new period in his life – he felt thrilled to the core.

He followed her inside, and in the darkness her naked body melted into his own.

There was nothing he could not achieve.

Paul sat outside on the deck of Bush Camp, pounding away on the keys of his typewriter. Inside his room was a file containing the hundred pages of film script he'd already completed.

His face had a gaunt, almost haunted look about it. He had not drunk or smoked since being released on bail. Every morning he spent an hour with the three lion cubs, then started working on the script again. He was a man possessed. This was the only outlet for the strain and tension building up in his body. He had always thought about making a film about his father and his relationship with lions – now he was working on a script in order to retain his very sanity. He immersed himself in the world of his father's diaries, notes and films. He didn't want to think about the coming trial – the possibility of the death sentence or, at the least, life imprisonment.

He had made twenty documentaries during the course of his career as a combat cameraman. Five had won major international awards: films on Vietnam, on the Rhodesian bush war, on the Soweto riots, on Afghanistan, and finally one on the Falklands conflict. All had been controversial and all had heightened his reputation as the world's foremost combat cameraman. Many of the men who had worked alongside him had died, and few of those who were left would work with him now. He was considered to be slightly mad.

But now he was producing something with a deeper meaning. Though the film would be about his father and his work with lions, it would convey a symbolic message for mankind. The

101

script hadn't evolved from any well-thought-out plan, but had been born out of Paul's own memories and his father's meticulously kept diaries.

Paul leaned back from the typewriter, got up and stretched. The long periods spent over the machine were hammering his back.

The trial date was in less than a month's time. He wanted the script finished well before then – he'd invited Charlotte to the reserve. He knew she had been suffering from the wave of bad publicity he'd been subjected to. At least, here in the reserve, he had escaped that.

There'd always been criticism of his father. Armchair conservationists had objected to what he was doing with his lions – people like Hyde Macleod and Dr Anne Madison, people with influence or a string of university degrees, but with no genuine experience of what they were talking about.

He stared out across the bush and watched a small buck moving timidly towards the artificial waterhole. The buck was afraid of predators – danger, that was the price of freedom in every aspect of life.

He knew that, if he was sentenced, he wouldn't see Charlotte again for a long time. He wouldn't be here, he'd be locked away in a cell, out of contact with everything that made his life worth living. He'd never lived indoors, always preferring the open and a life that was filled with risk. The thought of imprisonment made him feel desperate.

He hadn't appointed a new attorney, or even counsel. His only real support came from Mkhulu and Johannes.

Mkhulu's voice echoed again and again in his subconscious. Mkhulu had become more than a friend – he was now Paul's support system, keeping him writing whenever he felt tired or depressed. He thought of the endless dialogue between them:

'You must never feel guilty, Paul. What you did was right. It was as if Cilliers killed your child – your daughter. You never had a chance to develop a true rapport with Shiva, Cilliers took that away from you. There was no other way you could have reacted.'

'But, Mkhulu, the bloody world – a court of law – doesn't see it that way.'

'I pray for you every night. I pray that someone will help you.'

In the days that followed Paul pushed himself harder. He was barely conscious of what he was typing, the script just poured out of him, a sublimation of all his frustrations. He drifted around only half-aware, ignorant of what was happening in the outside world, lost in the complexities of the script – linking existing film material with new material, developing the blueprint for a film with all the veracity and raw impact of his best documentaries.

He was scared of jail, of being alone and caged. He began to question the nature of justice. He knew that if the situation repeated itself, he would react in the same way. Perhaps he had become too close to Shiva. Yet every hour he spent with her cubs reinforced the knowledge that he had had to avenge the death of their mother.

Eventually, at two o'clock one morning, Paul collapsed over his typewriter. The script was completed.

Mkhulu came in later and lifted Paul over his big shoulders, taking him, half-asleep, into the bedroom. He covered Paul with a blanket and stared down at the deeply tanned face that reflected so much suffering.

'If there is any justice left in the world, my friend, I hope you find it,' he murmured, turning down the paraffin lamp.

The large Mercedes whispered along the razor-straight tarmac road, the sunlight creating dappled reflections on the windows. It was a magnificent machine with fine coachwork and a massive engine. Behind the wheel sat a man in his mid-thirties. Closely-cropped dark curly hair surrounded a hard face with a distinctive hook nose that was faintly intimidating. The lean hands held the wheel firmly, keeping the car on its course, and the dark eyes never wandered from the road. As he drew up at the border post, his car attracted a lot of attention from the customs officers, especially the air suspension, which let the body sink over the wheels when the engine was turned off.

He went through the border gates, looked down at the dirt track that crossed the Limpopo, and parked his car under some trees. He lay back in the broad leather driver's seat, stretched, and then consulted his maps. Finally he got out, took a leather holdall from the boot and locked up the car. Then he trudged along the sand track, across the dry bed of the Limpopo, over to the Botswanan border.

At the customs post he filled in the entry form for Botswana and shoved his Israeli passport across the counter. The black customs official looked through it cursorily, then at the form.

'Mr Katz, you're going to see Paul Norton on Klaw?'

'Right.'

'Where's your transport?'

'My car won't make it across here. I'll be walking.'

The man laughed good-naturedly. 'Sir, you're obviously new in Africa. This area is wild. You can't walk here.'

The dark eyes of the Israeli caught his own. 'You're wrong, I've lived here most of my life. Tell me, how do you and your assistants get here in the morning?'

The official found the glance unnerving and shifted his eyes away. 'I walk, white man.'

'Then I'll walk as well.'

The black man gripped his arm. 'White men do not walk. It is dangerous. Come, I will drop you on the border of Mr Norton's farm.'

David Katz watched the black man as he drove slowly along the dry dirt road across the expanse of open bush. 'Do you know Paul Norton?' he asked.

The black man nodded his head.

'What sort of man is he?'

'He has courage. He works with the lions.'

David Katz smiled to himself. 'You like him?' he said. 'A man accused of beating and raping a black woman?'

The man made no reply to this. Then he said, 'Who are you?'

'I am a lawyer, I have come to try and help him.'

There was a pause before the black man said simply, 'We know he is not guilty.'

They pulled up at the side of a dirt road turning off to the left. David Katz saw a battered sign with the word 'Klaw' painted on it, hanging loosely from a tree. Far in the distance he saw a huge rock formation, with a magnificent stone lodge at its edge.

104

'Straight up the road, Mr Katz. He's in Bush Camp, not at Rock Lodge which you see ahead.'

'Why don't you take me there?'

'It's not a good idea to be seen to be too friendly with Mr Norton.'

'But you like him?'

'Yes. But that is between you and me.'

David Katz watched the customs official drive off, and then turned up the dirt track, sweat breaking from his brow in the scorching midday heat. In the distance he heard the noise of another vehicle. Perhaps it was Norton, and he wouldn't have to walk so far. A little while later he turned to see a vehicle coming up quickly behind him, and he jumped off the track as a Land Cruiser shot past him, showering him with dust, then pulled to a standstill further ahead.

The driver, a dark-haired man in bush kit, got out of the cab and blocked his path. David recognised him as Hyde MacLeod. They'd met before in the courtroom – Hyde had been accused of whipping some of his farmhands. David had lost the case but he'd known MacLeod was guilty, and the memory still rankled – he wasn't used to losing his cases.

Hyde MacLeod stood nearly six inches taller than he was, and pointed a shotgun at him.

'You're trespassing.'

David Katz didn't show the slightest trace of fear, he was used to dealing with intimidation. Throughout his career people had threatened him, and a shotgun pointed directly at his face was a lot less worrying than an anonymous phone call at two in the morning telling him he was going to die. And he came from a family that was used to persecution; fifty years before, his father had lost his brothers and sisters, as well as his own father and mother, in Dachau. The scars were on David's soul – and the determination to live, to survive, was etched deep into his subconscious.

Now he said coolly: 'You're breaking the law, Mr MacLeod. You could lose your firearms licence and face up to three years imprisonment, plus a fine of up to five thousand pula. Pointing is a criminal offence.'

The gun barrel moved away from his face. He had an

105

advantage: Hyde plainly didn't recognise him. He watched as Hyde's upper lip flared in anger, and thought about the story he'd read in the *Sunday Times* – the story that didn't make sense to his well-honed legal mind, especially as he'd had personal experience of Mr Hyde MacLeod's behaviour in the industrial court. The man was like a raging bull.

'If you move your vehicle,' David Katz said, 'I'll be generous and forget this incident ever happened. Otherwise, I'll walk back to the police station at the border post and lay a charge against you.'

The barrel of the rifle came up again and was pushed into his nose. 'Get out of here. Don't come back.'

David watched Hyde's finger on the trigger. Then he stared straight into Hyde's dark eyes and saw in them the mentality of the coward, the bully.

'Want to discover how Paul Norton's feeling right now?' he said. 'Pull the trigger. In Botswana they're not shy about handing out the death sentence.'

The rifle barrel dropped. David fought back his anger. He wanted to go for Hyde MacLeod, and he knew he could, but he also knew what that would do to his reputation as one of the leading advocates at the South African bar. And how it might affect his current plans.

He watched Hyde walk over to his Land Cruiser and start the engine.

'Fucking yid . . .' David caught the words over the noise of the engine.

'Oh, you'll have cause to regret saying that, Hyde MacLeod,' he said under his breath. Then he picked up his holdall and continued walking along the track.

That incident, more than anything else, convinced him that he had made the right decision to find out more about this peculiar case.

He never left Johannesburg except on business, and he generally worked a sixteen-hour day, six days a week. He took Saturday off to do his shopping and to go to *shul*. Sometimes he thought he should work on Saturdays too, but his grandmother had said that would be excessive. God alone knew what she would think of what he was doing now. Actually, she'd probably approve.

His family had a long history of subjection to privation and intimidation, which was perhaps why he felt it was his vocation to use his talents to help others. His grandmother, who had raised him, had wanted him to be a doctor – in her eyes he had failed her by becoming a lawyer. And nothing he ever did would change her mind, so he'd just had to get used to it.

He came up to another battered sign saying 'Klaw Bush Camp', hanging from a tree. He was getting the impression that this reserve was just about as rustic as it was possible for such a place to be.

He trudged on. There was something very pleasant about the silence. He thought about his Mercedes parked back at the border – it was his one indulgence. Otherwise he lived simply, his philosophy being that everything he owned should be able to be packed into the boot of his car. The stories his grandmother had told him as a child, of the sudden necessity of flight from a pursuing enemy, were etched in his memory. His grandmother . . . She had had such an influence over him, yet he had defied her so many times. They would fight and fight, but a fierce love always held them together. When he had got his LLB with the highest marks ever recorded in the law faculty of the University of the Witwatersrand, he had really thought she would be pleased.

'Oh David, imagine what a doctor you could have been!' was her only comment.

He laughed easily now, thinking about her in the openness of the bush. She was incorrigible. And he might not be a doctor, but he had sworn his own Hippocratic Oath all the same – and he was bound indissolubly to the members of his family who had died.

He walked on, thinking again about Hyde MacLeod. All his thoughts about the case had been confirmed by the incident that had just occurred. But why should a man like Paul Norton refuse legal representation? Why plead guilty to the murder and not guilty to the rape?

He turned the bend and found himself looking across at Bush Camp, elegant and spacious, set above the dry river bed on its huge black poles. Wire-netting was stapled to the poles, and within its confines he saw three lion cubs sleeping in the shade. Suddenly an enormous black man with an artificial leg below his right knee, appeared from nowhere.

'Good afternoon,' David said quickly.

He stared at the huge torso, the proud muscles that gave the man the appearance of a heavyweight boxer. This encounter was totally different from the one he had had with Hyde MacLeod an hour earlier.

They shook hands and talked briefly about the reserve, the weather and the general state of things. David was just about to ask if Paul Norton was around, when their conversation was interrupted by an oath.

'Fuck!' – the word echoed around the bush. David looked up to see a lean, big-boned man, about six feet tall, stride down the ramp from the main deck. The face was weather-beaten, the blond hair slightly too long for a man in his forties, the blue eyes mesmeric.

Norton looked down at him with thinly veiled loathing. 'Are you some arsehole from MacLeod?'

'No,' David said, smiling icily, 'I am not some arsehole from MacLeod.'

Paul stared at him, a puzzled expression on his face. 'Have some tea with us,' the big black man said pleasantly. Paul Norton continued staring, then extended his hand.

'Paul Norton.'

'David Katz.'

David tested the firm handshake and looked into Paul's slightly mad blue eyes. He decided he liked him.

They sat at the long wooden table made from railway sleepers on the stoep, and Mkhulu went into the kitchen to make tea.

'You're having problems?' asked David, looking across into the room opposite, at the desk strewn with papers, and the typewriter.

'No. I just slept badly.'

'You're writing a script?'

Paul glared at David. He obviously didn't want anyone to know what he was working on. 'I won't tell anyone else,' David said reassuringly. 'I know it's difficult, my father used to write.

He was a very, very difficult person to live with, especially when he was writing.'

Paul stared again at David, who refused to be unnerved. At last he said: 'I've finished, but I'm not happy with it.'

'If you've got that far, you can't turn back. You have no choice but to go on and revise it.

To David's relief, this seemed to relax Paul. Mkhulu brought the tea and sat down with them.

'I like old things,' Paul said suddenly, looking at David's leather holdall, 'especially old things that are used and not hidden away.' He paused. 'Are you sure you've come to the right place? Hyde MacLeod runs a very luxurious game lodge. Perhaps you're booked to stay there?'

'I almost didn't make it here . . .' David said. 'Hyde MacLeod threatened to shoot me if I crossed onto your land.'

'The bastard!' Paul rose from his chair, clearly ready to drive over to the MacLeods' reserve immediately.

'Relax, my friend, I think you're in enough trouble already.'

'You're a lawyer?' Paul asked suspiciously.

'Well, yes. Actually, I'm at the bar.'

'Ah, Leo Steyn must have put you up to this.'

'Er, no. In fact this is rather a delicate matter.'

Suddenly, Paul's whole attitude seemed to change. 'I'm sorry,' he said, 'please forgive me. Now I know where I've heard your name before. I have great admiration for your work.'

David's name had appeared in the press a number of times during his legal battles to save men on death row. As an advocate he handled mostly civil rights work, and had fought some of the big cases of the last few years.

David decided this was the moment to jump in, feet first. 'So why have I come to see you?' he said. 'Well, first, I don't think you're going to escape the death sentence. You shot a man in cold blood – a premeditated action. Secondly, you stand accused of raping a black woman. Yet you summoned witnesses to the scene of your crime. Tell me – and this is critical – have they matched your semen to that found in the body of the raped woman?'

The voice cut through the stillness, and Paul stared away, over the bushveld to the horizon. He is trying to shut my words out of his mind, David thought; he knew Paul must be afraid of the coming trial.

Suddenly a voice said: 'I will answer that question.'

David spun round to see a wizened black man staring at him. 'Who are you?' he asked quickly.

'I am the father of the woman Paul supposedly raped. I paid his bail . . .'

David nodded, and turned back to Paul. 'Mr Norton,' he said, 'I have never done this before, you must understand. It is against the rules of my profession to solicit work. But you see, I have many friends who are journalists, and one of them told me about the story that his paper suppressed. It was the story about how the father of the woman you allegedly raped put up your bail money and now works for you here.

'I have also come up against Hyde MacLeod before, and I know it is his father who owns the newspaper that journalist works for. So you see, I have it on first-hand authority that Wayne MacLeod suppressed that story and encouraged a media campaign against you.

'In short, with the few facts at my disposal, I've decided I want to act for you.'

Paul stared again at him. 'You drove up from Johannesburg this morning?'

David nodded. 'I suppose I could have phoned you, but I preferred to come in person.'

'I don't know how to say this . . .'

'You haven't got any money?'

'No, not that. I just don't think you can do much, given the facts and the witnesses.'

'I didn't come here thinking defeat. I knew the facts; what I didn't know about was you. I came here because I wanted your case. I believe that in certain respects it was inevitable you shot the farm manager.

'Now if this case was being fought in the US, in front of a jury, I think you might get off. But I've checked your court date, and I know the circuit judge, and quite frankly I don't think you've got a chance.'

Paul seemed to sag a little.

'You raped her, didn't you, Paul?' David stared hard into his eyes.

'I would kill him if I knew that was true,' Johannes said softly in the background.

'You beat her and fucked her, didn't you, Paul?' David said cruelly.

In an instant Paul was on David, his hands round his neck. 'You bastard, stop it!'

'That's it, show you're a man of violence. Rape is a crime of violence, not passion.'

Paul collapsed, sobbing. 'Damnit, man, of course I didn't rape her. I was trying to save her life . . .'

David got up, massaging his bruised neck. 'And that's what I believe, but no one else does except Johannes. So we've got to fight this, fight it with everything you've got.'

Paul looked up at him. 'Let's fight.'

'All right, then.' David helped Paul up. 'First I want to read your script. I want to know everything about you . . . everything.'

While Paul went to fetch it, Mkhulu refilled David's cup, and David stared across at Johannes. 'The woman who died, the woman who was raped . . . she was your daughter?'

Johannes nodded.

'So Paul supposedly raped her and then got his lioness to kill her?'

'Paul didn't rape Thoko and Shiva didn't kill her – Thoko had hyena bites on her body. But that's not the full story – she was dying before any of those predators took her.'

David hunched forward. 'That wasn't in the papers, Johannes.'

'You know who owns half the papers in South Africa,' Mkhulu said.

David's face hardened. 'You're saying there are other stories that have been suppressed as well as the one I know about? Or are you saying that the reporters lied?'

'No. They just didn't dig that deep,' Mkhulu said.

'And what is it they failed to reveal?'

'That Thoko had lived in the bush here all her life,' Johannes replied. 'She'd walked that route a thousand times without anything happening to her.'

111

'Well, what about Paul's lioness? Her cubs were hungry. She saw an easy kill – a defenceless woman.'

There was a ripple of anger across Mkhulu's face. 'I have worked with lions all my life . . . I know that Shiva would never have killed her.'

'So what *did* happen?'

There was a long pause. At last Johannes spoke. 'Hyde MacLeod was waiting for her as she came home,' he said quietly. 'He raped her and beat her up.'

'Motive?'

'I had been working for Hyde MacLeod up to that time. The day before, I had shown Shiva and the cubs to Dr Anne Madison – she's a researcher who's working for Hyde. Hyde was furious when he found out; he hates Paul and his work with the lions – he's jealous of the publicity.

'So then Hyde accused me of stealing his watch. Charles Fox, his head ranger, planted it in my hut. When Fox found it there, he beat me and burned my belongings. Then he took me to the police station in Francistown and laid charges.'

'Are there witnesses to this?'

'Talk to Dr Madison,' Johannes answered quickly. 'She saw Charles Fox and his men burn my belongings. Anyway, she's also the key witness to Paul killing Cilliers.'

David sat forward again, and Mkhulu noted that his eyes had a curious sparkle to them.

'You will stand up in court as a character witness, Johannes?'

'Yes. I do not believe he raped my daughter.'

Paul came out back onto the stoep, and awkward smile on his face. He looked down at David, then handed him the script. 'My most important work is now in your hands.'

David got up. 'I can't take this away from you – have you got a place where I can sit and read it?'

'Use my study, I'm going down to see the cubs.'

Later, Paul drove David Katz back to the border post at Pont Drift. He had made no comment on the script, simply declared that he had a lot of work to do and must get back to Johannesburg. 'Your trial is in four weeks time,' he had said. 'I'll get all the details from your attorney, and then I'll find out the state's case against you. There's only one thing I need to know.'

'And what's that?' Paul had asked, somewhat nervously.

'Find out exactly where I can get hold of Dr Anne Madison.'

Paul drove slowly back to Bush Camp, thoughts whirling around in his head. Since David Katz's surprise visit he felt he could handle the tension of the coming trial a little more easily.

Back on the main deck he found Mkhulu looking out into the bush.

'So what do you think?' he asked him.

The black man scratched his head. He thought about the strange lawyer he had had tea with on the stoep. He thought about the questions David Katz had asked him.

'I think that man will save your life,' he said.

David Katz sat in his grandmother's flat, looking across the Hillbrow flatland. She was on the twelfth floor, and this room enjoyed a sweeping view to the south, over Johannesburg and across to the mine dumps in the distance.

He heard the clink of cups as she came back into the room. She was a diminutive woman of over eighty, but she still retained some of the beauty of her youth, and her fiery spirit. She sat down on her favourite chair, her back as straight as a rod, her grey hair neatly piled up on her head. The dark eyes twinkled – eyes like his own.

'Why did you take this case, David? It sounds impossible to win.'

David settled back on the old couch and sank deep in among the cushions, munching a piece of shortbread.

'He shouldn't die,' he said. 'He shouldn't even go to prison. I think he was justified in killing the man.'

'What is his name?'

'Paul Norton.'

His grandmother looked across at him in surprise. 'The combat cameraman?'

'Yes, that's right.'

She pulled on her reading-glasses and went into the next room. David sighed. His mother had been the chief librarian at

Johannesburg Library for many years, and she kept voluminous files on people and places, and a computer catalogue of information she thought important. Often he consulted her on research for his cases.

He helped himself to another shortbread, and looked up guiltily as she came back into the room.

'You eat so much, yet you stay so thin. Just like your father!'

David turned to stare at the photograph of his father on the mantelpiece. He fought down the surge of emotion, the bitterness, the sense of hopelessness. He wanted children of his own – but he didn't want to see them suffer. Sometimes all he could see was suffering.

'David. David . . . I'm sorry.'

'No, don't be. Maybe, one day, I'll have a family.'

His grandmother shook her head. 'You don't want one now, or you'd have one. You always get what you want. You're a fighter.'

David had many girlfriends but he never told his grandmother about them. She would only know if it got serious. He looked with interest at the piece of paper his grandmother held in her hand.

'I remember the case,' she said, sitting down again. 'It was in all the papers then.'

'What case?'

'Your friend Norton – the cameraman. When he was twenty, he caused a lot of trouble.'

That Sunday Paul revised over twenty pages. He sat back from the typewriter and looked through the window at the afternoon sun, bathing the trees a delicious orange.

He heard the noise of a vehicle in the distance, and it sounded as if it was travelling extremely fast. He rubbed his eyes and walked out onto the deck. He could hear Mkhulu playing his saxophone, and for a few moments thoughts of the coming trial evaporated from his mind and it felt good to be alive.

The noise of the machine obliterated the lazy sounds of the afternoon. Paul was just realising that it didn't sound like an ordinary engine when a motorcycle scrambler slid into view in front of the lodge, its rider caked in dust. As he tore his helmet

114

off and stormed up onto the main deck, Paul recognised David Katz.

'You bloody fool,' he spat. 'What other dirty linen is there in the closet?'

Paul coloured. He guessed what David had discovered. 'How did you find out?' he managed.

'You've been up on a murder charge before! You've killed before! That was why you didn't try to defend yourself, wasn't it? You know you haven't got a hope!'

Paul felt the memories swimming back – memories he did not want to resurface, memories he tried to forget, to ignore. 'All right!' he shouted. 'Go back to fucking Johannesburg! Forget about the real fucking world! Do you know what it's like out there?'

David looked up at Paul, eyeballing him. 'You sanctimonious arsehole. You think you've got a monopoly on human suffering? My people have suffered for two thousand bloody years, but we're still fighting. You fool! With what they've got on you, you'll hang!'

'Well then, go!'

Then the enormity of what David had said registered in Paul's mind, and he walked down from the deck into the lower area, to be with the cubs.

David sank down on the ramp, looked out across the sprawling wilderness, and groaned. He'd planned to leave after he had had his say, but now he felt guilty. Paul Norton was a complex, misunderstood man.

He felt a hand on his shoulder and looked up to see Mkhulu.

'My friend, we have a great problem,' David said softly.

'I think we should have a drink. It is a good time for a drink.'

The two of them sat in the final glow of the day, sipping whisky. There were no words between them; somehow the beauty of the sunset made language unnecessary.

Paul returned when it was dark. David hardly noticed him come onto the deck, he moved so quietly.

'I'm sorry, I should have told you . . .' Paul started.

David poured him a whisky. 'Tell me about it. How you remember it.'

Paul took the whisky, sipped it, and projected himself back to Angola, over twenty years before.

'I was a different person then. I was headstrong and impulsive. I'd barely passed my matric. I never spent any time on my school work. I had no real prospects. All South Africans had to do a year's military training then, but if you opted to join the Permanent Force for three years, you got a much better deal, so I joined the PF and got into the Reconnaissance Commando. I enjoyed it – the exercise, the discipline and the danger.

'We were helping the Portuguese in Angola. Off the record, of course. It was before the Portuguese pulled out. We'd fly in under cover of darkness, drop down by parachute, hit our targets and then make our way back to the border.'

David leaned closer. 'So what happened?'

'In that particular operation we'd dropped in with another unit. The objective was quite simple: the enemy had a large ammunition dump which we had to destroy.

'I saw that the men from the other unit had landed on the far side of the town, obviously a miscalculation on their part when the jump was made. I had to find out what was happening to them – I was in command. So I left my men to place the charges around the dump, and set off. We'd taken out the sentries as we moved in. It was a cold-blooded, ruthless action: they were soldiers, we were soldiers, that was the way it was then. Only later would I question our motives.

'I moved quietly through the little town; it was about two in the morning. There wasn't a single light on – I guess the inhabitants knew what was happening. It was a good rule in that part of the world to keep your mouth shut and stay silent. That way you lived longer.

'I moved silently among the houses. I loved the danger, living right on the edge – I still do. It was a challenge to move through the place undetected. It was when I was on the far side of the town that I heard the screams. My first thought was that the other unit must have been captured and were being tortured. Then I realised the screams were a woman's.

'I had never worked with that unit before. They had an

116

excellent hit rate, and I was surprised they hadn't already made it across town to the dump.

'The building the screams were coming from was on the outskirts of the town. It wasn't hard to find – it was the only place with a light burning inside. The screams continued uninterrupted. Then I heard the distinctive sound of a silenced weapon being fired.'

David pulled out a silver cigarette case, flipped it open and offered a non-filter cigarette to Paul, who declined. David placed a cigarette between his own lips and Paul struck a match, shielding the flame with his hands.

David inhaled and coughed. 'You remember all this very vividly?'

'I wish it would go away, it will always haunt me,' said Paul, slowly sipping his whisky, glad of the break.

'Please, go on . . .'

'I came up to the building. There were two bodies outside the front door, both women. One had her breasts cut off and had been killed by a shot in the head. The other had cigarette burns all over her stomach, blood oozing from her vagina, and her face was frozen in a scream. They must have bayoneted her up the rectum.'

David's cigarette glowed in the half-light. 'How could you see this all so clearly?'

'My eyes were accustomed to the dark. I have good night sight – anyone involved in covert operations has to have. Anyway, the window above the doorway wasn't curtained.' He paused. 'I drew my Browning, screwing on the silencer. Then I kicked in the door and swivelled, aiming behind it. Sure enough, there was a man waiting. I pumped two shots into him before I could stop myself. It was one of the men from the other unit.

'I swivelled back, taking in the room. In the centre was a table, and across it lay a woman, face down, naked and screaming. Her buttocks were a mass of bloody weals, and a bayonet had been thrust through her left breast and her blood was dripping onto the floor. The commanding officer of the other unit stood by, his trousers around his ankles, a bloody leather belt in his hand.

'He turned to look at me in astonishment. Then another man

117

burst through a side-door, naked, with an R1 in his hands. He was going to fire, so I shot him in the head.

'The commander screamed at me. I pivoted, side-kicked, and drove the heel of my right foot hard into his groin. His one testicle exploded as the heel struck home. It was his turn to scream. He lay on the floor, writhing in agony, and I went into the next room. A metal bedstead lay propped against the wall, with another woman strapped on it, facing outwards, her panties stuffed in her mouth. A soldier staggered back . . . he'd been shaving off her pubic hair with a bayonet – she was bleeding badly. He went for me, and I brought the butt of the Browning down hard into his face.

'Another man came at me from the side, armed with a knife. I feinted, the blade swished past my cheek and I head-butted him, breaking his nose. Gradually the rest of the unit appeared, coming through the hall, all in various stages of undress. I knew they must have done this sort of thing on every mission they'd been on – it made me sick just to think about it.

'They looked at me dumbfounded. "Outside!" I ordered, and returned to the front room. The commanding officer was on his feet and dressed. "You'll pay for this, Norton!" he said. I pulled the bayonet out of the woman's breast and her screams filled the room. I cut her loose from the table, all the time keeping my pistol aimed at the commander. The woman fell to the floor, then gathered herself up and ran from the room, screaming.

'I took the commanding officer outside. "It's all right," he said to his men, "I'll sort this out." Then he turned to me. "You're out of line, Captain Norton, striking an officer, killing your own men. You're going to pay for this."

'I could see his men moving forward, it didn't take much imagination to know what was going to happen. "Stop!" I screamed. "Kill him," the commander ordered. I raised my pistol and shot him in the head. The men backed away. I felt sick to the core. Nothing had prepared me for the brutality of what I had witnessed, and I felt no pity for the three men I had killed.

'The men slunk together into a pack. "If I ever find any one of you doing this again, I'll kill you," I said. They disappeared into the darkness and I hoped they'd be caught by the enemy. Then I

118

returned to my own unit and we destroyed the ammunition dump half an hour later – then started off back towards the border on foot. It took us over a week to make it back to the base – we lost direction at one point, and went over fifty kilometres out of our way.

'Well, the moment we walked into base camp, the military police appeared. They disarmed and arrested me, and I was dragged off to the detention barracks and kept in solitary confinement. The next day I was visited by an army lawyer who told me I was to be court-martialled and tried for murder. I stood accused of killing the commander of the other unit, and one of his men. I told the lawyer what had happened – he looked at me in disbelief. He said I was entitled to give my interpretation of the events that had led up to the killing of the three men, but that there were eight witnesses who were testifying to the contrary.

'It was a month before the trial was held. I was kept alone, in a cell that had no natural light. By the time I made it to the military court, I was weak and angry. And I knew, as I looked at the eight faces that turned as I came in, that I didn't have a chance.

'I concentrated on each of the witnesses in turn, eyeballing them as they gave their testimony. They knew they were lying, but no one else did. That was when I realised I was in very serious trouble. None of my own men had witnessed my actions, and the only testimony I could offer in my defence was my own version of events.

'By the fifth day of the trial I was certain that I would be convicted of murder as well as being cashiered. I stared at the men who had lied, I put all my energy into catching their eyes.

'I was convicted. I remember how I rocked on my feet as sentence was passed. Fifteen years. It was at that moment that one of the eight men broke. The one I'd thought least likely to. "We lied. He's not guilty," he cried.

'They called a mis-trial. All the charges against me were dropped and I was unceremoniously kicked out of the army. There was only one condition – my silence.'

David lit another cigarette. 'Give me the names of those eight men,' he said.

Paul rattled off the names, indelibly etched in his memory.

'I'll trace them,' David said. 'The case should be re-opened.'

'But it was over twenty years ago. Look, it's over.'

David leaned forward and grasped Paul's arm. 'The state's going to push for the maximum sentence – they'll use what you did in Angola to prove you deserve to hang, that you might kill again. We have to outfox the prosecutor, we have to outrun him; we have to get the truth about that old case out into the open. So Paul, you have to tell me everything about yourself, you can't afford to keep any secrets.'

'How did you find out about Angola?'

'Research. I always find out everything about my clients. You become cynical – most people have something to hide, and few tell the truth, very few . . . Trust me, the prosecution will find out about that incident and use it against you. They'll think that we shall try to cover it up, but we won't. It can be our first ace.'

Paul stared out into the shadows between the trees and caught sight of a leopardess, stalking something in the distance.

'Come,' he said, picking up his rifle from the table. 'I want to show you our leopardess.'

They walked down to the Landy. Paul placed the rifle in the clips across the dashboard and started the engine. Then they moved slowly forward, breaking through the bush. Only after Paul had handed him the infra-red spotlight did David manage to pick up the leopardess they were following.

'We must be pissing her off,' David whispered.

'She's not frightened of vehicles – there's no hunting allowed here. It's only when people shoot at them from vehicles, that animals become afraid of them – a Land Rover presents no real threat here. Of course, if we were on foot it would be different. A little more dangerous.'

'Would you rather be on foot?'

'Yes, but it wouldn't be fair on you . . .'

'Let's go on foot.'

Paul killed the engine and they climbed out. He slung the rifle over his shoulder, and took an infra-red torch off the dashboard. They set off, finding their way in part by the light of the moon. David was surprised at how easily Paul tracked the leopardess. He himself could see very little, and he felt uneasy. The security of being in the Landy was gone – perhaps he shouldn't have pushed to go on foot.

Paul wondered if he'd done the right thing – he was exposing David to unnecessary danger. They moved for half an hour, till Paul raised his hand.

'No sudden movements now,' he whispered. 'We're downwind of her. As long as you don't move too much, she won't see you. She's been following a buck. We're down near the water now, and my guess is she'll strike very soon.'

David peered into the darkness and saw the sleek form of the leopardess in the infra-red light. The lithe cat was moving towards the unsuspecting buck at the river's edge.

Then, in one fluid movement, it was over. The leopardess was on the buck, savaging its neck and raking the soft skin of its back with her claws. The buck collapsed, half-alive, and the leopardess took it in her mouth and climbed up a tree. David watched spellbound as the leopardess's claws bit into the bark. The buck she was lifting must weigh over forty kilograms.

The leopardess wedged the buck in a fork and then climbed quickly down again. Paul knew there could be only one reason why she would leave the kill so early – she must have cubs. It was then that he grew nervous. He just hoped he and David weren't near the cubs – they would be in grave danger if they were cutting the leopardess off from her young.

The leopardess disappeared into a nearby thicket and came out minutes later, holding a cub between her teeth. She carried him up the tree and let him feast on the now dead buck, then quickly returned to the thicket and fetched another cub. Then the leopard sat back in the branches, watching her young ones gorge themselves.

Far off, Paul heard the noise of a vehicle. He gestured to David to follow him into denser cover. Now there were voices in the air, and a bright white spotlight caressed the foliage of the trees above Paul's head.

The engine got louder, and there was the sound of breaking branches. A Land Cruiser burst into view and stopped under the tree. Now there was silence among the game viewing party, who sat in the open on tiers of chairs welded to its back.

Paul watched one of the viewers – a man whose unshaven face looked vaguely familiar. But he couldn't place him; perhaps he was just imagining things.

The ranger, whom he recognised as Charles Fox, played the spotlight up onto the leopardess and her cubs. It irritated Paul, the way Fox aimed the bright light right into the leopardess's eyes. It would take the cat at least thirty minutes to recover her night vision after that – but he wasn't about to protest, the leopardess wasn't in any danger.

Paul looked from the leopardess in the tree to Dr Anne Madison, who was sitting in the front passenger seat next to Charles Fox. There must be someone of considerable importance in the party for her to be brought along on a game drive – surely she wouldn't normally be involved in this sort of activity? Her face was beautiful in the stillness. Her voice drifted across to him; she was telling her party to remain silent.

Paul had hardened himself against her, knowing she would be the principal witness for the prosecution. But seeing her again brought on a quickening of his senses. He felt disturbed. He wanted her. The anger he had felt at her disturbance of his and David's vigil had already dissipated and was replaced by a sense of longing.

'She's beautiful,' David whispered in the darkness, echoing Paul's innermost thoughts.

Wayne MacLeod watched as the helicopter pilot eased the cyclic forward and the machine dropped quickly in altitude, skimming the bush – low enough to escape radar detection, he thought as they gathered speed. He only ever came in by air. The location of the factory was known to very few – its real purpose to even fewer. There'd been an over-zealous journalist, some years before, who'd threatened to expose the set-up – a nerve-racking episode. But then, fortuitously, the journalist had been involved in a fatal car accident.

The logistics of the set-up were remarkable. At first he'd thought that not having a road into the complex was a disadvantage, but then he'd realised it guaranteed security. A road would have been difficult to conceal, especially from the air. And no one thought twice about seeing his planes in the area; his airline,

CayAir, owned a fleet of air freighters that flew all over Africa, as well as Europe. The operation offered his clients a unique advantage. No one knew about it, and its products never featured in the Jane's annual review of weaponry.

Ahead of them now there was nothing but the endless expanse of the Kavango. He kept the area around the complex stocked with predators, a guarantee that anyone moving in the area on foot would have little chance of survival.

They skimmed across the browny-yellow landscape, and he was again satisfied with the camouflage. Hiding the runway had been the hardest part, and had only been achieved at enormous expense. It had been a question of finding a colour that blended in perfectly with the landscape. The main hangar was quite invisible from the air – a gigantic underground tunnel. Access was from what appeared to be from the air, a low hill – a hill whose sides slid back to reveal a cavernous interior. But the hillside only opened once a plane had landed, so the whole complex was totally invisible from the air. Wherever possible, however, helicopters were used to move in and out, rather than planes. The advantage of helicopters was that they could be hidden in their smaller hangars in under a minute after landing – thus lessening even further the chances of aerial detection.

The pilot radioed in his code on the special waveband, and waited for permission to land. Since it was almost impossible to detect the landing area with the naked eye, the pilot used a radar guidance system to locate the correct landing-point. As he came in, the sand appeared to open up; the pilot eased the chopper down, and a landing team quickly drew it into the underground hangar. Inside, the hangar was brightly lit, its walls an assembly of stainless steel panels that contrasted dramatically with the semi-desert outside.

Wayne MacLeod stepped down from the helicopter, bathed in yellow light from the spotlights on the ceiling. He stared around. There were three other helicopters – all high-powered and heavily armed, though from the outside they looked like standard civilian models. He walked over to a brightly lit cubicle and changed into dark green overalls. Then he talked briefly into a voice analyser, and a door at the far end of the cubicle slid open.

Dirk Jansen was waiting for him.

'Good morning, sir. A pleasant flight?'

'Excellent,' MacLeod replied, looking over the control room. Every section of the complex, and the surrounding area, was under surveillance. Foot patrols by specially recruited bushman commandos guaranteed excellent protection around the periphery.

Dirk Jansen was of medium build, wearing a beret that matched his weather-beaten face. He wore black bush-boots polished to a shine and laced up to the knee. Strapped to his waist was a .44 Automag, which MacLeod knew he used with particular skill.

'Sir. We had an infiltration, yesterday evening. They discovered the doors of the main hangar – naturally they cannot be permitted to leave. The course of action I must take is inevitable. However, I felt it would be prudent to consult you before I finally dispose of the problem.'

'Very good. Let's have a look at the culprits.'

Captain Jansen flicked a switch and the largest monitor cut to two men in bush kit, lying on the floor of one of the complex's concrete detention cells. Both men looked in good shape and well fed.

'Excellent. They were on safari?'

'Yes, sir. We have impounded their Land Rover . . .'

'We will proceed with the plan we formulated to cope with this eventuality.'

Moments later they were down at the detention cells. MacLeod opened the door and stepped inside. He held out his hand, and one of the men got up and shook it. Good, he thought, we're getting to first base already. The other man got up and followed suit.

'I'm terribly sorry about this. As you probably realise, this is a secret government installation,' MacLeod lied smoothly. 'Captain Jansen has given me your details. He tells me you have agreed you will say nothing to anyone about this place. Is that so?'

Both men nodded. MacLeod knew they would contact a newspaper the moment they were set loose – he would have done the same thing himself.

'Very good. You will follow me and Captain Jansen outside, your Land Rover has been filled with petrol . . .'

Both men relaxed visibly on hearing this, and five minutes later they were outside in the blistering heat, looking with evident relief at their battered old Land Rover.

'If you can just tell us where you want to get to, we'll give you an accurate compass-bearing . . .'

'Grootfontein,' the one with the beard said amiably. 'Who are you?'

Wayne MacLeod smiled. 'I'm General Sage.'

'I was in the Permanent Force. I've never heard of you.'

You fool, thought MacLeod. Aloud, he said: 'Ah, that's because I'm in special operations. Well, we wish you well on your journey, and not a word to anyone, of course . . .'

The two men climbed into the Land Rover and moved off into the heat haze. MacLeod turned to Captain Jansen.

'How long are you giving them?'

'I want them fifty or so kilometres away from here . . . I've filled the six jerrycans on the roof as well as both long-range tanks and the regular fuel tank.'

'How many litres?'

'About three hundred and fifty . . .'

Wayne MacLeod smiled. 'Ah . . . it happens so often. Too much petrol, the heat, and then an overheating engine.'

'Yes, sir. It'll probably merit a few lines on page five of the *Namibia Herald* . . .'

Patrick kept his foot down hard on the metal accelerator pedal. 'Bloody hell, I can't get more than fifty out of her!'

His companion groaned. 'Just keep going flat out. We have to get to Grootfontein as soon as possible. Those bastards are up to something . . .' He unfurled the map.

Patrick looked down at the instruments. 'Shit. We're overheating badly.'

There was a loud bang, and the vehicle rolled to a halt. Patrick smelt burning and wrenched the fire-extinguisher from the dashboard.

'Get . . .'

Before he could complete the sentence, the Land Rover ignited into a burning torch, engulfing them both.

Later, as the sun set, the charred remains of the Land Rover were testament to yet another unfortunate safari accident.

Down in the bowels of the earth, the silence was absolute. Wayne MacLeod looked at the plans that had been faxed through that morning. They were brilliant, absolutely brilliant. He shook out his long silver hair and stroked his nose. Then he looked up from the podium at the group of men who sat watching him in the darkened confines of the lecture theatre. An eerie glow from the lectern lit his face, accentuating the size of his nose and giving him the appearance of a hawk, waiting to pounce on its prey.

He switched on the overhead projector and the room was bathed in an icy light.

'This is what you came here to assemble. It's taken three years to develop it to this final stage, but I think, as you study the design, you'll understand why.'

He surveyed the faces bathed in white light, looking for the ones he might have to weed out at a later stage. Yes, there were about three whom he did not completely trust.

'You have the equipment and technology here to develop this blueprint into a real weapon. One of my other factories will develop the shell, and another associate will negotiate the acquisition of the nuclear warheads. Everything you require will be provided. The weapon must be delivered by the end of 1990.'

There was an intake of breath. He leaned forward on the podium, staring at each of them in turn.

'I didn't select you idly. I know you can perform, and I want to see a timing plan drawn up by the end of today. The delivery date is non-negotiable – our customer is a man in a hurry.

'Secrecy is essential – you have all been sworn to it. Our client may well be at war soon, and if his adversaries learn of the existence of this weapon, your lives will be in danger.'

The faces were grim. That was what he wanted. Let them shit themselves.

'Now, I'll show you a film.'

He switched on the video projector, and screams filled the

126

room. It was footage of a torture session. The victim was hanging by his testicles from a beam in the centre of a cell; every time he passed out, a doctor stepped forward and injected him, bringing him back to consciousness. The torturer worked on the victim with a pair of pliers.

One member of the audience staggered out, and the sound of his retching filled the auditorium together with the smell of fresh vomit. MacLeod switched off the video projector and turned up the lights. The man who had been sick came back into the room.

'That's what organisations like the CIA will do to you if they capture you. They want information; your life will be irrelevant. That man, the one in the film, was kept alive for over a month after that scene. Eventually he broke, and took another ten months to die.'

Wayne MacLeod was a consummate liar. In actual fact the session had been conducted by one of his clients on a suspected spy.

'Inside this complex,' he went on, 'I can guarantee your safety. Outside, I cannot. You have each been issued with a pill in a foil wrapper. I want you to carry it with you at all times, and if you are apprehended by one of the world's intelligence agencies, I suggest you take it immediately. Death will be painless and instantaneous. Far better, I think, than . . .'

He dimmed the lights and the auditorium was filled with screaming as the torture film continued. He let it continue for another five minutes, then turned it off again.

'Gentlemen, to work!'

The auditorium emptied quickly. MacLeod switched on the overhead projector again and studied the blueprint. Developing this weapon would be his most profitable venture yet. He had managed to keep this side of his business dealings secret throughout his entire career. That had cost a lot of lives.

Everything was now in place. One successful demonstration of the weapon's effectiveness, and its value would skyrocket. He needed the money desperately; his media empire was under attack and he was leveraged to the hilt. But, as always, the money would come at the last moment and his reputation would remain untarnished.

He walked back along the dimly lit, concrete-walled corridors to his bunker. This particular bunker was probably one of the finest in the world: a West German company, part of his consortium, had developed and perfected this type of nuclear shelter. Ten metres below the surface, with three-metre thick walls, it would protect its occupants from even a direct nuclear hit.

He took the lift down to his wine cellar on the bottom level. As the lift door opened, lights illuminated the giant cellar and the fountain bubbling away in the middle of it. He walked down the lines of bottles and selected a bottle of Chateau Lafitte 1953. He held it in his hands for a few minutes, examining the label, then went back to the lift. In his office on the floor above he opened the wine and poured himself a glass. He sipped at it, and gazed up at the ceiling for a few moments. Then he picked up the phone closest to him and punched in an international number.

'Vance? How are you? Good. I think the initial design is outstanding, and we shall now develop the cannon for testing. Yes, I insist that you should come out for that.'

He placed the phone down, lifted up the glass and inspected the contents.

'A very, very good year,' he said softly.

Paul had lost count of the days and nights he had worked. He'd poured his soul into finalising the script, thought about nothing but how the story had developed, taking on a life of its own. It had kept his mind occupied. He knew that if he'd started worrying about the coming trial, it would have overwhelmed him. He didn't want to think about the possibility of a lifetime in jail, or even the death sentence. He couldn't remember a period in his life when he had drunk so little and worked so hard.

Now, at last, it was over – the script was finished. He felt an immense burden had been lifted from his shoulders. He had done the one thing he'd been putting off for years – he'd written a script that summed up everything his father had believed in and fought for.

After he'd reread the script several times, he drove across the border to Messina where he made two photocopies. Then he couriered one copy to his agent in London and left another with the local bank for safe-keeping. The original he took back with him to Bush Camp.

Paul didn't want to think of the future, instead he focused on the evening ahead. He felt a sense of completeness as he drove back into the camp. He knew his father would have appreciated how he felt; his father had always wanted him to do a film on his work with the lions.

Mkhulu was waiting for him on the deck, his face long and drawn. Paul came up and put his arm around his shoulders.

'You're still thinking of Shiva?'

'Paul, she is with me in my dreams and she will never go from them. But no, you are wrong. It's not Shiva I'm concerned about, it's Dr Madison.'

Paul suppressed a momentary feeling of anger. How could Mkhulu feel any sympathy for this woman who was standing as the key witness against him in the murder trial, whose work, funded by Hyde MacLeod, was against everything his father had stood for?

'Forget her – she's no friend of ours.'

'Paul, don't say that. She's not like Hyde MacLeod. I hear she doesn't want to testify at the trial. Evidently she's had a change of heart – she supports your action. But I've heard that Wayne MacLeod's pressurising her to keep silent. I hear she's ill, and they're not exactly helping her to make a recovery.'

'Sounds like supposition to me.'

'Let us say I have my sources – the bush telegraph, call it what you will. I can assure you that what I'm saying is true.'

Paul thought of the time, nearly a month before, when with David Katz he'd seen her showing the leopard to a group of guests. She'd looked drawn then, almost in another world. He was weakening to Mkhulu's argument, he knew it.

'What's on your mind, then?' he said grudgingly.

'We must talk to her. Persuade her to see reason.'

Paul sighed – and Mkhulu swung round and gripped his shoulders, so that he felt the force of the powerful fingers digging into his neck muscles.

'They're trying to shut her up!' Mkhulu said. 'I think she knows what really happened.'

'She saw me kill Cilliers. I've already been through that with David.'

'I think she knows something more . . . But she's under their influence, Paul. But with our support . . . perhaps she might change her mind.'

Mkhulu released his grip on Paul's shoulders and stood proudly against the glowing red of the sunset horizon. 'You white people and your civilisation,' he said. 'You bring your religion and your laws into our lives, you tell us to behave like civilised men – but you lose the ability to feel. God, Paul, I have had enough of your self-pity. I would go to jail to get my leg back, but it will not happen. Well, I will risk my life to get to Dr Madison and try to talk her into telling what she knows, even if you will not.'

Paul shook his head. 'No, Mkhulu. It would be a mistake. It would be interfering with a witness. I'm sorry, but I can't go along with it.'

'You sit watching all the time. You have lost the courage to act. Why are you trying to ignore what's happening to you?'

'I killed Cilliers. Nothing is going to change that.'

'Damn you!' Mkhulu said softly, starting to walk away. 'I shall talk to her, then.'

'Hyde will kill you if he finds you on Cayzer.'

'Then I will die a man.'

The darkness closed in around Mkhulu as he moved slowly through the bush and across the boundary into the MacLeods' reserve. There was no moon, and the bush was particularly quiet. He was almost invisible in the darkness.

Time passed quickly and Mkhulu felt secure as he blended in with the landscape, his senses becoming more and more highly attuned. He began to feel like an animal – a feeling of primitiveness that he enjoyed.

He estimated he was now less than a kilometre from the private lodge. He heard scuffling, and then a weak, desperate female voice. His hackles rose.

The scene gradually unfolded before him, lit by the glow from the parking lights of a Land Cruiser. In front of it a man was wrestling with a woman on the ground. The woman was black –

no doubt one of the women who lived on the Cayzer compound. Then he recognised the man – Hyde MacLeod.

A jigsaw of disconnected observations came together in Mkhulu's mind, and the fate of Johannes' daughter Thoko, before she'd been savaged, became clear.

'No. No!' came the pleading voice.

'You know what happened to Thoko,' Hyde whispered menacingly.

Mkhulu moved in closer to them, almost on his hands and knees, concentrating on Hyde's exact position. He leant into the cab of the Land Cruiser and switched the parking lights off. Then he leapt onto Hyde, his bunched fist hammering into his face again and again. He sensed the woman break free. Hyde fought back, and to his horror Mkhulu realised the man was far more powerful than he'd estimated.

Time to forget the rules. He slammed his right knee hard up between Hyde's legs – Hyde yelled out in agony. Mkhulu forced his knee backwards and forwards, smashing into the bone above the groin, crushing the scrotal sac. Hyde's fingers latched around his throat in desperation, but Mkhulu was in control now, and he grabbed Hyde's little fingers and wrenched them back, breaking his grip. Hyde let out a piercing scream and then collapsed as Mkhulu stepped out of the darkness and felled him cold with a powerful right hook.

The woman had disappeared into the darkness. It took Mkhulu a few minutes to recover, and then he was on his way again.

Fifteen minutes later he had moved expertly through the perimeter defences of the private lodge, not in the least surprised to see that there were regular ground patrols by armed guards. The buildings were lavishly constructed and he could only guess at how much the whole complex must have cost to develop. It was built on sloping ground, looking down towards the Shashe river.

He climbed up one of the side-walls built from the local rock and then dropped onto one of the flat roofs that lay beyond. He sucked in his breath and stared down through the giant picture window. Wayne MacLeod was sitting with the unshaven man he had seen weeks before in the Land Cruiser with Dr Madison. In front of Wayne MacLeod and his guest was a huge computer screen, and on it the blueprint of some machinery. Mkhulu looked down at his watch, then realised he'd lost it. Damn. It had been a present from Lionel Norton.

He moved on, over more flat-roofed rooms and cabins, passing several swimming pools, a spa bath and a gymnasium. Then he looked down through another window, into a lounge area filled with women in various stages of undress.

Mkhulu whistled softly. Wayne MacLeod was clearly running the seamier side of his business from inside this bush complex, safe from prying eyes. He moved, on past a series of rooms filled with computers and electronic communications equipment.

Damn. He saw they'd put a guard on the cabin where Johannes had told him he'd find her.

Mkhulu drew in his breath, let himself down from the roof and stepped onto the walkway, walking towards the guard.

'Please, master, I need money.'

The guard raised his gun. 'How did you get in here?'

As the guard moved in, Mkhulu hit him a savage blow across the face and the man toppled onto the tiled floor.

He found a key for the cabin in the guard's top pocket, opened the door and dragged him inside. Then he darted into the bathroom, quickly stripped off his own and the guard's clothing, and put on the guard's uniform himself. Breathing heavily, he looked in the mirror – a guard to the life.

There was knocking on the bathroom door. He opened it, to find Dr Madison staring at him. She opened her mouth to scream, but his hand was across it before she could utter a sound.

'It's OK. I'm not going to hurt you. I want to talk. I work for Paul Norton.'

Her eyes relaxed.

'I'm going to release my grip,' he said. 'If you scream and they find me, I'll die.'

Dr Anne Madison pulled away from him and tightened the cord of her towelling robe. 'I think you should leave now, Mkhulu,' she said.

He hobbled into her room and stared at the computer monitor where she'd been working.

Into the silence he said: 'Paul did not rape Thoko.'

Anne turned on her heel and stared at him. 'Did you, then?' I thought you were about to assault me.'

Mkhulu shook his head. 'You clearly trust the MacLeods' story.'

'They have done nothing to harm me,' Anne said, sitting down on the corner of her bed.

'What did you think of what they did to Johannes, then?'

She stared away from him.

'Dr Madison,' Mkhulu persisted. 'You are a key witness. You know Paul didn't rape Thoko.'

A sharp knock on the door made Mkhulu spin round in fear. 'I think you'd better leave,' Anne said – and Mkhulu made for the sliding doors, pushing them open and melting into the darkness. Safe in the bush, he turned back and saw Dr Madison in Wayne MacLeod's arms.

God. What had he done?

Fahad studied the line of trees on the horizon; they looked ethereal in the first light of dawn. He found the relaxed pace on Wayne MacLeod's reserve a pleasant change from his usual breakneck run of commitments, even though his discussions with MacLeod had lasted most of the night. There had been two major points of disagreement: timing and money.

Design was just one aspect of the process, MacLeod had emphasised; development was quite another. He had stressed that the weapon would have to be tested after the first prototype had been made, and only from the results of that experiment could a final timing plan be drawn up. Naturally, the development programme would be headed and co-ordinated by Dr Vance Torr.

A faint knock on the door brought Fahad back to the present, and he turned away from the window. 'Come in,' he said softly, stroking his chin.

The door was unlocked and a tall, statuesque African woman stepped into his room. She was everything he had requested.

'Take off your clothes.'

She dutifully stripped in front of him, and he took in the superb lines of her body. Fahad was aroused by her size and her sensuality – he had had few African women.

'Take a bath, bitch.'

133

She looked at him in surprise, and he hit her hard across the face. 'I want you clean.'

Her lips trembled, and she went dutifully to the bathroom. He heard the sound of running water and saw the steam coming from the door. From his case he took a condom. Accursed things, but in Africa one could no longer take chances. Who knew how many men she might have been with, despite Wayne MacLeod's promises to the contrary. Fahad's main requirement had been that she was expendable – that she could disappear without questions being asked.

He laid the leather thongs out on the bedside table, along with the strop razor and the bottle of iodine. From his suitcase he took a large plastic sheet and unfolded it over the bed. He was intoxicated with the moment – excitement was coursing through his veins. His body cooled in anticipation. He set up the video camera in the corner of the room, the auto-focus lens aimed at the bed.

She came out of the bathroom, dripping. 'Kneel,' he commanded.

The rules were quite simple. She must feel pain, he must receive pleasure.

He dropped the leather slip-noose over her head and tightened it around her neck. Then he indicated that she should remove his underpants and begin to caress him. As he hardened, he tightened the leather noose around her neck and heard her breathing quicken. Without warning, he yanked the noose upwards the way he would a choker chain round a dog's neck.

She collapsed to the floor, clutching at her neck, her face contorted.

'Kneel!'

He watched as she struggled to her knees. He waited till she was on the verge of passing out, then eased the slip-knot so she could breathe again.

Now he drew the curtains, locked the door and pulled a nylon stocking over his face. Then he went over and switched on the video camera. He came back to her and kicked her hard in the stomach.

'This time, you try harder.'

She nodded desperately.

He was aroused now, looking forward to the next few minutes. He slipped a knuckle-duster on his right fist and slammed it into her head. She dropped back and fell to the floor.

'Lie face down on the bed.'

He attached leather thongs to her wrists and ankles, strapping her out to the four corners of the bed. He licked his lips as he took out a razor blade. He ran it down between her shoulder blades, watching the red line open up. Next he rammed a wad of cottonwool into her mouth and then raised the leather noose from around her neck and tightened it across her mouth, forcing the wad down her throat.

He relaxed again, her screams were muffled.

The plastic sheet became soaked with blood as he worked steadily, slowly skinning her alive. He took particular satisfaction from the paroxysms of her body, staring occasionally at the redness of her back.

He forced her buttocks apart and penetrated her savagely. Then he rode her, feeling the heat rise within him.

Now came the point of climax.

He reached for the bottle of iodine and unscrewed the cap. Then he cut the thong that held the cottonwool between her lips, and poured the contents of the bottle over her bloody back.

Her body arched with the scream. It was as good as he'd dreamed it would be. He reached for the knife, slit her throat and climaxed.

The power of life and death – it was the greatest power on earth. There was no feeling quite like it. Now he felt rejuvenated – ready for a long, delicious sleep.

He went over, switched off the camera and pulled out the videocassette. Another one for the President's personal collection. He returned to the bed, wrapped the bloody body in the plastic sheet and then expertly slid it into a black body bag. He placed the videocassette carefully in his briefcase, then picked up the phone, tapping in the numbers quickly.

'I have finished. You will dispose of the bag? Very good.'

Wayne MacLeod flicked the ash off his cigar. He was not in the best of moods. His client was proving demanding. Now Fahad talked of penalty clauses in the agreement, to compensate his government if the delivery dates were not met.

What was an agreement anyway? A piece of paper. Of course, he would agree to the penalty clauses, but at the same time he would raise the stakes. And, when the Supergun was ready, he would have another surprise for Fahad – that the price of the Supergun didn't include the shells, shells that Fahad could only obtain from him. For, as far as Dr Torr knew, the only purpose of the Supergun was for satellite launching.

Good – he swept Fahad from his mind. He had other problems to deal with. Like the attempted assault on Dr Anne Madison. Earlier in the evening someone had managed to penetrate the lodge's elaborate security system and threaten her. What worried him even more was what else the intruder might have seen. The breach of security was serious, very serious.

His thoughts were interrupted by a knock at the door of his office. 'Come in,' he muttered gruffly.

Hyde staggered in through the door, barely able to walk. His right eye was black and his mouth bloody.

'God! What happened to you?'

He waited for Hyde to sit down. Wayne MacLeod didn't believe in showing his son sympathy – he felt it encouraged weakness.

'I was stalking one of the leopards,' Hyde replied. 'I was standing next to the Land Cruiser when someone attacked me from behind.'

'What time was this?'

'Must have been just before midnight.'

'Mmmm, just before Dr Madison was threatened,' said his father running his hand through his long silver mane of hair.

Hyde couldn't disguise his unease, and MacLeod knew his son was jealous of his affair with Dr Madison. There was nothing he could do about that. He was determined to make a man of Hyde.

Hyde took something out of his pocket and laid it on the table.

'A Rolex. Where did you find that?'

'It came off the man who set on me.'

MacLeod picked up the watch and examined it. He turned it over and examined the case. 'Ah . . ."To Mkhulu, from L. Norton."'

Hyde smiled evilly. 'The black bastard! But how come Anne didn't identify him? She knows who he is, Johannes pointed him out to her.'

'Come to think of it, Hyde, she behaved strangely this evening. I think we should be concerned about her attitude. I'll get the police to show her Mkhulu's picture – that way she'll be forced to identify him.'

Hyde avoided his father's eyes. He wanted Dr Madison, and perhaps this might be a way to force her to comply with his desires. She couldn't change her tune now. Her written statement alone was enough to convict Norton of killing Cilliers.

He was looking forward to watching Norton's trial – he hoped the bastard got the death sentence. Then he'd get his hands on Klaw. He could pressure Norton's daughter to sell up rather than face a costly legal dispute over access rights. Yes, it could all be sorted out very tidily.

'Hyde, I wonder if Norton didn't put Mkhulu up to this?'

'I'm certain he did.'

'Mmmm. He's in enough trouble already. Well, the prosecution can just add interfering with a witness to the list of charges against him.'

'The bastard must be sweating – it's only two weeks to go. Perhaps he wanted to get Dr Madison out the way – after all, her testimony will put the rope round his neck.'

Wayne McLeod sat down behind his desk and picked up the phone. 'I'll get onto the police right away – you and Anne can make a statement.'

Everything was in perfect focus that morning: Mkhulu coming into his room dressed in a suit and tie, the smell of freshly ground coffee mingling with the sweet fragrance of the early-morning dew. Time was passing so slowly, it was almost as if he were young again. Vivid memories of his father returned to him – snatches of words spoken to him as a child.

'Always remain faithful to the truth, Paul, that's what is important. The survivors, the people who matter, are those who hold to what is right.'

He remembered the grip of his father's hand and the face that reflected so much of the suffering within – the loneliness of a man who could not communicate to the world all the anguish and pain he felt inside. Perhaps his father had seen too much. No, rather, the rest of the world had seen too little.

'It's time.'

Mkhulu's voice broke his reverie, and Paul walked slowly across the floorboards, down to the Landy.

Mkhulu had already loaded their cases in the back. For the duration of the trial they would stay in Louis Trichardt. David had advised this, saying that Paul would need a lot of rest as the trial progressed.

Now Mkhulu faced him and gripped his arms. 'My friend, I will always be here. I have spoken with Charlotte. Whatever happens to you, we will fight with David to keep Klaw out of the hands of the MacLeods.'

Paul looked away and then back into Mkhulu's impenetrable eyes.

'I know that you will do that. I have told Charlotte of our agreement – that this place is as much yours as hers.'

Mkhulu let his arms go and went round to the driver's seat. Paul took one last look at Bush Camp, then jumped into the Landy. And as they drove slowly along the dirt road he felt an impending sense of doom that nothing could dispel.

Fahad felt uncomfortable in the emptiness of the place. He liked the mountains, but this particular range surrounding the valley made him feel uneasy. In the distance were the white buildings that housed the pilgrims, and above him the palace.

Fahad gathered his white robes close to him as the chilly wind picked up again. He only came to Pakistan for high-level meetings with the head of the International Peoples Bank of Pakistan, the rest of the business was conducted through their regional offices in London.

Abed – the Master – the leader of the order and head of IPBP, was ruthless in the time he allocated to secular business matters. But at eighty years old, his mind was as sharp as ever.

Fahad had been waiting in the lower courtyard since first light, looking for the sign. Around him were pilgrims, also waiting to see the Master. He did not communicate with them. Many were

Americans, and there were also Germans, Britons and South Africans.

A horn sounded in the distance and everyone knelt, Fahad among them. The Master was one of the few men, apart from the President, who scared Fahad. The Master had a talent for finding a man's weak points and exploiting them to the full. This was all the more frightening for Fahad, for he knew the Master's only obsession was power. And he and his country were within the compass of that power.

The blue light added a distinctive quality to the mountains above, which, along with the cleanness of the air, heightened the feeling of spirituality that permeated the place.

Now a red flag appeared above the flight of steps leading up to the palace. Fahad moved forward, eager to be away from the pilgrims. He held up the sides of his white robe as he quickly ran up the steps.

A woman appeared, dressed in flowing robes, and took his arm. 'Why do you run? You know the Master resents it.'

Fahad would like to have beaten her, instead he whispered softly: 'My apologies. In my eagerness to see the Master, I forgot the dictates of the order.'

She showed him into a vast hall, lined with soaring marble columns. At the end were black curtains. Fahad took off his sandals, knelt, and kissed the floor. The woman disappeared and he rose, walking steadily forward. He came up to the curtains and parted them. He had to make his way through endless folds of black cloth till he came into the inner sanctum – to see the Master sitting among large cushions on the floor.

The place was eerily quiet. Fahad knew it was mechanically swept for listening devices every few hours, making it completely safe for any discussion. A curious smile appeared on the Master's lips. Fahad looked at the tightly wound turban, the mass of grey hair and the long grey beard. The Master was almost gaunt, dressed in a loose-fitting white shirt and cotton trousers. His feet were bare, and covered with callouses.

'Sit.' The command was whispered rather than spoken. Fahad sat down on the cushions and a servant entered with a pewter jug and cups. Fahad smelt jasmine tea. The servant poured for them, looked reverently into the Master's eyes and then departed silently with a wave of his hand.

'Loyalty, Fahad, is the most precious of all qualities.'

Fahad felt a stab of fear as he heard this pronouncement. 'Yes, it is important.'

'Important is an empty word. Loyalty is the desire totally to fulfil the expectations of your bank.'

Fahad nodded. The Master took his pewter cup and sipped at his tea. Fahad followed suit.

'I hear your project may take longer than expected?' the Master said. 'That I may have to wait further for final payment?'

'Torr is the best at what he does, so it is not a good idea to apply pressure . . . yet.'

'You require more funds?'

The Master stared directly at him and Fahad was disconcerted by the curious, narrow green eyes. They reminded him of a cat's – a very dangerous cat's. 'Dr Torr must be given all that he needs,' he replied. 'He never spends money on himself, only on the project. The Supergun must be properly developed to protect my country.'

'How much do you require?'

'Another hundred million dollars.'

'And Iraq does not have these funds?'

'My President wishes me to arrange further finance through you for the project.'

The Master remained silent for a long time. Eventually his eyes rested on Fahad again. 'You will negotiate suitable collateral. You realise your final interest charges will be over a billion dollars.'

'The oil revenues from the territories we are soon to annex will easily pay off this debt.'

They drank tea. The silence grew longer, and Fahad felt uneasy. He could feel the Master's mood changing, sense his anger.

'I agree to the new loan,' the Master said heavily at last, 'but there is another matter we must discuss. You have been very foolish.'

'How so?'

'My disciples inform me that you are allowing your carnal

140

appetite to dominate your body. It is the ultimate weakness in a man. You will be destroyed by it.'

'I am in control.'

'No. In Africa you killed a woman. I have evidence of it, and I will use it against you should you ever try to default on our agreement. I am sure your President would not approve?'

Fahad felt the coldness seeping through his body. He knew he was right to fear this man.

'You may leave,' the Master said.

Fahad rose, kissed the Master's feet and moved away. The servant escorted him outside.

'Go in peace,' the servant said softly, 'The Master has arranged the loan you requested.'

Paul lay in the hotel bedroom, staring at the ceiling. Sleep refused to come to him. He gripped the headboard and felt the fear coursing through his body. Now the true reality of what he was to face was coming home to him. He visualised the flight of steps that led down from the courtroom to the cells below. He wondered what it would be like to walk down those steps, having received sentence.

They would take his fingerprints again, and then he would be marched to a cell. How long he would remain there would depend on whether he was granted leave to appeal.

He had spoken to many men in the course of his career who had been destined to lengthy jail sentences or to death. He had always been a voyeur, removed from the action, not really able to understand the reality of it. Now it all felt very different. There was no escaping the trial – and what he had previously considered short jail sentences now seemed harsh and barbaric from his new perspective.

The decision to kill Cilliers had been taken in an instant, but the punishment for the crime seemed likely never to end. David had emphasised again and again how important it was that the judge got an accurate idea of Paul's emotional turmoil at the precise moment he pulled the trigger.

There was a soft knock at the door of his suite. 'Come in,' he croaked.

He opened his eyes and followed the line of light that was created as the door opened slowly.

'Charlotte!' he exclaimed in an agonised voice.

'Dad, why don't you take something to make you relax?'

He got up and held her in his arms. 'I want my mind clear for the trial. I don't want to feel groggy.'

She held out her hand. In it were two small capsules. 'These will calm you down. And I promise there won't be any side-effects.'

'Who gave you these?'

Her dark eyes flickered. 'David.'

He didn't ask any more. He took the pills, went to the bathroom and washed them down with a glass of water. He was glad that Charlotte had come. He needed her more than he realised.

'You're not going to die, are you?' she asked in the half-darkness.

He switched on the light and stared at her. 'David thinks I'll probably get a lengthy prison sentence,' he replied honestly.

'I'll visit you every time I'm allowed. I'll keep you going.' She took his head between her hands. 'Please don't look like that. It kills me.'

'It's not easy.'

'David told me how you'd be feeling.'

'You've seen him?'

'He took me out to lunch . . . He told me he was relying on me to be in court every day.'

Paul lay back on the bed wearily and Charlotte sat down on the edge of the mattress.

'I suppose he wants to keep my spirits up,' Paul said.

'He also wants to influence the judge. He wants him to know that you're a family man.'

Paul turned to look outside at the mountain range above Louis Trichardt, and at the fir trees on the hillside, swaying in the breeze; he wished he could erase this whole time from his mind

'You mustn't stop painting,' he said. 'Don't let what's happening to me affect you.'

Charlotte was almost ready for her next exhibition. He felt sick in his gut that he wouldn't be in Cape Town to see it.

'Has Mummy phoned you?' she asked.

He shook his head. 'For Helen I have ceased to exist.'

'But surely this is different?'

Paul got up and put his arms around her again. 'Charlotte, your mother and I should have got divorced long ago. She hasn't loved me for years – she just saw me as a means of support.'

'She'd been having affairs.'

He looked away. 'I knew every time I went on an assignment that there would be someone else. I think at first it was loneliness. Later I think it was her revenge for my not being there.'

'She said you were never there for her. Like that time she thought she had breast cancer. She said you would have left her if she had a mastectomy – that you were only interested in women for sex.'

Paul buried his face in his hands. 'I can't believe she said that to you.'

Charlotte touched his arm. 'Dad, stop trying to protect me. I've lost respect for her, not for you.'

He got up and walked around the room, running his hands through his hair and occasionally staring across at her. She looked at him. 'You'll never lose me, Dad. You're my hero, you know that?'

He squeezed her hand. 'Let's go out for a walk before the sun sets. I feel like a little exercise to keep my spirits up.'

They walked for over an hour, up the mountainside behind the hotel. Then they had dinner in the hotel dining-room with David.

Much later, Charlotte came to his room again with some things she'd had sent up from Johannesburg for him.

'Just some clothes, and a few mementos that I thought might encourage you.'

He looked through the silver framed photographs and stared at the face of the young man he had once been. He had had so much optimism then; he felt he could change the world with his films. He hated the creeping cynicism that had become a part of his soul. He was glad he'd completed the script – that, at least, might be something of lasting value.

Of course, there'd been the international awards for his work.

However, far from appalling people, his films had been used to glamorise war. He'd taken enormous risks to get his footage. He was always the one who went in front, and he'd been badly wounded on several occasions. He'd hoped his films might stop future bloodshed, but instead they were used to add to its appeal.

Charlotte nervously handed him a videocassette. 'I found this in your rucksack when I was giving your cupboard a spring-clean.'

He took the cassette out of its case and pushed it into his camera, which he then connected up to the television set in the room. He thought he'd destroyed the cassette – he'd forgotten there'd been two. Now the vision returned to haunt him. The Kurdish woman and her child, gassed in Halabje by an Iraqi unit. In an instant he was back there, in the valley, the breeze blowing softly and the silence all-pervasive. Had he abandoned the woman and child? Yes, in a way he had, forgetting their death, appalled by the continuing ferocity and violence of the war.

Charlotte sucked in her breath as she took in the images. 'Dad, where did you take this?'

He went over the story for her, leaving out a few details but trying to paint as accurate a picture as possible. He'd never talked to her about his work before; he'd always thought it enough that she could see it on film.

'But why didn't you kill those men?' she asked penetratingly.

'Because they might have killed me. There were a lot of them. Anyway, as a cameraman you have to stand back, record what you're seeing and try to remain impartial.'

She looked at the film again. 'But you came back to see her and the child. Were you in love with her?'

He looked across at his daughter. Soon he might be far away from her, isolated and brutalised in prison. He might even hang. There was no more time for hiding things.

'I had stayed with her for a month. Yes, I was in love with her. She was the wife of a Kurdish guerrilla leader – her husband had been killed in the fighting. I just felt an empathy with her.'

'Why did you leave her?'

Always questions and more questions from Charlotte. Wasn't it enough just to know he'd had an affair?

'I felt there was no chance that it could work,' he said at last.

'Why did you go back?'

He looked out of the window and up into the evening sky. It was a cloudless night and all the stars were clearly visible.

'I couldn't get her out of my mind – her face was always there. I had to go back. I had to make a decision.'

'You felt guilty?'

He looked across at her. Charlotte was like him; she was never satisfied till she'd got to the bottom of things. She'd make a good reporter.

'I felt more than guilty,' he said. 'I knew I should have obeyed my instincts. If I'd stayed, I'd have asked her to live with me, to leave the valley. Maybe she would have come, and then she'd be alive.'

'So that was when you started to fall apart, Dad.'

God, she'd exposed him to core. Was he that vulnerable now? 'Yes. I felt that what I was doing was pointless. I was just providing news entertainment and nothing more. The magic went out of what I was doing.'

Charlotte kissed him on the forehead. 'I'm sorry. I'll leave you alone. You'd better get to sleep, ready for tomorrow.'

The door closed quietly a few moments later, and Charlotte was gone. He looked around the drab room and felt very depressed.

He put on the video again – stared at the image of the woman and the baby. And then he wept.

You couldn't always be a bystander. That was why he'd shot Cilliers, because he couldn't be a spectator any longer. He'd had to take matters into his own hands.

He switched off the light and climbed into bed. Tomorrow he would be on trial for his life.

Judge Henry Bosman cast his eyes around his office directly behind the Louis Trichardt Regional Court. He looked out at the early-morning sunlight on the red tin roof of the building opposite, then he looked back at the room again – everything neat and tidy as he had demanded. If there was one thing Judge Bosman would not tolerate, it was disorder.

He had travelled north to Louis Trichardt from Pretoria on

Sunday, an easy drive that gave him time to contemplate the trial ahead. It had been given much publicity, and that irritated him. He felt that sort of publicity built in the public's mind a demand for a certain kind of verdict. Judge Bosman was not about to have his opinion swayed by such emotion. The crime was extremely serious: the defendant was accused of raping his victim, beating her and then callously standing back while his lioness ate her alive. Then, when the local farm manager shot the lioness, the defendant had shot him in cold blood.

He watched the clock turn to 10 a.m. precisely. One of his assistants came in, handed him his scarlet robe and then opened the door to the courtroom for him. His mind was relaxed now, and uncluttered by the minutiae of day-to-day existence. He would focus a lifetime of legal expertise on the case.

As he came through the door and into the room, there was silence, and the court rose in unison. He stared across at the public prosecutor, the counsel for the defence and at the accused. He sensed the tension in the air and kept quiet. Then, with a subtle nod, he indicated that everyone should be seated.

First the charges were read out. Then Judge Bosman stared at Paul Norton.

'How does the defendant plead?' he asked dryly.

Norton replied, and then the counsel for the defence immediately rose to confirm the plea.

'My client, Paul Norton, pleads not guilty on the charge of the rape and murder of Miss Thoko Sebi. He also pleads not guilty to the charge of murdering Mr Ryan Cilliers.'

Judge Bosman stared down at the man with the curly blond hair, the deep tan and the haunted blue eyes. He saw the determined face, the hardened jaw-line, and he sensed that Paul Norton was a man who went his own way.

'Why has the plea changed?' he asked. 'Your client admitted guilt when he first appeared in court.'

'My client never pleaded guilty to the charge of raping Thoko Sebi. As to my client's previous plea of guilty to the charge of murder, I should like to advise the court that my client was in a state of shock and not able to make a reasoned opinion.'

The judge folded his arms and stared down at David Katz,

sizing him up. He'd heard about Katz, who was reputed to be both persuasive and adept in the courtroom.

'I call on the state to present its case,' he said.

'On the evening of the crime, the accused abducted Miss Thoko Sebi, who was returning from her place of employment to her home. The accused waited silently in the bush and attacked Thoko Sebi. He beat her savagely and raped her repeatedly. She was naked, badly bleeding and probably unconscious by the time he left her. He then returned to his own reserve, Klaw, leaving her where he had attacked her, on Mr Hyde MacLeod's farm.

'The accused returned early in the morning with his lioness, which he led to Miss Sebi's battered body. The lioness then attacked and badly mauled Miss Sebi. The accused then summoned help, knowing that Miss Sebi was dying and unable to accuse him of the hideous crime he had perpetrated.'

The accusations continued, and Judge Bosman watched Paul Norton's face. He saw that Norton was almost white with the tension of the affair and that his eyes hardly moved. One of his hands gripped the edge of the wooden rail in front of him.

Towards the end of the morning, the first witness for the prosecution was called – Mrs Helen Norton. She was eloquent, and unafraid of her former husband's angry glare. She told Judge Bosman of Norton's affair with an African woman some years before.

Paul rose in anger.

'Mr Norton, you are in contempt of court,' Judge Bosman told him. 'You will sit down. Your counsel will note that if this occurs again, you will face further charges.'

Red-faced, Paul sat down in his chair, while Helen talked of his predilection for reporting violence, and told how his obsession with war reporting had slowly wrecked their marriage, forcing her to look for support elsewhere.

'Do you think your former husband could have committed murder, Mrs Norton?' the prosecutor asked softly.

David interrupted him quickly. 'Objection. The question is speculative.'

*

Witness after witness was called, and a picture emerged of a man of passion. Paul Norton was ruled by his emotions. By the end of the day the prosecution had still not completed its case and it was held over, to continue the next day.

Judge Bosman returned to his hotel, ate a solitary dinner and contemplated the day's proceedings. The case was more complicated than he'd imagined. The revelations about Norton's military career were particularly damning. True, the man was a distinguished soldier, but he had shot three South African soldiers in a fit of anger. The prosecution had proved, beyond a shadow of doubt, that Paul Norton was capable of committing murder. David Katz's cross-examination of the witnesses had done little to alter that impression in the judge's mind.

Paul remained in his hotel room. He didn't want to talk to anyone. A confusion of feelings crowded into his mind – things looked pretty bleak.

Late in the evening, David Katz dropped by. He seemed to know Paul wouldn't be sleeping.

'Why did your wife say those things?' he demanded.

Paul walked around the room. 'You have to understand that it wasn't a happy marriage. I was away an awful lot. Helen was always running off with some lover.'

David scribbled a few notes, threw his pad on the bed and rubbed his eyes. 'Why didn't you tell me about your affair with the African woman?'

'It doesn't have any bearing on the case.'

David got up and stared at Paul. He put his hands on his hips. 'When the prosecution finishes, he's going to say you're attracted to black women. That you've had an affair with one – maybe even against her will, because she was in your employment. He's going to say that you tried to seduce Miss Sebi, and when she resisted your advances you beat her up and raped her. Then you left her alone, and badly injured – your plan being to return and rape her again, and then let your lion finish her off.'

'That's ridiculous.'

Paul's eyes were red from lack of sleep. He ran his hands through his hair as he listened to David. 'What does all this mean?' he said.

'It means our case is getting weaker and weaker.'

'But I'm telling the truth!'

'I know you are. But the judge doesn't, and I've got to convince him. The trouble is that your past is catching up with you.'

David took a vial of pills out of his pocket. 'Take two of these now. You've got to get some sleep, I don't want you looking haggard. You've got to give the appearance of confidence.'

Paul laughed. 'So much for justice!'

David worked through the night in a cold sweat. He knew he wasn't handling the case well. His cross-examination of the prosecution witnesses had been less than adequate – and vague doubts had formed in his mind as to the veracity of Paul's statement.

Tomorrow the State would produce the pathologist's report. It was something David was dreading. There was no doubt that Thoko had been raped – it was just a question of who had done it.

Then there was Dr Anne Madison. The court had accepted that she would not be standing as a witness, and under normal circumstances her written statement would not have been admissable because she could not be cross-examined. But unfortunately a new Act allowing hearsay evidence in exceptional circumstances meant that her statement *had* been admitted; the 'exceptional circumstances' were the nervous breakdown that prevented her from being available as a witness.

Was Paul innocent of the charge of rape? David believed so, but perhaps there was something Paul wasn't telling. Maybe he'd had an assignation with the woman? Things just kept on coming up that Paul hadn't told him about. And if Paul's semen didn't match the semen found in Thoko's body, it still wouldn't conclusively prove he hadn't raped her – he could have used a condom.

David felt nervous – he had to pull himself together. God, Paul needed a miracle to help him now.

Paul looked into the eyes of Judge Bosman and didn't find any sympathy in them. Then he looked across at his doctor, who'd just been called to the stand by the prosecutor.

'Dr Carr,' the prosecutor said pleasantly. 'you are Mr Norton's general practitioner, are you not?'

The doctor nodded.

'Would you say that Mr Norton has a considerable drinking problem?'

'Yes, most definitely. I have told him on several occasions that if he doesn't cut down, he's destined for an early grave.'

'And what do you think is the cause of this drinking?'

Dr Carr took off his glasses and cleaned them nervously. 'My patient is a very emotional man. I think he drinks to try and sedate himself.'

'Would you say he lacks self-control?'

'That is evident from the excessive drinking – a destructive habit if ever there was one.'

'That is all. Thank you, doctor.'

David Katz rose. 'I have no questions.'

Dr Carr walked from the stand with evident relief.

The prosecutor was an odd-looking man with almost alabaster skin, black hair and heavy-framed black glasses. Paul thought that if he auditioned for a part in a horror movie, he'd certainly get it.

The prosecutor stood up again. 'I now call the State Pathologist, Dr Retief, to the stand.' Dr Retief was in his early sixties, and walked to the stand with a stick.

'Dr Retief, for how long have you been practising in your present position?'

'Over thirty years.'

'And you are, are you not, considered a world authority on your subject?'

'That is correct.'

'You have published books and papers on your subject at a prolific rate?'

'Also true.'

'Very good. You examined the body of Miss Thoko Sebi?'

'Indeed I did. The autopsy was thorough and my findings conclusive.'

'Conclusive in what respect?'

'Miss Sebi had been raped repeatedly and badly beaten – her

death was precipitated when she was mauled by Mr Norton's lion.'

The prosecutor adjusted his glasses, letting the silence build. 'What evidence have you that it was rape?'

'The roughness of the penetration. There was bleeding in the vagina as well as the rectum. She had also been subjected to anal rape.'

The judge looked stonily across at Paul, who did not show weakness.

'What else did you find?' the prosecutor pressed.

'She had been savagely beaten all over. There were sjambok marks across her shoulders – her wrists had been tied and she had been punched in the abdomen.'

'Anything else of relevance?'

'The body had been savaged while the victim was clearly conscious.'

'But the mauling by the lion was the cause of death?'

'Most definitely.'

'Thank you, Dr Retief. Now, as to Mr Ryan Cilliers, can you tell us whether you think the bullet was intended to cause death, or could it have been a shot intended to miss?'

'Mr Cilliers was shot directly through the heart. It was a fatal shot.'

'Thank you, Dr Retief.'

David Katz rose. 'Dr Retief, it is true that you found male semen in Miss Sebi's body?'

'Yes. That, plus many abrasions surrounding the vaginal area which indicated she had been raped.'

'Did you take a sample of the semen and have it analysed?'

'Yes, but there was no need. The accused had pleaded guilty.'

The judge coughed and spoke quickly. 'Dr Retief, you should know better. The charge of rape was only brought later, after your examination, and then Mr Norton pleaded not guilty.'

Dr Retief went puce. David intervened quickly. 'A sample of Mr Norton's semen was given to you. Did it match that found in Miss Sebe?'

'Er, no. But then Mr Norton could have worn a condom.'

'So you cannot prove who it was who raped Miss Sebi?'

'I should think . . .'

'Can you prove who raped her?'

Dr Retief took in a huge gulp of air. 'No.'

'That will be all.'

Counsel for the prosecution looked through his papers and then called the next witness, an expert from the SAP's Ballistics Division.

'The bullet that killed Ryan Cilliers came from Mr Norton's rifle?' he asked him.

'That is correct. I must add that Mr Norton's fingerprints were the only ones found on the murder weapon.'

David had no questions, and there was a chilly silence in the courtroom as the man left the stand.

'I call Mr Jeff Daniels,' the prosecutor said, 'of the Union Charter Assurance company.'

Paul saw a flicker of surprise on David's face. This he clearly had not been expecting.

'Mr Daniels, what was your relationship to Miss Sebi?'

'I am an agent of Union Charter Assurance who dealt directly with her.'

'Could you tell the court of her assurance situation?'

'Miss Sebi's initial policy was for one hundred thousand rand, the sole beneficiary being her father, Johannes Sebi. Over the past six months that amount was raised to three hundred thousand rand.'

'Did Miss Sebi explain to you why she had increased her policy?'

'Yes. She said she was worried about her father's ability to survive, should she die. She said that she had discussed the matter with him.'

'So Mr Sebi was fully aware that if his daughter should die, he would gain three hundred thousand rand.'

'Most definitely.'

'And immediately upon her death, her father approached you for an advance on the pay-out?'

'That is correct.'

'Did he tell you what he required the money for?'

'I believe it was so that he could meet Mr Norton's bail requirement.'

There was an intake of breath across the courtroom.

'Thank you, Mr Daniels, that will be all.'

David was looking grim. He put a few questions to Daniels, then the witness left the stand.

The prosecutor was looking pleased with himself. 'I next call Mrs Anderson, the manager of the Commercial Bank, Messina.'

A perfectly dressed grey-haired woman came to the stand. She looked uncomfortable and kept readjusting her hat.

'Mrs Anderson, you employed Miss Sebi and promoted her within your branch. How did you regard her?'

'She was the best employee I have ever had.'

Mrs Anderson burst into tears and gripped the edge of the witness box. The court was very quiet. The judge waited patiently for her to recover herself, but the sobbing continued. The judge raised his hand.

'We will take a break of ten minutes so that Mrs Anderson may compose herself.'

David grabbed Paul as they walked out of the courtroom, and led him quickly into an empty side-room.

'Paul, I'm sorry. I missed that.'

'Missed what?' Paul asked.

'The bastard's going to try to prove that you and Johannes conspired to kill Thoko in order to get your hands on the insurance money.'

Paul looked at an old Thomas Baines print of Victoria Falls, hanging on the wall. 'That's ridiculous.'

'Steel yourself out there, Paul. Don't act as if you're concerned.'

'Is it going well, David?'

'No. It's going very, very badly.'

Mrs Anderson came up to the witness box again, her face red but composed. Her grey eyes met those of the judge. She felt terrible; she had never been present at a murder trial.

'Mr Van Wyk, you may continue.'

The prosecutor rose smartly. 'Mrs Anderson, what were your plans for Miss Sebi?'

'I told her, the day she was murdered, that I had applied for her to move to our Sandton branch as an assistant to one of the managers. I could see she was overjoyed, but also concerned. I knew that her father was a tracker and loved the reserve where they lived.'

'Did she give you an answer?'

'She said she'd have to talk it over with her father.'

The prosecutor indicated that his questioning of the witness was complete. David let the silence build, his eyes resting gently on Mrs Anderson. At last he said, 'Mrs Anderson, are you married?'

'I was. My husband died a few years ago of an incurable disease.'

'It was a happy marriage?'

'Oh yes. We loved each other. Fortunately I have five children, and his memory survives through them.'

'Would you say you can tell if a person who works for you has a happy relationship?'

'Yes. I think it's important that people have a stable family, otherwise they're unhappy.'

'So, would you say that Thoko Sebi loved her father?'

Now Mrs Anderson's face was calm. 'I think she loved him more than anyone else in the world.'

'Do you think he would have opposed her decision to move, if she'd decided that was what she wanted?'

'No. As I said, he was very attached to the reserve, but I think he would have moved, because she wanted to give him the opportunity to be independent. She spoke of this many times.'

David continued his cross-examination of Mrs Anderson for several minutes, finishing on his most important point.

'Mrs Anderson, do you think Mr Sebi would have arranged the murder of his daughter?'

'No. I think she was worth more to him alive than dead. I believe he loved her as much as it is possible for a man to love his child.'

'Thank you, Mrs Anderson. That is all.'

Johannes Sebi rose from his chair at the back of the court and walked out into the sunshine. He sat down on the brick wall that enclosed the narrow garden next to the building, and stared at a black chicken pecking in the grass. Without warning, tears burst from his eyes. How could they dare to suggest he had conspired to have his daughter murdered? Then he thought of Hyde MacLeod, and the hatred welled up inside him.

Johannes knew Paul was innocent of the rape charge, but everything was turning against him. The money that Johannes had inherited from Thoko was being used as evidence of a conspiracy between him and Paul.

Counsel for the prosecution, having called all his witnesses, closed his case, and the court recessed for lunch. In the afternoon, the trial resumed. David called Paul to the stand.

Standing in the witness box, Paul looked out across the courtroom and through the windows. He watched a bird on the gutter of the building opposite, saw the sunlight on its wings and wished that he could be free from this moment. David's voice brought him back to reality.

'Mr Norton, would you please tell the court exactly how you found Miss Sebi's body?'

Paul went over the whole story. He told how Shiva had warded off the hyenas and how he had released a flare to summon help.

The prosecutor's cross-examination of Paul was determined, but Paul didn't crack under the strain. He handled the questions calmly.

By the end of the day, the atmosphere in the courtroom had changed. Judge Bosman had listened intently to Paul's testimony. He rose and announced that the case for the defence would continue the following morning.

Paul stepped down from the stand and walked from the courtroom with David and Charlotte. They were all tense, but at least now David was confident that Paul would be given a short jail sentence.

Paul slept fitfully that night, his mind filled with terrifying dreams and premonitions. First he dreamed of his father, teaching him to shoot with a rifle. Then he was in Halabje, in a cloud of poison gas, chasing after the woman and the child, trying to catch them, his hands going through them, touching nothing. Lastly he found himself in a thick mist that blanketed out all sound. He was walking with a pride of lions and he came to the entrance of a huge building. The door slid open effortlessly and he tried to walk inside, but the lions would not let him go in, they kept pushing him away from the place. Eventually he woke in a cold sweat and walked out onto the balcony, taking in deep gulps of air.

This would be his last day of freedom. He savoured watching the sun rise in the east, bathing the tree-tops light gold. He did not eat breakfast, he did not feel in the least bit hungry.

David drove him and Charlotte into town. They pulled away from the hotel, following the curving main road that led downwards through an avenue of blue-gums, then a long straight stretch that took them past a strange white pyramid sign welcoming them to Louis Trichardt. David turned right at the four-way stop, passing the local school, and Paul was aware of beautiful trees with orange flowers along the roadside. He wanted the journey to last forever, but already they were turning into Krogh Street and passing the police station with the flags flying outside. David turned right, passing a modern office block and pulling up in the diagonal parking lot outside the magistrate's court.

Paul got out, surveying the court buildings which were built on a slope – two storeys high at the front and three at the back. He looked up at the double doors, the side-entrance to the building. One sign outside said 'Department of Forestry' and another 'Director of Animal Health.' Paul wished that his business was with these and not with the law. He looked down to see that there were chickens eating the grass beneath the trees outside the front entrance.

David touched his arm. 'Come, Paul.'

He went inside, into a dimly lit hall with a sign at the back saying 'HOF'. He turned and walked up the stairs to the next level, passing a glass noticeboard and then moving through a metal detector wedged between the double doors. This morning every detail seemed razor-sharp; it seemed important to register everything. He looked down the passage and took in the view from a window – an entrance way between the two buildings, with cars parked to one side. He continued down the passage and turned into the courtroom. He looked up at the ceiling and studied the wooden frame that ran round it, a metre in from the perimeter. Then his eyes moved to the ceiling-mounted fan that was directly above where the judge sat with a white coat of arms behind him. The room was light but austere.

Time passed quickly, and before he was aware of it the courtroom was packed. Paul hated being in the dock, on parade for the gallery to see.

Counsel for the prosecution rose. 'I beg leave to produce two more witnesses.'

Judge Bosman nodded. 'Granted.'

Hyde MacLeod stepped forward from the back of the courtroom and took the stand. He took the oath solemnly, dressed in a dark suit; his unruly hair had been trimmed and he looked the epitome of respectability.

'Mr MacLeod, tell me, does Mr Norton have any reason for wanting to see you behind bars?'

'Yes. I have a legal case against him: he has lost the servitude to his reserve because he visits it so rarely. I have made him a generous offer for his reserve, but he has refused it. He told me he was going to fight me to the death on that point.'

'Thank you, Mr MacLeod, that will be all.'

The court erupted into conversation. Angrily Judge Bosman rapped his gavel against the wooden surface in front of him. 'Silence in court!'

David went on the attack, but he could not unseat Hyde MacLeod. It was clear to Paul that Hyde had been well prepared for his appearance.

'I call my final witness, Charles Fox.'

Charles Fox, dressed in his customary bush fatigues, stepped forward. He took the oath and faced the court. The prosecutor looked directly at him.

'On the night that Miss Sebi was savagely beaten and raped, can you tell the court where Mr Hyde MacLeod was?'

A slight smirk appeared on Fox's face. 'We normally don't talk about our gambling. After all, it's illegal. But that night we had a good game of poker going. I think we went on till about five in the morning. I made a lot of money, and Hyde lost a lot.'

Paul watched David Katz. His face was drawn, the dark eyes focused on the witness box.

'Thank you, Mr Fox.'

Again David went on the attack, but Charles Fox stuck rigidly to his statement, refusing to be thrown by David's line of questioning.

After David had completed his cross-examination, the prosecutor addressed the judge. 'I beg leave to call Mr Wayne MacLeod to the stand.'

Wayne MacLeod stepped into the witness box, an imposing figure with his long, black-streaked silver hair and expansive forehead.

'Mr MacLeod, you are a devout Christian, are you not?'

Wayne nodded.

'I'd now like you to tell the court about something that happened a month ago.'

Wayne stared hard at Paul. 'Dr Anne Madison, as you know, is an American lion expert who is doing research on our reserve. She has been traumatised ever since she witnessed Mr Norton shoot Mr Cilliers. I think she feared that Mr Norton might come after her. She was very attached to Miss Sebi . . .

Anyway, one evening, a month ago, my son Hyde was violently assaulted.'

'Do you know by whom?'

'Yes.'

MacLeod seemed reluctant to continue. Judge Bosman stared stonily at him. 'Please continue, Mr MacLeod.'

'It is a delicate matter. As you know, Anne – I'm sorry, Dr Madison – cannot appear in court because she has had a nervous breakdown. This was caused . . .'

'Mr MacLeod,' Judge Bosman interrupted, 'please tell the court who assaulted your son.'

'My son found a watch that had fallen from his assailant . . .'

The prosecutor handed the watch, encased in a plastic bag, to Wayne MacLeod. 'Is that the watch, Mr MacLeod?'

'It is. On the back is an inscription. "To Mkhulu, from L. Norton".'

Paul Norton swayed on his feet as the prosecutor stepped forward.

'What happened later that evening, Mr MacLeod?'

'The guard on Dr Madison's room was assaulted. His assailant then took the keys from him, dragged him into Dr Madison's room and changed clothes with him. This man then threatened

158

Dr Madison, telling her that Paul Norton was innocent of the rape charge. He said she must alter her statement.'

The prosecutor gestured to Wayne MacLeod to remain on the stand.

'I have here,' he said, 'a sworn statement made by Dr Madison that the man in question was Mkhulu, a servant in the employ of Mr Norton. I also plead that it was this Mkhulu who assaulted Hyde MacLeod earlier that same evening.'

Paul was appalled. Mkhulu was in trouble too now. He saw the prosecutor eyeing him.

'My Lord, I beg leave to call Paul Norton's servant, Mkhulu, who is in the courtroom.'

Mkhulu took the stand, swallowing deeply, and the prosecutor walked over to him and showed him the wristwatch.

'Is this watch yours?'

'Yes.'

'Did you assault Hyde MacLeod?'

'Yes,' Mkhulu replied weakly.

'Did you go to Dr Madison's cabin later that evening, assault the guard and then threaten her?'

'Yes.'

'Did Paul Norton know of your intention to confront Dr Madison?'

'Yes, but . . .'

'Did he try to stop you?'

'He said he wouldn't go along . . .'

'Please answer my question. Did he try to stop you?'

'No.'

'I have no more questions.'

David Katz rose immediately and the Judge indicated he should speak.

'I beg leave to postpone the trial,' he said. 'I should like to cross-examine Dr Madison.'

'Denied,' Judge Bosman said sharply.

Both David and the prosecutor completed their arguments, and then the Judge held the court in recess while he made his decision.

Paul felt terrible. How could Mkhulu have been such a fool?

159

After ten minutes they were all called back into the courtroom. David quickly squeezed Paul's hand. 'Whatever happens, remember it's not over yet,' he whispered nervously.

Once everyone was seated, Judge Bosman walked to his chair and the court rose. His judgement took nearly an hour to deliver.

In the matter of the State vs Paul Norton he passed the sentence of death on both charges.

Paul swayed on his feet. He heard Charlotte sobbing in the background. Every second seemed an eternity, he wanted to shout out his innocence.

'Mr Norton, you have an hour to spend with your relatives and friends in the courtroom, then you must go below.'

Paul stumbled into Charlotte's arms and she held him tightly. 'Oh God, Dad, this isn't happening!'

He smelt her, drank her in, remembered her as a child, tried to compress a lifetime of memories into a moment. His chest was wet with her tears.

'Daddy, this isn't right. Oh Daddy, how can they do this to you?'

Then Mkhulu was there, his arms locked tight around him and the dark eyes boring into his.

'I am sorry. I wanted to help you. There is no justice here, no justice at all.'

'Keep on, my friend, look after my reserve. Don't give up, please don't give up.'

Then David, his lips thin and white with anger. 'I'll fight this thing, Paul. I'll fight it with everything I've got. I'll go all the way to the State President. You're innocent of the rape and assault charges, damnit; that bastard Hyde MacLeod was lying about the poker game, and so was Fox.'

Johannes came forward and held Paul's hand. 'I know you did not rape her, believe me.'

Then the time was up. Paul felt firm hands pulling him away from Charlotte. 'Come on now, Mr Norton, you've had your hour.'

He looked down the line of steps that led under the courtroom, the steps he thought led into hell. He smelt the last air of freedom, then walked slowly downwards and felt the barriers closing around him.

Below the courtroom, his world changed. First they took his fingerprints again, each hand roughly held as the fingers and thumb were rolled in black ink, then pressed against the paper. Next, looking suitably shaken, he was forced to pose for his identity photographs. After that, he was shown to his cell.

He sat on the bench silently, staring at the wall as so many sentenced men before him had done. A coldness crept through his bones. A few hours later he heard the echo of footsteps in the corridor, the lock on his cell was undone and the door swung open. A grey-haired warder stared silently at him and placed a plate of food on the floor. Then the door closed and he was alone again.

He did not eat the paltry meal. Instead he thought what it would be like to be sitting on the deck of Bush Camp, watching the sun set over his reserve. Later, he felt the waves of resentment come, at the injustice of the sentence. He cursed Mkhulu's stupidity at trying to talk sense to Dr Madison. And most of all he questioned the impulse that had driven him to shoot Cilliers.

Sleep refused to come and he remained sitting bolt upright, taking in the fact that he had been sentenced to death. Eventually he dozed off, to be woken at four by the warder. His mouth felt dry and he sipped at the glass of water that had come with his meal.

Now he began to savour every moment of living. Each second was precious because now the inevitability of death had been brought forward. He studied his hands, still dirty from the fingerprint ink. He thought back to the courtroom, to the judge, and to the South African flag that hung dolefully to one side of him.

At half-past five the door to the cell opened and the warder barked out a command for him to step outside. He moved like an automaton and was shepherded out to a covered truck in the yard. He stepped into the back and sat down on the metal floor. There were no windows, only ugly wire grilles that kept the world outside safe from him.

The truck roared out of the yard and he careered around in

the back, desperately trying to get a hold to steady himself. The men in the cab turned and laughed at his predicament. Evidently this was their moment of fun, taking advantage of a new prisoner.

He stared out of the grille as the air rushed through it, looking at the countryside, knowing that this might be his last journey. David had told him they would take him to Pretoria Central, and he had guessed he would travel alone. Murderers were considered dangerous, and received special treatment. The crime of which he stood convicted was particularly appalling – apart from child molesters, rapists occupied the lowest rung of criminal society.

One of his first journalistic assignments had been to film a man who had just been sentenced to death: now some divine justice was allowing him to see the legal system from a different perspective . . . He lay back against the cold metal of the truck floor and dropped off into a fitful sleep.

Judge Bosman looked around the hotel room. He felt uncomfortable. The decision he'd made regarding Paul Norton had caused him several sleepless nights. He hated the death sentence in many ways, but he also recognised its role as the ultimate deterrent.

He glanced across at his writing-desk and the bound pages of his case notes. He had examined them carefully, and there could be no doubt that the rape had been premeditated. Norton must have known Miss Sebi would have to come across that section of land on the way to see her father, and his intimate knowledge of the area would have allowed him to position himself directly in her path.

The sentence, Judge Bosman thought now, was the result of his having visualised himself in the victim's position. He had imagined her trauma, the agony of being beaten and raped repeatedly, and finally the ghastly experience of being left bloody and conscious on the edge of the Limpopo – a place where predators constantly lurked. Norton must have stood coldly by, listening to her screams as his lioness feasted on her flesh. Then, as night turned into day, fear would have gripped him – fear that someone might not believe his story. It would have been at that moment that he fired the flare.

However, things had not worked out as Norton planned. First, Ryan Cilliers, the farm manager, had arrived, then Hyde Mac-Leod, who had radioed Dr Madison. No doubt fearing Thoko might live, Norton had sought to delay her being taken to hospital by threatening Cilliers. Then Norton shot Cilliers in a fit of temper after the farm manager had killed his lioness. Acting quickly, Hyde MacLeod had called the police, who had arrested Norton as he returned to the scene of the crime.

Dr Madison had obviously been severely traumatised by the incident. Norton must have realised how damning her testimony would be, and persuaded his servant, Mkhulu, to terrorise her into silence.

Judge Bosman shook his head. A man like Norton was dangerous – who knew what he might do on release, even after many years in jail? The pent-up bitterness might well result in another crime of violence. The death sentence had been his only choice.

However, one small doubt persisted in his mind. He knew that the counsel for the defence believed his client to be innocent – and Judge Bosman also knew that David Katz was no fool.

Mkhulu got up again, and gestured to David to move forward. The straps of the heavy back-pack bit into David's shoulders. He turned to see Charlotte some ten metres further back, keeping covered in the denser bush.

They crept on, moving softly through the dew-soaked grass in the early morning light. They were trespassing – if they were caught they would be liable for prosecution.

'Here . . .' Mkhulu hissed. He was crouched down on all fours again, staring at the sandy surface beneath him.

David hoisted the back-pack off his shoulders and then slipped off his boots. 'Stay back, and prepare the solution as I explained.'

Mkhulu worked quickly with Charlotte, mixing the powder and water into a putty-like substance. David then took it and poured it over the markings on the ground. Next, Mkhulu indicated where the scuffle had taken place, and pointed to the

163

dried blood on the sand. David took a scraping of it, and placed it in a sealed plastic packet.

'And you say the vehicle tracks lead directly from this point across to the place, half a kilometre away, where Paul found her?'

Mkhulu nodded grimly.

'Then lead on, my friend. It is important that both Charlotte and I are witness to this.'

They moved slowly, following Mkhulu as he made out the vehicle tracks that led off through the dense bush. On a thorn tree he found a scrap of Thoko's dress, obviously torn from her as the Land Cruiser swept past in the darkness, carrying her to her death.

David concentrated totally on the task in hand, storing up every little detail in his memory. He had to make absolutely sure that if he was allowed to put his case before the appeal court in Bloemfontein in eight months time, it was watertight.

He felt Charlotte's hand on his shoulder and stared into the dark eyes. He had felt for her when her father was sentenced, and had admired her self-control. The eyes bored into his.

'Is this really worth it, David? Or are you just doing this to keep his hopes up?'

He took her hand, feeling the sweat trickling down between his shoulder blades. 'You've got to believe, you know that. If you give up, you're finished -- that's what my father taught me. Only when you stop fighting for survival is your life over. We're all Paul's got. He's innocent of the rape, and the murder was done on impulse -- the charge should have been manslaughter. But first we have to prove that he wasn't guilty of the rape.'

She leaned forward and kissed him on the cheek. Then she turned and followed after Mkhulu.

David felt elated by her touch, by the smell of her. He was scared, because he had never felt so passionately about a woman before. Every time she came close, he was revitalised. And that only made him feel worse -- for he felt that he had let her father down. That was why he had promised himself that he would keep fighting for Paul till the end -- for better or for worse.

*

For the thirtieth time that day, lying on her bed, Anne Madison read the newspaper report of the trial. She could not believe the consequences of her actions. She had been under constant sedation for the past few months, hardly aware of the passing of time.

She did not believe Hyde's story that he had been playing a poker game on the night Thoko had been attacked – she knew Charles Fox was lying to protect him. It was clear that her absence from the trial – her failure to appear in court – had made things worse for Paul Norton.

She got up, pulled her suitcase from the wardrobe and began to pack her things. She remembered back to her time in training as a CIA agent – her heart hadn't been in it, and one day she had decided that enough was enough. She had left, and her father, Joe Colson, the head of the CIA, had disowned her. He had even demanded she change her name, so furious was he at her having let him down.

Now, again, she knew it was time for her to move on. She could no longer work for Wayne MacLeod. She needed time to think things over.

Later, Anne walked down through the big lounge area, where some of the distinguished guests greeted her. Cayzer was probably the most luxurious game lodge in Africa; guests could opt for total seclusion if they wanted it, but for most of them, the intimate atmosphere of the lodge was privacy enough. One ranger per guest was the rule, and rangers could be changed at a guest's whim. That was why Anne herself had occasionally had to work as a ranger – it was supposed to be a demonstration of how seriously Hyde MacLeod took the running of the reserve. Of course, as Anne had discovered, Hyde was actually totally ineffectual; it was Wayne who controlled the reserve. Even so, she knew that Wayne devoted very little of his energies to it – the majority of his time was spent in his communications centre, deep within his own luxury wing. Though what exactly he did there was a mystery . . . And every few days he would fly off in his Lear jet, or one of the fleet of helicopters that was based on the reserve's airstrip.

Often the guests on the reserve were Wayne's business clients – usually heads of state or government ministers, who revelled in the opulence of Cayzer. Now, as she walked quietly through the bush, Anne wondered again about how life had taken her into Wayne MacLeod's world, and how she had come to be having an affair with him.

She reached the wooden balcony that overlooked the waterhole, and quietly settled herself down to watch. She had sat here often over the past few months, making notes of her observations on lion behaviour.

A hand rested on her shoulder and she looked into the mesmeric blue eyes of Cade Korda – Hollywood's number one box-office draw. He was taking time off at Cayzer from the set of his latest movie. Anne didn't like him; she felt he was insincere, that his devastating looks covered up a very shallow human being.

'Morning, Anne. Are you feeling better?'

She smiled coolly.

'Wayne was telling me about what happened. I can understand how you feel.'

She said nothing, determined not to show the resentment she felt at Wayne's having talked about her nervous breakdown to this man.

'You're a very attractive woman,' Korda went on. 'Perhaps you should have been a model.'

'I never considered that as an option.'

In her view, modelling was one stage removed from prostitution.

'You could still do it.'

She looked deliberately gullible. Jesus Christ, he was probably planning to use her in some minor role and then fuck her! Good God, Wayne must have put him up to this. 'Do you think I could be an actress?' she said innocently.

His eyes flashed. 'Sure.'

She sensed that someone else was approaching and saw that it was the film director, Rex Zanders. He was around fifty, at the height of his powers. He doted on Cade Korda.

'Rex, did you know Anne wants to be an actress?'

Rex raised his bushy eyebrows and looked her up and down. 'What makes you think you've got what it takes?'

Anne breathed in deeply and resisted the momentary impulse

to knee Rex Zanders in the balls. 'I acted in a few plays at university . . .' she replied demurely.

'I'd be prepared to do a screen test with her,' Cade said enthusiastically.

Rex perked up at this. 'Well, if you feel warm about her, I'm prepared to give her a chance.'

She was boiling with rage. This was obviously Wayne's plan to end their relationship. With an easy excuse, she left them, and walked quickly across to Wayne's private dining-area.

Wayne MacLeod's back was to her, the long silver hair lying silkily on the broad shoulders, and for a moment she could imagine him on a war-horse, dressed in armour, carrying a sword and ready for battle. God, why had she got involved with him?

He shifted in his chair, sensing her behind him. 'Ah, Anne. I see Cade was talking to you.' The voice was refined, with only the hint of a Scots accent – and the look in his grey-blue eyes totally sincere. But now Anne was beginning to see behind the veneer.

'Did you ask Cade to offer me a part in his film?' she asked icily.

'Come on, sit down,' he said cheerfully. 'You need something to eat. You hardly touched dinner last night. Are you still not feeling well?'

She looked over the beautifully prepared table, at the assortment of exotic fruits laid out before her. Wayne MacLeod never stinted his guests; everything was done to the highest standard.

'I'd like an answer to my question,' she said.

'Anne. Sit down.' He pushed a hand-control unit, and a waiter appeared through a side-door. 'Sulliman, ask chef to prepare an omelette for Dr Madison.' The man disappeared soundlessly.

Anne sat, but she was now beside herself. Wayne thought he had her worked out: everything she needed was provided for her. Wherever she was on Cayzer, help was literally seconds away, and any wine, any food, any book or video, could be provided almost immediately. This sort of attention was something Wayne MacLeod prided himself on – and suddenly, Anne had begun to loathe.

She thought about how the MacLeods treated their workers –

how the squalor they lived in contrasted with the opulence afforded to the guests.

'You think Cade will offer you a role?' Wayne MacLeod said.

Her heart skipped a beat. Her every movement was monitored. 'If you must know,' she replied stonily, 'I don't want one.'

'Anne, you are paid to help us promote lion conservation. Cade is Hyde's guest – Hyde wants him and Rex Zanders to shoot a feature here, promoting our work with the lion. If you read your contract again, you'll see it specifies that you must help us with promotional work.'

God, how she loathed him. 'So?'

'Well, I think you'd better co-operate, don't you?'

She finished her omelette quickly. She did not like what was happening. She was just a pawn in Wayne MacLeod's game – he'd been using her from the beginning. How the hell could she have fallen for him?

She spent her day down by the waterhole, making detailed observations on the bird life. She decided she definitely didn't trust Wayne MacLeod any longer – but she also decided she wasn't in a great hurry to leave. Questions popped up in her mind. Perhaps Paul Norton hadn't been lying – perhaps he had been set up.

After dinner that evening she began to feel a little more at ease. Was she just imagining things? She walked back towards her luxury suite and shook out her hair. The cool air of the evening revived her. Maybe she was being too hard on Wayne . . .

She unlocked the door to her cabin, stepped inside and switched on the light. She sucked in her breath as she saw Hyde MacLeod sitting on the couch, a glass of whisky in his hand.

'Hallo, Anne. Did you have a good evening?'

'Get out!'

She heard a noise from the bathroom, and Charles Fox walked into the room.

'How dare you two come in here!'

Hyde rose to his feet and moved towards her. 'Shut up, bitch!'

Before she could react, he hit her hard across the face and she fell to the floor. Her mouth bloody, she tried to get up, but Hyde's foot caught her hard in the stomach. Winded, she couldn't scream out, and the next moment Hyde had stuffed his handkerchief into her mouth. She tried to fight him off but he was far too strong for her.

Then Charles came up and took out a wide roll of sticking-plaster, and taped her mouth shut. Desperately she lashed out and caught Charles's knee.

'Bitch!'

Charles pushed her roughly to the floor. She felt Hyde's hands ripping off her clothes and exploring her body. She sagged to the floor, and saw them stripping off their clothes. Her gun was hidden under the mattress . . . She dragged herself over to the bed and pulled it out, aiming at Hyde's head. She ripped the plaster off her mouth and shouted, 'Move, and I'll shoot!'

Hyde looked across at Charles. 'I told you to check if she had a gun.'

Charles pulled his pants back on and buttoned up his shirt. Hyde followed suit.

'Out, both of you.'

Charles slunk quickly out of the door, but Hyde stood staring at her. 'You keep your mouth shut, Anne,' he said. 'Because if you don't, nobody will believe you anyway.'

'You bastard!'

'You asked for it. You've been provoking me ever since you got here.'

'I'm going straight to Wayne!'

'And you think he's going to believe you? I was playing poker with Charles all evening. And you were hungry for a man, seeing that my father's not balling you any longer.'

Her finger trembled on the trigger.

'Yes, that's right, Anne,' Hyde sneered. 'He's got a new mistress.'

So that was why Wayne had been so distant. She saw Hyde's eyes exploring her naked breasts, and held her left arm across them. 'Get out of here!'

He left, slamming the door behind him, and she bolted the door, then ran into the bathroom and turned on the shower. She washed and washed herself, but she still didn't feel clean. She scrubbed herself raw, and then staggered into the bedroom and lay on the bed crying.

The bastards.

Her mind turned over slowly. They were banking on the fact that she'd be too scared to tell anyone her version of the truth.

She thought about Paul Norton. There was something elemental about him. She remembered the trial photographs – the look of determination and desperation in his haunted blue eyes.

Questions about Norton's trial began to ask themselves in her head. Hyde said that if she didn't keep her mouth shut he would say that he and Charles had been playing poker. Wasn't that his alibi for the night Thoko was raped? Was Hyde guilty of the rape? There was definitely a strong bond between Hyde and Charles Fox.

The next morning Anne forced herself to behave normally. She took Cade Korda down to the waterhole and showed him where the animals rubbed themselves against the bark of the trees, and the hundred other things that were interesting to someone out in the bush for the first time. But all the time she was thinking about Hyde and Charles. Suddenly she guessed why Mkhulu had attacked Hyde that night he broke into her room – he must have come across him molesting a woman.

As the heat of the day grew stronger, Korda began to feel uncomfortable and suggested they return to the lodge. She drove back deliberately slowly, letting him roast in the heat – there was no canopy over the safari Land Cruiser, it was only used to take people out early in the morning, late in the afternoon and at night.

She thought about the irony of the situation. She was alone with a man so many women desired, a movie star who might offer her a role in one of his films, and all she felt was emptiness, isolation and despair. She gripped the big steering-wheel more tightly as she thought of Paul Norton in prison. Cade was an actor, Paul was genuine. She wondered what Paul was doing at that moment.

Paul sat on the hard bunk in his cell and felt dirty. The smell of sweat and urine was all-pervasive. It was the smell of captivity. Yet still in his nostrils was the memory of another smell, the smell that had hit him when he first arrived at Pretoria Central a week before: 'Ou Swaar', the smell of the polish that was used to black the prison floor.

He could remember every second of his arrival. It was as if he'd recorded a film of it in his memory – a film that he played back to himself again and again as he sat alone in his cell. His first impression was of the stone wall as the truck pulled up in front of it, sixteen feet high and stretching for eighty yards, with a guardpost high up at each end – the eagle eyes of the sentries always alert for some desperate soul foolish enough to try and make an escape.

The guard had bellowed at him to get out of the back, then led him roughly towards a Gothic arch in the middle of this formidable wall. A peephole opened, and the eye of a guard on the inside blinked as he took in the identity document held up by Paul's guard. One of the two huge wooden doors had swung open and the two of them moved in smartly. They were standing in an iron cage, like birds on display. Another guard stared across at them and lazily came forward to release them. He undid the lock, and the metal gate creaked open. They moved across the yard towards the entrance to the main prison.

For a moment Paul had stood, frozen. He knew he would not leave this place alive. But a rough punch in the back had brought him to his senses and he staggered quickly forward.

Once he was inside he had to climb two flights of stairs to reach the main hall. It was an empty, frightening room, the sense of despair almost tangible; the smell of the polish, 'Ou Swaar', seemed to carry within it the spirit of the place. He felt the desperation of men who had spent long years here regretting some action that had deprived them of their freedom. But for him there would be no boredom. Every minute would be precious, for his time was short.

Then his tousled blond hair was shorn, and he had to strip. His clothes and belongings were carefully listed and placed in a cardboard box. He was handed a pair of olive-green nylon trousers and an open-necked shirt, and put them on. He could not close the waistband of the trousers. The warden smirked.

'Don't worry, Norton, you'll find they fit in a couple of months. We'll get the fat off you.'

Lastly he put on the boots. They had obviously had several

previous owners, and were misshapen and uncomfortable to wear. He felt strange, wearing another man's clothes, but then he wasn't a man any longer, he was a prisoner destined for death row.

He was taken in the back of a prison truck to the south end of Pretoria Central – a prison specially reserved for 'condemns' – those whose fate was death. He was marched out of the back of the truck, through a huge sliding door into a courtyard. Its concrete walls soared up all around him. Then he was marched up a wide set of stairs towards a modern prison building – death row. He stood outside a set of wooden doors at the top, and was again examined through a peephole before being let in. The inner section was divided into barred cages that gave access to the main prison. Two warders approached the next door and unlocked it with separate keys. Paul was shown into this section, and locked in; then a warder approached from a side-passage, and unlocked yet another gate to let him through.

This prison smelt clean and antiseptic, almost too well-scrubbed. Paul had the feeling that here he would be treated for what he was – a man with not long to live.

He was shown into a lonely cell, and sat at a table that was bolted to the wall, trying to steady his nerves. Later, he slept – the first good sleep since he had entered prison.

He was woken in the darkness by singing – the chant of his fellow-prisoners for those men who were about to die. It bored into his soul and became a part of his unconscious – for he knew that one day, in the not too distant future, that singing would be for him.

Later came a noise that struck terror into his soul – the sound of the trap as those condemned to die that day dropped to their deaths.

Paul had thought that he had lived intensely before this, but now he realised how short those periods of intensely lived experience had been. This time was long-drawn-out and all-absorbing. He was drawn to the memory of his dead father, to the long hours the old man had spent with him as a child. His forgotten advice returned to him, and suddenly he realised that all experience is for a reason. His father's words echoed in his brain – the words of a man who had gone through hell and survived. His father's gift – or perhaps his curse – was the one he'd handed down to Paul: the gift of language.

Held in a Japanese prisoner-of-war camp, his father had survived because he knew Japanese, and understood the mentality of his captors. Paul's linguistic gift meant that here he could talk to his fellow-prisoners – most of them black and all of them 'condemns' – in their own language; he could know their fears. And he could speak to the warders in fluent Afrikaans.

He found that his sentence baffled his captors and his fellow-prisoners alike, for he did not match the character of the men he stood among. His life had been driven by the need to expose the worst side of human nature; he had stood for the very justice that was now about to cut him down.

Strangely, he found he got stronger. He had thought he might break down, but the inevitability of what was to happen to him eliminated all cause for worry. He concentrated on living, and extracted all he could from his surroundings. He was given some books to read, most of them religious.

He felt content that he had finished his script – at least most of his feelings about life had been encompassed in it.

He hated the noise of the warder's keys, the sound of the locks being opened and closed – a constant reminder of his containment. He dreamed of walking free with the cubs. Most of all, he felt remorse for what he had done. He realised at last that killing Cilliers had been wrong.

He vowed that if by some miracle he escaped the death sentence, he would live every day of his life to the fullest, and never stop fighting for what he believed in.

Dr Anne Madison steeled herself for what she had to do. She pulled the tight white sweater over her breasts and tucked it into the lycra micro-mini. Then she smoothed out her dark pantihose and slipped on her high heels. She took a heavy slug from the bottle of whisky, then screwed on the cap and took it with her as she closed the door to her cabin.

It was Monday night, and she knew that most of the camp staff went to bed early. Hyde was in Pietersburg on business. She moved up to the door of the thatched rondavel and knocked on it.

'Yes?' came the gruff reply.

She knocked again, a little louder. 'It's open!' the voice bellowed.

Breathing in deeply, she opened the door and stepped inside. Charles Fox was lying on his bed, dressed only in a pair of scants, reading a novel and smoking a cigarette.

He put the cigarette out on a tin lid on a box next to his bed, and got up quickly, looking nervously at her.

'Whadya want?' he asked suspiciously.

Anne, who felt like running a mile, touched his arm and sat down on the side of the bed. 'I brought you a present,' she replied, handing him the whisky.

This seemed to relax him; he was obviously scared she was going to confront him about his and Hyde's behaviour earlier in the week. She realised how gutless he was – the perfect partner for Hyde – and this encouraged her.

'I'm sorry, do you want me to go?' she asked, crossing her legs so that her skirt rode up a little higher.

'No. Care for a drink?'

She nodded, and he poured them both a neat whisky. Then he sat on the bed next to her. 'So, Anne. What's this about?'

She forced herself to kiss him, resisting the temptation to gag. His hands began to explore her body and she felt him relax. Good. She pulled away.

'Why hurry?' she said huskily. 'We've got the whole night.'

He laughed, and lay back. 'I thought you'd come to threaten me.'

'You were a fool. If you'd come on your own the other night, you could have had me with pleasure.'

His face lit up. 'It was Hyde's idea . . .'

He began to talk freely. She got up and poured him another drink to loosen his tongue. He didn't notice that she wasn't drinking. She let him slip his hand under her top and caress her breasts.

After an hour, the bottle of whisky was nearly empty, and Charles was talking freely.

'Yes, Hyde gets carried away all right. Mostly it's black chicks like Thoko . . .' He stopped in mid-sentence, realising he'd said more than he should have.

'Tell me, I'm no friend of Paul Norton's.'

Charles smirked. 'Hyde really nailed the bastard. You see, we'd tried to work out a way we could shoot his lioness. Hyde figured that if we could lure her across the Limpopo, then we could shoot her on the grounds that she'd been killing our cattle. Anyway, he got this tape of hyena calls – that's the way to lure a lion in.'

Anne poured him another whisky and felt her blood run cold. She couldn't believe what she was hearing. Paul Norton was going to hang for this.

'You see, Hyde ordered me to find a reason for kicking Johannes off the reserve, because Johannes had shown you Norton's lion. Well, after I'd sorted the situation out, Hyde remembered Johannes' daughter would be coming home that evening. He told me he was going to have some fun with her. He likes black chicks.'

Anne breathed in deeply. 'So . . .?'

'Well, that night Hyde came back at midnight, covered in blood and looking scared. He told me Thoko had fought him and he'd lost control – raped her and beaten her up. I suggested he kill two birds with one stone – use the hyena tape to lure Norton's lioness over the river towards Thoko's body. Naturally, the lioness would eat her, and then we'd have the perfect excuse to kill the lioness.' Charles looked at her nervously. 'This is between you and me, eh?'

Anne smiled salaciously, and nodded.

'It all worked beautifully, except that bloody Norton came over the border, looking for his lioness.'

Anne could hardly breathe.

'Listen, Anne,' Charles said, 'Norton deserves to die, he shot Cilliers.'

Five minutes later, Charles was comatose. And when he awoke six hours later he had a terrible hangover and the uneasy, though vague, memory of having said too much to Dr Anne Madison.

Anne packed her bags and left Cayzer the next day, claiming she had to go to Pretoria University to do further research on lion

175

behaviour. In fact she had no intention of ever returning. She was horrified by Charles's revelations.

Later that day, she booked into a hotel in Pretoria. She was quite certain what she was going to do. She wanted to talk to Paul Norton.

The following day she walked along the tree-lined streets to the grim outer wall of Pretoria Central. It made her shiver. She went back to her hotel and phoned up the department of prison services, who told her that only a man's next of kin and his legal counsel were permitted to visit him on death row. Undeterred, she continued her researches and found out that one of the doctors at the local hospital visited the prison regularly to examine the prisoners. Better still, he was always looking for a nurse to go with him – no one liked the job.

Anne went to the hospital, gave details of her qualifications, and volunteered. She got an immediate interview with the doctor.

Dr Villiers looked at her twice and adjusted his glasses. Then he scratched his bald pate.

'You are serious about this? You want to accompany me on a regular basis?'

Anne nodded determinedly, afraid he might turn her down.

'You've never done this sort of work before?'

'No, no. But I want to.'

'Come with me one time, then let me know if you think you can manage it.'

They started off early the next morning, arriving outside the prison just before eight. Dr Villiers looked up and down the outside walls with a grim expression on his face.

'Look at those walls, my dear. Inside there you will see a part of life that most people never glimpse.'

She felt numbed as she walked across the exercise yard, sensing the eyes of the warders on her. Next time she would wear pants, not a skirt. She realised that these men rarely saw a woman.

In the distance she heard singing. She touched Dr Villiers' arm. 'Why are they singing?'

'Those are the men on death row – they're singing for those who are about to be hung.'

She swallowed deeply and stopped to draw breath. This was something she had not thought about. In her mind Paul had been alone, the only man in the world condemned to die. But now she knew there were many, and that he was consigned to follow an endless, slow procession of men destined for the gallows.

They were shown into a grim little room that was the dispensary. Dr Villiers was searched, but she was left alone; a woman, it seemed, was above suspicion. Dr Villiers caught her eye.

'They don't have a female warder on duty today. Male warders aren't allowed to search women. I told them you're OK.'

The first man came in. He was young, and good-looking in a rough sort of way. His face was a mass of bruises. He whispered something to the doctor.

'It's all right, she's a trained nurse.'

She turned away as he stripped. He lay on the examination table, and she had to resist the temptation to gag . . .'

'Anal rape,' Dr Villiers murmured. 'It happens . . .' She steeled herself, and handed him a swab.

'Please, get me away from here! They'll get me again!' the man gasped.

The doctor leaned over him, very close, and whispered carefully. 'Don't fight them. They'll destroy you then. I'll speak to the head warder.'

The man limped out a few moments later, and the next filed in.

In the next two hours Anne learned more about life than she had in the last twenty-nine years. She resisted the look in each man's eyes, sexually assessing her. She switched off her normal self and became distant.

The last man in was black. He was curiously silent. The other prisoners had welcomed the chance to talk to the doctor, but this man was different.

'What's the problem, my friend?'

'I feel sick. I can't eat,' he mumbled.

'That's not unusual,' Dr Villiers said. He carefully slid a plastic container of pills into the man's hand. 'Take these,' he whispered, 'they will make you feel better.'

Anne tidied up the surgery, then followed Dr Villiers out across the courtyard. It was wonderful to be away from the place. When she reached Dr Villiers' car, she hung on to the roof, gasping for breath.

He patted her on the shoulder. 'It's usually older nurses who come, they're a little more hardened to accepting that sort of thing. I'm sorry, today was particularly bad, especially the first case. But you mustn't feel bad, Dr Madison. I'll understand.'

'What do you mean?' Anne said softly.

'Well . . . I'll understand if you say you don't want to come again.'

She looked up and touched his face. 'You come here three times a week. Why do you think I'm not capable of that?'

He broke into a half-smile. 'You're young. You have so much to live for. This sort of thing drags one down.'

'Dr Villiers, I will come with you every time.'

He took her hand. 'I have needed someone like you for a long time. You will find that there are highs as well as lows.'

He dropped her off at the hospital, and she sat by herself in the passage by the out-patients ward for a long, long time.

She thought of the last man they had seen – the black man – a man condemned to death. Then she thought of Paul Norton. She had to see him, that was all she knew.

David went through all the evidence again. He couldn't accept defeat; there had to be something he'd missed. But he could find nothing to hang an appeal on.

Eventually he gathered together all his notes and packed them into his wide black briefcase. He walked out of his chambers, past the doors of the Supreme Court, through the bustling streets of Johannesburg. He headed north, knowing with absolute certainty where he was going but not hurrying his pace. He would have to drive out to Pretoria tomorrow – he would have to do that. Leave to appeal had not been granted because there was no prospect of the court's decision being overturned.

The street took him upwards, towards Hillbrow, built slightly higher than Johannesburg, and one of the most densely populated areas in the world. Here, before the laws changed, black people had lived illegally, preferring it to the sprawling black townships that lay around Johannesburg. Sometimes as many as twenty people shared a flat here, some of them night-dwellers, some of them day-dwellers.

David was pleased to see that more and more of the apartheid laws were being scrapped, but he knew that discrimination couldn't be erased from the minds of men. If a person hated or disliked you for what you were, that could not be altered except through friendship or gradual education. He also knew, as a Jew, that his people's strength, their solidarity as a group, was precisely what isolated them from the world around them. There were many things he despised in himself to do with his Jewish background, but there were other things that made him proud to the core. Above all, he and his grandmother were survivors; they carried on the legacy.

He reached the doors of the synagogue, and for a moment wondered why he had come. He was about to turn away when the rabbi came out.

'I saw you from the window. You wish to pray?'

David nodded.

'You go to *shul*?'

David nodded again.

The rabbi opened the door, and David entered. He had always in the past felt oppressed in the synagogue, but now he felt free. The rabbi touched his shoulder.

'I will leave you to pray. But when you are finished I should like you to talk to me. Maybe I can help you.'

David sat for a long time in the silent synagogue. He wondered if he should move from criminal to civil work. It was one thing to lose a case, quite another to lose a man who had become a friend. David believed in justice because he knew that you couldn't change men. All you could do was enforce the law and protect the weak from the strong, the good from the evil, the just from the unjust.

He had been so certain of getting the appeal granted. He leaned his head against his closed hands and prayed again. There had to be something, something he'd missed. He had felt so certain that he could win Paul's case.

179

Eventually, exhausted, he got up and found the rabbi's office. Dressed in a charcoal-grey suit, the rabbi carried a natural authority. His brown eyes rested on David. 'Tell me what it is that troubles you.'

'I am an advocate . . .'

For the next hour, David went over everything that had happened. He talked about his beliefs – and now his despair.

'Do not give up,' the rabbi said when he had finished. 'Of course, you must tell your client that the appeal has failed. But tell him you will keep fighting, keep searching . . .'

David walked back to his chambers through the warm heat of the afternoon. He needed a miracle now to save Paul, that was for sure.

Anne found her visits to the prison exhausting. Dr Villiers relied on her more and more, and confided in her his concern for his patients and the abuses they were subjected to. Familiarity with the prison and its surroundings did not make the task any easier for Anne; even away from the prison she could now picture it perfectly in her mind, and the vision travelled everywhere with her.

They had seen ten prisoners that morning when Paul came in through the door. She didn't recognise him at first, though she went cold when the blue eyes rested on hers. He looked thin and drawn. It was unbearable to watch him going through this, and at first was glad that he did not recognise her.

'What's the problem?' Dr Villiers asked kindly.

'I can't sleep. I'm beginning to feel I'm going crazy.'

Dr Villiers peered into his eyes. 'I am not allowed to give you sleeping tablets, officially.'

The hard blue eyes rested on his own. 'Unofficially?'

'You might take them and commit suicide. Then I should not be permitted to come here any longer, I should be struck off . . .'

Paul's hand gripped the doctor's, and Anne wanted to scream. She would get him the tablets, somehow she would get them to him. She moved over to the doctor's bag, lifted out a vial of sleeping tablets and slipped them into the pocket of her trousers.

'I'll tell them to allow you to do more exercise,' Dr Villiers said. 'You'll sleep better then.'

Paul nodded grimly. 'Thank you.'

He got up, and as Dr Villiers went over to make a few notes, Anne moved forward. Her eyes locked on Paul's – and he recognised her in an instant. She pressed the vial of tablets into his hand.

'Take them, for God's sake,' she whispered.

'Why?' he asked, not moving his eyes from hers.

'Because . . .'

She saw a flicker in his eyes, then he turned and was gone.

The morning passed slowly, and when she eventually walked outside the prison with Dr Villiers she was close to breaking-point. He opened the car door for her, and they drove off. It took Anne some minutes to realise that Dr Villiers was not taking their normal route.

'Where are we going?'

'I'm taking you to lunch.'

'But I want to be on my own . . .'

'I think we need to talk.'

The restaurant was pleasant, mostly full of businessmen. Anne undid the ribbon that held up her long blonde hair and shook it out. Her eyes ran quickly over the menu, and she realised that the tension of seeing Paul had made her ravenous.

'Shall I order some wine?' Dr Villiers asked politely.

'Not for me, Doctor Villiers.'

'My dear, you need a drink.'

Her eyes caught his, and she sensed that he was not unaware of her plight. 'All right then,' she said. 'Thanks.'

He poured for her, and she sipped at the cool white wine, feeling guilty about the pills she had stolen.

'You know, I was going to give him the sleeping tablets,' Dr Villiers said softly.

Anne knocked her wine over, and a waiter came over immediately and cleared up the mess. A fresh glass was brought, and the wine waiter filled it for her.

'I don't know what you're talking about,' she whispered, arranging her hair.

He smiled. 'So you think I did not wonder why an exceptionally attractive – no, beautiful – young woman should elect to do the worst duty in the hospital with a cranky old doctor?'

Anne gulped down her wine. 'I want to leave,' she said.

'But what is wrong?'

She stared at him defiantly. 'You can't stop me coming with you!'

Dr Villiers laughed softly, and laid his hand over hers. 'You have helped me more than you know. I would never stop you coming to the prison with me. The only fear I have is that you might decide not to come.'

She brightened, and he poured her another glass of wine. 'Now,' he said, 'I want you to tell me why you want to get close to a man who sentenced to death for rape and murder.'

David walked grimly behind the warder. He hadn't slept the previous night. When he'd arrived at the prison that morning, he'd walked up and down outside before summoning up the courage to enter.

He smelt 'Ou Swaar', the smell that old-timers said never left your nostrils till the day you died. His footsteps echoed along the corridors, and in the background he could hear the clanging of bars and the murmur of men's voices.

He was led into a small room to the left of the main entrance hall, and waited for Paul to be brought to him. He rehearsed the words in his mind again: *I'm sorry, but I've failed to get your appeal granted. I'm sorry . . .* The words were hollow, and in the end inadequate to express the enormity of what had happened.

The door of the room opened and he was staring at Paul, standing in the sunlight. The door was half-closed, and two warders remained in the room, looking on. Paul looked grim but strong. David guessed he knew what was coming.

'Paul, this is very hard . . .'

'I saw her yesterday.'

David was stopped dead in his tracks. 'Who? Who did you see?'

A quickening of his pulse, a feeling of hope. 'Anne – Dr Anne Madison. She's working with the prison doctor.'

David's mind went into overdrive. He had left Dr Anne Madison out of the equation. Why had she come to see Paul? Surely, she would only have come if she believed he had been unjustly convicted. He would question her. This was what he had been looking for – a witness who might prove that Paul's interpretation of the events leading to his arrest was true.

'Where did you see her?' he asked eagerly.

'I couldn't sleep. I had to see Dr Villiers – she was with him.'

'Did she say anything?'

Paul broke down then, and David got up and put his arm round his shoulders. The two warders stepped forward, and David glared angrily at them.

'Don't keep it in, my friend,' he whispered to Paul. 'Let what you feel out. There are no heroes here.'

Paul gathered himself together. 'David, speak to her, but don't force her.'

'Paul, the application for an appeal failed, but I think the possibility of a new statement from her might give me a chance to try again.'

'I don't know . . . How will you find her?'

David didn't have to do much looking. He found the note asking him to call Dr Anne Madison when he returned to his chambers. Feverishly he dialled the number of the Pretoria hotel where she was staying – and later, as he sat in her hotel room, listening to the truth behind what had happened, he felt a white blaze of anger coursing through him.

'Get a sample of Hyde's blood, Mr Katz,' Anne Madison said. 'I guarantee you can match it to the semen found in Thoko's body.'

Over the next week David had detailed forensic tests performed, and Hyde MacLeod's blood did match the semen found in Thoko Sebi's body. But David knew that this would be inadmissible as evidence unless Anne was prepared to make a statement. That meant she would have to explain how she obtained the information. And he knew it would be impossible to keep the story out of the papers.

Early one evening David met Anne again in her hotel room.

'So,' she said desperately, 'unless I make a statement, all the evidence you've accumulated is worthless? Is that right?'

'I need you to tell the court what Fox told you.'

She held her face in her hands. 'Wayne will never forgive me.'

'Do you want to see Paul Norton hang?' he said. 'It's your decision to make, Anne, but I can't tell you what it's like to live in the knowledge that a man has died unjustly. I admire your courage in coming forward – but you'll have to stand up in court.'

He looked at the beautiful woman who sat stonily in front of him. He had said enough. Now it was up to her, and he prayed a silent prayer to the God that he did not always believe in to deliver a little justice.

Eventually she lifted her head. Her dark eyes were dry, her jaw was firm.

'Mr Katz,' she said, 'you've got your statement.'

He took her down, early the next morning, to the local police station. All he could think of was Paul sitting in Pretoria Central, going through hell for a crime he had been set up to commit.

The Appeal Court sat in Bloemfontein. Five judges presided, because of the severity of the sentence – and because of the publicity surrounding the case. Usually only written evidence was presented in this court, but now a key witness, Dr Anne Madison, was appearing – no one, except for David and the police, knew what her evidence would be.

The sombre atmosphere of the country's highest court appealed to David's idea of justice. Here, he felt, the law was upheld dispassionately.

The presiding judge leaned slightly forward and peered through his spectacles at Dr Anne Madison. 'What makes you believe Charles Fox's story?' he asked. 'He could have been boasting.'

'He and Hyde MacLeod had tried to rape me the previous evening. I hardly think he saw the need to impress me.'

The judge paged carefully through the account of evidence already given in the case, then nodded his head. 'Your new statement – that with the aid of an interpreter you now clearly understand Miss Thoko's last words to have been "Hyde raped me". . . Are you quite sure you remembered the words accurately? After all, you didn't know the language.'

'I am learning Tswana. I know quite a few words.'

The judge conferred with his colleagues, then turned to her

again. 'I believe you are telling the truth. You realise that Hyde MacLeod will now be arrested and charged with rape and attempted murder, and that you will be called upon to testify against him?'

'I will testify against him.'

'Very good.' The presiding judge looked down at his notes, then up again. 'What do you have to say to Charles Fox's testimony that on the night of the crime Hyde MacLeod was playing poker with him?'

Anne grimaced. 'They were both drinking, planning how to use a hyena tape to lure Paul Norton's lioness onto their South African land so they could shoot her. Charles told me that after that, Hyde left him to have some fun with Thoko Sebi.'

'Hyde MacLeod knew Miss Sebi would be coming home, across his farm on the South African side of the Limpopo?'

'He knew she always came that way – and he knew she wouldn't know that he'd dismissed her father.'

'Did Charles Fox say what Hyde Macleod intended to do after he had apprehended Miss Sebi?'

'He simply said Hyde was going to have some fun with her.'

The presiding judge examined his notes again. He saw that David Katz had photographs and several casts of the tyre-prints and scuffle marks from the spot where the assault had supposedly taken place. There was even some dried blood, found under examination to be Miss Sebi's. The tyre prints matched those of Hyde MacLeod's Land Cruiser.

'So your contention is,' he continued, 'that when Mr Norton found Miss Sebi, she had already been raped and assaulted by Hyde MacLeod. Mr Norton then had to fight off hyena who were attacking Miss Sebi, and once he had done so, he fired a flare to summon help. And you say that Hyde MacLeod and his manager, Ryan Cilliers, were waiting nearby to take advantage of the situation?'

'Yes.' Anne stared directly into the eyes of the appeal judges. They had to believe her. She wasn't lying. They had to believe her, or Paul Norton would hang and Hyde MacLeod would walk free.

David stepped forward. 'I should like to read certain sections

185

of Dr Madison's written statement that I believe are relevant to the proceedings.'

The presiding judge nodded his assent, and David began.

'"I always walk early in the morning by myself. At exactly five past six I saw a flare fly up into the sky. I ran back to my Land Cruiser."'

One of the judges gestured to David to pause. 'But she must have realised it came from across the Limpopo – on the South African side?' he said.

'Yes. But her statement corroborates that. I continue . . . "I could tell it had come from the South African side, but I guessed that whoever had fired it was in trouble. I had to help. I drove flat out down to the river, but I could see and hear nothing."'

David looked up. 'So, after a while,' he said, 'she decided to return to the main camp. You will note that during her drive back, she received a radio call from Hyde MacLeod, summoning her assistance. I would now ask you to refer to Hyde MacLeod's statement, which reports that he arrived at the scene of the crime at ten past six. So the two statements taken together show that it took Cilliers and MacLeod exactly five minutes to get to Norton. Well, I must point out that Hyde MacLeod says he was standing outside the main farm, talking to Cilliers, when he saw the flare – and the main farm is ten kilometres from the scene of the crime, and there are no direct roads. So if it is true that MacLeod and Cilliers were at the main farm, they must have travelled across country at an average speed of over one hundred and twenty kilometres per hour and pinpointed Norton immediately.'

The presiding judge looked up.

'There's a possible explanation for that – their watches could have been slightly out.'

David leaned forward. 'But they both affirm that Norton shot Cilliers at exactly six thirty-five in independent statements.'

There was silence for a moment. Then the judge said, 'You mention that you have incontrovertible proof that Hyde MacLeod was the man who raped Miss Thoko Sebi?'

'Yes, a sample of his blood matches the semen found in Miss Sebi's body at the time of her death.'

'Did Mr MacLeod consent to giving a sample of his blood?'

'No. It was obtained by Dr Madison from the MacLeods'

private blood bank in Pretoria. I would ask you to read her statement.'

David handed each of the judges Anne's sworn statement, and after they had conferred, the presiding judge stood up.

'I believe we have enough evidence to make a decision,' he said. 'Judgement will be given tomorrow morning.'

Paul sat alone in his cell. He thought of Dr Anne Madison.

He knew there had been publicity; her decision to provide new evidence had attracted international attention.

He had experienced more emotions in his eleven months on death row than he knew existed. Tomorrow he would know whether he was to live or to die.

Whatever happened, the morning singing of the prisoners would stay with him forever. And death, if it came, would at least be a release. God, what if they commuted his sentence to life? He could not live behind bars. That would be worse than death – a long, slow destruction.

He made a vow, that if he lived, he would make sure that his life counted. He would put his time to good use. And to Dr Madison he would remain eternally loyal, for she had come to help him when he had nothing.

The morning air was cold as David hurried across the parking area towards the appeal court. He had wanted Anne to come with him, but she had refused. She would wait in her hotel room for him to return.

He walked into the empty courtroom and prayed silently. 'Oh, God, if there is any justice in the world, let me win this case. Oh, God spare this man's life.'

He looked up to see the judges filing into the room, watching him. Their faces were deadpan. He knew what they must have gone through; he knew the difficulty, the agony of their decision.

The presiding judge, Mr Clive Davenport, a leading advocate, rose.

'In the matter of the State v Mr Paul Norton, we find the accused not guilty of the charge of rape. As for the charge of murder, we find him guilty. However, there were extenuating circumstances; there was collusion amongst the parties involved

187

-- a conspiracy that pushed Mr Norton to the edge of sanity. He is guilty of murder, but we believe he has suffered enough. We sentence him to five years in prison, suspended for ten years. He is a free man.

'I speak for my learned colleagues, Mr Katz, when I say we respect the courage and the integrity of your client.

'I have made arrangements for Mr Norton to be released from Pretoria Central tomorrow morning. I hope, and so do my colleagues, that this is the last time in his life he may have to go through such an ordeal.'

Paul was woken, as he always was, at four. He knew he would hear if the appeal had been successful at nine that morning. The time dragged terribly. He wondered whether he would remain sane if he heard that the death sentence was confirmed.

At eight thirty, the warder came and opened the door to his cell. Paul followed him dutifully, expecting to be taken to the office where he usually met visitors. Instead he was taken to another room, where a cardboard box was given to him, and a sheet of paper.

'Will you check that the articles are as you left them?'

Paul looked up at the warder, dumbfounded. 'Am I being moved to another prison?'

'From nine o'clock, you're a free man, sir.'

The doors that led out onto the main road slid open, and Paul walked out carefully, swaying like a man who has been at sea for many months and has just put his first foot on dry land.

The sense of confinement was gone. The air smelt sweet. His clothes hung around him loosely as he moved. He sensed the people passing by in cars in the main road staring at him. He knew he had changed forever – the last eleven months had been sheer torture. He crossed the road, scarcely able to believe that he could go where he wanted to. On the other side he saw Charlotte coming towards him, wearing a thin cotton dress, her dark hair blowing in the wind. Her eyes met his and he drew close to her, folding her in his arms.

There was no need to say a word.

Then David came up and hugged him. Paul saw the exchange

of looks between David and Charlotte, and realised there was something between them. That made him feel good. Then Charlotte led him by the hand to the car park, and he got slowly into the passenger seat and David drove them back to Johannesburg.

Paul looked at everything with new eyes – the trees and the sky had a freshness that he wished would last forever. His home in Johannesburg seemed like a palace. Charlotte drew him a hot bath and he sank into the foam, his skin tingling as the smell of the prison was drawn out of it. He washed his hair again and again, feeling the life return to it. Then he shaved very carefully, enjoying the cleanness and freshness of the bathroom.

He slipped on the towelling robe and came out into the main room. The doors to the balcony were open and he could see the mine dumps in the distance, silhouetted against the stark blue highveld sky.

Later he walked in the garden, staring at the leaves of the trees. Charlotte cooked him lunch, David opened a bottle of wine. And he was deliriously happy. Then he sat down on the couch and fell into a deep sleep, and dreamed only of the greenness and the feeling of freedom.

He awoke to a red sunset, the light filling the room and covering Charlotte, who was sitting in an easy-chair reading a book. He said nothing, but instead lay watching her for a long time. She had moved here just to be near him. Why did she love him? He had hardly seen her as a child – he'd neglected her, as he'd neglected Helen.

'Are you feeling good, Dad?' Her voice was deep and husky as she laid down the book and came over to him.

'Am I feeling good? I'm feeling wonderful.'

She went over to the dresser and opened one of the drawers. 'This arrived for you a week ago.' She handed him an unopened letter.

He looked up at her questioningly. 'Didn't you see what was inside?'

'That's for you. I just saw that it had a film company's emblem on the envelope and guessed it must be about your script. Your agent has been calling every day.'

Paul took the envelope and ripped it open. He recognised the letterhead, Roland-Emery, Britain's most successful film production company. He read the letter again and again, trying to keep control. They wanted to make the film! They felt it had great potential and they were prepared to sign a contract immediately!

'I'm going to London.'

'Going to London? But . . .'

'Charlotte, they're going to make my film! And they're giving me complete control of the production . . .'

Charlotte's face did not reflect his own elation. 'Let them make the film here,' she said. There's no need for you to leave. You need a rest, Dad. You must spend some time on Klaw.

Paul shook his head. 'I want to get away from this place. I'll work on the script in London – I'll do all the pre-production work there. Anyway, their facilities are better. And I want a change, I want to enjoy my freedom.'

'But, why not here? You've got the cubs, the reserve . . . That's what the film's about. That's your life, Dad.'

'I have to get away. . .'

'Dad, I want to stay on Klaw. Mkhulu's agreed to it.'

'Whatever you want . . .' He said, puzzled.

'Dad, you don't have to worry about me. I love you. Look, I understand. That film is yours – but I do think that if you want to go to London, you should take Mkhulu.'

He held her shoulders tightly. 'You've waited so long for me . . .'

'Dad, you've been through hell. You need time to find yourself. I'm not going to wall you in. If you need me, I'll be on Klaw.'

'And what about David?'

'Dad, it isn't over yet. The legal battle for Klaw is only just beginning. Hyde MacLeod will be arrested today, and his father isn't going to forgive you . . . Dr Madison was his lover, and now she's turned against him to help you. David's agreed to fight for Klaw, and I must support him all I can.'

Part II

Paul sat back from his computer and stared out of the window at the pouring rain. He'd rented a mews house in Kensington, a few streets away from Harrods and very close to Hyde Park. Roland-Emery's offices were in Bowater House, only a block away, so the situation was perfect. Each day he would run in Hyde Park for an hour, whatever the weather, and then get down to work. It was a long time since he had left Pretoria Central, but he still relished every minute of freedom.

The final script was almost completed. He had been working on it for over six months in collaboration with Dave Emery, the chief producer at Roland-Emery. Paul felt he had more stamina than ever before – the time in Pretoria Central had hardened his resolve.

Now he got up and slipped on his anorak. He needed a break. He went downstairs, picked up his small video camera and then let himself out. He always carried a camera with him – often the best footage came when one least expected it.

The hard mid-afternoon drizzle didn't deter him as he walked quickly down the road, and he kept up a brisk pace, shaking the last vestiges of the scene he'd been working on from his mind. He thought about Dr Anne Madison. She had applied to him for a job on Klaw just before he left for London. He'd been intrigued by the request, and when he met her face-to-face he'd realised she was the ideal person to assist Mkhulu and Johannes with the rehabilitation work. In fact she was the perfect person to give their work credibility, for it was she who had been the most outspoken critic of his father's work.

He'd enjoyed talking to her. There was no question that she was attractive. They kept in touch; she wrote to him regularly, and spoke to him occasionally on the phone.

Two weeks ago Hyde MacLeod had been sentenced to ten years imprisonment. Paul guessed that Hyde wouldn't cope with prison particularly well, but perhaps it might make him think twice before assaulting another woman.

The legal battle for Klaw was going well. The Botswanan authorities were sympathetic to Paul, especially because of his work with lions.

Yes, he was glad Anne was on Klaw. She was enjoying working with the cubs, and that was what counted. And he could tell that her attitudes towards conservation were changing, now that her academic knowledge was being enriched by genuine experience. Of course, in a way he was jealous – he was losing out on the experience of himself rehabilitating the lions. But he knew that if he'd been there himself, Anne would not have experienced so much, or developed such a close rapport with Mkhulu and Johannes.

He thought of her as he walked through the drizzle, the way she walked through the bush barefoot, her blonde hair flowing over her shoulders . . . Suddenly he felt very empty – alone. What was he really doing here, away from the people who mattered in his life?

In the weeks following his release he saw a lot of Charlotte and David Katz. With Charlotte he felt closer than ever before, and for David he felt the beginnings of a deep friendship. But all too soon he had to leave for London to work with Roland-Emery on the final draft of his film script and attend the inevitable complex pre-production meetings.

Now David was fighting Wayne MacLeod in the civil court of Botswana for the access rights to Klaw – a protracted battle into which MacLeod was prepared to pour vast sums of money.

Paul knew that David was close to Charlotte. He was surprised she liked the talented young lawyer, but very, very pleased, and he sensed from her letters that David was becoming more and more a part of her life. He thanked God for it. David was Charlotte's intellectual equal, but had a maturity and a strength that she still lacked.

He focused back on London. He wasn't walking in any specific direction, he just needed a break from the exhaustive process of tightening the script. He went through a gap in the wall and headed north.

He was walking through Rutland Gate, an exclusive square just north of Knightsbridge, when a Mercedes Pullman saloon caught his attention. It was parked outside the front entrance of the largest house in the square – one of the few that had not been converted into flats.

Paul looked up at the large balcony filled with pot-plants and thought what a fine view of the square it must have. His eyes drifted back to the Mercedes – it radiated wealth, with a huge radio antenna on the back. A dark-suited chauffeur was slowly polishing the bonnet.

The door of the house opened – and the chauffeur smartly folded up the yellow duster, placed it in his pocket and quickly opened an umbrella. A very tall, intellectual-looking man with white hair came out, followed by a dark-skinned man dressed in a navy-blue double-breasted suit of the finest cut – in dramatic contrast to the two-day stubble on his chin.

'I cannot accept any more excuses, Dr Torr,' the dark-skinned man was saying.

Paul caught the words through the drizzle. For some reason his curiousity was aroused, and he took the video camera from the main pocket of his anorak and began filming.

He looked again at the dark-skinned, unshaven man. Surely he had seen him somewhere before? The dark eyes were restless, on the watch, and they suddenly focused on Paul. A ripple of anger crossed the man's face. Paul made to lower his camera and ejected the videotape into his left hand, instinctively pocketing it. Before he realised it, a heavily built, blond man had sidled over to him and blocked his view.

'What you filming, guv?'

'What I want to,' Paul replied, standing his ground.

The burly man closed in on him and smashed his fist hard into Paul's gut, so that he toppled forward and dropped his camera. The man gripped his arms and expertly frog-marched him down the road and into an alleyway.

Paul felt the grip lessen and tried to break loose. The man's knee came up fast, smashing into his groin. He collapsed onto the wet tarmac, and smelt urine on the pavement. Then he fell unconscious as the man's boot impacted into the side of his skull.

Paul came round to see an old lady looking compassionately down at him. 'The drink will be the end of you,' she said, wagging her finger at him.

He dragged himself to his feet. He had a dull pain in his scrotum and a blinding headache. His wallet was gone, so was his watch. And he had no doubt that they'd taken his video camera as well.

'Fuck it!'

The old woman backed off. 'I'm not drunk, damnit!' he shouted. 'I've been mugged!'

She opened her handbag, and a ten-pound note was pushed into his hand. He could see she was embarassed. 'You must tell the police,' she said anxiously.

'Later . . .'

Staggering, he, followed her out of the alley. In the distance he saw the large house, lights burning behind the curtained windows. He felt the videotape in his pocket, and smiled. At least he had a record of them, whoever they were.

'Are you sure you're all right, young man?'

'I'll be OK. Thank you.'

She hailed a taxi for him, and watched it disappear into the darkness, its rear lights blurring against the road in the pouring rain.

Paul limped painfully home to his mews house. His next door neighbour, Jessica, was arriving home as he staggered up the steps.

'Paul! My God, what happened to you? Do you want me to take you to the hospital? You look terrible.'

'No . . . I'll be all right,' Paul replied dully. It was only when he faced the front door that he realised he wouldn't be able to get in.

'Oh, bugger it, they took my keys,' he said desperately, and fell down the steps.

Jessica ran over and helped him up. 'You are coming inside with me, now.'

He made it inside and collapsed on her settee.

'Paul, what happened?'

'I was mugged. They took my keys.'

Jessica made him a cup of tea and then ran him a hot bath. 'You're staying here tonight, Paul. You can get a locksmith in the morning.'

He knew better than to object and made his way up to her bathroom. Alone, he undressed painfully. The whole area around his groin was badly bruised, and when he looked in the mirror he could see why Jessica was so concerned. There was an ugly cut across his forehead and one of his eyes was black.

He thought about the whole incident again as he lay in the hot water, recovering his strength, a silent rage building up in him.

He woke later in Jessica's spare room, in a cold sweat. He'd been back in the valley. Clouds of white gas had been rolling down the sides, and there was screaming from the huts. He saw her running towards him with the child. At first he thought she was going to make it, then the clouds had enveloped her and she'd fallen forwards.

He breathed a sigh of relief. It had only been a dream, but it was disturbing. He touched the cut on his forehead. His body ached all over – was there anywhere the thug hadn't kicked him? He lay awake, unable to get back to sleep.

Why had he had that dream now – what had prompted his mind to go back to the valley, to the horror of the gas attack?

He lay staring at the ceiling. Where had he seen that man before?

Fahad looked at the picture projected on the television screen. He pulled out a Sobrani, inserted it carefully between his sensuous lips and then flicked on the slim gold lighter. He inhaled deeply, the taste of the tobacco making him feel a little more at ease.

'Our security is excellent. No one could possibly have known about the meeting.'

On the leather couch in the basement room lay an enormous man. He had a greying beard and a huge gut, and was permanently sweating. He exuded a combination of garlic and wine smells. Fahad looked at the hairs of the man's stomach, visible in the places where his shirt bulged open between the buttons.

Josh belched loudly and Fahad turned his nose up in disgust.

197

He did not like this Englishman, but he was the best at what he did, so he had to put up with him.

'That man obviously did,' Josh said. 'And he's nobody's fool.'

Josh flipped on another slide. The picture of Norton had been reduced and next to him was a fact file.

'Maybe he'll back off, Michael slapped him around hard enough,' Fahad said casually.

'No way. Not Paul Norton. He's been around – Vietnam, Afghanistan, Northern Ireland, The Falklands, Soweto . . . He was a captain in the elite South African Reconnaissance Commando till he was court-martialled for killing three of his own men. More recently he murdered another man – he's just spent a year on death row in South Africa's notorious Pretoria Central, the hanging jail. Six months ago he was released – and guess whose testimony sent him to jail originally?'

Fahad shook his head and lit another cigarette.

'Wayne MacLeod's son – Hyde.'

Fahad broke into a fit of coughing. 'Josh, we have to frighten him off. What if he makes the link between me and MacLeod?'

'This man isn't afraid of danger. He loves it.'

'I'm not happy.'

Josh lifted Paul's vidoe camera off the table. 'We got the camera,' he said, 'but we didn't get the film Norton shot of you and Torr together.'

'So get the film. Then kill him.'

Josh switched off the projector. 'Not so fast. This isn't Iraq. When people die in London, questions are asked. If Norton was acting on a tip-off, we're in trouble; it's the inside informers who are the most dangerous. And remember, Norton has good reason to hate Wayne MacLeod.'

There was a slight twitch above Fahad's eyebrow. 'The security on this project is watertight. You realise what happens if one word of what we're doing gets into the hands of the media?'

Josh sat up and rested his feet on the floor. His shoes were tiny, incongruous for his enormous size. 'With respect, that's my bag,' he said. 'If we find there's been a leak, there are numerous ways to close it, believe me.'

Fahad breathed a little easier. Josh was very good – he had never failed to do what was required. It was just that things were getting very, very tense. President Saddam Hussein was getting edgy – he wanted his weapon. He had now paid out over half a billion dollars and the Supergun was still not completed.

Fahad had the inside track on Dr Torr. He knew the doctor wasn't taking them for a ride – Torr was a professional who took pride in his work. The doctor's only loyalty was to those who provided the funds for him to realise his dreams.

Another four weeks and they would commence testing. Fahad could feel the excitement coursing through his veins. He looked forward to returning to Africa.

The man in the car on the other side of the road had not moved for the past four hours. Paul looked carefully through the condensation on the window of his study. He had been working hard all morning, and his desk was covered with papers. Next to his computer lay the print-out of the revised script. Now all he had to do was work with a film editor, going through all the existing footage they had of him, his father, the lions and Mkhulu. The idea was to work in the present, constantly flashing back to the past. It was an ambitious project, part documentary, part feature film.

Till now the mugging incident had receded to the back of his mind. He'd probably just been in the wrong place at the wrong time. He needed to work on his film – that was all that really mattered.

But now he was suspicious again. He'd first noticed the car when he went for a run at six that morning. Why was the car still there? And with the same person inside?

He looked through the window again. The man in the car raised a small set of binoculars and looked in his direction. Paul dropped below the window sill. Now his anger was rising. Was this surveillance linked to the mugging the week before? Maybe he should have reported it to the police.

He moved to the back of the room, slipped on his anorak, a pair of dark tracksuit pants and his running shoes. Then he crawled across the floor, out of sight of the window, and out into the hall. Moving quickly across the carpeted floor, he went into the back bedroom and over to the window that looked down over the access road running behind the mews. He was about to go downstairs and slip out of the back door when a sixth sense told him to beware.

He stood further back from the window and looked carefully down the access road again. On the corner with the main street was another occupied parked car. Shit. He waited patiently again, saw the driver pick up a pair of binoculars, survey the back of his house, and then reach for a flask of coffee. What was going on? His house was being watched from both sides – he couldn't get out undetected.

Paul went back downstairs to the wardrobe in the front hall, opened the door and took out a torch. Then he went up to the second floor and into the main bedroom. Fortunately the curtains were still closed so no one could see what he was up to from outside. He moved a chair into the centre of the room and opened the ceiling hatch. He breathed a sigh of relief as the retractable ladder came smoothly down, and he moved quickly up into the roof. He switched on the torch and moved carefully across the rafters. It was something he'd noticed when he'd helped Jessica put something in her loft – the wall that divided the loft of her house from his had a hole in it. The renovators must have used it when they were fixing up the block – it probably saved them a lot of time.

He moved carefully into Jessica's loft and saw that there was a also a hole in the wall that led into the loft of the last house in the row. Paul eased himself through and located the trap door. He pulled it open and found himself staring into a bedroom much like his own. He switched off the torch, let himself through the hatch and landed with a thump on the floor. His adrenalin was pumping as he moved quickly down the stairs to the front door. He didn't waste time. The car in front was still in position, the driver staring up occasionally at his house.

Paul walked off smartly down the road and caught a cab on the next corner.

He visited a friend of his in Fleet Street, and spent the rest of the day going through files of photographs, trying to get a fix on the tall man with the grey hair whom he'd seen outside the house in Rutland Gate.

It was already dark outside when he stumbled on the photograph of a high-ranking Iraqi military officer. How could he have forgotten that face? The man outside the house at Rutland Gate was the officer he'd seen at Halabje. One and the same.

Paul knew he was onto something sinister. Fahad would not be in London for a holiday. And he hadn't been beaten up for nothing.

As Jessica drove back from the casting session, she glanced down at her watch. It was almost ten. Her heart quickened. Perhaps she might bump into Paul Norton, the attractive film cameraman who lived next door.

As she walked up to her front door, she saw that the door to Paul's house was open – he must have forgotten to close it. She walked over, grasped the brass knocker and began to pull the door closed. Then she noticed that the curtains were closed but none of the lights were on. A vague feeling of unease crept over her. She thought about the time Paul had been beaten up. Instinctively she moved away from the door and back towards her own home.

There was a smell in the air, a man's cologne. She ran up the stairs to her own front door. She was going to call the police. Something wasn't right.

The explosion came without warning, and the force of the blast knocked her down the steps. She saw the front door of Paul's house torn off its hinges. Flames erupted from inside the house as she scrambled to her feet.

'Paul! Paul!' she screamed as she stumbled towards the doorway, the flames licking round the wooden frame.

Mr Matthews, from the house on the other side, appeared with a fire-extinguisher in his hands. Jessica tore off her raincoat and high heels and dived in through the door. The house stank of petrol, and the burning floorboards singed her feet. She moved up the stairs to the study where she knew Paul always worked. In the distance she could hear sirens. She moved quickly towards the study.

Where was he, where was he?'

The house was in chaos. Drawers had been pulled out, cupboard doors opened, and the floors were strewn with articles of clothing, papers and books.

She made her way through the smoke to Paul's study, and on

his desk saw the pile of precious film script. Gripping the smouldering papers, she hugged them to her. Her skin was hot and she screamed out in pain. She turned – and looked into a wall of fire. Then she blacked out.

Paul took a cab – it was nearly midnight by the time he made it home.

There was a policeman waiting outside. Paul looked up and saw blackened, smoking holes where the front windows had been. A dull feeling filled his body.

'Your house, sir?'

'Yes, yes it is.'

'Don't worry, sir. She's alive.'

'Who?'

'The woman . . . Jessica, I think that was her name. She went inside when the fire broke out, looking for you . . .'

'Oh, my God . . .'

He held her hand and watched the first light of day come through the windows of the hospital ward.

'Mr Norton?'

He turned to see the doctor staring down at him. 'Yes. Is she all right?'

'It's little short of a miracle. The firemen got her out just in time.

'Is she badly burned?'

'No, but she inhaled a lot of smoke. She's very lucky to be alive.'

Paul was thinking. He'd get the bastards who'd done this. He wouldn't stop till he found them. Whoever they were.

'Would you like us to call you when she comes round?'

'No. I'll just stay here. I'm glad she's all right.'

'OK, but don't try to rouse her.'

The doctor left the room and Paul was alone with Jessica. He knew that the fire hadn't been an accident. Every instinct in his body told him that it was connected with that assault in Rutland Gate. What had he seen that he shouldn't?

Damn, his bloody film script had been in there. He'd been meaning to copy it, but never got round to it.

Well, if the bastards were trying to frighten him off, they weren't going to succeed. There was something he'd promised himself on death row – that there weren't going to be any more compromises in his life.

He felt Jessica's hand touch his own. 'Paul, you're all right?'

He leaned over and kissed her on the cheek. 'That was a very brave thing you did.'

She turned her head to one side. 'Paul, someone had ransacked your house and deliberately set fire to it, there was an explosion.'

He grimaced, and held her hand tightly. 'I know it was no accident.'

'I've got some good news for you, though . . .' But before she could finish she drifted off into a deep sleep.

He sat next to her for a long time in the darkness, half asleep. He started to dream. He was back in the valley in Iraq, staring at the bodies of the woman he had loved and her child . . .

'No. No. No!' He sat up bolt upright, waking Jessica up.

'Paul, what's wrong?'

'Sorry, I was having a nightmare about the bastard I filmed coming out of that house in Rutland Gate – the one whose men beat me up. I saw him before, in Iraq. He was in the army – a high-ranking officer.'

'You're imagining things. You've been under a lot of strain.'

'Damnit, Jessica, the bastard gassed an entire village. It was his eyes I remember.'

She held his hands tightly in the darkness. 'I think you should leave this thing alone,' she said. 'Go back to Africa – to your lions.'

'Those people – the ones who beat me up, who set fire to my house, what are they up to that they think I've seen?'

'You're allowing your imagination to run riot. Finish your film – you haven't lost your final script after all . . .'

Jessica indicated a cupboard next to the bed, and Paul opened the door. Inside was a slightly charred pile of papers. Paul's face lit up.

'I don't believe this!'

He moved to take them, but she stopped him with a gesture. 'You only get them if you make me a promise.'

'And what's that?'

'That you forget this whole business – that you concentrate on your film.'

'If you insist.'

'I do.'

But he didn't keep his promise.

His script was accepted, but shooting wouldn't start till the following year. The film's producer, Dave Emery, wanted to meet Mkhulu face-to-face, so Paul called Anne the following morning and asked her to make the travel arrangements for him to come to London. Then he sent a telegram to Charlotte in Cape Town. He wanted her to find the Halabje video cassette – the one she had brought up to Louis Trichardt for him, just before he was sentenced.

He'd still got the video cassette of the two men leaving Rutland Gate. If the bastards thought they'd destroyed it when they fired his house, they were wrong: the cassette was in the safe at Roland-Emery's offices. Early experience had taught him that once you'd got footage you made damn sure you looked after it.

Next, he bought a set of high-powered binoculars and some night-vision goggles. And he replaced the camcorder video camera they'd taken from him with a better model.

Back at the hotel he'd moved into temporarily, while his house was being refurbished, he got down to work. As he did for all his assignments, he worked in A4-sized, hard-backed exercise books. He listed the sequence of events – his first sighting of the Fahad in Iraq, then the events in London. He worked slowly, his mind poring over every detail.

By now, he guessed, they thought they'd frightened him off, which was fine. It meant that they wouldn't be maintaining such a tight surveillance on him.

He gave himself a month. He was quite certain that would be long enough for him to build up an accurate picture of what he'd stumbled on by accident.

Sitting in the study of his Rutland Gate house, Fahad was beginning to sweat. Iraq had paid out nearly half a billion dollars for the development of the Supergun, and still the first testing had not taken place. If Fahad hadn't got the inside track on Dr Vance Torr, he'd have thought Torr was taking him for as much money as he could.

To consolidate her power base in the Midde East Iraq needed the Supergun – above all else, to launch a pre-emptive attack on Israel. Fahad knew just how critical to their strategy this was. In one firing they could prove that their weaponry was superior to Israel's – an event that would unify the whole of the Arab world against the Jewish state.

Surprise, as always, was what Fahad aimed to achieve. He was certain no one else could possibly know about the project – every single stage of the development process had been shrouded in secrecy. Yes, there had been the one recent worry in London, but Josh claimed he had sorted that out. Fahad had proposed killing Norton off, but Josh had advised that that was excessive. In London it could have resulted in the police asking a lot of questions – something they wanted to avoid. Instead, Josh had fired Norton's house, destroying the film Norton had taken of Fahad and Dr Torr together. In one move he had removed any evidence Norton might have been piecing together, and had no doubt effectively frightened him off.

Still, Fahad felt they should have disposed of Norton. To Fahad's mind, murder was the best solution to such problems, and he had killed so often that it seemed the most logical approach.

But now it was time to unwind. He slipped the video cassette into the player in his study. The quality of the picture was excellent, as he had demanded. He had dictated the scenario a month before, and now the video had been produced to order. It opened on a naked youth being whipped by his captor.

Fahad felt his palms moistening. He wished he could have been there, participating. The white was a giant, and the boy was putty in his hands. The camera zoomed in on the youth's face as he was subjected to a vicious attack. Writhing, the whites of his eyes bulging in terror, the boy's breathing became sharper, and Fahad saw his young body struggling, fighting for life. He gripped the sides of his chair as the screams escalated. Then the man's fists smashed into the youth's rib-cage. After that, a quick twist of the neck, a crack, and it was all over.

Sweating, Fahad switched off the recorder, and a children's programme appeared on the screen. He turned off the set angrily.

It was a month since he had last enjoyed such entertainment first-hand – he couldn't hold out much longer.

Dr Torr stared at the design on the computer screen. Every part of the weapon had to be perfect – this was his design credo: no compromises. He didn't care how hysterical Fahad became. The timing was irrelevant – he needed more money to develop the cannon to its ultimate state. The new super-computer he had just acquired opened up design possibilities he had never even dreamed of.

It was the rapid-fire option that occupied most of his thoughts. Why, after all, concentrate all one's efforts on a single satellite launching? Uniquely, his cannon would have the ability to fire off one satellite shell every minute, re-sighting taking place during the reloading operation. The entire operation would be controlled by computer.

Research was producing other dividends as well. Now he saw the barrel being substaintially shorter than in his original conception, and with the sabot containing not just a shell but its means of propulsion. This would make possible another important option – the ability to change the direction of the satellite shell once it was in the air.

Soon his dreams would be realised – and he knew he could never have done it working for a government agency. The project would have been vetoed because of cost. So much the better, he thought; this would show the United States how stupid they had been to reject him, to arrest and imprison him. And Fahad might be angry now, but when he saw what he was getting, Dr Torr was certain he would be a happy man.

The package arrived by courier the following morning. Paul tore open the envelope, read the short note from Charlotte and then pulled out the video cassette. Next, he went across to Roland-

Emery, collected the other video cassette, and booked one of their edit suites for an hour.

After fifteen minutes work he was able to bring the two images up next to each other.

It was him, there was no doubt about it. The man he had seen outside the house in Rutland Gate was Fahad, the officer who had been in the jeep in Halabje after the gas attack.

Paul used a special facility in the video edit suite to generate close-up Polaroid pictures of the two men outside the Rutland Gate house. Now he had to find out who the other man was, and what they were both up to.

He returned to his hotel and changed quickly, dressing in deliberately poor clothing he'd brought second-hand from the Portabello market – a tattered jersey, torn jeans and an old pair of running-shoes. He felt the day-old stubble on his face with satisfaction. His video camera, the night-vision goggles and the binoculars he put in an old sailor's duffel bag.

As he came out of his hotel room, one of the porters looked at him in surprise.

'Auditioning for a part in a film,' Paul said brightly.

'Oh,' the man said, 'you're an actor.'

'All the time.'

He caught the tube to Knightsbridge, then walked past his badly burned mews house and up towards Rutland Gate. This time there was no Mercedes Pullman outside. He couldn't see the men who had beaten him up either – but he had a definite feeling they were in the vicinity.

He moved slowly past the house and noted that the building diagonally opposite to it looked very dilapidated. There were wooden shutters across its windows, and he saw that several of the boards on the front window had been removed, then badly replaced. He guessed that the building was in use – a squat.

He looked up and down the road to make sure no one was watching him, then he pulled away a couple of loose boards and clambered inside the dark room beyond.

He was immediately confronted. 'What you doin', man?' a voice asked in a broad American accent.

'Looking for a place,' Paul said.

'Not here, you're not.'

Paul slipped the duffel bag off his shoulder. He was the same height as his opponent, but about half the weight; the man was black, and looked in pretty good shape.

'Look I've just arrived here,' Paul said. 'I just need a place for a couple of days . . .'

Paul kept his eyes on the other's face. The man could tell he wasn't afraid – Paul guessed he was used to throwing his weight around.

'Where you from?' the man asked.

Paul jumped in, feet first. 'South Africa. I'm a sailor.'

The black man laughed, then his face turned ugly. 'You've got that apartheid policy. You treat us like scum.'

Reluctantly, Paul reached inside his duffel bag and pulled out the bottle of whisky he'd brought. He handed it to the black man, who took it with alacrity.

'It's my last bottle.'

The black man unscrewed the cap and tasted the amber liquid. 'Mmmm. How long do you want to stay?'

'As long as I can. I haven't got a work permit.'

The black man laughed. 'Well, Mr South African, you can work for me.'

Paul felt distinctly uneasy. He didn't want to get involved in any criminal activity. The man saw his anxiety. 'Relax,' he said. 'I work at this pub. They need a man for behind the bar. You pay me fifty per cent of what you get – you get the job.'

'And I can stay here?'

'Yeah. But on the top floor.'

His heart leapt. That was exactly where he wanted to be. 'Sounds too good to be true,' he said.

The smell of sewage and dirt was overpowering as they went up the stairs. Paul could tell that the whole house was being used – and they'd just about wrecked the place. At the very top was an attic room. Paul stooped through the low doorway, following his companion inside.

'You can stay here. I suggest you get a lock for the door, otherwise you'll lose everything you got. I'm Sonny.'

Paul shook the outstretched hand and was surprised by the strength of the grip. 'Paul,' he replied with a grin.

'I'll pick you up at six, then,' Sonny said, and turned to go down the stairs.

'If anyone comes looking for me . . .' Paul started.

Sonny gave him a slow smile. 'I've never seen you,' he said.

He waited until the footsteps retreated down the stairs and then pushed the door closed. There was a bolt on the inside which he slid firmly home, then went across top the windows and looked down. He was higher up than he'd expected, but the view couldn't have been better: he was looking right down into the front of the house opposite, and he could also see the right-hand side of it, where the windows faced a disused church, and the access road.

Paul pulled out his binoculars and settled down comfortably, propping himself against the corner of the attic window so that he could keep a constant watch on his target. He lay back and prepared for a long wait. He didn't know what he was looking for; it was just a question of watching.

By midday he'd established that there were a housekeeper and a butler on the premises. That made his job even harder, because his target wouldn't be going shopping or making other little domestic trips. Paul couldn't even be sure that the house wasn't just a liaison point – a place for taking girlfriends to, and holding important meetings in.

Shortly after two in the afternoon a Range Rover pulled up outside the house, and two thickset men got out. Paul recognised them instantly as the men who had beaten him up. They didn't go in through the front entrance but moved around the perimeter of the property – he could tell they were looking for anything remotely suspicious. He was particularly fascinated by the huge grey-haired man who was obviously the senior of the two – despite his huge gut, the well-cut suit and upright gait suggested a military background. Paul eased the camcorder from his duffel bag and focused the zoom lens. He shot a couple of minutes of footage of him, wanting to be sure that it he needed to identify him in a hurry, he'd have the material to do it. He didn't bother with the henchman, he was only interested in the big fish.

He could tell by the men's movements that they were constantly on the look-out for trouble. No wonder they'd reacted the way they had when they saw him shooting footage of the two men leaving the house; they must have thought he was casing the joint. The grey-haired man was now standing quite close to the front entrance, his right hand feeling for something hidden beneath his left arm-pit. A gun.

The Mercedes arrived without any warning, and two men got out of the front. One was a uniformed chauffeur, and the other, who saluted the grey-haired man, Paul recognised as the thug who'd been watching his house.

Then the chaffeur opened the back door of the Mercedes, and out stepped the Iraqi.

Paul raised the camera to his eye and started filming. There was no doubt about it now, this was the officer he'd seen in command at Halabje. Now Fahad was dressed in a hand-tailored, double-breasted suit, and was immaculately groomed.

The grey-haired man and his thugs cast anxious glances up and down the street as the Iraqi was let in through the door of his house by the butler. Paul raised his binoculars to scan the upper windows, and there, sure enough, was another man, covering the entrance with a high-powered rifle.

Paul refocused his binoculars on the grey-haired man, who appeared to be talking to himself but was actually, Paul guessed, talking into a radio. No doubt all the heavies were radio-linked, taking their commands from him. And now that the Iraqi was inside, they were all melting into the background. The grey-haired man made his way round to the back of the house, continuing to issue orders to the rest of his force.

A van swept past, and Paul guessed from the long aerial on its roof that it was also part of the protection team. Nervously, he glanced back at the bolted door of his room. If security on the Iraqi's house was so tight, they would certainly be checking out every building surrounding it. But if he vacated the squat now, he'd attract attention. He decided he'd work a few nights at the pub, then tell Sonny he'd got a break elsewhere. That way no one would be suspicious.

It grew darker and darker. Paul glanced down at his watch and saw that it was nearly six. He guessed the other squatters would probably search his room after he'd gone, so he couldn't risk leaving his equipment around. He tried the catch on the window, and opened it with difficulty. The casement slid upwards and he was looking down at the slate roof. About a metre to his right was a leaded ridge running to the top of the roof. He felt the sweat on the palms of his hands as he gingerly moved out onto the tiles and gripped the ridge with his left hand. He didn't need to imagine what would happen if he came off.

Just above his window, some of the tiles were loose. He carefully lifted one up and saw that there was a hollow area six centimetres above the sloping ceiling of his room. He leaned back into the window and picked up the duffel bag with all his equipment in it, then placed it under the tiles.

A minute later he was back in the room. As he carefully closed the window he could smell the acrid smell of his own sweat.

There was a knock on the door and he started with fear. 'Come on man, it's time,' Sonny's voice barked.

'OK. OK.'

He unbolted the door and Sonny stepped in, looking around the room. 'You been smoking hash in here?' he asked suspiciously.

'No. I've been sleeping.' He hadn't hidden his equipment a moment too soon. 'Will my things be all right?' he remembered to say as he followed Sonny down the stairs.

Sonny laughed loudly. 'Hey, what you got, brother, that anyone wants? You're poor. You South African son-of-a-bitch.'

The black man had an easy way about him. Paul wondered how he'd come to be running a squat in Rutland Gate. He'd find out the answer in time, he was sure. He suddenly remembered he must check for messages at his hotel; there could be further developments in the pre-production for the film.

'Sonny, there's someone I have to talk to. I didn't know I'd find a place so quickly.'

'OK, you've got an hour, buddy. But if you aren't back by then, you're out.'

Paul made his way quickly round the corner and caught a cab back to his hotel. He had to pay the cab driver in advance, so effective was his disguise, and the receptionist at his hotel looked him up and down suspiciously.

'It's Paul Norton, room one-o-seven. I've been auditioning for a role as a vagrant in a movie.'

'Ah, I see, sir. Sorry, but you had me fooled for a moment!'

'Are there any messages for me?'

'No. But there's someone waiting to see you.'

A stab of fear. He'd been a fool – he shouldn't have checked into the hotel in his own name.

'He's behind you, Mr Norton, having a cup of coffee in the main lounge.'

Paul peered anxiously over some greenery and saw Mkhulu, dressed in a suit, sitting in the lounge. He breathed a huge sigh of relief.

'Ah yes, I know him. Thanks. Can I have the keys to my room, please?'

He walked over and touched his friend on the shoulder. 'Mkhulu.'

The black man spun round in his chair, spilling his coffee. 'Paul,' he said happily.' And then: 'My God, what's happened to you?'

They embraced and shook hands. 'Come up to my room,' Paul said. 'I haven't got much time.'

In the lift Mkhulu ran his eyes up and down Paul, as if he couldn't believe what he was seeing. 'What have you got yourself involved in now, my friend?'

'It's a long and complicated story – how are the cubs?'

'Hardly cubs any more, at more than a year old! And they are fending for themselves better than you are, I think!'

Paul laughed. 'You don't know how right you are.'

In the room, Paul flopped into an armchair and gestured for Mkhulu to do the same. Then he quickly recounted the events of the previous month.

'Anne thinks you're up to something,' Mkhulu said. 'She's worried – you know, she really cares about you.'

Paul gave Mkhulu an ironic smile. 'Well, her intuition is a hundred per cent right.'

Mkhulu grimaced. 'Be careful, Paul.'

'I can't drop this thing, Mkhulu. And the film's going well, so I've got the time.'

'I see. So while you have all the fun, you expect me to spend my time in London sight-seeing, do you?'

Paul leant back and laughed. 'Well, first we'll have to get rid of that suit . . .'

*

To Paul's surprise, Sonny agreed to let Mkhulu use the room as well. He looked the big black man up and down, taking in the artificial leg. 'Now you're a *real* nigger!' he exclaimed, roaring with laughter.

Paul left Mkhulu in the attic and set off with Sonny to start his new job.

The pub had seen better days, but it certainly hadn't seen better trade. It was packed with foreigners, drinking furiously and talking hard. Sonny was greeted like a long lost friend. He leaned across the bar to a bald-headed man with a large tattoo on his left arm. 'Hey, Vince, my brother here is looking for work.'

Paul sensed Vince's beer-sodden brain giving him the once-over. 'Where's 'e from, Sonny?'

'South Africa.'

This seemed to have the right affect. Vince lifted up the bar counter and gestured to Paul to follow him. They went into a back room area that stank of stale beer and was sodden with water; in the background three older women were furiously washing glasses.

'Can you add up figures?'

Paul nodded.

'You can serve, then. The prices are on the blackboard. You put any money in your pockets and I'll burst yewr bollocks.'

'I want to earn money, not steal it.'

Vince burst out laughing. 'All right, mate, get to work.'

Paul pulled pint after pint. He'd been with some heavy drinkers in his time, but the people in this pub were in the first league. He hated to think what they would feel like in the morning. He noticed that Sonny drank nothing except Coke, and sat in one corner of the pub, taking money from some people and giving it to others. He wondered if Sonny dealt in drugs. The black man seemed to be popular with everyone around.

Towards midnight the pace eased off, and Paul was frequently engaged in conversation by people too drunk to put a simple sentence together. He wondered how he'd feel after a week of this; he was sure he'd be smelling of beer for months.

Then a thickset man came in through the front door of the

pub, and the conversation suddenly dropped in pitch. Every eye was on him, he generated fear. As the level of talk picked up again, he looked around him – and Paul felt a cold trickle of sweat running down his back. He had recognised him at once as the grey-haired man he'd been watching earlier, controlling the surveillance team.

The man started chatting to Sonny, who tipped his head in Paul's direction a couple of times. Paul realised he was checking out who'd come to stay in Sonny's squat. He just hoped the man didn't recognised him, though with a couple of days beard on his face, he doubted he looked much like the man they'd duffed up a month before.

Sonny called the man Josh. Paul saw how he never relaxed; his back was to the corner of the pub and his eyes were constantly watching and assessing. Perhaps he *had* recognised him, but wasn't showing it . . . After what seemed an eternity, Josh got up and left.

Later, Paul walked back to the squat with Sonny.

'You did well, man,' Sonny said. 'Vince likes you. You've got a job.'

He felt a little easier. Perhaps he was worrying needlessly. It felt good to be out in the cold winter air, away from the sodden, smokey atmosphere of the pub; he almost wondered if he shouldn't just forget the whole business. He decided to sleep on it, and make his decision in the morning. He didn't like the look of Josh at all.

He staggered upstairs to his room. It was in darkness, and at first he thought Mkhulu was at the window, watching the house. But the room was empty.

Paul lit a candle Sonny had given him and took a careful look around. Everything was just a little too tidy for comfort – he could smell someone had been through the place. He wanted to have a bath, but there was nowhere to have one here. Sonny had said he could go to the public baths in the morning to clean up.

Where the hell was Mkhulu? Maybe they'd caught him spying on the house and beaten him up. If there was no sight of Mkhulu in the morning, he'd have to go to the police.

Paul carefully bolted his door and lay down to sleep – but after a few hours he was suddenly uneasily awake. In the darkness he

214

could hear a creaking sound. He wasn't imagining things, there was definitely someone coming up the stairs.

He had no choice. He had to get away. He had no idea who it was who was coming for him.

He moved across to the windows and opened it gingerly. Outside it was drizzling heavily. He felt like throwing up when he looked down at the lights below: if he slipped, he was dead. He closed the window behind him, then leaned across and grabbed the lead ridge.

He heard the door of his room burst open. There was no choice. He moved out cautiously – then slid, out of control, down the tiles. His bare feet touched the guttering, and he knew if it gave he was dead. It held.

Above him, a torch light flashed around his room and then the window was opened. He saw a face, covered in shadows, staring out. It was Josh, and he was looking down from the window to the Iraqi's house opposite. An ugly expression crossed his face. The only way he could know that Paul was using this room was from questions he'd put to Sonny.

Somehow Paul knew he could trust Sonny. In the morning he'd speak to him – try to persuade him to tell Josh he was harmless. It was important that Paul maintain his surveillance of the house to gather more information about the Iraqi and his friends.

Josh's face disappeared from the window, but Paul did not move; all his instincts told him to remain where he was, shivering in the drizzle. He guessed that Josh was not in a hurry and might still be lurking in the shadows, somewhere on the top floor of the house.

After an hour he finally made his move, his feet slipping against the tiles as he edged his way towards the window. If Josh was still around, one push would send Paul skittling down the roof to his death.

Eventually he pulled himself through the windows and sank to the floor, exhausted. There was only a limited time before he was found out – he knew that now. He had to discover what the Iraqi was up to that demanded such tight and ruthless security.

Maybe they'd got Mkhulu and were torturing him? Paul broke

into a cold sweat and moved to the door. He felt a hand descend on his shoulder and hold him in a vice-like grip.

'This place is full of snakes,' Mkhulu said in the darkness.

Paul shook with relief. 'Mkhulu. Thank God!'

'My friend, what have you got yourself involved in now? I sensed this place was not safe, so I watched the house from the park. Several men entered the house soon after you left. I left a hair across the door to this room and when I came up later, it had been moved. I think they do not trust you.'

Mkhulu flicked on his lighter and lit the candle. 'You must sleep now, Paul, I will keep watch for the rest of the night. I hardly think they can take the two of us.'

Paul nodded wearily. 'All right. But be careful.'

He blew out the candle and lay down on the dirty mattress. He thought about Dr Anne Madison, about how he missed the lions at Klaw, and wondered why he had ever come here.

He longed to return to Africa.

Josh sat in his Jaguar, smoking a cigarette. The squat had always bothered him. It was the only building on the block opposite that he couldn't keep under control – its inhabitants were constantly changing, and were difficult to threaten effectively. He had contacted the owners and come to an agreement with them: if he could get the squatters out, then they'd restore the house and turn it into private flats.

Josh regarded his work as an art-form. He always spent a lot of time creatively planning a job – like the one he'd just done on Sonny. Sonny was in his way – and the trouble was that he didn't respond to threats. But he reckoned he'd got him this time. Sonny would be in bad trouble now, and with any luck, he'd have to go.

Once Sonny was gone, he'd clear the other squatters out very quickly. He was looking forward to that. They'd do it at night, when no one was watching.

He felt the cold hand touch his face, and opened his eyes blearily. He was still exhausted from the previous night, Mkhulu, who'd woken him, drew away.

'Paul, we've got problems.'

He looked up to see Sonny standing behind Mkhulu in a state of extreme agitation. 'What's going on, man?' Sonny said. 'Where's my money?'

Paul dragged himself to his feet. Sonny's dark face was looking decidedly pale and the big body was trembling with tension. 'Calm down,' Paul said quietly. 'Come on, I'll take you to breakfast, and we can . . .'

Before he could finish, Sonny grabbed him by the throat. Paul raised his hands, chopped outwards, broke the grip and dropped down. Sonny collapsed over him. 'I'm gonna kill you, you thieving bastard!' he cried. 'Where'd you get the money to take me to breakfast?'

They wrestled on the floor, but Paul was no match for him, and Mkhulu had to lock his big arms around Sonny and drag him off.

'Sonny, I didn't take your money,' Paul gasped.

'Then who did? Batman?' Sonny said, struggling in vain to get out of Mkhulu's grip.

'Josh was here last night. Perhaps he took your money,' Mkhulu said gently, relaxing his hold. Sonny pulled away and sank back against the wall.

'You can't be serious.' he said.

'He was up here in Paul's room, looking for something.'

'And he didn't find you because you were in my room, stealing my money, Mkhulu.'

'What's so important about the money? How much did you lose?' Paul asked quickly.

'I'm the local bank, man,' Sonny said, glaring at him. 'I loan, and people pay me interest. I store money for people who ain't got a bank account.'

'Well, why would we steal your money and stick around? We could just have disappeared.'

Sonny stared at them long and hard. 'You aren't who you're making out. You've been lyin' to me, man.'

'Look,' Paul said, 'let's get some food.'

They went to a nearby restaurant and ate bacon and eggs until at last Sonny sat back pensively sipping his coffee.

'But why did he come up to your room?' he asked.

'Because,' Paul said, he wanted to know if I was watching the house opposite.'

'And why would you be watching the house opposite?'

'Because there's someone in there Josh is protecting, and I want to find out who.'

Sonny considered this for a moment. 'So you think that mother-fucker's got my money?' he said.

'That's my guess.'

Paul looked across at him. He had to take Sonny into his confidence. He wasn't going to get the information he wanted by just watching the outside of the house, he needed to find out what was going on inside.

'How do you fancy a little house-breaking, Sonny?' he said. 'We might even find your money.'

An hour later Paul had purchased a crowbar from a hardware store, plastic gloves and three pairs of pantihose. His idea was to make the break-in look like an amateur job, but to leave no clues. Speed was all-important. They'd strike at eleven that morning, when the security on the house was at its weakest and the Iraqi was out. Paul sensed that Sonny wouldn't let them down if they got into a tight corner.

They made their way out of the squat and into the churchyard that backed onto the side of the Iraqi's house, they moved surreptitiously through the rhododendron bushes that grew close to the wall. Paul eyed the kitchen windows, then pulled a crowbar out of his rucksack.

Sonny sniggered. 'Let's not make a mess, man,' he whispered. 'Please, let me do this . . .'

He took the crowbar, went up to one of the windows and expertly chiselled off the putty. Then he carefully removed the glass. He gestured to Paul and Mkhulu to climb through, and then followed them.

The kitchen was huge, with a big wooden chopping-table in the centre. Paul looked around at the expensively wood-panelled walls, then made for the door. It was locked. Sonny again gestured him out of the way, then he ran at it hard with his shoulder. The wood burst into splinters and Sonny rolled out into the passage, Paul charging after him. Mkhulu was about to follow when he heard the distinctive metallic noise that could only be made by a gun.

There was an explosion of bullets. Almost mesmerised, Paul watched Sonny roll over and over across the floor, smashing into the gunman's legs, toppling him, wrenching the gun from his hands and smashing a punch into his oesophagus. The man crashed into a banister, which immediately collapsed, and he fell down the stairwell with a heavy thud.

Paul was sweating, he'd miscalculated badly. 'Let's get out of here!' he shouted at Sonny and Mkhulu.

Sonny expertly handled the machine-gun. 'No, man! Who do these cocksuckers think they are?'

As the words burst from his mouth, two shots grazed his arm. Sonny ducked and swivelled, firing as he moved, and Paul heard a scream erupt down the passage. Sonny charged forward, smashing down another man who appeared from a doorway with the butt of the machine-gun.

Paul tried a door off the front hall. It was locked. Sonny's boot came up, smashed it open, and they both charged in.

It was a large, airy room that looked out over the Rutland Gate. It was furnished with antique chairs and couches, and had original paintings on the panelled walls. Mkhulu hobbled on and went through an archway into a further room dominated by a large oak partner's desk. Sonny followed him.

'Fuck!' Sonny shouted, suddenly. He snatched up a canvas bag that was lying beside the desk and turned to Paul. 'You were right, they did take my money!'

To Paul's left was a bank of television screens that monitored every room in the house, and the area outside. He stood entranced for a moment, looking at a large swimming pool, a stately dining-room, a sauna and spa bath, and a bedroom whose surface was probably greater than that of his entire mews house.

Then they heard a door slam below. Paul glanced at a monitor and saw figures darting along the hall. Then he heard Josh's voice, cold and menacing.

'Put the gun down, or you won't get out of here alive.'

A curious smile crossed Sonny's face. 'I don't think we're going to anyway,' he whispered to Paul and Mkhulu. 'Just stick behind me, man.'

Sonny raised the machine-gun and aimed it towards the stairs. He opened fire, and Josh and his men backed off into the front hall. Sonny showered the walls with bullets, disintegrating a large mirror.

Paul wondered how long they had to live. Sonny kept firing, and backed into the study beside him and Mkhulu. Out of the corner of his eye, Paul noticed another door, recessed into the panelling.

A man burst into the room with a shotgun, but before he could even fire, Sonny cut him down with a hail of bullets. They could hear Josh screaming orders from the front. Mkhulu crouched down and snatched up the dead man's shotgun. The odds had just gone up; now two of them were armed.

Paul looked again at the partner's desk and saw a pile of blueprints. He snatched a couple, rolled them up and stuffed them down the front of his shirt.

Sonny glared at him. 'Are you out of your fucking mind! Find us a way out of here!'

Paul shouldered the door in the recess and it burst open. He found himself in the passage next to the kitchen.

'Come on!' he screamed at Mkhulu and Sonny, and they sprinted across the kitchen, dived through the window and crashed through the undergrowth of the church garden. Paul heard Josh shouting in the distance, and a shot thudded into the wall of the church slightly above their heads.

Paul looked up at the second storey of the house and caught the flash of light from a laser sight. Then Mkhulu raised the barrel of the shotgun, traced the bead across the window and stroked the trigger.

The scream drifted down to them as they beat their way through the weeds and bushes to the front of the church. Paul vaulted the wall and hailed a passing cab – Mkhulu and Sonny piled in after him seconds later, concealing their weapons as best they could.

'Where to?' shouted the cabbie.

'Richmond. Where the bridge crosses the Thames. And move it.'

'That was a mean shot,' Sonny whispered quietly to Mkhulu.

'You handled that shotgun like you was born with it in your hands.'

'My father taught me that there are two skills that matter to a man,' replied Mkhulu, 'the ability to shoot straight, and the ability to work hard. The first will let you survive, he said, the second will earn you a living.'

Paul felt sick. They'd left at least three men dead in the house. And this was England, the heart of civilisation. They'd killed, and they would pay the price.

As the cab drove them through the London suburbs, the events of the morning flashed through Paul's mind again and again. He hadn't expected them to be repulsed with such violence. Whatever was going on in the house, it must be deadly important. He knew that Josh couldn't have recognised him and Mkhulu, but Sonny was another matter. Sonny was now in terrible danger – he would have to disappear.

'What you thinking?' Sonny whispered.

'That we've left three men dead.'

'If we hadn't, we'd all have bought it.'

'That doesn't make it any better. What if they call the police?'

Sonny laughed emptily. 'Don't think about it, man, just don't think about it.'

But Paul did. He couldn't believe that in such a short space of time he'd got himself into such unbelievable trouble again. He rested his hand on Mkhulu's shoulder; his friend's first visit to London hadn't got off to a very good start.

Paul gave the cabbie some more directions and eventually he dropped them beside the river at Richmond. Paul knew only too well that if the police put out a description of them, it wouldn't take the cabbie long to put two and two together.

'So where are you taking us to now?' Sonny asked quickly.

'You two wait here. I've got a call to make.'

He went across to a phone booth and quickly dialled Dave Emery of Roland-Emery.

'Dave, it's Paul Norton. Look, this may sound like an odd request, but I need to disappear for a while. You know when you took me for a drink on your house-boat you said that any time I wanted it, I could use it? Well, I'd like to call in the favour . . .

'Great. Thanks a lot. You say the keys are at the boat-house . . . ? Dave . . . No, don't worry, I'm fine.'

In just over half an hour they were on the house-boat, drifting down the river, totally exhausted.

Paul looked at Sonny. He had handled himself brilliantly, there'd been no fear in him when the attack came, and he'd used the gun expertly. Yet the man must be almost his own age, and living in a squat, surviving from day to day. Sonny returned his glance.

'You said you were poor,' he said, 'but you organised this boat pretty quickly. Who are you, Paul?'

He looked into the dark eyes. 'An over-curious South African combat cameraman.'

'But you were a soldier once?'

'For three years.'

'You never lose that, you know. I was one of the last to leave 'Nam. That was 1975. I was almost thirty. I knew how to fight and little else. There aren't any vacancies for professional machine-gunners.'

'So why didn't you stay in the army?'

'My record stank. No, sir, I was a good fighter, but I had a bad reputation off the battlefield. I was cannon-fodder. All right for taking risks, but no good back home.'

Paul spied a deserted section of river bank, where the grass was short. He guided the house-boat across to it, and moored it. They stepped onto the land and stretched out. Paul lay on the grass and looked at the grey clouds above him. He didn't want to think. He could imagine the headlines in the papers that evening: 'Mad Killers Strike In Rutland Gate'. With his past record, he wouldn't have a hope in hell, if they were caught, and nor would Sonny. As for Mkhulu, they'd most likely deport him.

He should have stayed away from it, not got involved. But that would have been against everything he'd decided on death row. He had to get involved, he couldn't just keep walking away.

Now it would be a question of waiting. If anything was going to be reported, it would happen fast. It would be in tomorrow's papers and on the news. If that happened, Paul knew they were finished. They would just have to run until they were caught.

*

Fahad felt the fear in his bones – terror that one of the intelligence agencies had decided to move in on him. Perhaps it was the dreaded Mossad. He'd felt secure in London, insulated from violence beneath the cosy blanket of civilization. There was no way he could have anticipated something like this.

The men were cleaning up the mess now. The bodies had already been disposed of. It was a frightening scenario: their attackers hadn't been armed, yet they'd taken out three men.

He feared the Mossad especially because they were as ruthless as he was. They understood his mentality and they knew how to hurt him.

There was a knock on the door of his study. 'Come in!' he barked.

Josh entered, and remained standing.

'So. What have you to say about this? I employed you because you were supposed to be the best. And you failed.'

Josh pulled out his silver cigarette case, offered a cigarette to Fahad and then took one himself. He lit up for both of them. Then eased himself onto the leather couch opposite Fahad.

'I'm as angry as you are,' he said.

'That is little consolation to me, my friend. If I had been here, they would have killed me. You exist to protect me.'

'However good your security is, you're never safe from fanatics. And right now you need me more than I need you.'

'If I'd been in the house, you would not have been able to protect me.'

'Wrong. As you know, our arrangements become tighter the moment you arrive.'

'And suppose I had arrived when this was happening?'

'My men would have known. The moment those men penetrated the rear door, my man on the top floor radioed your bodyguard, warning him to keep you from the house.'

Fahad felt his anger subside slightly. Yes, that was true. He had wondered why they were taking so long to return to the house. His driver had deliberately taken a circuitous route.

'So why was I not informed of this before?' he barked.

'My first obligation is to ensure your peace of mind.'

'I am now extremely agitated.' His lips parted in a wolfish grin. 'You have failed.'

'No, you are alive and well. I simply have to step up security. On the church side of the house, security grilles will now be installed on all the windows. But it will have to be done carefully. We don't want to attract attention.'

Fahad fiddled with the hem of his right trouser-leg. 'My neighbours . . . Have they complained about the shooting?'

'Your neighbours were out. There have been no complaints.'

'And the bodies of your men?'

'I would rather not elaborate on the niceties of my disposal techniques. Suffice it to say, they have vanished.'

Fahad took another drag on his cigarette. His confidence in Josh was restored. 'I want these men caught, tortured and killed,' he said.

Josh smiled. 'My thoughts exactly. It won't take long to find them – I know who one of them is. I'll use my contacts in the police to locate him.'

Fahad chuckled. 'I wish to participate in the torture, of course.'

'My pleasure, sir. Now, if you will excuse me, I must concentrate on upgrading security and briefing my new team.'

Josh returned to his office on the first floor and sat down at his desk. The calm expression was gone from his face and replaced by one of extreme agitation. The facts he had at his disposal were limited. The attackers had had their faces covered with stockings – he only knew that one of them must be Sonny because the only thing taken was the bag of money Josh had stolen from the squat the previous night.

The attackers had effectively overpowered three very highly trained, professional bodyguards. All three of the attackers must have had extensive combat experience, including Sonny. From this Josh could only draw one conclusion – that the squat must have been used for surveillance purposes.

He picked up his phone and dialled a number quickly. 'Gideon,' he said. 'I want a house cleared. Yes, immediately. I want a search conducted, and any occupants removed. It's a squat.'

He gave the address, and put down the phone. Then he thought about the previous evening at the pub. Sonny had talked about the new man who was staying at the squat – and when Josh had investigated the house later, he'd had the uneasy feeling he was being watched.

His men were already out on the street now asking questions, looking for clues to where the three men had fled to. Perhaps, just perhaps, they might get lucky. Then he might get a few answers to his questions.

He went over the facts again – everything that had happened over the past week weeks. Then it hit him. Of course! He should have thought of Norton! Come to think of it, the man who'd been working behind the bar could have been him. And Norton had combat experience – he would know how to handle himself under fire.

Josh called up all the information he'd compiled on Paul Norton on his computer. He smiled, and dialled Roland-Emery's number.

'Hallo, I'm looking for Paul Norton. I'm an old friend of his from South Africa. I wanted to surprise him.'

He was connected to Dave Emery. The man seemed reluctant to help him, but Josh wasn't going to give up so easily.

'Dave, I'm surprised Paul never mentioned me to you, we go back a long way . . .'

'Look,' Dave Emery said at last, 'he doesn't want to be disturbed, right? But he's on my house-boat. No, you can't miss it. Navy blue with the name *Yukon Belle* on the side in gold leaf.'

The noise of the boat woke Paul. He opened his eyes and caught sight of the craft, far in the distance. It was moving a little too close to the shoreline for comfort . . . He nudged Sonny, who was snoring noisily.

'What's the problem, man?' he asked sleepily.

'Hide!' Paul shouted.

They both dived into the bushes as the boat got closer. Mkhulu was still on the house-boat, but there was nothing they could do about that.

Paul saw two men on the main deck of the approaching boat. One was steering and the other was scanning the shoreline with binoculars. Paul cursed as he realised that their own boat wasn't

225

as well hidden as it could have been – it was lying in a prominent position against the shoreline.

The noise of the motor-launch got louder, then there was the sound of the throttle being backed off as the craft drifted in towards the shoreline. The man at the front put down his binoculars and picked up a submachine-gun. Paul cursed his stupidity. They should have got away, and now they were trapped. He looked round for Sonny but couldn't see him anywhere.

The man with the submachine-gun leapt out onto the bank, and Paul shrank back into the bushes. The man went over to where they'd been sleeping and felt the ground below the crushed grass.

'I think we've found the cocksuckers!' he screamed.

The pilot took his hands off the wheel and raised a machine-gun. 'I'll cover you.'

The man moved forward towards the bushes where Paul was hiding. Moments later he felt the cold metal of a gun barrel against his neck.

'Out you come, unless you want to die.'

Paul felt sick. He staggered out and received a violent kick in the kidneys. Then, as he slumped forwards, the butt of the machine-gun slammed into his neck. Where the hell was Sonny? What was Mkhulu doing?

There was a splash in the water, but neither the pilot nor the man attacking Paul took much notice. Then the launch tipped slightly – and as the pilot spun round, there was Sonny, and Sonny's fist was slamming his solar plexus . . . As the pilot collapsed onto the desk, Sonny pivoted the machine-gun directly at Paul's attacker.

'Leave off him, buddy,' Sonny said.

The man laughed, and kicked Paul hard in the face. Then the train of bullets took him in the gut, lifted him up in the air and followed him as he slammed down into the ground.

The pilot staggered to his feet and whipped out a pistol, but Sonny's boot caught him between the legs. The pilot bent double as Sonny swivelled, and slammed a side-kick into his gut, sending him flying off the side of the boat. The man rose out of the water some minutes later, face down.

Mkhulu emerged from the inside of the house-boat.

'Looks like someone spoke to your friend who lent us the boat, Paul,' he said quietly.

Paul was still doubled-up from the beating he'd taken. 'My God!' he gasped. 'That was close.' He dragged himself onto the deck, groaning.

'We're OK for now,' Sonny said, staring across the water. 'But those bastards aren't going to leave us alone, are they?'

Fahad waited anxiously in his study, his eyes scanning the screens that monitored the pavement outside and the hall. He saw the familiar tall, gaunt figure with the white hair step out of a taxi and move quickly to the front door. He heard the bell, and watched the security guard go to the door. Dr Torr flashed his identity card, and the guard let him in and frisked him.

A minute later there was a knock on his study door and he opened it to see Dr Torr towering over him. The doctor looked tired – there were dark half-moons under his eyes. Fahad hoped there weren't fresh problems; he had enough of his own already.

They shook hands quickly, and then Fahad directed him to the easy-chairs in the front lounge that adjoined his study.

'A drink?'

Dr Torr nodded. 'I'll have a mineral water.'

At least, thought Fahad, the doctor had no other vices. Just a passion for spending vast amounts of money on his projects . . . He tried to smile, but he knew he was almost at the end of his tether: the attack on the house had made him realise that time was running out despite Josh's assurances to the contrary, he could only believe that the Mossad must be onto him.

Dr Torr sipped at his mineral water, then removed his glasses and cleaned them with a handkerchief. Fahad walked over to the window and stared across at the tall trees in the park, wondering if his men had found their attackers yet.

'I have good news for you, Fahad.'

A faint smile crossed the Iraqi's face. At least he knew what was going on with Dr Torr – the signs of stress were the result of overwork. 'Good news?' he said.

'My plans are complete,' Dr Torr announced. 'Naturally, the

227

development of the prototype has been moving steadily ahead at Wayne MacLeod's Namibian installation, and I think we should be able to witness a test firing within three weeks.'

Fahad was pleased, but didn't show it. He turned sharply from the window. 'But when, my friend, will the Supergun be operational?'

'By December. As promised.'

'December?' Fahad shouted. 'Are you crazy? That is too late.'

'Too late for what?'

Dr Torr's eyes rested on him and Fahad realised he had given too much away. He must cover up his indiscretion.

'I am hoping to appease the President,' he said. 'He is uncomfortable with the vast amount of money that has already been spent on your project with nothing to show.'

Dr Torr pressed his fingers together as if praying, and rocked forwards. 'Why don't you invite him to the test firing? I have no doubt the demonstration will appease him. The Supergun is not a dream, it is fast becoming a reality.'

Fahad kept his face stern, but smiled inwardly. 'You will come here, then, when it is time for the testing? We may travel there together, Dr Torr.'

'As you please. And I hope President Hussein can attend as well.'

'That would not be well-advised. He is paranoid about security, and out of Iraq I cannot guarantee that his life will be safe.'

Dr Torr nodded, and then drew a tube from inside his overcoat and handed it to Fahad. 'I have here the final blueprints. I have also given you a clear breakdown of how the latest funds have been allocated. The barrel of the gun, especially the breech, was hard to develop. However, I have worked closely with some of MacLeod's engineering companies and I can now confidently say that it will handle the explosive force generated by the shell on detonation.'

'The rate of fire is the same?'

'Yes. One a minute. The entire operation will be computer-controlled.'

Fahad looked out at the park again. Why had Josh found

228

nothing so far? He wanted to know that every one of the men who had broken into the house was dead.

'Are you listening to me?' Dr Torr demanded.

'I am sorry. There have been security problems.'

Dr Torr adjusted his glases, then drew his hand through his silver hair. 'Security problems?'

'There must have been a leak at your end.'

Dr Torr suppressed his anger. 'You have not been to prison – I have. And I can assure you that every person who works for me has been screened. You realise, don't you, that if anyone in Western Intelligence grasps the true potential of the Supergun, we are in terrible danger?'

'You exaggerate.'

Dr Torr raised his eyebrows. 'I'm surprised, after all you have spent, that you do not fully understand the capabilities of what you have bought. However, the test will educate you.'

'We are going to use the gun only for defensive purposes.'

Dr Torr lay back in his chair. 'My dear Fahad, do you seriously think the nations of the West would believe that, knowing the tension growing in your country, and given their own need for ever more oil? *We* know the Supergun is for satellite launching, but others might think differently.'

Fahad kept his face deadpan. Of course, Torr must never find out that they intend to use the Supergun to fire nuclear warheads, with Israel as the target. Because if he did, he'd refuse to work on the project. Fahad knew exactly why the American military did not like dealing with Dr Torr – the man was too much of an idealist. But that did not matter to him – he had Maria to control the doctor. He had inside knowledge of the man's most private thoughts. He said, 'You would do best to keep your thoughts to yourself, Dr Torr.'

'Well,' the doctor said, 'I can only reiterate that if there is a leak, it does not come from my side. Most people believe that the Supergun concept is outdated, and I have published nothing in the last ten years to invalidate that argument. Any leak, of course, would be extremely dangerous. But I can assure you that if you do have a security problem, it can only be of your own creation.'

Fahad knew Dr Torr's usefulness was almost at an end. He

would have to be disposed of; the man was too clever and knew too much. His death would also be a useful diversion, deflecting the prying eyes of Western Intelligence from the Supergun project itself.

'I look forward to the testing,' Fahad said neutrally.

Dr Torr got up, towering over him. 'Don't make the mistake of underestimating my ability,' he said. 'I could always go directly to your President for a comparison of accounts, and I wouldn't be surprised if you had been taking some of the money for your own use. I find your constant bickering over costs extremely suspicious.'

'How dare you make such a claim,' Fahad said slowly.

'I will deliver your weapon on the date you requested. Any further pressure from you, and I will go directly to your President. I want to know that he has been correctly informed as to the progress of the design.'

The front door closed moments later, and Dr Torr was gone. Fahad was in a blind rage. Dr Torr was fast becoming a liability. And the problem was that he couldn't risk Dr Torr finding out about his agreement with Wayne MacLeod – that MacLeod was working on a nuclear shell to be fired from the Supergun. Thank God he had Maria watching the man!

He stared down at the black-and-white chequerboard tiles of the hall. The whole businesss was really like a giant game of chess, and so far, he was still the one with the most pieces on the board.

He walked slowly up the stairs to Josh's office and let himself in.

'Did you hear all that?'

Josh put down the headphones and nodded. 'So what have you decided?'

'I have decided that once his plans have been completed, Dr Torr should disappear . . . Dr Fassbinder is quite capable of supervising the final development of the weapon . . . the atomic shell. By the way, did you notice that black pilot's case he carries with him all the time? Dr Fassbinder says that's where he keeps the plan for the sabot – the combination of shell and missile that will be fired from the cannon. Without those plans, the Supergun is useless. They are his insurance policy.'

Josh smiled thinly. 'You just tell me when that policy runs out. 'I'll arrange the time and the place. And I'll make sure the bag gets back to Dr Fassbinder.'

Fahad grinned. 'Josh, my faith in you is restored.'

Paul put the phone down and stared across the river. He didn't like involving anyone else, but he had to find a secure place for the three of them to stay. The house-boat was out of the question now, that was clear.

He had gone through all the options and come up with the most elegant solution. Whoever was after him would never believe that he would return to his mews house – and anyway, it was still being refurbished. So, he decided to go one better and move into the house next door. When he'd broached the idea to Jessica on the phone, she had agreed immediately. Mkhulu and Sonny could used the spare bedroom on the top floor, he could share with her. He wasn't about to object.

They made it back that night to Jessica's house. He knocked softly on the door, and as soon as Jessica opened it she said, 'Paul, there's someone here to see you.'

'What . . .?'

Mkhulu and Sonny filed into the hall, and Jessica opened the door to the lounge. When Paul walked in he saw Anne, sitting in a chair, facing him. She got up, tears running down her face. 'Oh Paul, where have you been? I've been so worried about you!'

He kissed her gently on the lips.

'Paul,' she said, 'what are you doing here, when David Katz is fighting to keep Klaw out of MacLeod's hands? Thank God for Dave Emery. He had the sense to phone me . . .'

Feelings he had no control over swept through his body. Why hadn't he stayed on Klaw with her? She was more beautiful than he'd remembered – now she had come to London to see if he was all right. He thought back to the time when she had visited him in Pretoria Central. He'd been in love with her even then.

'Anne . . . I've got involved in something I just can't leave alone.'

Now her face darkened. 'God, who do you think you are? Charlotte told me you sent for that tape. Now I find your house has burned down and you've taken time off from working on the film.'

She turned away, crying quietly. 'Paul, I love you. For God's sake, I'm scared you're going to die.'

He pulled her close to him and her lips locked on his and they were kissing passionately. He felt her warmth beneath the plaid skirt she was wearing and pushed her onto the couch. Her legs wrapped round his torso.

He gently removed her underclothes, the smell of her body driving him wild. Then he was kissing her again and wondering how he could be so in love. Time seemed to stand still and he felt as if he were floating on air.

He felt her nails clawing into his back. 'Paul. Paul. Oh God, please . . .'

Then he was inside her, dominating her, riding her. She stared at him, her eyes wide. His hands locked round her waist as his body convulsed and she groaned with pleasure.

He gripped her tightly in his arms, feeling her breasts push against him, and pressed his face into her hair. They sank back on the couch and said nothing, just stayed close.

He opened his eyes as she stroked his forehead.

He looked at her silently, realising how much he loved her, desired her. She had surprised him – it was better, much better than he'd imagined. He needed her.

'Paul . . . Jessica, she's very beautiful. Did you – '
'No.'

Paul looked at his face in the bathroom mirror. It was covered with a heavy stubble, and very dirty. He washed the dirt off and found a razor. As the stubble came off, he began to feel better.

He walked back down the hall, went through the bedroom door and sat down on the bed beside her. She drew in close to him, and he hugged her.

'Jesus, Paul. What have you got yourself into?'

Anne got up and brushed her hair in front of the mirror. Every time he looked at her, he felt more in love with her.

'When I came here,' Anne said, brushing her hair with long, even strokes, 'I was only thinking of you. Every day I've been thinking about how the money from the film will help you to carry on with the lion rehabilitation work. I imagined you working on your next project – not hanging around with a guy who looks like a heavyweight boxer. And you've got Mkhulu involved as well.'

'Anne, I've found out things – '

She turned and faced him, her eyes on fire, and he got up and kissed her softly on the lips. She returned the kiss, but didn't allow it to progress any further. Instead she eased him away and then began packing her case.

'I'm going now,' she said. 'I know you've got to work this thing out.'

He laughed uneasily. He hadn't realised just how strong she was.

'I'll sacrifice almost anything for you, Paul. But I can't stay here, wondering if you're going to come home alive.'

'Anne. Please . . .'

She kissed him. 'I'll be on Klaw. When you want me, come back to Africa. I love you. I'll always love you.'

She turned, avoiding his eyes, made her way down the hall and closed the door softly behind her.

Paul felt hollow to the core. For a long time he just stood there. Then he looked through the door to see Sonny staring at him.

The big black man walked in and laid his hand on Paul's shoulder, his brow wrinkling. 'If I had a woman like that to come home to, I wouldn't leave. I suggest you leave this thing alone, man. I'll go my own way.'

'Sonny . . . It's not that simple. We're involved. They know who I am, and they sure as hell know who *you* are. They're not going to leave any of us alone.'

'Sure, but if you want to go back to Africa – go. I won't take offence.'

Sonny went back up the stairs and Paul went into the lounge; the sound of the front door softly closing was still in his ears.

What was he doing? Sonny was right, she was an exceptional woman . . .

He could run for it. He could liaise with Roland-Emery from Klaw . . .

Then he thought back to Pretoria Central. He thought of Ton van Tonder, the man who had refused to die. They'd sung for him the whole night, and the place had sounded like a church, not a prison. He would never erase that singing from his brain.

The warders had come for Ton in the morning. Ton had been moved to his own cell the previous night – they never left a man who was about to die in a cell with other prisoners. He had heard the warders wrestling with Ton, the grunts, and the sound of a truncheon smacking flesh. He knew that the blow would have hurt the warder as much as the prisoner. Then there was silence, and he knew they'd failed to get Ton out of the cell.

Later, there'd been a muffled explosion, and Paul had crouched forward as the tear-gas hit his eyes. They'd gassed Ton's cell to get him out. He heard scuffling again, and then the dragging of heels. Ton was screaming, 'No! No! Sweet Jesus, no!'

Paul had collapsed against the bars, shivering. Would he go like that? he had wondered. Then later there was the sound of the trap, echoing around the concrete walls of the prison. Paul had vomited, knowing Ton was dead – Ton, who had sworn he would never die.

Now Paul was a free man. But the world of violence, a world he'd known all his life, wouldn't go away.

What was wrong with him? Most men would have been ecstatic to have a woman like Anne in love with them . . . He paced round and round the room, feeling disorientated.

No, he could not give this thing up. He'd promised himself on death row that, if he lived, he would live without compromise. Too often in his life he had compromised, and always he had paid a heavy price.

Anne must accept him for what he was, that was all there was to it.

He pulled a piece of paper from his pocket, crumpled and then uncrumpled it as he thought of Anne. Then his eyes focused on the paper and he remembered that he had snatched it from the study of the Rutland Gate house.

He smoothed the paper out on the lounge table. It was a blueprint. He stared hard at the design. It was the barrel of a cannon. He couldn't tell what type of cannon, nor could he decipher the notes at the bottom.

Inside his pocket he found another section of the blueprint. This sheet had a detailed drawing of a round object that looked suspiciously like a shell – there were some lengthy equations, too.

Perhaps this was what Fahad was so anxious to protect. It made sense; Iraq was known to be buying sophisticated weaponry. Paul decided to get expert advice to help him decipher the plans – then perhaps he might get to the bottom of the business.

In the taxi Anne felt very lonely. Part of her wanted to go back and forgive him. She loved him so much. She wanted to be close to him, feel his skin pressed against hers, hear him say how much he loved her.

She wanted to see him as the successful film director – the animal conservationist – the two of them on the reserve, rehabilitating lions together . . . And how had she found him? Creeping back to his beautiful neighbour's house, dog-tired and stressed-out. Who was the strange black man with him and Mkhulu?

Instinctively she'd known they were in trouble – dangerous trouble. And she had shied away from the danger.

What scared her most was what she saw in Paul's eyes. It was what she'd seen soon after he'd been released – a singular determination to do what he wanted. She wanted that energy devoted to her, and to his film-making. But Paul Norton had a nose for trouble, and when he found it, he couldn't leave it alone.

She remembered paging through a scrapbook of press-cuttings about him that Charlotte had given her. His life was an anthology of documentaries on death and destruction. Those press-cuttings told her more about the man than any of his award-winning films. It was what he chose to film that was fascinating – the worst aspects of warfare.

Charlotte had told her he'd wanted to expose war, to make people aware of all its horrors. But Charlotte had also told her about the three years he'd spent in the army, rising to the rank

235

of captain in the elite South African Reconnaisance Commando. She had sworn her to secrecy on the subject. Evidently Paul never talked about that time. Anne knew he'd been court-martialled – it had been in the papers during the trial – and she knew the reason for the court-martial. But whatever he might have been standing up for, he'd still been a soldier.

She guessed that as a cameraman he sometimes felt frustrated. Yet she sensed that he was also afraid of the violence within himself. Now, this strong, more violent side, far from being subdued by his time in prison, was coming to the fore. And she had to ask herself again, could she live with this man?

She crossed her arms and gripped her shoulders. What frightened her was the sexual attraction that drew her to Paul. She loved the uncontrollable side of him. However, living with it on a day-to-day basis might be another matter. But maybe living without it would be even worse.

Most of the men in her life before had been voyeurs, playing other roles. Paul was genuine; he was himself. She knew he loved her desperately, but that if she wasn't around, he'd find someone else. She sensed that if she hadn't been there that evening, he would probably have slept with Jessica.

No. The problem with Paul wasn't that he'd leave her for another woman, it was that he had this need for taking risks, and she didn't know if she could live always wondering if he'd make it back to her alive.

She thought of Klaw, of the lions. He never doubted that she would look after them – perhaps that showed just how much faith he had in her.

For the moment, then, she would lose herself in her work with the lions – that was the only way she could stay sane. She could only hope that Paul quickly got to the bottom of what he was involved in. Then he would come back to Klaw and perhaps they could build a life together.

Paul found the name of an armaments expert through one of his journalist friends in London. The man had seemed reluctant to talk to him at first, but the mention of the plans had changed that.

He rang the bell of the flat off Cadogan Square. 'Sir Donald Morgan', read the brass name-plate above the button.

'Yes, who is it?' The crisp, pukka voice erupted from the intercom.

'Paul Norton.'

'Very good. Take the stairs, you don't sound like a man who needs to use the lift.'

Before Paul could reply the door opened, and he made his way quickly inside.

The apartment was a spacious one on the top floor. Sir Donald was quite different from what Paul had been expecting, a big man, with huge hands and a deep bellow of a laugh. His eyebrows were sandy, thatched bushes that erupted from his forehead. His eyes darted up and down Paul before finally focusing directly on his face. He got the impression that he was being very carefully assessed.

They shook hands, and Paul wondered if it was Sir Donald's intention to break some of his fingers.

'Take a seat, old chap. Glad to see you have some military experience in your background.'

Paul looked at him in surprise. How had Sir Donald come to know he'd been in the army?'

'Security clearance, old boy. Let's say I was involved with intelligence, and leave it at that.'

Paul let his eyes rove around the room. There were flowers, and pictures of quite a few children and grandchildren.

'I'm sorry, but you won't find any clues except misleading ones,' Sir Donald said affably.

'So I'll never really know who you are?'

Sir Donald only smiled and said, 'Care for a drink?'

Paul glanced at his watch.

'Got work to do, have you?'

'No, but I usually don't drink before six. It's a habit from the bush.'

'Bugger tradition, what would you like?'

'Whisky.'

'I'll join you. I've got a very nice malt here. You'd like something with it?'

'No.'

'Good. Can't stand a man who weakens a good whisky,' Sir Donald said conspiratorially as he poured them each a drink. 'Look old chap', he went on, 'you don't have to look so ill-at-ease. Basically, I'm a scientist. My career's involved designing weapons, and analysing the weapons of our friends and enemies.'

Paul felt a little more optimistic. Perhaps he had found the right man – he was scared of being dismissed as a crank.

'So, what is it you want to talk to me about?'

'I'm working on a film about the arms trade, and some blueprints fell into my hands,' he lied.

Sir Donald narrowed his eyes. 'You know, that's a dangerous world. You realise you'd have to get security clearance before you could screen such a film in Britain?'

Paul felt his hackles rise, but Sir Donald said, 'Relax, old boy. I said that to protect you, not the British government. Anyway, you've whetted my curiosity. Let's see those blueprints . . .'

Paul opened his case and took out a file. He'd pressed the two blueprints flat to make them presentable. Sir Donald took them, ran his eyes over them and leaned back in his chair. 'Mmmm, I gather these are of a cannon in the prototype stage?'

'I'm really not sure, but I would think so. I thought you might be able to fill me in on that.'

'Come through . . .'

Sir Donald got up and led Paul through into his study. Paul followed, noting the trickle of sweat that was now running down Sir Donald's forehead. The big man laid the plans out on a draughting-table and switched on a light. Paul watched him examine the scale of the drawings.

'Jesus Christ!' he muttered under his breath. Then he turned to Paul with a smile on his face.

'The work of a lunatic,' he said. 'Great idea on paper, but in reality it would never work.'

He took the other page and examined that too. 'You can't get the rest of the blueprint?' he asked tentatively.

'No. There's no possibility of that.'

'Come here, then, and let me explain what I'm looking at. What this is, you see, is the design of a very big cannon – a Supergun. It's an idea the Germans were working on at the end of the Second World War, and there was a lot of interest in it in the fifties. But then came ballistic missiles.'

Sir Donald moved closer to Paul. 'Whoever drew these plans is way out of his depth. The basic plan isn't bad, but the problem is that no one in the world today could possibly want to build such a weapon.' He pulled the second plan onto the table. 'This is a section of a section. What you're looking at here is a design for a satellite shell that would obviously be fired from the cannon. Now that would be little short of lunacy.'

'Why?'

'Because the pressures developed in the breech of such a weapon on firing would destroy the satellite.'

Perhaps someone was taking the Iraqis for a ride, thought Paul. But Sir Donald's next comment made him wary of jumping to such a conclusion. 'I wish you had the rest of the plans,' he said to Paul. 'I find this fascinating. You don't know who the designer is?'

Paul shook his head.

'So how did you get hold of this?'

'I'm afraid I can't reveal my sources.'

Sir Donald drew back from the blueprints and stretched lazily. His next comment, Paul thought, was delivered a shade too nonchalantly.

'Mind if I . . . make a copy?'

'Not at all.'

The big man disappeared into a dark-room adjoining the study, taking the blueprints with him. He emerged a few seconds later.

'It'll take a few minutes. Why don't you relax in the lounge.'

Paul walked back into the main room and browsed along the bookshelves. He wondered what the Iraqi would be doing with the plans of such a cannon. He thought of the Kurdish valley – surely the Iraqis wouldn't hesitate to use such formidable fire-power for military purposes. Wasn't there a possibility that such a weapon could be used for firing chemical, bacteriological or even nuclear warheads?

Sir Donald came through with the blueprints. He folded them up carefully and handed them back to Paul. 'I hope I've helped you.'

'You're not worried about this?' Paul asked.

'You've shown me a section of a design that's thirty years out of date – today we launch satellites with rockets. No, to answer your question, I'm not worried at all.'

'So I could feature these in my latest documentary?'

The smile went off Sir Donald's face. 'As I pointed out to you earlier, you'd have to get clearance.'

'But you said this Supergun's thirty years out of date.'

'To develop a weapon like this would take years of work. It would be almost impossible to do it in secrecy, and would require a huge amount of funding. That sort of money can only be provided by a government, not an individual.'

'So what's the problem?'

Sir Donald pulled at his right earlobe. 'Well, let's say that by showing such plans to the general public you could cause speculation. True, the weapon's a white elephant. But rumours can be very damaging.'

'I don't follow.'

'When you deal with classified information, you have to be very careful. I suggest that if you do want to proceed any further with this matter, you liaise with me.'

Paul rose to leave. 'Well, thank you for your help, Sir Donald'.

'Not at all. If I need to, how can I get hold of you?'

Paul took out one of his cards. 'My house is being refurbished at the moment. But I should be in by next week.'

'Norton, a word of advice. Stick to war reportage – you'll run into more fiction than fact in the world of weapons design.'

They shook hands and Paul made his way down the stairs. He felt that Sir Donald hadn't been entirely open with him. The only logical way to proceed now was to trace the blueprints back to their source, and for that he would have to resume his surveillance of the Rutland Gate house.

Sir Donald looked out of his window and watched Paul Norton get into a taxi. He picked up the phone and dialled a number.

'Hallo, Chuck. Listen, old chap, something rather serious has come up. I think we should talk about it. No, not over the phone. Good. I'll see you in half an hour.'

*

240

Paul looked out of the window of the flat, peered at the house, and yawned. It was just after six in the morning. They'd been watching the house for over a week and seen nothing of interest. He, Mkhulu and Sonny had been at it day and night, taking four-hour shifts. They'd been lucky to find a flat in Rutland Gate through a letting agency. Paul had put the lease in Jessica's name to avoid suspicion.

There hadn't been a whisper in the press about the killings. It was as if they had never happened. This made Paul even more certain that he had inadvertently stumbled on something distinctly sinister.

Suddenly, two cars drew up outside the house in quick succession. From the first Fahad emerged, and from the second the man Paul had seen with him the first time. He was very tall, with white hair and clear-rimmed glasses. In his right hand was a large black pilot's case.

They were inside the house for just over an hour, then emerged, obviously in the middle of a heated argument. The tall man with the white hair shouted something at Fahad, then got into his car, slamming the door. Fahad turned on his heel and walked back into the house.

Paul decided to follow the white-haired man. He had to start developing some leads. He sprinted down the stairs, ran out of the door and got into his car.

Fahad closed the door behind him – the expression of anger vanished from his face and he smiled. Dr Fassbinder had already informed him that Dr Torr was going to ask him for a further injection of funds. They needed to do more development work on the shell – a prototype had been constructed, but its design was unsatisfactory. Fahad realised that if he didn't provide the extra funding the project would have to be aborted. And if the project failed he knew President Hussein would have him executed.

He now understood perfectly why the American government had found it impossible to work with Dr Torr – he could not keep to a budget. His reputation for devouring vast sums of money was well earned. But Fahad wasn't concerned – he knew the President's consuming passion for weaponry. He would just have to whet the President's appetite some more. Besides, they could invade Kuwait. That would double their oil revenue overnight, and cancel their huge debt to Kuwait. There would be little chance of immediate retaliation, because no one else in the Arab world could match their firepower. And by the end of the year they would have the Supergun, and from Wayne MacLeod the nuclear shells that would make them invincible.

They would have to pay. But once the completed plans were in Fahad's hands, Dr Torr's usefulness would be at an end. Dr Fassbinder could finalise the design of the nuclear shell that would decimate the Israelis.

Yes, it was a good plan.

Paul followed the cab with difficulty, weaving his way through the heavily congested traffic, darting between cars and trucks as he fought to stay close to it. He sensed that this man was a key to the puzzle. He needed to get close to him, find out who he was and what his business was with the Iraqi.

Eventually the cab pulled up at Kings Cross station, and Paul dumped his car in a no parking zone. He dashed through the crowds, keeping his focus on the tall man with the white hair. The man turned a corner. Paul fought his way forward and rounded the wall. He couldn't see him anywhere.

'Shit!'

His eyes combed the walls, looked through shop windows, but his man refused to appear. Then he noticed the sign that indicated lavatories down a narrow passageway. Paul prayed silently that that was where his man might have disappeared to.

He waited. Five minutes. Ten minutes. He cursed himself for not keeping closer. Then, without warning, the man came out of the passage.

Paul felt his pulse surge. He kept close now, following him to the ticket counter. He booked a first class, one-way ticket to Inverness on the eight-fifty InterCity. Paul did the same.

He then waited till the man had gone down to the platform before darting across to the autoteller and drawing some money. Next he went to enquiries, paged through the InterCity timetable and found that there was a Hertz car hire office at Inverness station. He had to be totally prepared on his arrival in Scotland. His subject might have a car waiting, and God alone knew where this man might be going to. He found the Hertz number in Inverness, went to a call box and reserved a car for his arrival at five-twenty that afternoon.

The train left on time at eight-fifty, and Paul sat in the seat he'd reserved in first class – at the far end of the carriage. There weren't a lot of people on the train. His man was at the other end of the carriage and was already working at his table.

Paul waited till the train started moving, then made his way to the dining-car. As he passed his subject, he looked down at what the man was working on. He froze. It was the same section of blueprint that he'd stolen from the Rutland Gate house. Paul knew he was looking at the designer of the Supergun.

In the dining-car he had a full English breakfast and then went back to his seat. His subject was still hard at work.

Paul stared at the passing scenery for a while, then dropped into a fitful sleep. The conductor had to wake him to announce that lunch was ready. Paul moved back to the dining-car – and experienced a moment of unease when he realised that his subject had vanished. But then Paul saw him at the far end of the dining-car, and relaxed. He wouldn't fall asleep again – his subject could easily have eluded him by getting off at one of the stations on the way.

Paul ate ravenously, casting an occasional glance at his quarry. The man looked more like a minister than a weapons' designer. He was oblivious to everyone else in the dining-car, his only interest was in the plans laid out beyond his plate.

Paul knew he would have to be patient. He needed to put a call through to Mkhulu or Sonny, to tell them where he'd got to. He also wanted them to get his film of the man and see if they could have him identified without arousing suspicion.

Paul finished his coffee and moved back through the carriage to his seat. He fought to keep his eyes open but, desperately tired, he dropped off into a deep sleep and dreamed of Anne.

He felt a hand on his shoulder and looked up into the conductor's eyes.

'Come on, sir. You're in Inverness.'

'Oh my God,' he blurted, and leapt up, scanning the carriage. His quarry was gone.

Paul thundered down the carriage, leapt out of the door and onto the platform. He found himself in the centre of the station; in the distance he could see cars in the street beyond the entrance. He ran up to the first railway official he saw.

'Where's the Hertz counter?'

'Just over there, sir.'

Paul sprinted hard, knocking several people flying. He caught sight of the distinctive white hair disappearing through the front entrance.

The breath burst from his lungs as he sprinted through the crowds, past the John Menzies newsagent and some circular red seats in the centre of the concourse. At the front entrance he saw a red sports car turning left out of the car park and moving into a traffic jam. His man was in the passenger seat.

Desperately, Paul turned round and sprinted back to the yellow Hertz desk. He eyeballed the blonde at the counter.

'Mr Norton,' he gasped. 'I telephoned ahead. I need my car right now.'

'All right, sir. Follow me.'

She walked briskly along the side of the platform and turned right into an open, car park. 'Here's your car, sir.'

In the distance, on the road that ran past the car park, Paul saw the red sports car flash by. He snatched the keys from the woman and leapt into the driver's seat of the Ford Sierra.

'I'm late . . .'

He started the engine, spun the rear wheels and roared off in hot pursuit of the red sports car. Already he could see its tail-lights, and he shot across a roundabout to the accompaniment of hoots from the angry motorists he'd carved up. Then he swung to the left, taking the Ullapool turn-off, and headed north on the motorway, past the Mercury Hotel and towards the white suspension bridge that crossed between the Beauly and Moray Firths. He kept his foot hard on the accelerator pedal, and cursed himself for not hiring a faster car. Down to his left he saw the lights of the Inverness Industrial Estate, and beyond, the huge expanse of water that formed the Beauly Firth.

He shot over the bridge, the white supporting rods flashing past in his headlights, and noted a tourist information centre on his left as they moved onto the Black Isle in the Ross and

244

Cromarty District. He was sweating now – if the sports car went any faster, he'd lose it. At least the traffic had thinned out and he was able to keep it in sight.

Paul had been to the Scottish Highlands several times before, and the rugged beauty of the country appealed to him – not that he could see much of it now, in the darkness of a winter evening. He closed in on the sports car, which he identified as a Lotus. If they wanted to, he knew they could lose him in seconds.

At Tore, the Lotus moved fast into a roundabout and swung first left along the A832 to the Muir of Ord. It was a narrow road, but the Lotus maintained its lightning pace. After nine kilometres they shot through the village, crossed a bridge and turned hard right. Paul kept his foot flat on the accelerator. The Lotus pulled away, then indicated left and turned off the road. Following, Paul swept up to a turreted entrance, shot through it, and saw the rear lights going down another road between some trees. There was nothing to do except keep going. If they'd seen him, too bad.

He passed a sign pointing in the direction he was going. It said 'The Dower House'. And suddenly he had to slam on the brakes as he shot into a gravel drive and saw a single-storey house in front of him. Bloody hell, if it was a private dwelling he'd just have to say he'd lost his way.

The white-haired man and his companion, an attractive woman with dark hair and a pale complexion, made their way to the front entrance. Paul got out of his car and started walking across the gravel.

'Dr Torr, Dr Fassbinder, it's good to see you,' an attractive Scotswoman in her forties greeted them.

'Thank you. I'm looking forward to dinner,' Dr Torr replied, and following her, he and Dr Fassbinder went inside and disappeared down a passage. Paul walked to the entrance and stared into the lounge, which was elegantly furnished and had a roaring fire in the hearth.

'Yes sir, can I help you?' the Scottish woman asked.

Paul spun round. 'Er yes. I was wondering if you were full tonight?'

'Just yourself, is it, sir?'

'Yes, I'm in Scotland on business.'

245

'Well, you're in luck, we do have a room. Would you like to fetch your things, and I'll show you.'

'Thanks, but I'll get my bags later, I have a few telephone calls to make.'

The woman showed him to his room, and the moment she had gone he phoned the London flat. It was a relief to hear Sonny's voice on the other end of the line.

Paul quickly explained what had happened, then got down to the real reason for his call.

'I want you to see a friend of mine tomorrow, Sonny. He works for the *Sunday Times*. There are two names I want him to research.'

Sonny took down the details carefully. 'Your producer rang,' he said. 'He said they want to start shooting the film next January.'

Paul had forgotten about the film – he'd forgotten about almost everything. 'Anne didn't call?'

'No, man. Mkhulu's taking over here, I'm sleeping at your mews house tonight – they've finished the redecorating and I'm sure you don't want any more unwelcome visitors.'

'Good. I don't know when I'll be able to call you and Mkhulu again.'

'Look after yourself, Paul.'

Josh waited in the shadows till the lights had gone off. He smiled to himself. Revenge was something he'd always particularly enjoyed. He'd been made a fool of, but it hadn't taken him too long to put the pieces together. Now it was just a question of doing some cleaning up.

Fortunately, it seemed the damage was minimal. They'd stepped up the security at the house – there was no chance of a repeat of what happened – but still, he was maddened by the breach of security. He was angry with himself; he'd become complacent, and let his client down.

Now he pulled the black balaclava over his face, smoothed down the black jersey and slipped on the thin black cotton gloves. In the darkness he was invisible. He liked the feeling of the silenced pistol in his hand. This was what he did best.

The front door lock of Norton's mews house was easy, but as

he worked at the tumblers, a woman emerged from the house next door. Her startled eyes caught Josh's. In one move he was over the fence and had delivered a hard chop across the back of her head, laying her out cold on the step.

Josh climbed back over the fence, opened the front door, passed through the hall and moved up the staircase, heading for the door on the first floor. Already his pulse was racing. He liked a clean operation, nothing left to leave a clue.

He tapped the butt of the gun against the wood, tapped again, then waited.

'Who the fuck is that?'

Josh darted away from the door, moving slightly up the stairs. It was going to be very satisfying.

Sonny's face appeared at the door. 'Over here, you black cocksucker,' Josh whispered.

Sonny moved forward, and Josh pumped two bullets into the centre of his forehead. The black man crumpled to the floor with a dull groan.

Josh made his way carefully around the house. He wanted Norton, but the bastard wasn't in. Then Josh saw the notepad and the names written on it: Dr Torr and Dr Fassbinder. He froze. He'd fucked up.

Feverishly Josh searched the place for more clues, combing each room. He found Norton's study, but the place was empty – they'd obviously just moved back in after the fire. Norton must be staying somewhere else.

Josh sank down into a chair. If Fahad found out that Norton had Dr Torr's name, Josh knew he wouldn't just get fired, he'd probably get murdered. And even if he got out of the business alive, his reputation would be finished.

He tore the piece of paper with the names on it from the notepad, and put it in his pocket.

After going round the house one more time, he came back to Sonny. He needed to make an impression – he had to warn Norton off. He pulled out his knife and slit the waistband of Sonny's trousers open. The knife sliced easily through the soft flesh and Josh drew back, admiring his handiwork.

He left the house quietly, closing the door carefully behind him. The woman from next door was still lying unconscious on her doorstep, blood running from her mouth.

Josh grinned, then moved into the street and melted into the darkness.

Paul lay awake in the bedroom, staring at the white vaulted ceiling. The walls of the room were covered with a pretty blue wallpaper and in front of him was a small television. He liked the style of the place and hoped that one day he could bring Anne there on holiday.

The evening meal had been magnificent. Fortunately he'd been shown to a table at the far end of the dining-room from Dr Torr and Dr Fassbinder. In between him and the doctors was a party of six who, judging by their conversation, were enjoying a hunting and fishing expedition.

Paul had deliberately finished earlier than the other diners, and taken coffee in the lounge. He'd then gone through to the small reception hall and paged idly through the visitor's book. He'd given a fictitious name and address. He noticed that Dr Torr and Dr Fassbinder were leaving the following morning.

Returning to his room, he leaned over the bed and picked up the phone. He dialled 607 and tapped in the time he wanted a wake-up call – five in the morning. He couldn't afford to take the chance that they might leave early.

Paul woke at five, bathed, dressed, and moved into the lounge to read. He breakfasted at eight and paid his bill in cash. He didn't want Dr Torr to catch sight of him – he had no idea how long he'd have to tail the man, and he wanted to remain as anonymous as possible.

Paul was determined to find out if the Supergun was under construction. He was certain that Dr Torr was intimately involved in the project, and knew that if he stuck close to him he'd eventually find out just what was going on.

The drive at The Dower House was a long, curving affair, and Paul found a turning off it where he parked his car. In the quietness of the early morning he had more time to reflect on what was happening between him and Anne. She couldn't expect him to stop following up what he'd uncovered. He knew the

Iraqi had no moral scruples – if the weapon did have nuclear capability, he was quite certain that Fahad would not hesitate to use it.

He opened his wallet and looked at the photograph inside – Charlotte. Then another image flashed across his consciousness – the dead woman and her child, lying on the road in Halabje. There came a point where you could not walk away any longer and remain a man.

The Iraqi was a man capable of perpetrating the grossest atrocities. He had to be stopped – for despite Sir Donald's assurances to the contrary, Paul felt that the development of the Supergun had sinister implications.

He looked out of the front window of the Sierra. The greenness was all around him; condensation dripped off the windows of the car. He wished he was with Anne at that moment. He thought of making love to her, and that made him feel very alone. He envied Dr Torr and his girlfriend – he imagined them in bed together, enjoying early morning coffee, lying naked next to one another beneath the starched white sheets.

Suddenly he felt very hollow. He thought of Klaw, of the lions and the bush. What the hell was he doing here?

The noise of a car coming up the gravel drive broke into his thoughts. Dr Fassbinder was driving, Dr Torr was in the passenger seat reading the morning paper.

Paul started the engine. He didn't have time to waste. Would they turn left or right at the top of drive? He accelerated hard and caught the flash of the left rear indicator light as the sports car turned into the main road and headed north. Fortunately there was a light mist that enabled him to keep close on their tail without attracting attention.

They sped along the A862 till they reached a roundabout at Maryburgh, and turned left onto the A835. On his left, as he passed through the town of Garve, Paul caught sight of a loch. There was a moment of unease as he swept past the turning to the Kyle of Lochalsh, but then he saw the Lotus ahead of him again.

He switched on the radio and listened to the news, his eyes watching the Strathgarve Forest on his right.

'Today', the newsreader said, 'the Iraqi ambassador in Washington, Mohammed Sadiq Al-Mashat, met with US officials at the State Department Headquarters. Ambassador Al-Mashat down-played reports of Iraqi troop movements. However, the US Assistant Secretary of State for Near Eastern and South Asian Affairs, John Kelly, voiced his country's concern over reports that nearly one hundred thousand Iraqi troops were massing on the borders of Kuwait.'

A cold sweat broke out across Paul's forehead. His mind was putting the pieces together and he didn't like the conclusion it was coming to. He pressed harder on the accelerator, keeping the sports car clearly in view.

Kuwait was a rich prize for any country. He knew the figures. At the end of 1990 Kuwait had reserves of 95 billion barrels of oil, slightly less than Iraq. Yet Kuwait was a small country, nestling on the south-western borders of Iraq and facing the waters of the Persian Gulf.

Paul switched off the radio and concentrated on the road ahead. He began to enjoy the drive. He passed through a cutting and headed up into the hills. The weather was slightly overcast and he was aware of the grey cloud above him. A river came up on his left, then the country flattened out, and it started to rain.

On his right he saw a hotel, the Aultguish Inn, and behind it an enormous dam. As he travelled higher he saw a sign indicating the Glascarnoch Dam and then beyond this an open stretch of water – Loch Glascarnoch.

The water of the dam was at a low level, judging by the white rocks he could see at its edge. He passed a concrete structure, towering above the water on huge legs. His eyes moved back to the road and noted the white sticks with red markers on the top – guideposts for the snow-plough when the weather got really bad.

He came to the top of the mountains, and then the road started to work its way down through a bleak, barren landscape. In front of him was another loch.

He noticed a red light glowing on the dashboard. How long had it been on? He stared down at the fuel gauge in horror. He was almost on empty. Shit! But surely the tank had been full?

The engine coughed – and the Lotus disappeared into the distance. His car back-fired, then the engine cut out.

Desperately Paul turned the starter, then he put the car into third and dropped the clutch – but the engine refused to take. At the next incline the car ground to a halt.

'Damnit!' Paul shouted.

He leapt out and went round to the back. The fuel cap was missing. Someone must have siphoned petrol out of his car the night before. Had he been followed?

And then a car pulled up behind him, and the driver got out. A lean, dark-haired man, dressed in casual clothes.

'Have you got a problem?' the man asked in a broad Scots accent.

'I'm out of bloody petrol.'

'Ach, not to worry, I've got a wee drop in the back.'

He disappeared round to the back of his car. Paul felt the sweat running down his face. He was going to lose Dr Torr; it was a total disaster.

'Here we are. Five litres – enough to get you to Ullapool without a problem.'

Paul almost wrenched the yellow plastic container from the man's hands. He poured the contents into his tank, stuffed a twenty-pound note into the man's hand and jumped back into the car.

'Hey, hold on! That's too much . . .'

Paul started the engine and accelerated down the road. He edged the needle up past 160 kmh and kept on the pressure. A line of cars came up ahead – he swung out to the right and then saw a pantechnicon coming straight for him. He swerved up onto the right-hand verge, heard the paintwork scrape against the side of the vehicle, then he was through. The car smashed down back onto the tarmac, and he kept his foot flat.

His eyes scanned the road ahead. A light drizzle began to fall. The area was thickly forested and he saw a sign to 'Lael Forest Garden'. Fortunately there were no significant turn-offs. He might just be lucky. But he couldn't see the Lotus, and soon signs appeared announcing he was close to Ullapool.

He entered the town with the beach on his left and a line of houses and shops to the right. In front of him he could see the pier stretching out into Loch Broom. He saw a Caledonian MacBrayne ferry moored next to the pier, its back section open and a long line of cars and trucks driving on board. Paul accelerated down the road, to find his way blocked by the traffic going onto the ferry. The two doctors had to be on board – they must have left The Dower House early because they wanted to catch the ferry.

The drizzle turned into hard, driving rain. Paul ran into the ferry offices and saw a woman at the counter, behind a glass screen.

'Where does this ferry go to?' he gasped.

'Stornoway, on the Isle of Lewis. Is it a ticket you'll be wanting?'

'For me and the car.'

'A return?'

'Yes.'

'All right, that'll be eighty-eight pounds fifty. Your car will be on standby – if you don't get on, I'll refund your money.'

Paul went back to his car, turned right to overtake the traffic jam, and drove into the ferry car park. What if he didn't get on? He'd first have to go on foot and hire another car in Stornoway. He fingered the four pink tickets he'd been given, then watched an endless procession of cars and trucks going aboard the ferry. Eventually an official came up to his car.

'You're in luck, sir. There's space for you.'

Relieved, Paul started the car and drove into the bowels of the ferry, parking his car behind a large truck. He got out and followed the other drivers up to the main deck. He couldn't see the Lotus amongst the cars on board.

Out on the main deck, he looked down at the crowd of people on the shoreside, waving goodbye to the ferry.

The boat pulled out into Loch Broom and then headed north-west into Annat Bay. Paul watched the seagulls flying overhead, then moved to the upper deck, his eyes combing the passengers. No sign of them. Eventually, in desperation, he joined the queue for the bar. From where he was standing he could see the lounge and he searched the place for the couple without success.

Finally it was his turn at the bar. He ordered a whisky, then took it to a table in the bar lounge. He leaned back and took a sip. The whisky tasted good, warming him up on the inside. He had the creeping feeling that his car might have been deliberately sabotaged. But then why leave off the filler cap? If he'd noticed, it would have given the game away.

He went over what he'd heard on the news again, about Iraqi troops massing on Kuwait's border – and realised that he was onto something important. After all, he, Mkhulu and Sonny had broken into a house and killed several men, yet there'd not been a single report of it on the news. By chance he'd also stumbled on the blueprint for a weapon that could alter the balance of power in the Middle East. He sensed that the Iraqi wanted the development of the Supergun kept very quiet. And that could hardly be because he was using it to launch satellites.

Paul contemplated his drink – and then looked up into the eyes of Dr Torr. The doctor was sitting opposite him with his girlfriend, Dr Fassbinder, drinking a Guinness. Paul shifted his eyes away and felt his pulse racing. He couldn't believe his luck.

He felt the energy coming back and the excitement. He was going to follow this thing right through to the end.

Fahad went through the papers on his desk again. He had always been meticulous. There was no doubt in his mind that two of the blueprints were missing. He'd been a fool – he should have kept them in the safe.

The phone rang, and he snatched up the receiver angrily. It was President Hussein.

'We are going to return Kuwait to the fold of its motherland,' the President said.

'You are going to invade?' Fahad stammered, scarcely able to contain his excitement.

If he had been present at a meeting between an Iraqi delegation and the Crown Prince of Kuwait, he would have understood why. The Crown Prince had deliberately insulted Saddam.

'The Crown Prince will not sleep in his bed tonight,' Saddam muttered angrily.

'And the additional funding for the development of the Supergun?'

There was a silence at the end of the line, and then the words came down like manna from heaven. 'Spend as much as you like, Fahad. I am about to wipe out our debt to Kuwait. Your project has top priority.'

Fahad put the phone down slowly. What would it matter now if someone had taken some of the blueprints? He must push for the completion of the Supergun in as short a time as possible.

His mind worked quickly. What if the Mossad had the plans? Well, they would know who had drawn them. Only one person was capable of designing such a weapon – Dr Torr. Thus it would be remarkably simple to silence their fears. When Dr Torr was assassinated, the Israelis would believe that the project was stillborn.

Fahad thought of Dr Torr's girlfriend, the brilliant Dr Fassbinder. She would carry through the plans when Dr Torr was assassinated. Naturally, he had not told her that Dr Torr was to be killed, for he sensed she was close to the man – after all, she was sleeping with him.

Fahad smiled to himself. He would turn the loss of the plans into a strategic advantage.

Wayne MacLeod studied the coded fax very carefully. He could feel the excitement in the trembling of his hands. This was better than anything he could possibly have expected! There was no more haggling over the price, just a lot of pressure for early delivery.

Everything had been carefully planned. The Supergun parts were already complete; it was just the shell that was lacking. Even better, the parts were already in Iraq, smuggled in over the preceding months – a fleet of transporters could arrange delivery at a moment's notice.

MacLeod had a lifetime of experience in the weapons supply business. He knew that when hostilities broke out it became almost impossible to make deliveries. So, long ago, he had evolved the strategy of landing his consignments where they were wanted well before the final contract was signed. If the agreement fell through, no one would be any the wiser; if it was successful, he could guarantee the arrival of the merchandise.

In this particular instance he had been especially careful. The balance of power in the Middle East was precarious. One moment Britain, the United States, France and Germany might back a country – the next, they could turn against it. His factories in the West Midlands had manufactured the various sections of the Supergun and then exported them – but one of the dangers now presenting itself was that Britain could turn against Iraq and begin investigating any weapons supplied to it.

Wayne leaned back in his chair. He was quite safe. It had been a stroke of genius to involve the Prime Minister's son in the early stages of the contract. The price, a few million pounds in commission, was a small price to pay for the silence of the father. The Prime Minister could not afford such negative exposure – that his son had taken what was basically a bribe to sell a high-technology cannon to Iraq. Wayne could imagine how the Israelis and the Americans would react to such a revelation. He was sure that the British Prime Minister would be forced to stand down.

It was now vital that the testing programme for the Supergun should start as quickly as possible. He had already decided on a target small town – the ideal environment to show the effectiveness of the weapon. And what was more important, he had already filmed the area, so he could show Fahad a frighteningly realistic 'before' and 'after' scenario. The film would be a sophisicated sales tool, and the ultimate method of blackmail. Should the British make the slightest move to close down his intricate network of arms supply factories in the Midlands, he would release the film, with detailed revelations of the Prime Minister's son's involvement – especially in the acquisition of the necessary security clearances for manufacture and for export.

To guarantee payment from the Iraqi side, he had video footage of Fahad indulging in his gory fantasies. And as for the International People's Bank of Pakistan – he had that completely under control. With his contacts in the British banking establishment, he could bring down the IPBP anytime.

In the end, it was all a question of timing. He had already decided on the value of what he had produced. Now the perfect situation had developed for him to demand a suitably high price. The completed nuclear shells would not be delivered until he had received further payment from the Iraqis.

War was excellent for business . . .

*

As the ferry approached Stornoway harbour, Paul shared none of the elation of his fellow travellers. He watched as the gulls that had followed the ferry throughout its journey were joined by others from the island, to the accompaniment of much shrieking. Getting off the ferry was going to be a worrying business. He was scared that he might lose the Lotus again – he must drive his car off as the passengers were disembarking. He approached one of the crew members.

'I'll pay you ten quid to drive my car off. I've got to run ashore to make an urgent call.'

The man peered at him, considering the offer.

'Make it twenty,' the man said.

Paul handed the money over and then quickly moved back to the covered area. Dr Torr and Dr Fassbinder were standing at the front of the queue. The boat closed in slowly against the landing-point and the passengers began to disembark.

Paul kept close to the doctors, shivering with cold. It was raining heavily and his jacket was sodden. They went up to a Range Rover, and Dr Fassbinder got into the driver's seat. Paul looked back at the ferry and saw that the vehicles had only just started to come off. He turned back to see the Range Rover go past the Caledonian Hotel and take the A859 turn-off to Ness.

Paul sprinted back to the ferry, found his car with the sailor sitting in the driver's seat.

'There you are. What's your hurry?'

'I was supposed to follow my friend. I'm late. Please . . .'

The man got slowly out of the driver's seat. Paul wanted to hit him.

'I live here,' the man said. 'Perhaps I can give you directions? Who are you looking for?'

Bloody hell, he was going to lose them! 'They left in that black Range Rover as the boat arrived,' he said through gritted teeth.

'Oh, that would be Dr Torr.'

Paul was taken aback. He thought the doctor's hide-out – wherever it was – would have been veiled in secrecy. 'You know where he lives?'

'Amhuinnsuidhe Castle. You take the Ness turn-off just past the Caledonian, go through the town, and at the roundabout

256

take the A859 to Tarbert. Then just as you come down the road into North Harris, you take the right turn to Hushinish.'

'Thanks.' Paul leapt into the driver's seat and gunned the car forward. He couldn't believe his luck. He followed the sailor's directions, glimpsing Stornoway Castle across the waters of the harbour, shrouded in dark green undergrowth and trees. Then he was on the A859, heading south-west.

What little traffic there had been in Stornoway vanished, and he had the road to himself. He crossed a cattle-grid and passed some warehouses on the right, keeping to the forty-mile-an-hour limit. Suddenly the scenery turned bleak, and a sign saying 'Watch Out for Blasting' came up on the left. In the distance he saw a quarry. Out of the forty-mile-an-hour zone, he floored the accelerator and moved fast along the road.

Five minutes later he spotted the black Range Rover in front, and was forced to draw further back to escape detection. He grew concerned as he realised he was heading into sparsely populated territory. It was important that he maintain his anonymity for as long as possible.

Now he drove very carefully, letting the Range Rover get far ahead of him. The terrain became rocky, and there were quite a few sheep wandering about with distinctive blue or red branding-stains on their wool. He crossed another cattle-grid, then a new double bridge that ran parallel with the old one. The town of Baelie Aileen came up, and he saw a big expanse of water off to the right. The Range Rover started pulling away and Paul drove flat-out to keep up. After another cattle-grid, he passed through some plantations of new trees and the road became a single track.

It took all his concentration to maintain speed. One wrong move and he'd be off the road, or have a head-on with a vehicle coming in the opposite direction. Down in the distance he saw Loch Seaforth, quiet and majestic.

He breasted the top of a steep hill and then started heading down the other side. He guessed he was close to Tarbert now. The road wove its way downwards, passing another quarry operated by Macaskill Contractors, and then he saw the Range Rover taking the turn to Hushinish. The sailor had been one hundred per cent right with his directions.

The road to Hushinish was even narrower, and Paul looked down into West Loch Tarbert and saw a high brick smoke-stack, the last remains of an old whaling station. He caught the sun shining down through the clouds, glistening white and silver against the waters of the loch. Outside the car he could hear the wind howling over the boglands. The isolation and the beauty reminded him of Africa.

He went over another cattle-grid and then passed a block of rock that looked almost like one of the Easter Island sculptures. The road became more and more twisting, and to exceed forty miles an hour would have been suicidal.

In the distance he saw bad weather moving in across the mountains. He came over another hill, the side of the road marked by concrete posts and metal railings, and saw white horses dancing across the waters of the loch. He pressed on, passing a smaller loch to his right, then a stone quarry. At every turn there were stacks of neatly cut peat-sods, forming cairns all over the bogland.

A little white school building with a red tin roof clung to the hillside, next to a stone bridge. Paul felt as if he had entered another world – and then almost lost control of the car as he rounded another tight bend. He gripped the wheel and saw the wreck of a car far down the hillside. He could not afford to lose concentration.

Soon after this he crossed a small concrete bridge with green metal railings, and saw there was a turn-off to the Cliostair Power Station. Ahead was a cattle-grid, with white gates flanking it on either side, and stone battlements running up the hillside and down to the stream on the left. A white signboard was bolted to the battlements: 'Entry for Residents Only. Amhuinn-suidhe Castle. MacLeod Estates.'

MacLeod. Warning bells sounded in Paul's head. Could there be a connection with Wayne MacLeod? He remembered his father telling him that MacLeod came from the Hebrides.

He pulled up on the right and got out. A man in a Harris tweed jacket, carrying a double-barrelled shotgun and a walkie-talkie, came up to him.

'You're not allowed to park here.'

Paul forced himself to act casually. He couldn't afford to lose his temper and draw attention to himself.

'Oh,' he said. 'Is there nowhere I can park?'

'Aye. If you just go up the road to the power station, you can park on the left. What is it you're wanting?'

Paul smiled. 'I'm here on a walking holiday.'

'Well, you're free to walk above the power station, but I'd be careful if I were you. There's a lot of hunting on the estate at present.'

'Thanks. I think I'll go somewhere else!'

'Good idea.'

Paul reversed, and turned round. He planned to return later, unobserved.

Dr Torr felt better as they pulled up in front of the castle. The sea air was bracing; he rolled down the window to breathe it in. He relished the isolation of his castle and the freedom it gave him to concentrate on his designs. Its very inaccessibility was its biggest advantage. Fahad could never bother him here. And the front that he had established in the local community – that he was the leader of a religious group – further enhanced his privacy.

His team would be waiting, hoping that the final development work on the Supergun could go ahead. Of course, it would only take a matter of days and then the blueprint could be faxed to MacLeod. Then he would fly to Namibia to supervise the commencement of the testing programme. Every little detail had to be covered.

He knew how many scientists were sceptical of the viability of a Supergun. But his team believed totally in their ideal. It would be a joy to see how the critics reacted once they witnessed the awesome capability of what he had conceived. It would vindicate him, once and for all.

He ran his eyes over Maria as she walked to the white wooden front doors of the castle. Yes, he was certainly excited by her, but that excitement was nothing compared to the feeling of power he would get after the first firing of the Supergun.

*

David held Charlotte tightly in his arms and listened to the sounds of the bush. He knew Paul was in danger – Anne had come back from London almost out of her mind with worry.

Charlotte's hair brushed against his face. He felt himself rising, felt the sap burning as her moistness pressed against him. Again he penetrated her, feeling the release that only she could bring. Her head arched back, her breasts pushing into his chest, her body intoxicating him beyond comprehension.

He had sensed that there was an electricity between them from the moment they set eyes on each other. He had come up to Klaw on the pretext that he needed more information to fight the servitude case for Paul, but in reality he just wanted to see her again. They both knew that.

That first evening they had retired to separate bedrooms. For a long time he lay reading, not his usual law reports but a book on lions by George Schaller that Paul had lent him. Then she had come to him, naked and unafraid. He had folded her in his arms and drawn her close. They had made love again and again, and each time was better than the last. He felt he'd found something that had been missing from his life for a long time.

'What are you thinking?' she asked softly.

'That I need you. That if you left me now, I'd be destroyed.'

'Why should I want to leave you?'

'Because my culture is different from yours. Because you're beautiful, and there are a lot of men who are desperate to have you.'

She stroked his brow. 'I've only made love to a few men. I never want to make love to another – just you.'

He closed his eyes and wondered where the emptiness had gone. Every day of his life he had felt that emptiness, and had worked harder and harder to escape it. He closed his hand around hers.

'Charlotte', he said, 'long ago I promised myself that if I ever felt happy, even slightly, I would go back to Israel – just for a year. I want to give something back. Do you understand?'

'Of course,' came the reply, without a moment's hesitation.

'It'll only be a year. Can you wait a year?'

'What are you saying, David?'

'That then I would come back to marry you. I promise.'

She took his hand and examined the fingers. 'I am free to do what I like.'

'Charlotte . . .'

'You can go for a year', she said, 'or even a lifetime. But if you go, I want to go with you.'

He looked into the darkness. 'It's hard there, Charlotte. I don't expect you to have to put up with that.'

'If that's what you want to do, I want to do it too.' She rolled over and knelt astride him.

'Charlotte, I think you're slightly crazy.'

She rested her hands on his stomach. 'No, not crazy. Just very, very happy.'

Paul checked into the Cabarfeidh Hotel in Stornoway, totally exhausted. Tarbert would have been closer to the castle but he guessed that the doctor's security team might well check up on who was staying close to his home.

He glanced down at his watch. It was after five in the afternoon. He picked up the phone and dialled the number of his house in London. The number just rang and rang – he wondered where Sonny was? They'd made an agreement that he'd stay in the house between six and eight every evening, to take calls.

Paul sank down onto the bed in his room and switched on the television. He found the programmes boring, and was just about to switch off when a newsflash caught his attention.

'This morning Iraqi troops sped across the border into Kuwait, moving along the six-lane super-highway towards Kuwait City. Reports say that Iraqi jet-fighters and attack aircraft covered the invading force that is now engaging targets within Kuwait itself.

'An emergency session of the United Nations Security Council drafted Resolution 660 condemning Iraq's invasion of Kuwait and demanding Baghdad's immediate withdrawal.'

Paul switched off the set and lay back on the bed. Suddenly events were taking on a new perspective. Naturally Iraq would be happy about her ability to hold Kuwait, she had a huge army developed during the war with Iran. But he sensed a belligerence in the act of occupation that suggested Iraq was suddenly particularly confident of her military prowess.

*

261

Jessica came round in the casualty ward of the hospital.

'Are you all right, dear?' asked the nurse pleasantly. 'They say you slipped.'

Jessica felt the bruise on the side of her head, and suddenly she remembered exactly what had happened.

'No, I was attacked!' she protested. 'Get me a phone, I want to call the police.'

The two uniformed policemen stood outside the front door of Paul's mews house with Jessica. 'Madam, you're quite sure you're not imagining this?'

'Listen, I saw a man breaking in, and he knocked me out.'

The bigger of the two put his shoulder to the door and it swung open. 'Would you be so kind as to show us around, madam?'

Jessica stepped in and switched on the hall light. 'Oh my God, no!'

She almost fell over the mutilated body. Someone had cut off the man's sex organs and stuffed them in his mouth. She started to cry uncontrollably, gripping the banisters.

The policemen were shocked too, but recovered more quickly. 'All right, madam. Take it easy.'

She got control of herself after a few minutes and heard one of them talking on his radio.

'Yes, that's correct. The house belongs to a Mr Paul Norton.'

He listened for a while, then went up the stairs and closed the door. Then he gestured to the other policeman to follow him so that they could talk in confidence. There was more, talking into the radio: We'd better arrange collection and then an autopsy . . . The woman? Yes, she's still here.'

Jessica watched a delivery van draw up outside. A dark-suited young man moved into view. He swept back a lock of long black hair and came up to her.

'Jessica, please relax,' he said.

She stared at him. 'Who on earth are you?'

'We're calling an ambulance for you,' he said soothingly. 'There's no need to be afraid.'

She looked into his dark eyes and saw nothing. 'What's

going on?' she said desperately 'Where's Paul Norton? Who *are* you?'

He led her back into the house, to the body. 'Do you know this man?'

She averted her eyes. 'He came to stay in my house a few days ago with Paul. I think he was called Sonny but that's all I can remember.'

They walked through to the kitchen together. The dark-haired man sat down on the edge of one of the kitchen units, raised his right knee and held it between his hands, swaying backwards and forwards. He stared at her. 'Are you having an affair with Norton?'

'Mind your own fucking business!'

The man looked at her coldly. 'A savage murder has been committed in this house. You are probably the last person to have seen the murdered man alive. You are also a prime suspect.'

'You really suspect me of mutilating a man in that fashion? Are you out of your mind?'

There was something about this man she didn't trust. He was putting on an act; he wasn't genuine.

'I've been on a film shoot,' she said. 'I have alibis for almost every hour of the day – in fact, for most of that time I'm on film.'

The man nodded. 'I said you were a prime suspect, I didn't say I was going to arrest you.'

'Can I talk to my attorney, please?'

He laughed, but didn't move. Only his mouth was laughing, his eyes were deadly still. 'I wouldn't do that if I were you,' he said. 'Paul Norton's in serious trouble. He's been dealing in classified information.'

'How come you know so much about him?'

'He has a criminal record. He was beaten up, and his house caught fire under mysterious circumstances. I think that's enough to warrant interest, don't you?'

Jessica went across the kitchen and looked into the hall. The body was gone; the hall looked as though it had never been there.

'Don't worry, Jessica, we'll sort this out,' the man said. He got down and walked past her, out of the house. Then he turned back.

'And please don't leave the country without contacting us, We'll probably need you to help us with our investigations.'

Jessica went back to the phone and called the local police. 'I want to report a murder . . .'

Detective-Inspector Nobbs looked around the house again, and then at the beautiful woman who sat opposite him. He could watch her all day – but then he had work to do.

'Look, madam there's no body. No evidence of a murder. You can't expect me to launch an investigation.'

Jessica fidgeted nervously. 'A van came and took the body away. There were two policemen with me in the house, and then a plain-clothes detective arrived . . .'

'Names? If you can give me names, then maybe I can make something of this.'

'Oh, why don't you believe me?'

Detective-Inspector Nobbs raised his eyebrows. 'Listen, love, I'd like to believe you, but there's no proof of what you say. Please understand, I'm sympathetic, but this has every appearance of being a hoax. Wasting police time is a serious offence, you know.'

'How can you be such a bastard?'

'And so is swearing at a police officer.'

Jessica shook her head. She was close to tears. 'I don't know what's going on any longer . . .'

Detective-Inspector Nobbs got up and squeezed her hand. 'Look, love, why don't you rest for a couple of days? Perhaps you'll feel better then. All right?'

When he'd gone, she slumped down onto the settee in a daze. Where in God's name was Paul?

He pulled the knitted cap down over his head and leaned over the bank of sodden grass. The padded green anorak he'd bought in Stornoway protected him from the damp but not so much from the cold. He stared down at the castle.

Dr Torr was no fool. You couldn't see what was going on inside the rooms of this executive fortress. And the sprawling expanse of closely cropped green turf that lay around the walls precluded any possibility of approaching it unnoticed.

On the highest turret, on the right-hand side of the castle, a guard was stationed, armed with a sniper's rifle equipped with a high-powered night-sight. Flanking this guard, at ground level, were two other guards, dressed in Harris tweed, making constant foot patrols. Paul had only spotted the guard in the turret after careful observation. Dr Torr had engineered a rumour that he was running a unique spiritual order within the castle's walls; a guard armed with a sniper's rifle hardly fitted that image, so the man was invisible to all but the expert observer.

Paul noted that the castle had its own emergency generator. As well as the road he'd come on, the fortress was accessible by air and by sea – there was a helicopter landing-strip on the front lawn, and a small harbour on the east side of the castle walls.

Paul rose, and made his way back across the moorland side-stepping several bogs. He was concerned about Sonny. Phone call after phone call to the house had met with no reply. He couldn't understand what had happened – he'd instructed Sonny and Mkhulu to maintain their watch on the Rutland Gate house and report if anything unusual occurred.

He made it back to his hotel in Stornoway after dark, and the moment he was in his hotel room he put a call through to London. The phone was answered on the fortieth ring. It was Jessica.

A wave of apprehension swept over him. 'Jessica, what's wrong?' he asked, hearing her silence when he mentioned Sonny.

He sucked in his breath when he heard how she'd found him. Then she went on to describe the behaviour of the policemen. Paul began to feel uneasy – several vague clicks on the line alerted his suspicions. The phone was probably tapped; he must do what he could to mislead the listeners.

'I'll see you in a minute, darling, at your favourite restaurant,' he said. Then he rang off before Jessica could reply.

Putting the phone down, he pulled off his sodden anorak. He was sweating. Suddenly he no longer felt comfortable. Why were the police acting so strangely? He opened a hard-backed exercise book he'd bought that morning and started detailing his observations.

The style of Sonny's murder had all the hallmarks of a revenge killing – revenge for the bodies at Rutland Gate. After all, Sonny was the one known to Josh – he'd been in the most danger. Paul felt a terrible grief for this new death on his conscience.

He dialled another London number, the number of Jessica's favourite restaurant; they'd eaten together there on a number of occasions. He breathed a sigh of relief as the maître d'hôtel answered the phone.

'Hallo, Marcus. Yes, it's Paul Norton. Look I know this may sound a little strange, but I need to speak to Jessica Potter. Ah, she's in the restaurant. You'll call her? Thanks.'

A few minutes later Jessica's voice was on the line. 'Paul, what's going on?'

'I don't know, but I think I've stumbled on something very important.'

'But why are the British police covering things up? Paul, this is very dangerous – leave it alone.'

He realised the wisdom of what she was saying – but he couldn't leave it alone. Not now. There was something about the whole affair that spoke of a larger and more sinister plot – something that he was determined to unravel.

'Paul, for God's sake, you've been through enough already.'

'Jessica, I want you to do something. I'll give you my phone number here. I want you to take it to a flat in Rutland Gate and give it to Mkhulu. Ask him to call me immediately. If you can't find him at that address, then contact me again. And if anyone else asks you how they can get hold of me, say you haven't got a clue.'

'All right, Paul, but I think you're out of your mind.'

Paul put the phone down, and switched on the television. He wasn't budging from the hotel till he heard from either Jessica or Mkhulu. He ordered dinner in his room.

At nine that evening, three hours later, his phone rang. He heard Mkhulu's voice on the other end of the line.

'My friend, I know that Sonny is dead. I went to the house. And when I found him, I thought it was best to leave his body where it was – we're in enough trouble already.'

At least Mkhulu had handled the situation well. By not reporting Sonny's death, he hadn't implicated himself.

'Did Jessica tell you what happened with the police?'

'Yes, Paul. I think we're in very serious trouble.'

Paul wondered if they were. It seemed as if the British police were very concerned to cover things up. And he had thought the main danger came from the Iraqis.

'Listen, Mkhulu, I contacted a weapons expert before I left London. He said the plans I'd snatched off the Iraqi's desk were for a cannon that could fire satellites into space. But I think it's going to be used to fire nuclear projectiles.'

'You've lost me, Paul.'

'Look, Iraq has just invaded Kuwait. If they have this Super-gun they could drop a nuclear shell on Israel. That would win them the support of the rest of the Arab world.'

'And start World War Three?'

'It's quite possible.'

There was a long silence on the line. Paul was worried about Mkhulu. Sonny was dead, how long would it be before they found Mkhulu?

'Paul, where are you?'

'On the island of Lewis in the Outer Hebrides.'

'What about your film? What about the lions? What about Anne?'

'My film will be made, even if I die. The lions will survive – you, Anne and Johannes will rehabilitate them.'

There was a groan on the other end of the line.

'Mkhulu? What's wrong?'

'When they killed your father, I said to myself, "No more violence, Mkhulu, no more violence." But I am as much a man as you and I see this thing cannot be left alone.'

'I know you're with me, but for the moment I think it would be safer if you returned to Klaw.'

'Paul, just remember, if you need me, wherever you are, I'll be there.'

Paul drove into Stornoway that evening – he felt like a drink. He found a small pub near the harbour, packed to capacity with people of all ages, most of whom had had a lot to drink.

He went up to the bar and ordered a whisky. A tall, lean young woman with a haughty face caught his eye.

'You're a stranger, then?'

'Yes.' He paid for his whisky and turned towards her. 'You live here?'

'I've got no time for the British, why don't you go home.'

A young man sitting near the woman gave Paul the hairy eyeball. Never one to resist a challenge, Paul moved closer to the woman. 'For your information,' he said, 'I'm South African.'

She smiled. 'And you're desperate for a woman?'

'Probably less than you're desperate for a decent man.'

Her face reddened. The young man was up, and latched his right hand round Paul's throat. Paul smiled, and expertly sent the young man flying across the floor with a judo throw. To his surprise the man staggered back to his chair, smiling.

'I respect a man who can give as good as he gets.'

The woman leaned back against the bar counter, her firm breasts pressing against the thin wool jersey she was wearing.

'Can I buy you a whisky?' the young man continued.

'Certainly,' replied Paul, much astonished at the offer.

Another hour, and he was getting on like a house on fire with everyone at the bar, including the young lady, who he found out was called Megan.

Paul dropped a few questions about Dr Torr and got an instant response from a lean, bearded man who hadn't done much the whole evening except prop up the bar and drink.

'Coont!' the bearded man swore aloud, then moved closer to Paul. 'Peter Killick's the name . . .'

They shook hands. Killick seemed to have taken a shine to Paul, much to Megan's annoyance. Paul slipped his arm away from round her waist. He sensed Killick might prove a useful lead.

'You know Dr Torr, then?' he asked.

'In a manner o' speaking. I rewired his bluidy castle and he calls me back every day. It's his focking computers. He says they put him in touch with the universe.'

Paul continued the conversation. He mentioned that he knew a lot about electrical work, taking a professional interest in Killick's problems. 'What's Dr Torr's girlfriend like?' he asked.

'Listen, if ye're so interested, why don't ye come with me tomorrow. I've got work to do there and I need someone skilled in the electrics to help me.'

The pounding on his bedroom door woke him. His head ached, and he was aware of Megan's naked body next to his. Gently he got out of bed, staggered to the door and opened it.

Peter Killick glared at him. 'Come on, man, there's work to be done!'

He glanced at his watch. Shit. It was after seven. 'Look . . .' Paul mumbled.

'Listen, you Sassenach bastard. Drop yer bullshit and get down to me van in five minutes – or I'll cut yer goolies off.'

He dressed quickly. It would only be a day, after all – then he could be away. He kissed Megan and let himself out of the room.

Killick's van banged along the narrow roads, its red trim revealing its former life with the British Post Office.

'Aye, Paul, I know ye were of two minds, but I can't take a man who goes back on his word.'

Peter took the occasional slug from a hip-glask as he drove. Eventually he offered some to Paul who took a large gulp. He felt better as the amber liquid trickled down inside him.

'Aye, lad, there's naught better than a wee dram before work. Especially with Dr Torr. He's a strange creature, that one.'

'What do you mean?'

'Aye, yer'll see for yerself. He and his girlfriend and their strange band. I wonder what they get up to behind closed doors.'

He gripped Paul's arm and pulled him nearer. Paul smelt his whisky-sodden breath.

'There's a legend that people disappear inside o' that place and never reappear. 'T'was the hunting lodge of the MacLeods till a few years back, then along comes the good doctor, who pays a princely sum to change it round. But we don't complain, because on these islands there's little enough work for a man.'

Paul's mind went into overdrive. 'Was it Wayne MacLeod who owned it?'

'Aye, the very same. The long-haired bastard!'

Now what was Wayne MacLeod doing, selling his castle to a

man who designed weapons? It was more than a coincidence, of that Paul was certain.

They narrowly missed a stone wall and Peter concentrated on driving, releasing his grip on Paul's arm.

'They're a suspicious lot,' he went on. 'I'll say ye're my brother from the mainland. Say ye've been at sea for many a year, which accounts for yer strange accent.

Paul nodded. He was having second thoughts about the wisdom of accompanying the drunken Scotsman. He wondered if they'd even make the castle alive if their present rate of progress was anything to go by.

The van rattled its way along the A859 and then swung off to the right down the B887, taking the road to Hushinish. Paul took another swig from the hip-flask as they narrowly missed going over the edge of the hill.

The van slipped and clawed its way along the road to the castle. Several times Paul felt like wrenching the wheel over to avoid disaster, but felt his spirits rising as the castle walls approached.

The same guard in the Harris tweed jacket who'd stopped him two days before came up to Killick's window as he pulled up at the gate. Paul picked up a newspaper from the floor of the van and buried his nose in it.

'Who's the man with you?'

'Me brother. He's come to help.'

The man waved them through. They went down the narrow, winding tarmac road and parked on the gravel drive in front of the castle.

Paul got out and walked up to the sea wall. He looked across to the left and saw the river running over the rocks and down into the loch. Miniature cannons pointed out towards the open sea through gaps in the sea wall.

'Come on, ye're not a bluidy tourist!'

Paul helped Peter unload his equipment and they trudged across to the large white front doors. Killick banged his tool box against them chipping off some paint in the process. 'Open up, coonts!' he yelled. But he was immediately silent as the bolts slid back and the door opened. A lean, blond man in a white laboratory coat stared at Killick with distaste.

'Dr Torr said that if you'd been drinking, I wasn't to let you in. Drinking destroys the soul as well as the mind,' he said in a precise English voice.

Killick spat on the flagstones, and the young man took a step back. 'Aye, lad, I was drinking last night. But today I'm sober.'

'And your assistant?'

'He's not the drinking kind.'

Paul looked up and saw a man on the upper battlements. Hanging from his shoulder was a Heckler and Koch HK33 light assault rifle, fitted with a Litton night-sight. The man vanished in a second. Paul guessed he was not for the general public to see.

'This is my brother, Ian Killick, who's been ten years at sea and none the better for it.'

The young man ran his eyes over Paul with distaste, and sniffed. 'I suspect he smokes. Does he know that smoking is not permitted inside the castle?'

Paul nodded in acknowledgement. Then he followed the young man and Killick through the hall. He immediately understood why Dr Torr had chosen the castle as his base – it was quiet and isolated, the ideal environment in which to write a book or design a weapon.

Dr Torr stepped into the hall without warning.

'Killick, I'm not impressed with your workmanship. As well as the other things two of the lights in the main study have failed – I want them fixed, and fixed properly.'

'Very good, sir. It's the damp that causes the problems.'

'The damp in your whisky-sodden brain, no doubt. I have had enough of your excuses. You will not be paid till everything works – do you understand?'

'Very good, sir.'

They were shown into a large room which Paul guessed was the refectory. Several of the neon lights above were flickering continuously. An extension ladder was brought, and while Paul held it steady, Killick worked on the light units. It was a miracle he didn't fall off.

The next job was a lot more difficult. They trudged up the carpeted main staircase and then out onto a balcony that led up to the battlements. Killick wrapped a rope round one of the stone buttresses and handed a climbing-harness to Paul.

'Ye know how to rappel?'

Paul nodded.

'Well, let yourself down the wall, replace the broken bulb in the spotlight, and then go down to the ground.'

Now Paul discovered why he'd been brought along. There was no way, in his drunken state, that Killick could have balanced against the wall and changed the light. The wind blew Paul backwards and forwards as he slipped down the stone wall, ignoring the ground far below him.

He stopped by the first window he came to and looked in. The room was filled with computer terminals. He saw several operators at work on designs up on the screens. Dr Torr was definitely not the religious guru he claimed to be to the islanders. These might be his disciples, but the only thing they worshipped was weapon design.

'What the fock are yer doing?' Killick cried from above.

Paul looked up, smiled, and let himself down to the spotlight. Changing the bulb was an uncomplicated business and he was down on the ground five minutes later. He walked back round to the front door and was let in by the young man.

'You know which way to go?'

Paul smiled, and walked back towards the staircase that led to the battlements. Taking care that he wasn't being followed, he slipped down a side-passage and opened the first door he came to. It was a study, and there were air tickets lying on the table. He quickly looked at the destination. Windhoek in Namibia – the flight was booked for two weeks time. The tickets were for Dr Torr and Dr Fassbinder.

He opened the first drawer of the desk and saw a buff folder filled with papers.

He heard steps in the passage, and froze. He stuffed the folder into his jacket, then he closed the drawer, moved to the light switch and unscrewed the cover. Dr Torr walked in.

'What the hell are you doing here?'

'Just checking.'

'Didn't Killick tell you this area is out of bounds?'

Paul managed a foolish grin.

'Get out of here immediately!' Dr Torr said grimly.

'But what about the light-switch cover?'

'Oh, put it on.'

Paul worked slowly as the doctor looked on. His eyes caught piles of blueprints lying on the floor, similar to the ones he had stolen from the Iraqi's house.

He smelt an exotic fragrance, and Dr Fassbinder walked into the room.

'What is this man doing here?'

'He's Killick's brother.'

'I don't want him here. I want to see his papers.'

Paul felt uncomfortable. He sensed these two wouldn't lose a moment's sleep if he had to be sacrificed to maintain secrecy. He tightened the fitting-screw on the light switch and moved out into the passage, walking quickly back to the steps that led up to the battlements.

'Where've you been?' Killick asked gruffly.

'I lost my way.'

'Tell me, laddie, can ye tie yer shoelaces in the morning without an instruction manual?'

This joke seemed to amuse Killick, who chuckled on for several minutes before recovering himself. 'All right, there's one more outside light to fix.'

They walked over to the other side of the battlements and Killick pointed to the back chimney. Paul saw a spotlight high on the side of it. He wondered how they would reach it. Then Killick pointed to the narrow ridge that ran along the top of the two slanting roofs.

'Off you go, lad. It's simple enough – like walking the tightrope.'

Paul moved out onto the lead strip that couldn't have been more than a couple of inches wide. If he slipped off, he'd plummet down the side of the roof and go straight over the edge.

'OK, don't forget a bulb and a screwdriver. At the base of the chimney ye'll find there are wire rungs built into the wall. You climb those up to the light.'

Paul looked uncertainly upwards, and Killick slapped him hard on the back. 'Why d'ye think I needed an assistant?'

Paul moved forward, slowly and surely, towards the ladder.

Further across the roof he was buffeted by the wind, and was conscious of the terrifying drop below. Almost at the end of the ridge, he saw the metal rungs of the ladder – heavily rusted loops of metal butted into the stone wall. He moved off the roof and felt the rusted metal of one rung flaking off in his hands. Now, flattened against the stone wall, he worked his way quickly towards the light. He unscrewed the glass cover and slid it back. Then his hand unscrewed the light bulb, let it drop, and screwed in the replacement.

He looked across to see Killick talking to Dr Torr. They both looked up at him. He guessed they were discussing his venture into the forbidden area. Killick would be telling the doctor that he didn't tell Paul to fix the light switch.

Paul moved quickly down to the ladder. As he touched the top of the roof, his foot slid away. He heard Killick laughing. He swung backwards and forwards, his feet scrabbling against the roof tiles for a grip.

Eventually he made it, and walked quickly along the ridge of the roof. Only when his feet touched the stone surface of the battlements did he breathe easily again. He didn't say anything to Killick. He waited till they were back at the van, then he slammed his fist into Killick's stomach.

The Scotsman slumped forward, and Paul grabbed his hair and slammed his face hard into the bonnet of the van.

'You bastard, I nearly killed myself!'

Killick staggered back, then aimed a right hook at Paul's head. Paul feinted, swept his right foot across and hit Killick just beneath the knees. The Scotsman teetered over, and Paul hammered in two more blows to his skull, knocking him out cold. He was tired of being pushed around, tired of fighting fair.

He dragged Killick's unconscious body into the back of the van, and drove slowly back to Stornoway.

'You Sassenach bastard!' he heard from the back as he turned into the town.

'You weren't at the top of that chimney, Killick. I didn't find it funny.

Stopping outside his hotel, he let the Scotsman out of the back, expecting another fight. Instead Killick extended his hand.

'No hard feelings, lad, you did a good job.' They shook hands, then Killick paid Paul for his day's work.

'Ye'd work with me again?' he said.

'No games, though.'

'No games.'

Paul made his way up to his room. He knew he'd better get away before Dr Torr made any investigations; he sensed Torr wouldn't have bought Killick's story about his being his brother. He quickly packed and checked out. He would sleep in his car next to Stornoway harbour – but he told the receptionist that he was going to stay with a friend who lived on Harris.

He went out into the car park. In the shadows, he saw Killick's van. He walked over – and found Killick slumped over the steering-wheel. Paul opened the door and shook his shoulder roughly.

'Wake up. It's time you went home.'

'No, I don't feel like it,' Killick muttered, reeking of whisky.

Paul sensed the man was in a pretty bad way. He could kill himself, driving home drunk in the darkness.

'Come on,' he said, 'I'll drive you.'

Killick made no reply, only fired the engine.

'All right,' Paul said, 'you drive, but just let me put my bag in the back and I'll go with you.'

Paul picked up the haversack he'd bought in town, which he'd packed with the few clothes he'd acquired, and his notebooks, and tossed it in the back. He jumped into the passenger seat and Killick accelerated off, heading back to Tarbert.

'Where do you live?' Paul shouted above the din of the engine.

'Govig Bay.'

Paul slipped the ordnance survey map he'd purchased out of his jacket, switched on the interior light of the van and scanned the map to find Govig Bay. Killick angrily switched off the light. 'Listen, you silly coont, it's past the castle.'

Paul wondered if that meant Killick had gone miles out of his way to pick him up that morning. But he guessed the Scotsman had probably slept in his van in Stornoway the previous night.

Killick produced his hip-flask. Paul tore it out of his hands and tossed it out of the window.

'You bastard!'

'You've had enough to drink, any more will kill you.'

Killick growled, and went on driving.

Much later they approached the castle once again. Paul touched Killick on the shoulder. 'Mind if I hide in the back?'

Killick eyed him strangely. 'No – just climb over the seat and bury yourself under me tools.'

A little while later Paul heard Killick pulling up at the entrance to the castle grounds. To his relief, the guard let him through without incident.

'You can come out now,' Killick shouted.

Paul scrambled forward and looked through the windscreen at the narrow road lit by the faint headlights of the van. After a couple of miles Killick took the left turn to Govig.

'You were born here?' Paul asked.

'Aye, and I'll die here.'

The road wound its way down across a tiny harbour swept by high winds. Killick pulled up next to a large caravan that had been cemented into the rock face.

'Home.'

When Paul went inside, he expected to see chaos. Instead the place was a picture of neatness and order. He went over to the brick fireplace that dominated the back of the caravan's lounge. Along the top of it were pictures of Killick in climbing gear, on the summits of different mountains.

'Why didn't you fix that light, you're obviously a good climber?'

'I was testing ye. I took ye for a man of courage – I saw the way ye handled Megan in the bar. There's not many that get the better of her.'

'Why don't you?'

Killick suddenly seemed entirely sober. 'I wanted to see what you were made of. Megan's my daughter.'

Paul stared at him, trying to guess his age.

'I'm sixty, lad,' Killick said. 'On this island, if ye survive yer youth ye live to be a hundred or more.'

He chucked some peat into the hearth and set light to the papers he'd crumpled beneath it. A pleasant smell filled the room. Paul leaned back in one of the easy-chairs. Maybe he'd been over-reacting, he thought. He could have spent the night in a comfortable bed.

He woke the next morning to the sound of the wind drumming against the sides of the caravan and rain lashing the windows. Killick came through from the kitchen with a mug of coffee.

'Here, this'll warm ye up.'

Paul took the mug gratefully and gulped down some of the hot coffee.

'Who are ye, Mr Norton?' Killick said quietly.

Paul knew instinctively that he could trust this man. He explained to Killick what he did for a living.

'Aye, now I remember seeing ye documentary on Rhodesia. Ye've got nerve all right. So, ye think there's something going on at the castle?'

Paul realised that Killick could be a useful ally. He explained to the Scotsman Dr Torr's real business.

When he had finished, Killick nodded. 'It makes sense. Ye see, I'm just an electrician, and I do a good job on the islands. But that Doctor Torr's got all these bluidy computers and they need constant power – so he blames me for fluctuations in the supply. I wondered what he used them for. MacLeod's forever visiting him, and I wouldn't put anything past that bastard.'

Paul looked at his watch. 'I want to get off the island today.'

'No problem, I'll take ye back to Stornoway. And there's something else . . . Late last night they phoned, looking for ye. I said I didn't know where ye were – ye'd gone out drinking in Stornoway.'

'Who phoned?'

'Security – from the castle.'

Paul realised he'd been a fool. He shouldn't have booked into the hotel in his own name: when they checked things out, Torr's men would put two and two together very quickly – they'd soon realise that he and Killick's brother were one and the same.

'Look, I have to get off this island fast.'

'All right, let's go.'

When they got to the hotel in Stornoway, Paul's car had disappeared. He didn't go to reception to ask about it, he just knew he had to get the hell out of the place before something happened to him.

Killick drove him down a side-road and pulled over. 'If ye catch the ferry or the plane, they'll get ye. This place is just too small for ye to get out unnoticed on regular transport. Now, a friend of mine's got a trawler – I'm sure he'd drop ye on the mainland.'

Paul nodded. Under the circumstances, this was his only option.

Fahad was sweating. He hardly used to sweat at all, but often now his shirt would be soiled by the middle of the day and he'd have to shower and change. The Americans were putting the pressure on Iraq, that was for sure. And it looked as though they'd get quite a few of the Arab states on their side. Fahad didn't want that, nor did President Hussein.

Kuwait was Iraq's by right. And after the Crown Prince's insulting comments, President Hussein had had no choice but to invade. In fact, as far as Fahad was concerned, Iraq had been astonishingly conciliatory in its discussion of a restructuring of the terms of its debt to Kuwait. Now they had no obligation to pay back the money they owed the Kuwaitis. However, the Americans were playing tactical games.

Fahad wanted to buy time. Iraq's bacteriological, chemical and nuclear weapons were still under development. And he knew that the testing programme for the Supergun could not be rushed – Dr Torr had explained the dangers of speeding up the development process.

Yes, he remembered only too well the problem they'd had with rushing things – like using their chemical weapons before they had properly tested them. They had fired mustard gas on an Iranian unit based on a mountain top. Then, when they climbed the mountain in order to force the Iranians off, they themselves had been showered by their own still settling gas. They had had to back off in a desperate retreat.

Fahad felt bitter. He remembered the war with Iran – a war the Americans had encouraged them to fight. It had cost over five hundred billion dollars, leaving Iraq with a debt one and half times its gross national product.

Fahad did not believe the Americans would ultimately go to war – they were seeking to put pressure on Iraq via the diplomatic route, making alliances with the other Arab states. And if the Americans did choose to strike, they would need to mobilise a huge fighting force even to stand a chance of winning.

Iraq was geared for war, with the fourth largest army in the world – one and a half million troops. They were stronger than almost any other nation in the Middle East, only Israel came close on levels of fighter-aircraft and tanks.

Israel was the old enemy. Fahad knew his strategy must be to focus the Arab nations on the destruction of Israel, but in order to do that he had to show them that Iraq had the power to devastate Israel. After the experience of the Six Day war, the Arab nations were wary of engaging the ferocious Israelis. But Fahad knew that Syria in particular would like to regain the Golan Heights, lost to Israel in the war.

He had to have the Supergun by the end of the year. It would shift the balance of power in Iraq's favour and it would demonstrate to the Arab states that Iraq did have the power to take on the West. And once that feeling of confidence grew, he would not have to encourage it – the promise of the higher oil prices that a united Arab coalition could force on the rest of the world would be too attractive to resist.

The Supergun would give Iraq the vital element of surprise. It would stun the West into paralysis, and allow Iraq to accelerate its other weapons development programmes.

In the end, it was all a matter of timing.

The test firing was to be in two weeks time. Then Fahad would know that Iraq finally had the power to devastate the Israelis.

Sir Donald Morgan took the files back and placed them in the safe behind his desk.

'Interesting, Chuck?'

His American counterpart leaned back in his chair, a giant of a man with a harsh crew-cut, a bullish face and dull grey eyes.

'You Brits have always had a way with words, Donald. We've had our own particular problems, but I don't believe it's possible to make this Supergun. I'm sorry, Donald, but in my experience

279

plans like this are disinformation. Anyway, where would a weapon like that be built, and who would design it?'

'The Iraqis can do it – they've been importing the parts.'

'Give me proof. Show me evidence of a successful test-firing. Listen, Donald, if we move in on this thing and it comes out, it'll blow our relationship with the other Arab states out of the water. We can't be seen to be favouring the Israelis, and by interfering with Iraq's ability to buy a satellite-launching device we'd be doing just that. Right now, all we're insisting on is recognition for Kuwait's independence – that the Iraqis withdraw their forces.'

Sir Donald leaned forward, linking his hands together and resting his chin on them. 'You'd like us to handle it? We've been monitoring the situation. Certain of our operatives have positions in the companies that have been supplying Iraq.' He rose, took out another file and handed it to Chuck, who read through it carefully.

'Boy, you guys have certainly made a lot of money out of Iraq. But I still think the Supergun is a joke. We've had dealings with Dr Torr, and in our opinion he's good at spending other people's money and little else.'

Chuck reread the last pages of the intelligence report. 'Listen,' he said, 'this bastard Norton is bad news. He caused a lot of trouble for us in Vietnam. He has left-wing tendencies, he's hot-headed. Combat newscameramen like him are dangerous – they think they're fighting their own war. Then suddenly you've got classified information on the nation's television screens and it all becomes embarrassing, very embarrassing.'

Sir Donald leaned back in his chair, keeping his hands together and his eyes on his colleague. He knew he'd said enough. There was more, but the American wasn't being co-operative. Nor would he have been, he realised, in the same position. He respected Chuck Conroy, he was one of the best.

'Donald, if you guys handle this and it goes wrong, we can always take the opposite side. And if it goes right, then we can claim a little of the credit. You and I know that your people have been supplying military technology to Iraq – hell, you've even made the components for this Supergun. It could be very,

very embarrassing. I'm sorry, but I really don't want to get involved.'

Sir Donald reddened. 'You bastard!'

Chuck shook his head. 'We're playing for big stakes. Our relationship with the Russian President's healthy at the moment, so we can't afford to take chances. None of us wants war, but if it happens, we want to stay squeaky clean. We're wary of the Middle East. Another Vietnam is something that isn't going to happen.'

'I think that's a very negative viewpoint.'

'Well, negative or not, I'm going to leave the whole matter alone.'

'What? Are you crazy?'

'I don't see that there's any benefit in it for us. What do you want?'

'If it turns nasty, if that Supergun does turn out to be more than a satellite launching-system, then I want a promise of assistance.'

Chuck closed his eyes for a few moments. Then he looked up. 'I promise, if you get into trouble I'll do everything I can to get you and your guys out of it.'

Sir Donald showed Chuck Conroy to the door and then walked back to his rocking-chair. He sat down and lit up his pipe. Rocking himself backwards and forwards, he turned the problem over in his mind. He did all of his thinking in this chair.

Unlike many others, he respected President Saddam Hussein as a political strategist. Iraq was heavily in debt after fighting a war against Iran that the CIA had probably encouraged him to start. Saddam's missile capability was weak; his missiles were Soviet Scuds with a limited range. Saddam had now modified his Scuds so that they could reach Israel, creating two variants – the Al-Hussein and the Al-Abbas. The problem was that both got their extended range by reducing the warhead and increasing the fuel.

There was also the little-publicised Condor 2 project – Iraq had joined forces with Argentina and Egypt to develop a long-range ballistic missile. But Condor 2 was probably taking a long time to get off the ground.

Patience was now required. Sir Donald had everything under

control. He would just keep his eyes open and wait to see if anything happened. Anyway, he was quite sure that Paul Norton would produce fireworks – sooner or later.

The helicopter touched down on the landing-strip in front of Amhuinnsuidhe Castle and Wayne MacLeod stepped out, his mane of silver hair blowing in the wind. He breathed in, and smoothed down his tweed jacket. He would enjoy a weekend's salmon fishing, do some business with the local council, and most of important of all, go through the final details of the Supergun programme with Dr Torr.

He was greeted warmly by Dr Fassbinder, who showed him in through the front entrance. He was glad to see, from the sentries on duty, that security was being maintained at a high level.

'Vance is at work on another design,' Maria Fassbinder said. 'You know how he hates to be interrupted . . .'

MacLeod could accept Dr Torr's eccentricities, what mattered was that his work was outstanding. He followed Dr Fassbinder into one of the reception rooms and was pleased to see that all the work had been displayed for inspection in anticipation of his arrival.

'I know you'd rather be alone than have someone looking over your shoulder.'

'Thank you, Maria.'

He waited till she had closed the door, then began his inspection . . .

After an hour, MacLeod turned to the final designs with satisfaction. Dr Torr's satellite launching shell was a work of genius. The testing, Wayne was certain, would be revelationary; Dr Torr had designed and developed many different weapons over the years, but nothing in this league. This was the ultimate military product – no other arms dealer in the world could offer his clients such unprecedented fire-power. Naturally, Dr Torr was unaware of their true plans for the Supergun: it was Dr Fassbinder who was Fahad's agent, who would complete the final design of the nuclear shells.

Manufacture of the weapon had been complicated. Over the years MacLeod had acquired control of armaments companies throughout Europe. Ownership was achieved through nominees and different holding companies, carefully constructed to disguise MacLeod's own majority interest. Most of the companies already did covert work for their respective governments, which meant that their operations were protected by security legislation. In the West Midlands MacLeod controlled two operations that formed the nucleus of the Supergun project – Ron Winters Ltd and Chesterfield Forgemasters. The products of both these companies were protected by the British official secrets act.

Early that January, Forgemasters had turned out sixteen barrels, 39 ms long with an interior diameter of 76 cms. Eight of these had then been transported by road through Europe to Jordan, where they had been taken over the border into Iraq. The other eight had been transported by boat to Windhoek in Namibia. In both cases, the cargo in transit was described as 'high-pressure piping'.

Meanwhile, at Ron Winters' Halesowen factory outside Birmingham, the breech for the weapon was manufactured, along with the special 'collars' designed to link the sections of the gigantic barrel together. These collars were part of the genius of the design; they allowed for a smaller initial breech charge, then accelerated the flight of the shell up the barrel with supplementary charges activated by capacitance detonators.

Ron Winters had also delivered a separate shipment, Project 569 – a consignment of seventy-five forged barrels to Iraq. These were for the manufacture of another of Dr Torr's designs, a mobile artillery piece capable of lobbing small 52-kilogram shells over an incredible 750-kilometre range.

In Belgium, another covert division of the MacLeod Group, BRG, had manufactured a special liquid propellant that would be used to fire the shell from the Supergun. Consignments of this had also been shipped to Namibia and Iraq.

In Coventry, Winston Developments, yet another company under his control, specialised in the manufacture of shells and missile fins. They had already exported numerous computer-controlled lathes to Iraq for supposedly non-military applications, and were currently engaged in training Iraqi technicians at their factory. In reality, Winston was assisting Iraq in developing its own weapons industry, and had enabled the country to produce its own shells and missile fins. It was a neat arrangement, complementing MacLeod's other weapons sales to Iraq.

Wayne MacLeod stared out of the window at the waters of Loch Leosavay. Though Fahad had mentioned that he could produce the correct material for the nuclear warhead inside Iraq, MacLeod was sceptical. Not that it really mattered, because MacLeod had his own source of nuclear material suitable for constructing a warhead, and he knew that in the end Fahad would have to buy it from him. As Dr Torr had said, quality was non-negotiable. And Fahad couldn't afford to take risks – his first strike against the Israelis had to be totally effective.

The final assembled Supergun would be ready for testing in two weeks' time, as would Project 569. Fahad would be present at the firing in Namibia, and MacLeod looked forward to upping the price once the effectiveness of the weaponry had been demonstrated. He knew he could ask whatever sum he chose: the value of the Supergun to Iraq in the current situation was almost infinite.

Hyde MacLeod sat in his office, brooding. He felt terribly frustrated. True, he had been lucky to get off with a suspended sentence on appeal, but it had also prevented him from taking his revenge on Norton. If anything happened to Norton's lions, he would be suspected. And because of all the negative publicity, the legal action to gain control of Klaw was dragging in the courts. The Botswanans were clearly in favour of Paul Norton's keeping his reserve – the lion was Botswana's national symbol and they liked the positive publicity generated by Norton's rehabilitation work.

He heard shouting outside, and pushed the intercom. 'Ursula, who's making that racket?'

'Sir, it's Mr Van der Spuy. He wants to see you, urgently.'

'I'm busy at the moment.'

But he smiled when he heard who it was. He'd been trying to get Van der Spuy for a long time.

On the wall of Hyde's office was a large map of the Tuli Block. He now controlled all of it, apart from two farms – one belonging to Paul Norton and the other to Willie van der Spuy.

Hyde got up and went to his private bathroom. He groomed

himself and applied a little cologne. It was important to appear totally unruffled in the face of hot-headed behaviour. He was going to enjoy himself; Willie van der Spuy was easy meat.

He strode back into his office and sounded the intercom. 'Send him through.'

'Very good, Mr MacLeod,' Ursula purred. Hyde could hear Van der Spuy's shouts in the background, and Charles Fox's laughter.

Van der Spuy burst through the door, his bush-shirt soaked with sweat. His brown eyes darted round the room to find Hyde MacLeod lying back in his chair with his feet on his desk.

'Yes?' Hyde said tiredly.

'You've got to help me!'

Hyde belched loudly. 'Yes?'

'I've got this forty-five-year-old woman. She's in a terrible condition. We were going through a donga on a game-viewing drive when she was thrown forward against the roll-bar. Her face is smashed in. I need to use your runway to bring in an emergency rescue service – you've got the only tarred runway.'

'You're asking me if you can use my airstrip?' Hyde hated Van der Spuy. 'You're asking me to bolster up your piddling little outfit? You shouldn't bring in guests if you can't afford to look after them.'

'You bastard!' said Willie, charging forward.

Hyde pushed a button under his desk and two black rangers burst into the room, firmly gripping Willie's arms. Then Hyde opened the top drawer of his desk and pushed a neatly typed agreement over the leather-tooled top.

'Of course I'd like to help,' he said, grinning. 'I have a helicopter here with full medical facilities on board. But naturally, I expect your cooperation. Just sign this agreement and your lady will be well cared for.'

Willie tried to break loose but the men held him firmly. 'What agreement?' he said.

'Let's just say that you've wisely agreed to sell your farm at a market-related price. Really, I'd hate to see the liability suit against you if the woman dies . . .'

'Every guest signs a disclaimer.'

Hyde leaned back and roared with laughter. 'Ah, that'll look good in the press, won't it. Willie van der Spuy invites his guests to sign away their lives.'

'Fuck you!'

'No, my friend,' Hyde said very coolly, 'fuck you. Sign, or the lady dies, and with her your reserve.'

Willie felt the grip on his arms lessen and shook himself free. Hyde MacLeod's aides were well trained, they knew when their boss had his victim by the balls.

There was a faint tap at the door. 'Come in,' Hyde drawled, looking at his nails.

In burst Willie's wife, Teresa, as white as a sheet.

'What's wrong?' Willie asked desperately.

'She's blacked out! For God's sake, she's dying!' She turned to Hyde. 'You've got to let us use your helicopter!'

'Oh yes, of course, Teresa, but your husband's refusing to co-operate.'

'What?'

'He wants us to sign away the bloody farm,' Willie sobbed.

'Do it,' Teresa commanded, staring hard at Hyde MacLeod.

Willie staggered across to the table and quickly scrawled his name along the bottom of the agreement. Then he grabbed Teresa and made to leave.

'Not so fast,' said Hyde, 'you two are co-owners. The agreement isn't binding unless Teresa signs as well.'

She turned round, holding back the tears, and he grinned at her. 'You didn't think I'd make such a basic mistake, did you, my dear?'

She signed quickly, then turned on her heel.

Hyde leaned back in his chair. He heard the chopper start and then fly overhead. Life was full of opportunities, it was just a question of exploiting them.

He got up and walked to the window. Willie van der Spuy was slumped over the wheel of his Land Rover, Teresa leaning on his shoulder. The man was clearly broken.

There was a cough behind him and he looked up. Charles had come into the office.

'Well done, Charlie.'

'Thanks. They walked right into it. I'd been following them on trail for the last five days. There were leopard cubs in the bush on the other side of the donga, so I just deepened the donga slightly and made the downward slope a little muddier. It was like giving candy to a baby, they just went right in. You should have seen the way that woman smacked the roll-bar – I could hear her bones splintering.'

Hyde went back behind his desk and picked up the agreement.

'They have to be out in four weeks. I'll screw them down on the price and schedule the purchase payments over a twenty-year period. They won't be able to meet their overdraft commitments, which will force them to liquidate – then we'll bail them out, picking up all their equipment for next to nothing.'

Charles looked out of the window at Willie van der Spuy holding Teresa in a desperate embrace.

'Pitiful, isn't it?'

'Pity is for suckers. Go out and tell them to get off my property. I don't enjoy the company of losers.'

Charlie's laughter echoed around the room as he made for the door. Hyde had certainly come back on top form.

Peter Killick roared round the corner and slammed on his brakes. The road was full of sheep. He pressed his hand on the horn, then heard a tap on his window. He turned and looked into the twin barrels of a sawn-off shotgun.

'Out of the van, Killick,' ordered the bearded man holding the shotgun.

Peter opened the door and stepped out. The man handed him a bottle of whisky. 'Take a drink,' he ordered.

'I'd rather not join ye.'

The man whipped the shotgun round and expertly rammed the butt into Peter's gut. 'Drink, bastard!'

Peter coughed, throwing up some blood. His gut was on fire with pain – another blow like that might finish him. He clutched at the bottle, unscrewed the cap and took a drink.

'That's a good laddie. The whole bottle, if you'll oblige.'

Peter felt his head spinning as he drank.

'Get in the seat!' came the order.

He fell into the driver's seat, scarcely able to focus on the road in front. The butt of the shotgun came up and smashed into his right ear. 'Now, where's that bastard who came with you the other day?'

'Who?'

Without warning the man pulled out another bottle of whisky and smashed it across the front of Peter's face, breaking his nose and the bottle. The stench of whisky filled the cab. Peter was sobbing now.

'I don't know where he went,' he gasped. 'I met him in the pub.'

'Just as I thought.' The man laughed, leaned across him and released the handbrake. 'On your way, Killick.'

He pushed the van forward and it rolled towards the next corner, with Peter slumped over the wheel, groaning.

The van ran off the edge of the road and soared into the air, then smashed and tumbled its way down the mountainside.

Later the bearded man walked slowly down and found Killick's unconscious, bloody body lying against a stack of peat. Miraculously, Killick was still alive. The man put down his shotgun, gripped the collar of Killick's jacket and shoved him head first into a nearby burn, watching the bubbles burst from his mouth as he slowly drowned. Then he backed away and contemplated the waters of the loch.

He doffed his cap as he saw the laird looking down from the road above.

'A terrible accident, Mr MacLeod.'

'Aye, and another unsightly wreck on the mountainside.'

Anne squeezed Paul close to her and closed her eyes. He had come all this way specially to see her, to tell her he loved her. She knew now that she could not stand being without him.

She'd hardly been able to contain her excitement when she saw his plane coming in to land. She'd driven out to the sand strip in trepidation, to find him standing next to the plane with a bunch of red roses.

He'd kissed her softly, then pushed her down onto the sand, tearing off her dress as she giggled like a young girl, overcome by the electricity of the moment. His hands had caressed her buttocks and she'd sighed, arching her head backwards, then leaning forwards and undressing him. He'd rolled her over, cupping his hands under her breasts. Then he'd teased her, holding back, letting her excitement mount.

Then, when she could stand it no longer, he'd covered her, forcing himself into her wetness as she screamed out in an animal passion. His body had convulsed, pushing her across the sand so that her elbows burned.

She caught sight of his eyes opening.

In one deft movement she slipped away from him, rolled over again and began caressing him with her mouth. She felt her body seething with desire, out of control. She moved upwards and locked her mouth over his in a long-drawn-out kiss.

He thrust inside her and the waves of passion burst. Her hands floated across his body.

'Don't stop! Paul! Oh God, don't stop!'

She pushed her body up against his, her nails clawing into his back, raking it bloody. She could not live without him. There was no other man on earth who could make her feel like this.

Then she felt him explode inside her again and drew him tightly to her.

'Oh Paul, don't go. Please don't go.'

She awoke the next morning, the strains of a Miles Davis album echoing around the bedroom. Rain spattered against the dry wood of the deck and the sky outside was overcast. The place where Paul had lain next to her was still warm and she pushed her face into the masculine smell of his pillow.

She knew a man like Paul Norton did not like to be controlled. She guessed that the other wife had resented his independence. But she envied that wife for the child she had borne him; she knew how attached Paul was to Charlotte.

In the last months, living and working with the lions, she had gained a fresh understanding of life. At first she fought the primitive instincts that began to take hold of her, but then she began to enjoy giving in to them.

He came through into the room, naked, carrying two mugs of coffee, the overcast sky visible through the window behind him, the smell of the dawn, of Africa, in the air.

'Paul, thank you for coming back . . .'

289

His eyes crinkled up and he smiled. 'You make me sound like a chauvinist.'

'You are a chauvinist. A divine chauvinist.'

He stared out at the bush. He loved the smell of the earth in Africa when the rain had just fallen. Then he felt sad. He thought of Sonny – someone he'd known such a short time and had wanted to know better.

He'd woken before dawn and joined Mkhulu beneath Bush Camp, spending time with the cubs. They'd discussed the business side of running the reserve. Mkhulu had worked hard at getting the operation running – there were already paying guests staying in Rock Lodge. He was glad he'd told Mkhulu to come back to Klaw – in London he would have been in terrible danger.

'Paul, don't think about it. All right?' she said softly, knowing instinctively what he was thinking about, brushing her hand against his cheek.

'Perhaps I should have stayed in Africa?'

'Then you'd have found something dangerous to occupy you here. You have a nose for trouble.'

He looked down and saw the book next to her bed. It was a book about Vietnam, about him, written by a journalist who'd been a good friend – a journalist who'd disappeared in Colombia, following a lead on the drug wars.

'You've been reading . . .'

She stared into his eyes. 'I thought you were against the Vietnam war.'

'I was, in a way.'

'Your films don't show that, darling. That picture of you, on the rooftop outside Saigon, watching the evacuation. You looked sad.'

He stared again at the window. He'd never talked about it with Helen, never really discussed it with a woman before. It was a part of his life he kept to himself.

'You must understand, I was appalled by the killing,' he said without emotion. It was the copybook reply he'd always used when someone got a little too close to the truth.

'You went there when you were twenty, after three years with the South African Reconnaissance Commando. And you only left that because of the court-martial. You fought in Vietnam as a mercenary – the camera work only started later . . .'

His face tensed up.

'Paul, don't hide from me.'

'How did you find out?'

'David told me . . . He found out about it while he was working on the appeal.' She kissed him on the forehead. 'You worked in Vietnam for a long time. And you didn't see much of Helen, especially after Charlotte was born.'

'She didn't understand . . .'

'Understand, Paul? I'm surprised she didn't drop you years before.'

He put his coffee cup down heavily on the bedside table. 'That's unfair . . .'

Anne leaned back on the pillows and stared at him. He had to admit she looked gorgeous, even if she was angry.

'What gives you the right to demand loyalty from a woman, while you do as you please?' she said.

He gripped her arm hard.

'Paul, you're hurting me.'

He pulled her back on the bed, fighting her.

'You're hurting me, you bastard!'

'So don't you like the real me?' he said fiercely. 'Don't you bloody understand, it's a side of me you don't want to see.'

She stared at him, her green eyes flashing. 'You've worked with lions, Paul, you'd think you'd have learned something from them. It's the lioness that always does the killing. I'm not afraid of killing. I want to know what you're thinking, what you're doing.'

He let her go, staring at the way he'd bruised her wrists. Now she was crying.

'What do you think I've felt like?' she cried. 'You're getting involved in something – I can feel you slipping away, just as she must have felt you slipping away. No wonder she had affairs – sitting around all day, wondering if you were going to come back in a body-bag.'

He got up. 'I don't want to hear any more of this, I'm going out.'

Anne leapt off the bed, turned the key in the lock, then tossed it out of the window. 'You're not going anywhere.'

He sat down on the bed, surprised at the force of her feelings.

'You are going to talk to me, Paul Norton. I want to know about those years in Vietnam. I guessed you were a soldier – not just a cameraman.'

He lay down against the pillows and she lay next to him. He stroked her head. 'I was in love with Vietnam,' he said. 'I didn't want it to end.'

'But what took you there?'

'I'd been court-martialled. I believe I did the right thing. I suppose I wanted to see what it was like for other men fighting a war a lot of people didn't believe in. One day I was on patrol with a news cameraman. He got shot, and I picked up his camera – and I was hooked. Next thing I knew, I realised I could get more excitement out of filming than out of fighting.'

'And your wife and your child?'

'I was doing it for them . . .'

'Paul, that's garbage.'

'All right, I'd discovered something that really excited me. I'm addicted to danger – I can't walk away from it. I find war fascinating.'

She looked at the scars on his body, felt the scars hidden under the hair on his scalp.

'You're not afraid of death . . .'

'No. Those months I spent on death row – I think that was worse than death.'

Anne drew herself up next to him. 'I don't want you to hide anything from me, that's all I ask, Paul. I think I understand you – what drives you. But for God's sake, Paul, be careful – I don't want you ending up like Sonny.'

'I'll stay here a few days with you, Mkhulu and Johannes. Then I've got a rendezvous in Namibia.'

'And what about me? Isn't there some way I can help you?'

He touched her cheek. 'By staying here. I still don't trust Hyde MacLeod. I wouldn't put it past him to try something else to get us off Klaw, even though David's confident he'll win our case.' Her brow wrinkled. 'By the way, I didn't tell you, Hyde's just succeeded in forcing Willie van der Spuy to sell.'

'Jesus, how?'

She told him the story.

'The bastard,' said Paul. 'In the end he always wins.'

Dr Vance Torr felt out of place at the meeting of the *Comhairle nan Eilean*, the council of the islands of Harris and Lewis, and the United Kingdom's youngest local authority. He had come here on Wayne MacLeod's express instructions. MacLeod had explained to Vance that although the Hebrides was his home and he wanted to help the community, he did not want to be seen doing charitable work because it might be construed as weakness. So he had asked Vance to assist him in this matter, which could be of great help to the islanders.

The Reverend Duncan Macgregor, convener of the council, sat at the head of the table; to his immediate left was Dr Johnny Lauder, director of finance.

'Johnny, I'm not sure about this loan,' Reverend Macgregor said slowly. 'In 1988 we questioned you about irregularities. Now, are you sure this IPBP bank is a safe place to deposit our money?'

Dr Lauder turned to Dr Torr. 'I think, Duncan, that I should refer you to Dr Torr. Before forming his own church on this island, bringing us both work and prosperity, Dr Torr was a successful international businessman.

'Dr Torr, would you like to explain to the council your views on the International People's Bank of Pakistan?'

Dr Torr rose. He always liked to have an audience. 'I can vouch that your money is one hundred per cent secure with IPBP,' he said. 'I have consulted a colleague of considerable reputation and he has assured me that it is a bank of the highest standing.'

'And look . . . Look at the rate of interest they're giving us,' Dr Lauder added quickly.

'Aye, well, you're the numbers man, Johnny. Just as long as our money's safe.'

Dr Torr left the meeting five minutes later, pleased to have helped the islanders make a wise investment decision.

*

293

Dr Lauder leaned back in his leather executive recliner and stared over the Stornoway roof-line. Wayne MacLeod had been as good as his word – he had persuaded Dr Torr to convince the council of the wisdom of investing in IPBP. The council had now committed over twenty-four million pounds to the IPBP in return for a guaranteed rate of interest higher than that offered by any other bank. Dr Lauder had taken a discreet commission of twenty per cent on the deal. Not bad, he considered, as the money had come mostly through amounts raised for capital projects at a substantially lower rate of interest. He was using money to make money for the islands, and becoming a wealthy man in the process. He had a lot to thank Wayne MacLeod for – in private, of course.

David left the court elated. Hyde MacLeod had been using one of the country's finest advocates, Bartle Fridjhon. But it was clear to David from the beginning of the proceedings that Fridjhon had not been expecting his line of attack.

On Hyde MacLeod's behalf, Fridjhon argued that Paul Norton had neglected Klaw, rarely visited it, and had no real interest in the property. Fridjhon had argued that Paul hadn't visited the farm at all in 1988 – that he had deservedly forfeited the servitude.

David had given the Botswanan court evidence that Paul was now developing Klaw into an exclusive game reserve. He stated that Paul had made a commitment to develop Klaw, and since that time Klaw had been the only reserve in the Tuli Block to employ anti-poaching units, giving employment to the local people and protecting the wildlife. Paul had also divided ownership of the reserve between himself and his two black rangers, Mkhulu and Johannes. Mkhulu had been appointed manager, and backers had been approached to fund the project.

David also pointed to the work that had already been done, and made it clear that the reserve was already accommodating paying guests in Rock Lodge. Paul Norton was also busy directing a film that would draw international attention to the Tuli Block and promote tourism. He further argued that Hyde MacLeod's action was malicious – he had tried to force Paul out by denying him access to Klaw, and when Paul refused to capitulate, Hyde had then committed his father's huge financial resources to a legal action he knew they could not win, but which would cripple Paul financially. Paul would then be forced to sell Klaw to Hyde MacLeod. As evidence to support this line of argument, David pointed to Hyde MacLeod's deliberate engineering of events in 1988 so that he could have Paul's lioness destroyed.

All the time, David knew that Mkhulu, Johannes and Charlotte were behind him in the gallery, watching the proceedings with rapt attention.

Now, outside in the sunshine, David felt good. Mkhulu came out of the court and pumped his hand.

'So, we have the servitude.'

'Better than that, we have a ruling that the clause defining the rights of servitude in the original ownership agreement between both reserves is unreasonable. Klaw now has servitude over Hyde MacLeod's property in perpetuity.'

Johannes, who had just come up beside Mkhulu, smiled broadly. 'Why do we bother to continue? This is an expensive business.'

'Ah, expensive for Hyde MacLeod. I'm now going to sue him to pay for our costs.'

Charlotte ran up and threw her arms around David. 'Well done, darling!'

'For the fee, it was nothing.'

Charlotte looked at him quizzically. 'I thought you said you were going to waive your fee?'

'Ah, yes. Well, Paul has already settled my account.'

'Good God, David, you know he's short of money. I don't know how you could accept it. What was the price?'

'Permission to marry you.'

Wayne MacLeod relaxed in his seat and stared out of the window of his private jet. Puffy white clouds rested against an azure horizon. He'd enjoyed his weekend's hunting on Harris. Four hours before, he had flown into Stornoway airport by helicopter, then boarded his private jet and taken off for Africa.

He sipped at his whisky reflectively. He was looking forward to the testing session in Namibia. Security wasn't going to be the problem he'd thought it might be – the new Namibian government was as open to bribery as the old one had been. Yes, he thought, governments changed but the mentality of the men in power stayed the same. Perhaps they might be interested in the Supergun, once it was fully developed. He was quite sure they could afford it – after all, he'd just tied up a deal with them to buy an executive jet like his own.

A light flashed to his left and he picked up the phone.

'Ah, Hyde, good to hear from you. Is it all over?'

His face creased as he listened. 'But you told me it was a walk-over!' He punched the side of the chair hard. 'David Katz again? That bloody Israelite. Listen, I don't care what it costs, just keep the case going . . . What do you mean, we've got no case? I don't bloody believe this. I told you – we can't lose.'

His irritation grew as his son spoke on. 'I now have to pay to cross his land – pay for the right? What's this, a joke? He can't sue us for costs? Hyde, I'm not accepting this, you hear! Sue Fridjhon! I'll make his name dirt for this!'

He slammed the phone down hard, knocking his whisky over. 'Damnation!'

He poured himself another. Bloody lawyers, whether you won or lost, they always got their fee.

He moved to a swivel-chair in front of his desk and typed in a command on the computer keyboard. A detailed map of the Tuli Block flashed up on the large screen in front of him. He studied it for a few moments. Klaw was the biggest property in the whole reserve, and even more important, it was in the centre of the reserve – the easiest access to half the farms he'd bought was through Klaw. He could get to these farms by travelling around the perimeter of Klaw, but that would double the travelling time. And now, because of the way the case had gone, if he went over Norton's land he had to pay for the servitude!

Hyde had certainly buggered things up. It was time to take matters into his own hands again. He couldn't allow a man like Paul Norton to get the better of him. Norton was a trouble-maker – he didn't want him in the centre of his mega game farm, that was for sure. MacLeod knew what he had to do – find Norton's weak point and apply the needle.

He picked up the phone again and tapped in a number. He had to wait a long time before the connection was made.

'Ursula, get me Hyde.'

A beatific smile crossed his face. Let's see how Norton handles this, he thought to himself. Perhaps he'll think again about selling his goddamned farm.

Mkhulu drove down to the waterhole in the burning heat of the middle of the day. He liked to have this time to himself. There were five guests on the reserve, all staying at Rock Lodge.

He, Johannes and Anne had been running the reserve as a game ranch for the last two months. Charlotte had handled the advertising and promotion of the reserve through a well-known Johannesburg tour operator.

A reserve run by black men was unique. Overseas visitors were already clamouring to go to Klaw because of excellent reports in the international travel press of its ability to deliver a unique bush experience. Everything was done to the highest standards, and compromise was avoided. The object was to let the guest experience the bush – not to let him feel he was in a five-star hotel. Johannes brought a wealth of experience with him from Cayzer; Mkhulu offered a rare depth of insight that came from living in the bush with Lion Norton. Anne added glamour, and a formidable international reputation as a lion authority.

Mkhulu and Johannes were determined to avoid all the things that characterised so many of the game lodges in Africa – the big ranch with the smooth-talking rangers, and the sense of always being slightly away from the reality of the bush. Their intention was to make each guest feel as though he was in a home away from home in the African bush.

Wild animals roamed freely around the base of Rock Lodge – there were no fences, and the immediacy of the danger added to its attraction. After a few days, they found guests would ask to walk, rather than travel in the Land Rover. Now that he was back, Mkhulu conducted some of the walks, but Johannes took the majority of them.

In the evenings, instead of traditional dancing, they would play African jazz records to the guests, giving them the flavour of the new Africa. And Mkhulu would often play on his sax next to the camp fire, while the guests listened, spellbound. Mkhulu was determined to leave them with a feeling for the real Africa, instead of building on misconceptions.

Now, alone in the intense heat of the midday sun, Mkhulu felt good. He was getting a lot of satisfaction from running the reserve – already they had a year's guests booked in advance. There was really nothing to worry about . . . Except Paul. What had his friend got himself involved in? Surely Paul was happier here on Klaw with Anne than in London?

He got down from the Land Rover and walked towards the waterhole. He heard the noise of a rifle being loaded, and looked around. Nothing except the noise of the insects in the heat. He must be imagining things.

He leaned down and looked into the water. He saw his reflection and studied it for a long time. It was only after a while that he became aware of another reflection behind him. Spittle landed in the water next to him and he swivelled on his good leg, catching sight of a big black man behind him, an AK-47 assault-rifle in his hands.

'The word, my friend, is that you must leave.'

Mkhulu squared up and faced the man. He did not show fear. it was not his way to be afraid.

'You're on my land,' Mkhulu said. 'It is you who must leave.'

When the man opened his mouth, Mkhulu saw that his teeth were filed into points. He knew his kind. He had come from Zimbabwe, across the Shashe River. But what was he doing here? Was he poaching?'

The man spat again, this time in Mkhulu's face, then brought the butt of the rifle into his chest. Mkhulu arched backwards, drew his knife and rammed it into the man's gut. He saw the horrified look on the man's face as he ripped the knife across, disemboweling him.

Mkhulu wrenched the rifle from the man's hands and dropped flat against the ground. In the same instant as a burst of fire came from the bush, Mkhulu squeezed the trigger and brutally returned the compliment.

Another man reared up, and Mkhulu continued firing, turning the body in the air. He had no doubt that these men would kill him, and as a cripple he had no second chance.

He began to crawl towards the Land Rover. He had to get

away as quickly as possible. A shot rang out and he felt a dull pain in his leg.

Oh my God! Not my good leg. Please God, no!

He rolled over, levelled his rifle and fired into the bush. Another scream followed.

Now he was in agony. But he wasn't going to die. Inch by inch he dragged himself across the sand. The pain began to blind him. It was then he heard the dread crunch of another boot on the sand, then felt the weight of it against his arm. He looked up to see a rifle pointed at his head.

'You will pay for this, cripple,' said a cruel voice.

Two men came from the bush and grabbed his arms. They dragged him down to the waterhole and flopped him face-down in the mud. Mkhulu held his breath, but after a minute he could hold no more and started to gag. They lifted him up as he began to black out.

He caught sight of the man who had put his boot on his arm; he was smoking a cheroot and looking on. A wave of his hand and Mkhulu was forced underwater again. He came up nearly dead.

'Why?' he screamed.

The man laughed. 'We get paid good to do this. We enjoy seeing you die very, very slowly, cripple man.'

'Who paid you?'

The man laughed again, then gestured for him to be ducked.

The shot burst out of the bush. The man's head erupted in a shower of blood. Mkhulu's captors dropped him and made to run. He felt himself sinking into the mud, his arms were too weak to push himself out. Oh God. He felt the world becoming red, he heard explosions in the background. He started to cough as the water came up his nostrils.

Almost blacking out, he was wrenched out of the water and pulled back onto the sandbank. He opened his eyes blearily to see Johannes staring at him with fear in his eyes.

'Mkhulu? Mkhulu?'

He reached up, and Johannes pulled him upright.

'I heard shots, I drove over as fast as I could.'

'Where are the others?' Mkhulu asked fearfully.

'They are dead. There are no more.'

Mkhulu's eyes took in the pump-shotgun in Johannes' hands. At nine years old Johannes had first learned to handle a gun; he had fought in the struggle for Rhodesia. Now that deadly skill had saved Mkhulu's life.

'My friend, I thank you.'

'What men attack a cripple?' Johannes asked softly.

Mkhulu did not reply, instead his eyes combed the bush. Then he looked down at his bleeding leg. He was quite certain that this attack was connected with Norton's fight with MacLeod. If he had died, he would have been a victim of terrorism, no questions asked.

Of course, this would be in all the papers. The guests would not come. He cursed quietly. He had thought the hard times were over, especially after the court case had been won. But he had been wrong. The fight had just begun.

Hyde MacLeod cursed out loud. He peered again through his binoculars. He had wanted Mkhulu dead but he was still very much alive. His father had ordered him to control this operation, and he had failed.

Hyde thought of his own trial, of the humiliation. He hated Paul Norton with a vengeance. Now, as the feelings of frustration over his failure to kill Mkhulu overwhelmed him, he felt an all-consuming desire to indulge himself.

He fired up the Land Cruiser and drove back to the main camp. There was an American woman who wanted him. But she didn't interest him at all, there was nothing about her that aroused him sexually. He needed to feel power, and he knew he could not indulge himself with a guest.

But it was only three hours till dark. And it was Friday night. There was no doubt in his mind about what he would do.

Mkhulu drew the blackened killing-knife from its scabbard and honed the blade. He worked the oilstone gently back and forwards till the edge of steel was so sharp he could use it to trim the hairs on his face.

Already the phone calls had come, and he had answered honestly, not trying to bluff his way around the reporters' questions. But instead of vitriol, there was sympathy. He realised it was because he was black, and white men felt guilty about exploiting his misfortune.

The guests had been surprisingly supportive, too. He had explained to them what had happened and told them they were free to go. He also explained that the incident was unusual and unprovoked, and he saw the looks on their faces – the fear. He drove them slowly to the runway, helped them load up their luggage and watched their charter plane take off, flying up into the sky, heading for Johannesburg.

He spent the rest of that afternoon sitting on the sand of the runway, thinking. Later, driving home in the darkness, a plan had formed in his mind. He knew his enemy well.

As he parked the Land Rover in front of Bush Camp, he thought of Paul. In his heart he knew that Paul would have been with him. He looked again at the knife. The man who'd given it to him had died – a white man who'd fought alongside him in Rhodesia long ago; a man of courage.

Mkhulu remembered the incident; they'd both been through a lot by then. Jan had crawled forward with a grenade, moving in on the enemy. There was no chance, for they were surrounded. In the open ground in front of them, Jan had edged forward till the sniper fire caught him in the waist, paralysing his legs. Then, knowing they would come, he'd lain there, waiting for the enemy, with the grenade between his teeth, and his right hand on the pin. Behind him, in the undergrowth, Mkhulu had crouched, quiet and sweating. Eventually the men had come, men of his own colour.

Jan's timing had been perfect. He must have pulled the pin from the grenade as he heard their steps. As they kicked him, he rolled over and screamed out in rage. Then the grenade exploded, killing him and his attackers, leaving Mkhulu safe to escape under cover of darkness.

Mkhulu looked at the knife Jan had given him and turned the blackened blade in the light. He slipped it into the scabbard strapped to his leg, and went out into the darkness. He was dressed only in dark shorts and a T-shirt. The metal of his artificial leg glimmered in the moonlight.

He knew exactly where to go. It was the place where David had taken the tyre prints – a quiet, deserted spot on the eastern banks of the Limpopo, on one of Hyde MacLeod's South African farms. This was where the local people would walk in the darkness. It was the route the women who worked in the town took when they returned home for the weekend.

He cursed his artificial leg, knowing how much faster he had been able to move before he lost it. It was three hours before he made it to the spot.

In the darkness he heard whimpering and then pleading in Tswana, the local language. His lips drew back in a bitter smile. For once, he had been right, he had come to the correct place.

The sound of the quirt cut through the darkness, followed by its slap across raw flesh. 'Ahhhh!' came the pitiful scream.

Mkhulu edged closer and made out the forms in the darkness. Hyde MacLeod, naked from the waist up, was holding the quirt in his right hand. Below him, splayed flat across the bonnet of the Land Cruiser, was a naked black woman. Hyde dropped the quirt and explored her naked body with his hands. She whimpered desperately, powerless to stop him.

'Just do as I say and you'll live.'

She acquiesced, and he untied her hands from the spare wheel on the bonnet. Then, as she rose to her feet, he slapped her hard across the face and she dropped to her knees. Hyde unfastened his trousers and dropped them, along with his underpants.

'That's right, just as I instructed you.'

Mkhulu crept slowly forward as Hyde's pink buttocks were revealed in the moonlight. The woman moved round to lick Hyde from behind. Mkhulu could tell from her coughing that she wanted to retch; he was now only a yard from her.

Hyde's trousers lay around his ankles – his pistol on the bonnet of the Land Cruiser, just within his reach. Mkhulu moved forward silently, gently pushing the woman away and forcing the tip of his blade up into the bone beneath Hyde's testicles.

'One move, bastard, and it goes up your anus,' he hissed.

Hyde rose on his toes, powerless, his penis still erect. Mkhulu took the pistol from the bonnet and slipped it in his pocket.

'Get dressed,' Mkhulu said to the woman in her own language.

Hyde tried to make a move and Mkhulu pressed the blade in harder.

302

'Oh my God, please!'

The woman appeared in front of Hyde in the moonlight, smoothing down her dress. In one subtle movement, Mkhulu whipped away the blade and clamped his left arm hard across Hyde's neck. His arms were strong from using crutches, and he knew Hyde would never break his grip. He saw the hatred in the woman's eyes, but there was also fear. Her husband worked for the bastard – there was no way she would ever speak out. Mkhulu thought of Johannes' daughter, Thoko, and of what Hyde had done to her.

He forced his right hand down and with the blackened blade, he sliced off Hyde's testicles in two swift, flowing movements.

Hyde's scream was terrible. The black woman ran off into the darkness in terror. Mkhulu pushed Hyde away from him and cleaned the blood-wet blade against his leg. Then he melted into the darkness, Hyde's screams echoing through the blackness of the night.

Wayne MacLeod scratched the area behind his right ear nervously. The whole thing had backfired horribly. True, there had been negative publicity surrounding the attack on Mkhulu, but the second attack on Hyde had been far more damaging. Hyde's screams, when the rangers brought him back to camp, had cleared the guests out of Cayzer in less than twenty-four hours.

Hyde had been flown to Johannesburg for major surgery. It had been touch and go for four hours because he had lost so much blood. Unfortunately, the press had been primed by the first attack on Klaw, and there were reporters in the area the day after Hyde was attacked. They asked questions about Hyde's injuries, and before Wayne could stop it, the story was in all the papers.

MacLeod felt a coldness creeping over him. Hyde wouldn't talk about what had happened, and the savagery of the wound had all the elements of a Mau Mau atrocity. Hyde wouldn't explain what he had been doing or how many men had come up on him in the dark.

MacLeod guessed that the killers they'd paid and brought in to kill Mkhulu had gone out of control. He was sure they had mutilated Hyde as payment for the death of their comrades.

MacLeod was not slow to take revenge – he'd already set the wheels in motion. He wanted those men hunted down and brutally slain. But what he wanted most, he could not have: Hyde would never produce a son now. And Wayne wanted a man, a male to continue the MacLeod dynasty.

Hyde lay in the coolness of the private ward and stared fixedly at the picture of some daisies that hung on the wall opposite him. He thought about the final results of the operation – now there was only dullness where once there had been excitement.

In his mind he replayed the moment over and over again: the sudden pressure of the knife blade and then the terrible pain; the smile on the woman's face.

Every day was a fresh humiliation for him. The tender looks of the nurses merely fuelled his ire. This was worse than being a cripple. His father had not come to see him because his father could not accept failure.

Now he had a terrible hunger, a craving for food. Every time he felt the dullness, he ate. He was not a man any longer, just a sexless being.

He looked down at his legs, strapped to the sides of the bed so he could not cause himself pain. Urinating was agony – and was followed by the humiliation of having to ask for the bed-pan to be removed. It was the look on the nurses' faces that hurt most of all. He was no longer regarded as a man. He was exposed for what he was – weak and cowardly.

The pity was killing him.

David walked across the shimmering tarmac towards the plane, following Charlotte. In a way, he could not believe his dream was happening. It was something he'd thought he'd always be planning but would never do. He looked back at the terminal buildings of Jan Smuts airport as they wavered in the heat-haze. Of course, he was only saying goodbye for a little while. Once you'd lived in Africa, you could never really leave it behind.

It was strange, how life worked out. He'd applied for a position at the University of Jerusalem as a law lecturer. He'd sent off his application in a negative frame of mind: so many people would like the post, so many talented people wanted to live in Israel – applications from all over the world would pour in with his own. But only a week later he'd received a call. The university wanted him, the head of the faculty was at that moment in South Africa, and would David be interested in an interview?

Charlotte had urged him on. In fact she'd gone to the interview with him, because she knew the fact that he had a *shiksa* for a wife might tell against him, and she felt that if she met the head of the faculty in person, it might help. Something had certainly helped, because he'd got the job.

Now he was walking up the covered steps towards the cavernous interior of the SAA Boeing 747, wondering how it had all happened so fast. He'd told Charlotte he wasn't going till the legal battle for access to Klaw was over. To his surprise, the whole matter had been settled in a month.

This was going to be the first chapter of their life together. He just hoped fate would be kind to them.

Paul settled down into his seat, stared through the window at the rain-drenched tarmac, and thought about Namibia. It felt good to be going back – he was looking forward to the emptiness of the place, the isolation.

He opened Charlotte's letter. It had only come the day before and he had saved it to read when he had time on his hands. As he read the lines now, his brow wrinkled. He was concerned about her and David's decision. Paul knew the situation in the Middle East was tense – he felt they'd chosen a dangerous time to go to Israel.

United Nations sanctions had been applied on all trade with Iraq except for medicines and food needed for humanitarian purposes. Tension was building in the area. Naval force had been used to ensure that the sanctions against Iraq were effective. But the whole region was scared of war with Iraq – people were only too aware of the country's military strength and the ruthless nature of President Saddam Hussein.

The reports from Kuwait were frightening, to say the least. There were rumours of mass atrocities, of rape and pillage. No mercy was being shown – it was clear that President Hussein was a tyrant of monumental proportions.

Paul realised the potential of Dr Torr's Supergun, but so far had no real proof that it had been built. However, Fahad's involvement left little doubt in his mind that the finished Supergun was being assembled somewhere in Iraq – but where?

Until three days ago he had thought he might be over-reacting, and that, as Sir Donald claimed, the weapon might prove to be a white elephant. But the file he had stolen from Dr Torr's castle had proved illuminating. Basically, it had been filled with dates, times and telephone numbers. It hadn't taken long to discover that the telephone numbers were for factories in the West Midlands area, and one in Belgium. Deeper investigation proved a little more difficult – each of the companies' products was protected by the British official secrets act. If he pushed his enquiries further, he would draw attention to himself, and judging from previous experience, Paul decided that was not a good idea.

Using a bogus name and reference, he had visited each of the companies in turn, and what he found was disturbing. Together, they could certainly have fabricated the components for the Supergun. And the only company he could not visit, the one in Belgium, specialised in rocket propellants and high-explosives. One of the companies, Chesterfield Forgemasters, had actually given him a sales video on a special pressurised oil pipeline they had manufactured for a Middle Eastern client – to Paul it looked suspiciously like the barrel of the Supergun.

In Birmingham, Paul had decided on another angle of attack in his investigation. He'd contacted the customs office, to see if he could find out where these companies were exporting their products to. But that had drawn a blank; someone of influence had definitely made sure that the Supergun project was veiled in secrecy.

He folded Charlotte's letter up and put it in the breast-pocket of his jacket. What, he wondered, was Fahad up to?

Fahad paced up and down the floor outside the vast reception room of the Baghdad palace. President Hussein had summoned him to an urgent and confidential meeting, and he was afraid; Saddam was even more ruthless than he was himself. Saddam had occupied Fahad's position – head of the secret police, the

Mukhabarat – and it was Saddam who had turned it into the formidable, terrifying force that controlled Iraq.

He was ushered into the main room, and Saddam looked him up and down.

'You look nervous, my friend,' he said.

Fahad gave a faint smile. 'Life has been tough lately.'

'Ease and prosperity are things we shall all have to forego,' the President said, 'if there is war. We shall never be defeated, we will sacrifice everything for victory.'

'And I shall never be found lacking in my support,' Fahad said.

'Words slip easily off the tongue,' Saddam countered, 'it is behaviour that counts.' He stared at Fahad. 'I have now spent over five hundred million dollars on this Supergun project, and what have I to show for it?'

'The first testing is only a few days away.'

Saddam laughed emptily. 'I am not impressed. I want to meet Dr Vance Torr. I want the testing to be done here, in front of my own eyes.'

This was what Fahad had feared.

Fahad baulked. He most definitely didn't want Dr Torr dealing directly with the President – he needed to control the situation himself. And how could he explain to Saddam that Dr Torr would not be designing the nuclear shell – that he would be totally opposed to the idea?

'Dr Torr is a scientist,' he said nervously. 'He prefers to keep a low profile.'

Saddam came up to Fahad and squeezed his shoulder hard. 'My friend, I do not know whether I can trust you any longer.'

Fahad stood stiffly to attention. He would be assassinated if the President didn't trust him – he had to turn this conversation to his advantage.

'If there is any area in which I am lacking . . .' he began.

'Now you behave like my subject, and that I like. You understand, of course, Fahad: I need followers for my cause, not men who would seek to undermine me.' Saddam nodded his head, thinking to himself, and then stared at Fahad again. 'I have lost confidence in you. I want to see results.'

'The testing schedule cannot be changed,' Fahad replied anxiously.

Suddenly Saddam's rage exploded. 'You dare to contradict me! I want to see results, I tell you! Till that time, consider yourself grounded and stripped of all command!'

Fahad staggered out of the room. He had underestimated the President's wrath. The world reaction to their invasion of Kuwait must be disturbing him, along with the refusal of many Arab nations to co-operate with him. The Supergun was now a necessity.

And this meant that he had no choice but to arrange a live firing with conventional ammunition. Dr Fassbinder would have to organise it without Dr Torr's knowledge.

Maria Fassbinder lay on the bed, watching Vance Torr hunch forward over the computer screen, his fingers tapping away at the keyboard. Until Vance, every man she had been intimately involved with had been her mental inferior. With Vance it was different. He was just as gifted as she was in physics, aeronautics and mathematics, but what made him exceptional was his imagination. He was never daunted by complex problems, instead he attacked them head on, thinking up a solution that no one else could have reached – the right answer, the perfect answer.

In other ways, he was like a child. She manipulated him with ease – but this gave her little satisfaction. She realised he was not interested in petty matters and refused to clutter his mind with them. Politics held no interest for him. A student prodigy, he had been the youngest person ever to graduate with a doctorate from his university. From an early stage in his career, artillery had interested him, and he had built the world's biggest and most powerful gun. He had fired shells higher into the atmosphere than anyone else had ever done. But it was this, his latest project, that was the realisation of all his dreams.

The design of the Supergun was the ultimate expression of his art. She knew perfectly well why he could not sleep: the design of the shell was critical to the project. It had to withstand the enormous pressures generated inside the barrel on firing. One of the secrets of the design was the base-bleed formula that eliminated the vacuum behind the shell as it rocketed forward up the barrel, boosted on its course by further charges. In effect, the base-bleed formula doubled the range.

With its wide bore, the Supergun would be able to launch satellites into space for a fraction of the cost of a conventional rocket launch. With a rocket, most of the explosive forces were dissipated on blast-off, around the base of the rocket. With a Supergun, these forces were contained within the barrel and used to propel the shell forward. So the Supergun kept launch costs low, because none of the explosive power of the propellant was lost.

Torr turned to look at her, his face weary. He switched off the monitor and came over to the bed, lying down beside her. He held her tightly in his arms. For a long time they did not speak, but lay listening to the rain and the wind lashing the walls of the castle.

'I am afraid,' he said finally.

'But why? We are perfectly safe here.'

'I know, but that time I spent in jail – when they prosecuted me for selling technology to South Africa – I also had that feeling then. Intelligence people encouraged the sale in the first place – behind the scenes, of course. Then I became their scapegoat. They used me as an example. I've never felt secure since then.

'There are a lot of people who want to get me. I was always critical at university, especially of the bureaucrats, and I made plenty of enemies. Maybe it's an irrational fear, but I'd like you to make me a promise.'

Her heart skipped a beat, and conflicting emotions filled her. She had not reckoned on becoming so attached to him. Fahad was ruthless, and she had to follow his orders.

'You are being foolish,' she said. 'There is nothing to fear.'

'All the same . . .'

'All right, I will listen.'

'The Supergun. You must see the project through to its completion. You must supervise the firing of the satellite. I want you to prove my critics wrong.'

'But I know it's possible, Vance . . .'

'I know, my love. But no one else does. It will be a final vindication.'

She remained silent. It was possible. But that was not the objective of the programme. The Iraqis had no intention of ever launching satellites with the Supergun – for them it was a nuclear weapon, pure and simple.

He gripped her arms. 'Promise me that if anything happens to me, you will see that they launch a shell into space.'

'I promise.'

She turned over, and felt a deadness in her soul.

Paul put the phone down and stared around the crowded international lounge at Windhoek airport. He couldn't quite credit what had happened to Mkhulu. Perhaps he should abandon this whole project and return to Klaw. They might have won the legal battle against Hyde MacLeod, but the fight to keep the reserve solvent had only just begun.

Really, what was he doing? He should be fighting his own battles, not other people's. He moved towards the passenger services desk. His mind was made up – he would book a ticket back to South Africa.

He jostled with the crowds of people coming into the concourse. A plane from South Africa had just landed – maybe he could get a seat on a return flight. Suddenly it all seemed so logical. He must forget all the business with the blueprints and the gun, return to Klaw and start filming what was happening there in preparation for his film. Anne was right, he'd been crazy.

Then he saw him across the concourse, the last man he'd expected. Wayne MacLeod.

Paul stared across at the passenger services desk, then back at Wayne MacLeod, who was now moving swiftly across the concourse. What was MacLeod doing in Namibia?

Perhaps he should just see what MacLeod was up to? After all, MacLeod was his biggest enemy, the one who'd been trying to close his reserve down. If he could find out anything more about this elusive man, it might just help him get the edge over MacLeod.

He turned, following MacLeod across the concourse, keeping a discreet distance behind. He pulled his dark glasses from his top pocket and slipped them on.

Outside, it was blazing hot. He watched MacLeod slip into the back of a sky-blue Mercedes, and felt the sweat drip from his brow as he made his way rapidly to the car hire counter. He kept one eye on the Mercedes as he pulled out his cards.

'You want to take advantage of our fast check-in facility, sir?'

'Yes,' Paul said breathlessly.

'You can take the blue Corolla then, Mr Norton. Mr Norton . . .'

He snatched up the keys and sprinted across the parking lot. It didn't take him a minute to find the car. He got inside and started the engine. But he needn't have worried – the Mercedes was now stationary, parked about 100 metres from the terminal building. Paul sat in his car and waited.

Paul wondered who MacLeod was waiting for. There were no planes due in till the next day. Earlier in the morning a flight had come in from London, but the passengers had already left. Paul lifted the tiny set of Nikon binoculars from his bag and focused them on the Mercedes saloon. He couldn't see what MacLeod was up to behind the smoked-glass windows.

Then a door opened at the side of the building and a group of men came through. Paul lifted his binoculars and went cold. It couldn't be . . . but it was. In among the bodyguards was Dr Torr, and he was moving towards MacLeod's Mercedes. Then the door of the car swung open, and MacLeod was out and pumping Dr Torr's hand.

Paul sucked in his breath. Why had he been such a fool? Wayne MacLeod owned the castle on Harris. So was Dr Torr working for Wayne MacLeod?

He thought hard, especially about Anne's observation of the secret meetings on Cayzer. Then he thought of the companies he'd investigated in England that had been making the Supergun parts. They'd all been owned by nominees, but he'd sensed a larger force behind the whole operation. And now it was staring him in the face.

Over the years there'd always been rumours about the way Wayne MacLeod had made the money to buy his media empire. Now, in Paul's mind, suspicion became certainty: Wayne MacLeod had made his money by arms dealing.

The Mercedes moved away quickly, followed by a minibus for

the strong-arm contingent. Paul kept far behind, anxious not to blow his cover.

He felt the sweat running slowly down his face. He would never have seen Dr Torr if he hadn't been tailing MacLeod – Torr must have slipped off the other side of the plane by special arrangement. Paul gripped the steering-wheel tightly. He wasn't going to leave this thing alone now. MacLeod was involved with Torr, and Torr had a deal with the Iraqis. He was going to find out what was going on, even if it killed him.

He was hard-pressed to keep up with the Mercedes which was moving north now at an easy 160 kmh. Paul held the accelerator flat till they were out in the open, then dropped back a considerable distance. His car didn't have air-conditioning, so he rolled down the windows to keep himself cool.

They passed through the town of Okahandja after a couple of hours, crossing the railway line soon after, and pressing on northwards in the direction of Otjiwarongo. They continued moving fast. Fortunately there was other traffic heading north, so Paul's wasn't the only vehicle following the Mercedes.

A few hours later, the sign for Otjiwarongo came up. Paul knew the area well from the time he had spent in the South African army, fighting in the troubled areas of Angola, north of the Namibian border. He liked this desolate desert country. The Otjiwarongo district itself had been a reserve for the Herero tribe and was still largely occupied by them. The town was founded when a police station was built on the banks of the river during the time when Namibia was German colony. In the local tongue, the name Otjiwarongo meant 'the place of the Kudu'.

Now he was feeling dry. He dreamed of drinking an ice-cold beer, but there was to be no such relief for him. The Mercedes swung off to the right, heading for Grootfontein. Far to Paul's left, over the horizon, lay the Etosha Pan. He had spent months there – every time he got leave from the army he had hitched a lift down to the Etosha reserve and spent his time watching and tracking game. So this was familiar territory – he knew the local people and their language.

He returned his thoughts to the present. He knew the direction of the road ahead. They could only go as far as Grootfontein on the tarmac, then they'd have to swing to the south-west, heading up towards Ovamboland and the border with Angola. He was sure Wayne MacLeod must own a farm in the area – a lot of wealthy South Africans had sold their huge hunting-reserves here when Namibia gained its independence, and MacLeod could have picked up land for next to nothing.

For many farmers it was a sacred annual pilgrimage to go hunting on these lands. Paul surmised that MacLeod might well be entertaining Dr Torr in this way.

Vance Torr felt extremely comfortable in the generous leather seats of the air-conditioned Mercedes, and even more comfortable when Wayne MacLeod poured him a whisky.

'It seems very strange to me,' he said, 'that I should come to this inhospitable place to enjoy a "wee dram".'

MacLeod was about to drop a couple of ice-cubes into the neat whisky but he raised his right hand. 'Please, even in this heat it would be sacrilege.'

He took the glass and raised it. Wayne added some ice to his own whisky. 'In Africa I like my whisky cold.'

Vance cast him an annoyed glance 'I hope you haven't compromised on the manufacture of the Supergun as well.'

MacLeod's expression changed immediately. It was clear that the comment made him angry. Vance Torr knew MacLeod prided himself on being a perfectionist – but the Scotsman was above all a shrewd businessman, and Torr guessed that quality would suffer long before his profit-margin was allowed to.

'Cheers, Vance,' MacLeod said quickly, with a forced smile. 'You will find your exacting specification has been followed to the letter. After all, the operation is managed by the same men who designed the G5 and G6 cannons.'

'The men you stole from my Canadian facility,' Vance replied angrily.

The memories would not go away. He had lost almost everything when the CIA turned on him, exposing his dealing with the South Africans in the late seventies.

'Not my crowd, lad. That was Armscor,' MacLeod said, a little too quickly.

'You were involved in Armscor!'

'A consultant like yourself . . .'

Torr decided to change the course of the conversation. The past was behind them, he didn't want to dwell on it. 'This is a beautiful country,' he said, looking out of the window.

MacLeod relaxed, glad that Torr had dropped the contentious issue. 'I bought these reserves when Namibia gained her independence,' he said. 'I hunt here regularly.'

'And what about your Botswanan reserve? Surely the hunting's just as good there?'

'Yes, but it's not politic to hunt there. Hyde's reserves support conservation.'

'You are involved in conservation?'

MacLeod smiled. 'Yes. It's . . . how shall I put it? . . . a strategy for present survival. I like to know the other side's argument.'

Torr was disturbed by this revelation. Was MacLeod merely exploiting him for 'present survival'? He would have to be on his guard. Perhaps it had not been such a good idea to take up residence in MacLeod's castle – it put him too much within the magnate's power.

'The weapon is ready for testing?' he said, changing tack again.

'It was off-loaded at the rail-head at Tsumeb two weeks ago. My team have been linking the sections of the barrel together. I was informed two days ago that they were ready to make a test firing.'

'What about the telemetry and recording instruments?'

'In place already. I use this facility to test my other weapons.'

Torr looked out at the stark, savage beauty of the semi-desert landscape, composing his thoughts. 'Other weapons?' he said.

'I have been working on modifications to them for export purposes. The G6 cannon in particular.'

Torr again felt anger. Armscor manufactured the G6, or 'Kalahari Ferrari' as it was more popularly known, and it continued to irritate him that he did not gain any royalty from sales of the G6, because it was *his* design. Armscor, however, claimed it for their own, giving him neither royalties nor recognition. He was proud in the knowledge that he was the world's best designer of artillery, and he wanted to go down in the history books for his achievements. Academe had shunned him

– enduring fame, he knew, was the best way to exact his revenge on them.

'Is Iraq one of your customers for the G6?' Torr asked.

'Yes,' MacLeod replied guardedly. 'But, you understand, this is a sensitive issue.'

Torr felt his face redden. MacLeod had already criticised him for talking of his achievements to the technical press. Here there was a conflict of interest, but MacLeod had sworn him to total secrecy on the Supergun project.

'I do not talk of these things any longer, Wayne – with the Supergun there's a lot at stake. Naturally, that's why we are only developing it for satellite launching. The United States doesn't believe such a weapon can be successfully developed – if they knew how far we'd progressed, they would be very, very concerned.'

MacLeod smirked. 'I guess in a few months time there'll be some very red faces in the Pentagon.'

Torr leant back in his seat. 'So, when do we start testing?'

'Tonight, we go to Fort Namutoni. Tomorrow, I'll show you the Etosha Pan. Then, effectively, we'll disappear.'

'Ah, I wondered how you would ensure security!'

'This is a big country. It's easy to get lost in – and it's easy to spot the opposition in, too.'

Paul looked in his rear-view mirror for the tenth time in as many minutes. The Range Rover had swung in behind him after he'd left Tsumeb. There were two men in the front, both dressed in khaki and wearing dark glasses. The Range Rover was a new model and Paul guessed it didn't belong to the Namibian Parks Board.

Now there were just three vehicles on the deserted stretch of road – the Mercedes, his car, and the Range Rover. If he didn't play his cards right, he would be in serious trouble; the driver of the Mercedes must have realised he was being tailed, and radioed for reinforcements.

Paul knew from his experiences in London that to continue tailing the Mercedes would be suicidal – he'd have to take a calculated risk that the Mercedes was heading for Fort Namutoni.

He flattened the accelerator pedal and swept past the Mercedes, keeping his eyes on the road ahead. The needle nudged 180 kmh, and he breathed a sigh of relief: his hire car had greater reserves of power than he'd realised. Then he looked into the rear-view mirror again.

Shit! The Range Rover was hard behind him, keeping pace. They weren't buying his tricks. He'd just have to hope that his next plan of action was a little more effective.

The gates of the Etosha National Park came up, with the rangers' quarters just beside them. He stopped at the gate. The Range Rover was right behind him. His mouth went dry.

'Yes, sir?' asked the ranger, appearing as he pulled up.

'I'm here to see Kurt Hamza,' Paul said.

'You're a friend?'

'Yes.'

'Swing left just after the gate.'

'Where's his place?'

'Where it's always been.'

Paul looked into the rear-view mirror and saw the ranger wave the Range Rover through behind him. Sick with apprehension, he drove down to the left. Would Kurt remember him? It had been how many years? Ten, fifteen?

The house came up, children playing outside and a pretty, dark-haired woman in the garden. Kurt was married? Kurt had children?

He pulled up and looked again in his mirror – to see the Range Rover stop a little distance behind him. He could sense the men watching. He opened the door slowly, and the woman looked up, the two young boys looked at him warily. He locked his eyes on hers and hoped to God that she liked what she saw.

A warm smile, hazel eyes and pearl-white teeth. She was attractive in a wild kind of way. He took in the strong, sun-tanned legs and the firm breasts pushing against the khaki shirt.

'Yes? Can I help you?' The voice surprised him; English, a London accent. He liked her immediately.

'I'm an old friend of Kurt's.' He held out his hand. 'Paul, Paul Norton . . .' She smiled. 'He's talked a lot about you. He's inside, nursing a hangover.' She bit her lip, a curious, attractive movement. 'I've seen your film on Vietnam.'

'That was a long time ago.'

There was a strained silence between them. He knew he was an alien, an invader. This woman loved Kurt and she was probably scared of his past – the past that Paul was a part of. He sensed she was making a decision. Whatever it was, he'd accept it. All the time he sensed the eyes of the men in the Range Rover watching him.

He held her gaze. Her eyes shifted to the area behind him and he guessed she was assessing the situation.

Then the smile floated back across her face and she embraced him. He loved her for that. She'd probably saved his life. He heard the noise of the Range Rover starting up and then the sound of its gear-train as it reversed. He was safe. God, it had been close!

'Go inside, Paul,' the woman said. 'He'll be overjoyed to see you. I'll get you a beer. You look as though you need it.'

He went into the house, and the memories flooded back. The coat-hanger on the wall made from antlers . . . The black-and-white photographs of the desert . . . The old Oberndorf Mauser rifle mounted high on the wall . . . He respected the fact that she'd left the house alone. She hadn't tried to alter the way Kurt lived.

He made his way down the corridor to the study.

There he was, hunched over an old black typewriter, staring at the blank expanse of white paper. Then he looked up, pushing back the long black hair now flecked with grey, and stared at Paul.

'Man, I don't believe this . . .' Then the big voice bellowed down the hall: 'Paul, you old bastard!'

Kurt was up and lumbering towards him, larger than ever and now with a big paunch. They embraced.

'You must see my children . . . Kurt! Gary!'

The two boys appeared in the passage, still looking suspiciously at this intruder into their home.

'Lads, this is Paul Norton, he'll be staying with us for the next few days . . .'

They returned to his study and Paul looked at the books of poetry that stood proudly along the single shelf. Kurt grinned at him. 'I still don't make any bloody money from it . . . Ah, here's

Susan with a couple of cold Windhoeks. Isn't she beautiful, Paul?'

Paul looked at Susan and smiled. 'Yes,' he said, 'She is. Thanks for the beer, Susan.'

She winked at him and slipped out of the door.

'Now tell me, Kurt, you old bastard. How did you corner her?'

They staggered out into the moonlit night. Paul couldn't remember how many beers they'd had, but the feeling was very good. He wanted to cry, and he wanted Anne with him now. Again he wondered what the hell he was doing chasing Dr Torr and Wayne MacLeod.

'Why do you stay here, Kurt?' he asked.

'Why the fuck do you think? I need this place, Paul. I can't leave, it would kill me. *Ja*, the pay stinks; I suppose I should teach at the university – I was offered a post lecturing on conservation in Jo'burg. But man, can you imagine me living in that hell-hole? God, I'd die.'

I almost did, thought Paul.

'Your wife . . .?' Kurt asked.

'We're divorced.'

'I'm sorry, man. No, wrong, I'm not sorry. I don't think she loved you. I remember you coming here on your honeymoon.'

'I'm involved again . . .'

Kurt drew closer. 'What does she look like?'

Paul opened his wallet and took out the picture of Anne – it had been taken by Mkhulu. Kurt took it carefully and moved back towards the house, studying the photograph under the outside light. He shook his head. 'I'd like to meet her.'

'Why?'

'Ask her what she saw in an old dog like you?'

Paul slapped him hard on the back.

They made their way through the moonlight to the garage and got into Kurt's Land Rover. The engine started quietly, muffled for game-watching, and they drove silently out towards the pan. The cool air sobered Paul, and he took in the immensity of the landscape. Kurt drove on, heading round the edge of the waters, then pulled up slowly.

Kurt held a finger to his lips and they left the vehicle and walked barefoot across the sand. In the distance Paul heard the growl of a lion. They moved soundlessly for a long time. There were no landmarks, yet Kurt knew exactly where he was going. There was another growl, and Paul saw the stretched-out, sleeping body of a lioness three metres to his left.

He touched his friend's arm. Kurt was a tracker without compare, he'd learned his craft from the Bushmen of the Kalahari. But his ability with lions came from inside; it was something you couldn't learn – it was a matter of instinctive courage. Paul had known only two other men, who had the gift of being able to move among the most deadly of the predators without harm – his father and Mkhulu.

They came up to a clump of bushes, and behind them Paul saw the cubs – two of them, lying next to their mother. He sucked in his breath. He hadn't expected to see anything as beautiful as this. Suddenly he felt sad. Why could he not live like this? Why could he not go back and remain on Klaw?

The lioness rose slightly, and growled. Unafraid, Kurt moved forward and scratched the tummy of one of the cubs, who flopped over onto his back.

After half an hour they withdrew, to sit down under a tree.

'Now we wait for sunrise,' Kurt said softly.

The sun came up in the east, a fiery orange ball of light. A buck crossed the sand and drank tentatively from the waters of the pan.

They watched the lionesses creep forward, while the lion watched from a distance. Too late the buck sensed the danger, turned and started to run: the closest lioness leapt forward on her great hind-legs and raked her claws down the animal's flank. Then the others moved in to feast on the raw flesh.

There was no sadness in the death, it was simply inevitable. The cubs were allowed to enjoy the leftovers.

Paul wished that Anne could have been with him to experience this moment: the yellow light on the water, the magnificent animals and the companionship of an old and trusted friend.

Later Paul felt the heat of the coming day, and Kurt gestured to him to move slowly back to where they had left the Land Rover.

They were back at his house at ten, to be greeted with sounds of sizzling bacon and eggs. Kurt went into the kitchen where Susan was cooking in a black bikini and an apron. He put his arms around her from behind and hugged her to him. Paul felt a stab of jealousy at their intimacy. He wished again that Anne was with him.

'So what do you think of our lions, Paul?' Susan asked pleasantly.

'They're very, very beautiful. I'd forgotten about Etosha. I envy you, living here.'

'You're talking to a man who has his own private reserve,' Kurt said jokingly.

'You're both welcome there any time, Kurt, for as long as you like. Just remember that. The boys as well. And that's not an idle promise.'

Kurt removed his arms from Susan and slapped Paul on the back. 'You know what this bastard's going to do, Susan?'

She looked up from her cooking and Paul wanted to melt, she looked so gorgeous.

'What, Paul?'

'I'm going to direct a film about my father's work with lions. I've sold the script and we start shooting early next year.'

He saw the flicker of sadness cross her face and he knew why. Kurt was talented – a natural raconteur – but his creativity was intense and pure, finding its perfect outlet in poetry – his work only appreciated by a small audience. Paul's work on film was seen across the world.

'That's a great achievement, Paul,' Susan said. 'Kurt's told me how much he learned from your father . . .'

Suddenly he felt guilty, invading their house and their lives with his presence. They were happy together – Kurt might not have had commerical success, but they had a good life.

Paul pulled out a kitchen stool and sat down. 'You have so much here . . .' he said. 'So much that I envy.'

Susan served up the eggs and bacon. Then she joined Paul and Kurt at the kitchen table.

'The boys have gone back to boarding-school,' she said. 'Kurt never says goodbye to them, he just can't do it. So we're grateful for your coming, even if it was a surprise. I read the papers every day while you were on trial – I always thought there was more to what had happened – I've always wanted to meet you.'

They talked for a long time, especially about Paul's experiences on death row. And as he talked to them he knew he would only have friends like this in Africa, because only they could understand the true meaning of the word 'freedom'. Only they had the experience to understand what it had felt like for him to be kept in a steel cage under threat of death.

Eventually Kurt got up. 'Paul, stay here with Susan for the morning, I've got to go into Tsumeb to sort out a few administrative problems.'

As Kurt showered and shaved, Paul helped Susan clear up the breakfast table.

'So, are you going to tell me how you came to be here?' she asked. 'When you drove up, there was a strange expression on your face . . .'

Paul laid his hand on her arm. 'Maybe I should go. I'm bringing problems you don't need.'

'You're a friend. If I can help, I will.'

He knew he could trust her just as he could trust Kurt – and it was a relief for him to talk. He heard Kurt driving off to town. Susan made coffee as he unfolded his story. Later, as he told of the dealings of Fahad, MacLeod and Torr, her face darkened.

'Paul, there's a big farm to the north-east of Tsintsabis, bordering on Angola and Botswana. It's run by an international businessman and no one is allowed on the property. The African people in the area tell of bangs and flashes happening every day – we all know it's some sort of weapons testing facility. Perhaps it's better that that's all we know – the war to the north was very hard.'

Again Paul was assailed with doubts about involving them in what he was doing. With Kurt and Susan he felt at home, happy, yet he knew his very presence brought danger to them.

'You're right, you know, Susan – to put the war behind you.' But in his heart he knew he could never put war behind him. Without danger, his life had no meaning.

Paul slept for the rest of that day, exhausted from the previous night. The quietness of the place was relaxing, and Susan left him alone.

He woke to see the orange light of the setting sun projected against the wall of his room. He stretched, and took a shower. There was the delicious smell of meat cooking on a braai, and he went out into the garden. Kurt chucked him a beer.

'Feeling better? You obviously can't take the pace any longer, my friend.'

Susan came out of the kitchen with salads and some cutlery. 'Leave him alone, Kurt. No one else I know has your stamina.'

Paul laughed, and took a long sip from his beer. Then he turned his face to the darkness and wondered what Dr Torr and Wayne MacLeod were up to.

Wayne MacLeod stared out across the flat expanse of the pan. The hum of the Land Rover's V8 engine was vaguely soporific. The driver kept his eyes on the edge of the pan, aware that MacLeod would pounce if he made the slightest mistake.

The sun was dropping down towards the western horizon, the late afternoon light giving the area a surreal quality. MacLeod turned in the passenger seat and shifted his eyes to Dr Torr, who was sitting behind.

'This is where we disappear,' he said, grinning.

'Surely it would have been easier to fly directly to the test facility?'

'Security is my business. I am a respected businessman, taking you on a hunting safari . . .'

Dr Torr looked irritated, but MacLeod couldn't have cared less. 'My men suspected someone had followed us from the airport,' he said. 'Now they think they were mistaken – but there's no point in taking chances. You have an international reputation – you're the best designer of artillery in the world – and I don't want any intelligence people sniffing around my developments out here. So, to all intents and purposes, we're off on a hunting safari across Ovamboland and Kaokoland.'

This seemed to relax Dr Torr. Since his spell in an American jail, MacLeod thought, Dr Torr no doubt realised that the need for secrecy was paramount – and after all, his security arrangements benefited both of them.

322

He felt a glow of pride as the sleek, white executive jet came into view, standing out dramatically against the pan. The retractable steps came down on cue, and the pilot, co-pilot and hostess appeared at the top of them.

Wayne watched Dr Torr out of the corner of his eye. He could see from the expression on the doctor's face that he was impressed. This was important; the more the doctor's ego was stroked, the better he performed.

'Fitting transport for the world's greatest artillery designer?'

'I am impressed.'

'It's a short flight to our destination, but I felt it should be achieved with style,' MacLeod said deferentially.

They stepped on board. The cabin was quiet as the pilot completed his pre-take-off drill.

The jet took off effortlessly, and the hostess appeared.

'Dr Torr, something to drink?'

Dr Torr ordered a whisky. When the hostess returned with it, he nodded appreciatively to MacLeod. 'Thank you, my favourite malt.'

MacLeod followed the movements of the hostess's body as she walked elegantly back to the rear of the compartment. Then he gestured to Dr Torr to look out of the window.

'If you thought your test facilities in Canada were outstanding, wait until you see what we have here. Down below you can see the runway lights of my private air-strip – there's nothing to compare with this in the whole region.'

'You realise that the firing will be picked up by intelligence satellites?' Dr Torr said nervously.

MacLeod relaxed. He had already covered that angle – but he wasn't going to tell Dr Torr. It was better that Torr never knew how much influence he had; after all, he was just a pawn in the larger game. He said casually, 'Who cares? Perhaps it'll bring in some more customers? We're not breaking any regulations. No one will be able to find out who we're selling to, anyway, and by the time they do it'll be too late.'

'The risk is yours.'

MacLeod pretended to look concerned, but in reality he knew he was safe. He was selling weapons to almost every country across the globe – and he had too much on too many people for anyone ever to risk trying to prosecute him.

They touched down smoothly, and Wayne showed Dr Torr to his suite – a luxurious air-conditioned oasis with terracotta-tiled rooms that gave onto a courtyard with a bubbling fountain.

MacLeod phoned him after an hour. He wanted to make sure that the doctor felt completely at home – he intended to get the most out of him.

'You're happy with your accommodation, Vance?'

'It couldn't be better.'

'Would you like some company?'

MacLeod calculated that in Dr Fassbinder's absence, Dr Torr might like some female entertainment. Dr Fassbinder was in Iraq, where she was supervising the development of the Super-gun. Whatever changes Dr Torr decided to make after the test firing, she would immediately put into effect on the sister weapon in Iraq.

'No, I need to rest,' Torr said shortly.

MacLeod did not reveal his disappointment. He had hoped that the doctor would succumb to temptation, and that this might be used to create a rift between him and Dr Fassbinder. Fahad had mentioned that Dr Fassbinder might be falling in love with Dr Torr; proof of infidelity would give them a chance to kill Dr Fassbinder's growing infatuation with her victim.

'Right, then. I'll see you in the morning.'

MacLeod drew back the sliding windows of his room and stepped out into a courtyard that overlooked the vast landscape beyond the development complex. Soon the Iraqis would have the nuclear weapon he had promised, and he would have made close to a billion dollars on the deal. But even better, he now had a method of launching satellites into space for a fraction of the cost of a conventional rocket launch. And that was something he knew he could sell for an even higher price.

Paul wasn't taking chances. He knew how high the stakes were, and he couldn't afford to gamble that the men who had tailed him from Windhoek had given up their surveillance. So he spent the next few days on safari with Kurt and Susan.

They crossed the Namib desert by Land Rover and entered the

Skeleton Coast National Park. Out in the wilderness again, Paul felt the tension slipping away from him. He fished with Kurt in the sea off the Skeleton Coast, and in the evening they cooked their catch over the glowing coals of an open fire. Paul's skin took on a tawny colour from the intense sunlight and he felt better than he had done in years. He gained a renewed strength from the wilderness and realised it was where he really belonged.

Then, all too quickly, the time was over. They drove back through the Etosha National Park, his friendship with Kurt stronger than ever before, with Susan adding a new dimension.

Darkness masked the feverish activity that had overtaken the installation. Torr glanced across at MacLeod, who was looking tense. He could guess why. If his calculations were out, the barrel of the Supergun could explode on detonation. But he himself was not in the least concerned. He'd never made a miscalculation in his career – he was totally confident of his ability.

He felt a surge of pride now as he surveyed the huge barrel pointing to the sky. The initial charge would send the shell upwards, then secondary charges would boost it on its course up the barrel, then an in-board rocket – linked to telemetry and guidance systems – would put it faultlessly into orbit.

The hydraulic lifts hissed with the loss of compressed air, then guided the barrel a few degrees further into position. Of this system he was particularly proud. One of the potential draw-backs of the Supergun was its enormous weight, but he had refused to let this become an obstacle. True, the Supergun was too heavy to be transported, but the hydraulic lifts allowed it to be aimed in any direction, the barrel traversing a three-hundred-and-sixty degree circumference. And after firing, the muzzle withdrew below ground-level into a nuclear shelter.

Torr had known from the very beginning that the greatest weakness of the weapon lay in its immobility – after a single firing, enemy surveillance systems might pinpoint the Supergun's position and retaliate. However, with the hydraulic lifting system the Supergun could be withdrawn to perfect safety.

MacLeod came up behind him, looking across at the video

and computer screens that completely covered the main wall of the control centre.

'I have chosen a safe target, as you instructed.'

'Good. I am only interested in the accuracy of the hit. The distance of four hundred kilometres is perfect. You're sure no one will be hurt?'

'Solely for your information, doctor, it's a deserted stretch of land in Western Zambia.'

'Just give me the co-ordinates. I'm using a conventional shell.'

MacLeod laughed. And gave him the pinpoint co-ordinates of the church steeple in the town of Kalabo. Unknown to the doctor, the destructive potential of his dream was about to be realised.

Kurt and Susan had gone to bed. Paul was sitting alone outside the house, sipping a cold beer. He felt fate had brought him to Etosha. For the first time in years, he experienced a feeling of inner peace. The night was perfect, and he could see the canopy of stars stretching off to the north-east.

Suddenly, the earth shook, and in the distance there was a distinct rumble. On the horizon a shaft of flame shot up towards the heavens.

He dropped his beer and stared at where the flame had been. Kurt and Susan came out. In seconds, the silence returned.

'It's those bastards on the border, I'm sure of it,' Kurt muttered.

'You've heard this sort of noise before?' Paul asked, surprised.

'No. But I've heard stories about some sort of weapons facility out there, far in the north-east corner, almost on the Angolan border.'

Paul made the connection in a flash. *That* was what Dr Torr and Wayne MacLeod were about. It had to be that. The explosion and the flame – they had to have come from the Supergun.

Susan stared at Paul's face and saw the anguish. 'Leave it alone, Paul . . . Go back to Anne.'

'No, I can't. I know too much. God alone knows what they'll do with that weapon.'

'Weapon?' Kurt asked, shocked.

'You don't want to know any more about this, my friend. But I'll have to ask for your help. Do you think you can take me to this place you're talking about, this weapons facility near the border?'

Kurt smiled grimly. 'Oh yes, we'll get there. And if you need help to get those bastards, I'm your man.'

Kalabo lay sleepy-calm in the moonlight. The church spire cast shadows across the little town, and apart from the occasional bark of a dog there wasn't a sound, or a sign of activity.

A strange whistling sound broke the silence of the night – and then the church exploded in a mass of flame, shards of metal ripping outwards to flatten everything in their path. For a surrounding kilometre every dwelling was flattened, and people died as they lay sleeping. A fire fanned through the town, destroying everything in its wake, sending people screaming out into the open.

In the distance a man in a four-wheel-drive vehicle recorded the event with a video camera. After fifteen minutes he switched on the radio mounted into the dashboard of his vehicle.

'Cub to Lion, Cub to Lion.'

'Lion reading you.'

'A direct hit. Repeat, a direct hit.'

He switched off the radio, and then packed up. Five minutes later he drove off into the darkness.

MacLeod opened the first bottle of vintage Pommery. Dr Torr was smiling from ear to ear, hardly able to disguise his excitement. They had tested only a fraction of the Supergun's potential.

MacLeod thought of what he had in his possession. He could shell Pretoria if he wanted to – he'd have nations the world over begging on their knees for this technology. That was the beauty of the whole system. The gun on its own was worthless – only the technology to manufacture and guide the shells gave the system its value.

He had watched entranced as the technicians guided the shell towards Kalabo. But the true satisfaction came with the radio report: a direct hit at four hundred kilometres range. It was terrifying to contemplate the implications of such accuracy from an artillery piece.

Now the fun could begin. Fahad and Saddam might have the cannon, but for the technology to fire it, they'd have to pay up. It was just a question of upping the stakes. MacLeod knew Saddam hadn't got time to mess around, that he needed the technology fast. The Western powers were consolidating their position against Iraq's invasion of Kuwait, and if Saddam didn't withdraw, war was a definite possibility. But of course, Saddam couldn't withdraw. He needed Kuwait's wealth to pay off his fourteen-billion-dollar war debt, the result of his conflict with Iran.

MacLeod stared across at Dr Torr. The man had proved his worth. His technology was now stored in the computers of the test facility. It was the same with the G5 and G6 – he had everything the good doctor had to offer.

The firing would have been noted, and the intelligence networks would begin their investigations. The disaster in Kalabo would probably not be linked to the firing – after all, no one believed the technology was available to fire a shell over that distance – but if it was, the intelligence people would be led to believe that Dr Torr was the man behind it.

MacLeod poured the doctor another glass of champagne. 'It's your victory, Vance, all yours. In two days time Fahad will show President Saddam the results, then I can begin my negotiations.'

'But, of course, I shall continue my development programme.'

Wayne slapped the doctor on the back. 'Of course, old chap. You can go back to your eyrie in Scotland. You'll never have to worry about funding from now on.'

MacLeod smiled to himself. Soon the doctor wouldn't have any worries at all.

President Saddam Hussein struggled to restrain his temper. 'What do you mean,' he said, 'a new contract?'

Fahad stepped back and drew MacLeod's report from his case. Fahad had already sorted out the financial side of the deal – the IPBP had agreed to extend their loans to Iraq, but only on condition that there was a further increase in the already crippling interest payments.

328

'Mr President, the development costs of the Supergun have crippled MacLeod. With the test firing in Namibia, all his funds have been exhausted,' Fahad said nervously. 'It would be crazy for us to back out now.'

'You know how much we have already paid,' the President said, staring stonily at him.

'Sir, this is a mould-breaking project, one that even the United States government was scared to take on because of the financial implications. But I knew that you appreciated its true potential.'

Fahad paused, bent down and took a video cassette from his case. 'I've brought with me graphic evidence from the test firing. Before we continue this discussion, I think you should view it.'

President Hussein nodded coldly. He gestured to Fahad to follow him into his private viewing-theatre.

The room was icy, belying the yellow light from the solid gold candelabra mounted on the walls. There were seats for twenty people.

Fahad handed the video cassette to the projectionist and then seated himself next to Saddam at the back of the theatre. The lights dimmed ominously.

The video opened with a close-up of Dr Torr's face. The doctor launched immediately into his discourse, his voice rising with passion.

'You are about to witness history. Something that designers of artillery have dreamed of for the last fifty years. A cannon whose range and power is greater than any other on this planet.'

The camera moved in closer on Dr Torr's eyes. MacLeod's cameraman had fully exploited the doctor's persuasive powers, and Fahad noted that President Hussein was totally captivated.

'You will now witness a test firing that breaks all previous world records for artillery,' Torr said. Then a slow cross-fade introduced footage that captured the awesome spectacle of the test firing. Fahad knew several cameras had been used at the firing-point – one close to the launch and one much further away, to show the immense jet of flame that issued from the barrel. The dramatic sound-track ensured that none of the impact of the original firing was lost.

Fahad felt moved again as he watched. He imagined how the ground would have rumbled as the Supergun belched out its shell.

Next followed a series of computer-animated technical drawings, showing how the shell had progressed up the barrel. Then the film cut back to Dr Torr again.

'You have witnessed the test firing of the Supergun,' the doctor boomed. 'The computer animation graphically displayed how successive charges are used along the barrel to boost the shell on its way, instead of one larger initial charge. This is the revolutionary part of the design – for by reducing the pressure in the barrel, it is now possible to place a satellite within the shell. Because of the lower pressure in the barrel, anything held within the nose of the shell is perfectly safe. Proof of this lies in the fact that the guidance system worked perfectly once the shell had been launched.

'Most designers of artillery consider the development of a Supergun for satellite launching impossible – on the grounds that anything held within the shell would be destroyed or badly damaged by the forces of the firing. Now you have proof that they are wrong. And you will soon be in possession of a weapon that the superpowers considered impossible to develop.'

The video cut to a small African town at night, peaceful under the light of a full moon. A strange whistling sound filled the air, followed by a horrendous flash of light and an explosion that devastated the entire town. A fire-storm whipped across the surrounding bush, burning everything in its path.

The video ended, and the lights faded up.

President Hussein turned to Fahad, his face alive with enthusiasm.

'Magnificent! Magnificent! I take back my earlier comments. You are back in command. Now I understand.'

Fahad breathed in deeply. Allah be praised!

They drove north, towards the border with Angola. The memories of his time in the elite Reconnaissance Commando of the South African army came back to Paul – the harsh training and the intense camaraderie, the excitement of danger and action, then later the atrocities and the court-martial.

He felt Kurt's hand dig into his shoulder.

'I know what you're thinking about, my friend. Forget it, leave it behind. We all admired you then, and I still do. But that's the past. Times have changed, there's a new dispensation here, and in South Africa.'

'That war was pointless, Kurt.'

'No, it wasn't. That's where you make a big mistake. All wars are fought to establish bases of power.'

Paul thought about what was happening in the Middle East. He thought of Charlotte and David in Israel, of the explosion in the night, the giant sheet of flame heading up towards the heavens. He thought of Fahad and Halabje, and he didn't want to think any more.

'You reckon no one will see us?'

'They'll see us here, Paul, which is fine. I come up here often. I like to know what's going on and make sure there aren't any poachers in the vicinity.'

Paul gripped the grab-handle on the dashboard as they went over a particularly bad bump in the sand. He guessed that Kurt, a hard man who forgave little, wouldn't go easy on poachers.

Kurt looked across to the horizon and then swung the wheel over to the right.

'Now we head towards the Kavango. We'll cross the Grootfontein-Rundu road, then I'll hide the Landy in a place where no one will find it. After that, we're on foot.'

It was midday when they parked under a rock face, stripped off their clothes and put on camouflage gear. Kurt handed Paul a pistol.

'What's this for?'

'Survival, my friend. You've told me enough already – these boys don't mess around. And I'm sure they won't appreciate your filming their facilities.'

Kurt slung a Musgrave hunting-rifle over his shoulder.

'You don't have to get involved, Kurt.'

'Of course I have to. This area's in my blood. I've fought here all my life.'

They moved out through the bush, maintaining a fast pace of around six kilometres an hour. Paul felt the sweat running off him as the straps of his pack dug into his shoulderblades. He enjoyed the exertion, pushing his body hard. Soon his skin gave off the sweet smell that was a combination of sunburn and sweat, a smell he'd always liked.

In the distance they heard the sound of a helicopter, and they both dropped flat. The sound came closer, then faded away. Paul guessed it must be a routine patrol around the perimeter of the huge reserve.

'Paul man, relax. They won't be expecting any visitors from this direction. They obviously keep an eye on the road traffic, but we came from Ovamboland, so no one knows we're here. If anyone makes enquiries about where we are, Susan will say we've gone down to the Skeleton Coast to do some fishing.'

By the time darkness came they had found shelter in among some rocks. They both unfurled their sleeping-bags. A fire was out of the question – the light would give them away.

'We'll get up just after two this morning and move in under cover of darkness. No one will be around then. I know where the perimeter fence is, and I want to cross it before it gets light.'

They ate a meagre supper of biltong and fresh fruit. Then they settled down into an uneasy sleep. Paul closed his eyes. There was one image he couldn't erase from his mind – that great sheet of flame reaching into the heavens.

Paul felt someone shaking him, then turned to see that it was Kurt. He looked down at his Rolex. It was only twelve. What was going on?

'Shhh.'

Paul rose noiselessly, drew the Browning and followed Kurt to the edge of the rocks. In the darkness he saw a group of men, then heard the bark of a dog.

'The bastards are covering this area. They've got tracker-dogs. Just pray they don't pick up our scent,' Kurt whispered, raising his rifle over the edge of a rock.

'I thought you said you knew this area . . .'

'I do. I played here as a child. But things change.'

The men moved closer. Paul raised the muzzle of the pistol almost to his lips and thought how he would play it if it came to a fire fight. He couldn't be with a better man than Kurt.

They could hear their voices now. They were speaking English, telling jokes, getting closer. He could hear the dogs panting, smell the sweat on the men. He and Kurt remained deadly quiet, waiting for the moment when they would have to spring forward and open fire. But the moment did not come and the men moved slowly away into the darkness, their voices fading into incoherence.

'Jesus Christ,' Paul murmured softly as he lowered his gun. 'I never expected security as tight as this.'

They both bedded down again and slept for another couple of hours. Paul woke at two and roused Kurt. They were on their way in five minutes, Kurt expertly navigating his way as though he were walking in daylight.

They pushed on quickly, closing in on the heart of the giant reserve. Daylight came fast, and they were forced to take cover under some thorn trees. Now they moved more slowly, scanning the horizon for a helicopter or plane on patrol – a nerve-racking business that severely exhausted them.

At eleven, with the heat of the day intensifying, they decided to rest.

'Perhaps we should have flown over . . . Taken pictures,' Kurt said, sweat dripping from his face.

Paul took a swig from the water-bottle and handed it to him. 'We would have seen nothing. And that's what they expect – people in the air. Coming in on foot we still have the element of surprise.'

'Getting in is one thing. Getting out alive may be another, my friend.'

The rest of that day and the following night saw them continuing to edge their way forward. First Paul would flag, then Kurt; each would urge the other on. Sometimes they would laugh crazily as the isolation began to affect their souls. It was almost midday on the following day when Paul caught sight of some flat, sand-coloured structures in the distance.

'That has to be it,' he croaked through his parched lips.

Kurt sank to his knees under a tree. 'Let's rest till nightfall, my friend. If anyone spots us now, we're dead.'

Paul pulled out his binoculars and studied the distant structures. They looked like low-lying concrete bunkers, painted to blend in with the harsh landscape. On some he could see perspex domes, obviously designed to let in external light. He couldn't see a road or an airstrip in the vicinity, and guessed that the only way into the complex must be through underground tunnels. He also realised that there would be movement sensors and metal-detectors in the vicinity, and maybe even land-mines.

They moved forward again in the fading light of the day, Kurt leading the way, his eyes studying the ground carefully for any sign of land-mines. A kilometre further on, he waved Paul back and got down onto his knees. Slowly, using his fingers ever so softly, he scraped back the sand in front of him. He worked carefully, barely breathing. Paul saw the plastic top of the mine revealed as Kurt blew the sand away.

'My God . . .'

'They aren't taking any chances. The ground ahead must be full of these little bastards,' Kurt whispered.

'I'm sure it's just a perimeter minefield. They'd want to make patrols . . .'

Kurt looked back at Paul and smiled. 'You should have stayed a soldier. Of course, there'll be a pattern. We just have to work it out.'

Paul took the lead, crawling on his hands, studying the earth ahead in the fading light. Ten metres on he spotted an irregu-larity in the sand and raised his right boot to indicate that Kurt should back away. Softly, with the fingers of his right hand, he smoothed away the sand. He didn't think about what would happen if he had made a mistake. It was the same type of mine as Kurt had revealed, and under it was a primed grenade. The ultimate dirty trick. He lifted it out, holding the arm down.

He guessed from the pattern of the mines they'd found that the rest must be laid in a diamond grid. He identified the place where he thought he'd find the next mine and moved slowly in that direction. Sure enough, there was the slight indentation in the sand.

He and Kurt moved more confidently now, certain of the position of the mines. Eventually Kurt found vehicle tracks parallel to the minefield and they knew they were through.

They marked in the sand their entry-point back into the minefield, so they wouldn't be disorientated on the return journey.

It was ten o'clock when Paul finally touched his hand against the wall of the first concrete bunker. Kurt studied its surface and shook his head.

'I don't think we're going to find a way inside.'

Paul nodded. 'I think you're right, but let's do a tour of the installation before we come to any final conclusions.'

They moved slowly round the walls in the darkness, searching for windows or doors that might give them access to the interior, but found nothing.

'What about climbing up?' Kurt suggested. 'It's not so high, and there's a ledge where it joins the roof.'

Paul looked at him grimly. 'We'll be very exposed, but we've got no choice.'

Kurt cupped his hands together and Paul stepped up, grasping the top of the concrete wall closest to them. He pulled up and looked around, sucking in his breath.

He was looking at a huge and sophisticated installation. In the distance he caught sight of gardens and a pool . . . Then he saw a watch-tower; he guessed they'd be using night-sights, and immediately lay down against the concrete roof.

'Come up,' he whispered to Kurt, dropping his hand down over the edge.

Kurt pulled himself up and looked with disbelief at what he saw before him.

'God alone knows how much this cost to build.'

Paul edged forward – and without warning, sirens erupted. They both froze against the rooftop.

'This is all we need,' Paul said mirthlessly.

They heard motors starting, and the hiss of hydraulics. 'Sounds like a convoy of trucks, but I don't see a road near here,' Kurt whispered.

In the distance Paul saw something rising up into the sky out of the ground. It looked like the top of the leaning tower of Pisa. Then he realised it was the barrel of a gigantic gun. Spurts of gas erupted from its snout, and again warning sirens sounded.

Then there was a terrifying sequence of explosions. Paul looked up to see a sheet of flame spurt upwards from the barrel as it bedded down backwards with the force of the shot. Almost immediately they were showered with miniscule bits of debris, and Paul smelt burning.

'My God,' Kurt stammered, 'what is is it?'

'It's the most powerful gun on earth,' Paul whispered back. 'A Supergun. And it clearly works.'

'Yes, it works very well,' said another voice behind him. 'Both of you stay flat.' Paul felt hands exploring his body, and he was relieved of his Browning. Then he saw the same guard search Kurt just as thoroughly.

'All right, both of you, on your feet.'

They were marched across a series of roofs till they reached one of the perspex canopies, which opened as they approached.

'Down below, and no funny business.'

As they moved down the metal steps, Paul pivoted and struck the guard. Kurt moved sideways as the guard fell past him down the steps and crashed onto the concrete floor. Kurt went quickly down the steps – and another guard moved in as his feet touched the ground. Kurt knocked the weapon from his hand and they wrestled on the floor. Then Paul came down the steps fast and struck Kurt's adversary on the back of the head.

'All right,' Paul shouted, picking up his Browning and the guard's riot-shotgun, 'we'd better find the way out, fast.'

They both knew the roof would be certain death – they'd be sitting ducks for a helicopter attack. Kurt tied up their assailants, then they made their way cautiously out of the room.

They found themselves in a long, deserted hall with double doors at the end of it. They burst through the doors, to find themselves in a vast tunnel that seemed to go on for ever, lights running along its walls. They sprinted down it, hearing shouts in the distance, and Paul felt the breath bursting from his lungs as he pushed himself forward. Then came shots – bullets ricocheting down the tunnel.

Kurt dropped down, swung round and returned fire. The noise was deafening, making Paul's ears ring. Then Kurt was up again, running with him as fast as he could go.

The end came up fast, a huge door that looked as if it belonged in the bowels of a ship or a submarine. Paul swung the circular handle around and, miraculously, the door came open.

They were staring at a helipad and vehicle car park. At the

side Paul saw a collection of motorcycle scramblers. He jumped onto the closest one, turning the starter as Kurt leapt on the back. The bike exploded into life and Paul accelerated away as a group of armed guards burst out of the tunnel. Kurt aimed the shotgun at them and fired. Paul felt the recoil buck the bike, but held his course. Kurt fired again, anxious to buy them as much time as possible, his eyes flitting over the landscape as he tried to figure out their location.

'Swing right!' he screamed over the noise of the bike engine.

Maintaining his speed, Paul swung the bike hard off the dirt road and into the veld. Now they bounced up and down as he hit stones and bumps.

'Just keep going. We've got to make the main road to Grootfontein. They won't want to get too close to the army base there.'

Paul gritted his teeth and held the handlebars tightly, focusing on the lie of the land ahead. Not far off they heard the ominous rumbling of a motorised vehicle.

Kurt looked back, and almost fell off the bike. In the distance he saw a 'Kalahari Ferrari', a motorised cannon, come out onto the road. It pulled to a standstill and the barrel swung upwards. Kurt guessed it was sighting on them and about to open fire. He didn't give much for their chances – the weapon had a range of over forty kilometres and could drop shells with pinpoint accuracy.

'They're going to shell us! Change course now!'

Paul swung to the left and dropped down into a dry streambed. He hadn't seen the gun but he knew Kurt had spotted something dangerous.

Over the edge of the donga Kurt saw the muzzle of the mobile cannon spout flame. There was a sickening noise in the air as the shell hurtled towards them. He wasn't prepared for the noise or the force of the explosion when it happened. The ground shook and Paul lost control of the bike, pitching them both into the bottom of the donga. The blast travelled across the earth above them, shrapnel screaming in every direction.

Paul felt blood in his mouth, and leopard-crawled towards Kurt, who was lying face-down on the ground. He rolled Kurt over, relieved to see his friend was still breathing.

'I was winded by the fall,' Kurt stammered. 'We've got to keep moving. Those bastards are going to zero in on us again in a couple of minutes.'

Paul ran back to the scrambler, desperately trying to kick-start it. In the distance he could hear the engine of the motorised cannon moving in towards them. The scrambler's engine burst into life and Kurt staggered to his feet. He was on the back of the scrambler in seconds. 'Keep down in the donga,' he shouted. 'That's what saved us. We're below the spread of fire.'

Paul gunned his way down the narrow, sandy gorge. Then sand walls began to drop and they became more and more exposed. The gun roared again and they both clung to the speeding bike, waiting for the impact.

This time the shell landed close to them, blowing the bike away from under Paul. He screamed out in horror, then something hit him hard on the head and he lost consciousness.

Paul opened his eyes and saw blackness. His mouth was full of sand and he couldn't move. He knew he was suffocating. Panic began to grip him but he measured his breathing, knowing he must conserve air. He worked his right hand and got some of the fingers moving. Using every ounce of strength within him, he began to flex his body. After a superhuman effort, he realised he had about an inch of movement. He pushed the sand from his lips with his tongue. The explosion must have buried him in the sand. How deep down was he? How long had he been out?

He began to wriggle, fighting off the terror of his situation. He must free his arms, give them some leverage, so he at least had a fighting chance. He counted to sixty, then expended every ounce of energy he had in his forearms, scrabbling with his fingers at the same time. Then he rested, and repeated the process after another count of sixty. The danger of his situation was all too apparent to him. If he was fairly deep down he might clear a space for himself, only to have the ground above collapse in on him again. But he didn't think of that, he only thought of surviving.

He had no way of marking the passage of time, no way of knowing how long he had before his strength and his air supply gave out. He was reduced to the level of an animal fighting for life.

After hours of effort, he managed to turn his head. This was a major step forwards, but it was also when he realised how hard it was to tell in which direction he should dig to escape his sandy tomb. A few pieces of sand fell on his face and he guessed the direction lay above him. Now he struggled to achieve a standing position, fighting the pressure of the earth above him. Many times he felt like giving in, but then fought on.

His hands scrabbled upwards, finding looser earth at last. Like a mole he burrowed his way forward, his breathing becoming more excited as his progress increased.

His right hand touched air and he knew he was out. With desperate movements he fought his way from the earth and lay panting in the moonlight, staring at the pile of stones that marked his sandy grave.

He drifted into an uneasy sleep and woke as the first light of dawn broke across his face. It was then he saw the burial mound parallel to his own. Desperately he dug into the sand with his hand, hoping against hope that it wasn't Kurt. But then, in the heat of the day, he uncovered the face, and knew his friend was dead.

Every association with the Supergun brought death. He knew that those developing it would stop at nothing to achieve their final objective. He had to stop them.

Fahad always entered the SAAD 16 complex with a feeling of quiet satisfaction. Here was proof that Iraq had the finest weapons technology in the Middle East. To a stranger it was an odd-looking place, with the buildings arranged in long lines, stretching off into the distance. But the linear layout of the complex was important for two reasons: if there was an attack it would be difficult for the enemy to pinpoint key sections of the base, and in the event of an accident damage to the complex would be minimised.

He took the lift underground and walked along the labyrinth of corridors to the office of Dr Maria Fassbinder. He resented the enormous salary they had to pay her for marking Dr Torr, but they needed her because only she could run the complicated electronic monitoring equipment and guidance systems Dr Torr had developed.

'Everything is in place,' she said when she saw him.

Fahad felt the stubble on his face. She always seemed to be one step ahead of him. 'Dr Torr has now successfully test-fired the Supergun in Namibia,' he said. 'Are you quite sure you are capable of continuing the project here, without his assistance?'

Dr Fassbinder smiled, her dark red lips pouting. Then she smoothed back her black hair. 'Fahad, relax. I just have to get the final designs for the shell from Vance.'

Dr Torr never let the designs for the shell out of his sight. He carried them with him everywhere in a black leather pilot's briefcase – a briefcase that was never away from his side.

Fahad ground his teeth and hid his rage. He didn't like the power that Dr Fassbinder now had over him – and he was jealous of her affair with Dr Torr. Dr Fassbinder had slept with Fahad in the past, now she wasn't interested in him.

'Maria, how do you propose to explain to Dr Torr the new direction the project is taking?'

Dr Fassbinder looked at the map on the computer screen. 'In a few weeks the nuclear shell will be ready,' she said. 'I shall explain to Vance that this is vital to Iraq's interests and will not interfere with the satellite launching programme.'

Fahad grinned. If only she knew the real plan!

In only a few days she would be back with Dr Torr at their castle in Scotland. Wayne MacLeod had given Fahad detailed plans of the castle's layout, and from these Fahad had devised a way of disposing of Dr Torr, and regaining Maria's loyalty.

He left Maria to her work and made his way out of the complex. There was nothing to worry about. Even if the Israelis retaliated with ballistic missiles, he knew the Supergun was safe – SAAD was more secure than a conventional nuclear bunker.

Fahad was particularly proud of the way they had installed the Supergun. Its barrel was located underground, seated in a gigantic dish. It could be moved to any point on the side of the dish, while its base remained in the centre. Special hydraulic lifts could also elevate the barrel to a vertical position for satellite launching. It was an incredible engineering feat. Each time the Supergun fired, it would produce a recoil force of 30,000 tons.

This force was transferred down the barrel via recoil cylinders that pressed into a reinforced concrete base over sixty metres deep. The recoil speed would be about twelve kmh, but what mattered was that 30,000 tons of movement would have to be stopped in two-and-a-half metres. Ten tons of propellant would be needed to fire every shot.

Fahad reckoned that one firing would be enough to prove the point, then the Supergun could retreat beneath its protective covering, safe from enemy retaliation.

Supplies of all materials necessary for the construction of the installation had come via Wayne MacLeod's network of holding companies and subcontractors – a business labyrinth that would take even the most sophisticated intelligence agency years to break down.

Fahad stepped into the helicopter and lifted away from the base. Everything was in place. Now he must give orders for the termination of Dr Torr – an action designed to fool the intelligence world into thinking that the Israelis had effectively terminated the development of the Supergun.

Sir Donald Morgan held the phone tightly, covered the mouthpiece and looked across at his American counterpart.

'You want me to make the decision?' Chuck Conroy said with an air of fatigue. 'I thought Norton might have sorted the problem out.'

'It appears that Norton has gone out of circulation. He disappeared in Namibia. I think we can forget about him.'

'And now you've heard that the Mossad want to bump off Dr Torr? Well, personally I've never liked that smart-assed bastard.'

Sir Donald took his hand off the mouthpiece. 'I will contact you in another five minutes,' he said into the telephone. 'No, I have not cleared the matter.'

He put the phone down, linked his hands together and rested his elbows on the desk top, staring at the American.

'No,' Chuck said, staring back at him. 'You make the decision, Donald.'

'We do nearly half a billion pounds of business with Iraq every year. I don't believe they have the capability to build a Supergun, let alone launch satellites from it.'

'You said you saw the plans with your own eyes . . .'

'I saw plans, that was all. Not the final product. It would probably take ten years to develop.'

'Donald, as you know, we have close ties with the Israelis. But what if it was discovered that we'd bumped off Dr Torr? Then you'd see war in the Middle East.'

'So, you'd rather wait for the Mossad to do your dirty work?'

'You know, when it comes to that sort of thing there's no one to touch them. They'd do a nice, clean job, with no negative publicity.'

Dr Torr walked across the castle lawns and down the steps to the waters of Loch Leosavay. He felt at peace with himself.

The last sunlight of the day pierced the clouds and made the waters of the loch look like liquid silver. The moment captured much of what he considered was important about life – it symbolised that in everything there was a beginning and an end.

Now, at over sixty years old, he was close to achieving his dream, to launching a satellite into space from a big gun. He knew the ramifications of this would be far-reaching. It cost roughly $10,000 for the Space Shuttle to launch a kilogram of payload into space – with his Supergun the same cargo could be put into space for $600. Iraq now had technology that would be the envy of the rest of the world.

He knelt down and touched the water to his lips. It tasted good, like the whisky he loved so much. He had been stupid to be worried about security. Here at the castle he was entirely safe, and in Baghdad he would have absolutely nothing to worry about either.

He cast a final glance at the waters of the loch in the fading light, then took the path back up to the castle.

A few minutes after Dr Torr's departure, two frogmen came out of the waters of the loch. The smaller of the two pulled off his mask and looked cautiously around, the larger man went back into the water and lugged a long, hand-guided, torpedo-shaped craft onto the stone beach. They carefully opened their craft, surveying its contents with safisfaction. The smaller man silently peeled off his wet-suit, changed into a black tracksuit and then drew a pistol from the torpedo. While he stood guard, the larger man went through the same motions. They talked to each other quietly, their olive skins glistening in the evening light. Then, with a last exchange of glances, they made their way towards the castle.

Torr mounted her once more. He felt young; the success of the project had given him a new vitality. With her he enjoyed the physical act of sex – her passionate cries, the final stimulus that triggered his release.

He sank down into the sheets next to her, cradling her in his arms.

'Oh darling, that was so very good. God, I've missed you,' she purred softly.

'I felt alone, too, this time. I wished you could have come with me to Namibia instead of going to Baghdad. But I think someone was tailing me, and at least I knew that, in Baghdad, you would be safe.'

She raised herself on one elbow, a scared expression on her face. 'Why didn't you tell me? We should have stepped up security. Fahad should have provided you with a bodyguard.'

'He offered me bodyguard, but I turned it down. I like to preserve a measure of privacy.'

She held his hand tightly. 'Vance, you should have accepted. The Israelis are very dangerous.'

'If they want to get me, they'll get me.'

'You must move to Baghdad, immediately,' she said quickly. 'There you will be safe.'

'But I don't want to live in Baghdad, I want to be here, in my castle, with you.'

Her face suddenly appeared much older in the moonlight that streamed through the window. 'Don't be a fool, Vance. You are a marked man.'

Unsettled, he got up and walked around the room. Suddenly he was afraid. He had thought she would allay his fears, instead she had intensified them. He walked to the door that led onto the battlements.

'I need some air. This conversation is pointless. All that matters is our relationship.'

'I'm sorry, my love.'

He let himself out onto the battlements – and sensed a movement in the shadows.

'Who the . . . ?'

The explosion knocked him slightly forward as five bullets smacked in quick succession into the back of his skull. He was dead before he hit the ground.

Maria came out of the bedroom, shotgun in hand, but before she could fire the assassin was on her. He pressed the muzzle of his pistol into her head.

'One move. You die.'

She dropped the shotgun, and he released her, and pistol-whipped her around the head. She struggled, but was no match for him. He pulled off his tracksuit pants and bent her over the back of a chair. The nose of pistol was pushed savagely into her ear.

'One word from you, bitch, and I kill you.'

He penetrated her roughly, forcing her down hard against the back of the chair so that she could hardly breathe. When he had finished she collapsed to the floor and lay watching him. Another man appeared from the shadows. This one drew a knife, pushed it into her throat and forced her to perform oral sex. Finally, pulling his tracksuit pants back on, he raised his pistol to her head and pulled the trigger.

The pistol dry-fired, and he laughed.

'If you ever think of using your knowledge against Israel, you German bitch, you will die.'

Then they were gone from the room, and over the battlements, while she staggered to her feet and sounded the alarm.

On the balcony outside, Dr Vance Torr lay dead in a pool of his own blood.

Paul handed the customs official at Lusaka airport a ten-dollar note, took his case and made his way across the crowded concourse. His face was a picture of desolation. There were black bags under his eyes, his hair was unkempt and his face unshaven.

It had been unadulterated hell: telling Susan that Kurt was dead, trying to console her and then realising it was useless.

He'd taken her to the boarding-school so she could tell the boys. She was strong, he knew that, but there was only so much a person could bear and she was at the limit.

He'd said goodbye to her at Windhoek airport. He would be back, he'd said, and he wasn't lying. The two of them had given him so much in such a short space of time, and he was deep in Susan's debt.

From Windhoek he'd flown directly to Jan Smuts, and from there to his house. He'd worked like a demon in the *Star* newspaper library, piecing together the reports of the previous four days. It had almost missed his eye – the short account of a mysterious fire in a remote Zambian village. More enquiries had led to contact with a Zambian journalist. The journalist hadn't been to the scene of the fire, just given a brief report of its occurrence. Paul sensed he hadn't been interested in investigating further.

After that, Paul had made a few phone calls to London, and with the help of an investigative journalist friend had confirmed the link between Wayne MacLeod and the various arms manufacturing concerns Paul had linked to the Supergun programme. Now he was about to carry out some investigations for himself.

He hired a Land Cruiser and headed out to the west, leaving the copper belt behind. It was a 650-kilometre journey to Kalabo and he pushed the vehicle flat-out. Time and again he would run into road blocks, wait for hours and usually have to offer a bribe to get moving again. By nightfall he had made the town of Kaoma and had booked himself into a dismal hotel.

When he finally made it to his room, he took out his portable radio and tuned in to the eight o'clock news on the BBC World Service. He lay on the mattress, which sank in the centre. He knew by the morning it would have given him chronic backache, so he opted to sleep on the floor.

He listened to the build-up of events in the Middle East. Tension was running high, and it didn't look as though Iraq was going to pull out of Kuwait. But he was certain the United States and Great Britain were anxious to avoid going to war with Iraq. The balance of power in the Middle East was precarious; a war might unify the Arab States against Israel, and it would also push up the price of oil dramatically.

345

Tired, he had dropped off into an uneasy doze when suddenly he was up and staring at the radio.

'. . . Dr Torr was regarded as one of the world's top authorities on ballistics, and it is believed that he was working for the Iraqi government. With tension running high in the Middle East, claims have been made that he was the victim of an Israeli hit-squad. In Scotland, police on the Isle of Lewis are searching for the killers. Robbery is believed to have been a possible motive.'

Paul went over all the details of what he'd uncovered. He'd witnessed the firing of a powerful and dangerous weapon – a weapon that was clearly in an advanced stage of development. If anyone wanted to stop what was happening, it wouldn't be enough to eliminate Dr Torr. But then maybe no one else knew what Paul did.

He had to get to Kalabo the next day. If he uncovered what he thought he would, he'd contact Sir Donald in London. The information would have a direct and frightening bearing on the Middle East situation.

Wayne MacLeod looked carefully through his binoculars at the leopard cubs outside the complex, then he handed the binoculars to Fahad.

'Perfect, aren't they?'

Fahad grunted; he had other things on his mind. President Hussein was in a blind rage over Dr Torr's death and was demanding reprisals.

'Fortunate about Torr, he was beginning to get difficult,' MacLeod said quietly, as Fahad looked through the binoculars.

'You know his assassins raped Maria?'

'Ah . . . Nice touch. Naturally, she blames the Israelis?'

'Of course. She's on a plane to Baghdad right now. She wants to push the button.'

Paul arrived at Kalabo as daylight was fading. What he saw deeply disturbed him. The town was in ruins, having been apparently devastated by a huge fire. A local informed him that the fire was a message from heaven – that God had spoken, showing his wrath by turning the church into a great ball of fire and then sweeping the flames through the town.

Paul wanted to examine the ruins of the church, but in the darkness he could see next to nothing. He drove back to the motel on the outskirts of Kalabo and retired to his dirty, thatched rondavel – a depressing place with a broken ceiling-fan, the stained carpet below it littered with dead flies. He turned off the gas-lamp and lay down on his bed, listening to the sounds of the night. Sleep refused to come.

Just who had assassinated Dr Torr? Had they killed his girlfriend as well? The news report had made no mention of her . . . His mind turning over these and other speculations, Paul finally drifted off into an uneasy sleep.

He rose with the first light of dawn, packed the Land Cruiser, then drove into town. He pulled up at the church. In the centre of the charred ruin someone had propped up the blackened altar cross. It reminded him of the charred cross in Coventry cathedral – a stark testimony to the horrors of the blitz.

At the back of the church was a huge crater. Paul slid down into it, his feet sinking into the pool of rainwater that had gathered in the bottom. Then he looked up, across to the south-west, guessing from the shape of the crater that that was the direction the shell must have come from, scoring an almost direct hit on the church steeple.

He sensed that he was not alone, but when he looked around he could see no one. The atmosphere in the small town made him feel uneasy; he was the only white person in the place. He guessed MacLeod would have had someone here at the time of the firing, monitoring the landing of the shell. But that person would have left after recording the successful strike.

Paul took out his video camera and started filming, making sure no aspect of the destruction was missed. This was evidence he could use to prove the efficacy of the Supergun.

As he left the church, a black military officer accosted him.

'Identification, please . . . Why were you taking pictures?'

Paul looked into the dark eyes but could not read them. Squat and overweight, the man was blocking his exit from the church. In the background Paul saw two other soldiers, armed with automatic weapons. He should have been more cautious.

Paul scratched his nose and summoned up an embarrassed

smile. 'I'm with a religious magazine programme. We report occurrences that appear to be acts of the Lord.'

The officer looked sceptical. 'I want identification. What's your name?'

'Reverend Paul Norton.'

'You have identification?'

Paul produced his passport. The man looked at it, grinned, then put it in his pocket.

'I want that back!' Paul demanded angrily.

'No. I need this for the moment. We shall have to detain you.'

Paul produced fifty dollars, which the officer took unashamedly, snorting with pleasure. The passport was returned.

'I want the film, too,' the man said. Paul handed over another fifty dollars. 'Thank you, Reverend Norton, you understand the ways of the world very well.'

'Sinners are the same the world over,' Paul said piously.

The officer drew his pistol and aimed it between Paul's eyes. 'People disappear here, Reverend,' he said with a sickly grin on his face.

Paul raised his hands. 'I'm sorry, I talked out of turn. I'll be on my way . . .'

'That's a very good idea, Reverend. Just make sure you don't shoot any more film.'

The soldiers in the background melted away, and Paul breathed a sigh of relief – he had diffused a potentially ugly situation.

'Has anyone else been taking pictures?' he thought to ask. 'A tourist like myself?'

'No. You're the first.'

Paul walked back to his Land Cruiser, leaving the officer standing amongst the ruins. He gave him a final wave and started up.

It was time to leave Kalabo. It would be a long drive back to Lusaka.

Captain Lunga made his way back to the barracks. He did not think Norton was a minister – church people could not afford to pay bribes. Anyway, Norton's bribe was insignificant by comparison with the large amount of money that had been deposited in his bank account in Lusaka several weeks before. The money was his, and all he had to do in return was make sure that no one complained too much about the damage to the town, and identify any suspicious visitors.

Back at the barracks, he went to his office and picked up the phone. He made a long-distance call. Any information, he had been told, anything suspicious, and he must let them know.

Wayne MacLeod did not like Birmingham at all, but he owned many companies in the vicinity of the city and that meant he had to visit it fairly often.

Each company was part of a gigantic web that fabricated different parts for his arms manufacturing consortium. Taken individually, each of the components made by the separate companies could have a multitude of different, innocent uses, but brought together they produced a formidable array of weaponry.

He glanced at the stands that surrounded him inside the National Exhibition Centre, then stepped up onto the display of his latest acquisition – Troy Air. The presentation was of components for the aeronautical industry. Troy Air specialised in the highly profitable production of advanced composite and carbon-fibre aircraft parts, which all the major airlines were using in their new aircraft as they gradually replaced their fleets.

Only MacLeod and a handful of his most trusted engineers knew the real value of Troy Air. Carbon-fibre was a vital component in missile technology, especially in the design of missile nose-cones. This was technology nations like Iraq had problems getting their hands on – technology they had to have if they wanted to develop their own ballistic missiles. They would pay a fortune to acquire it – just as they would pay a fortune to acquire the filament winding machine Troy Air had recently purchased on the legitimate grounds that they required it for making radomes – the protective housing for radar antennae on many aircraft. However, as MacLeod knew only too well, filament winding machines were also used for building the nose-cones of missiles, and could not be sold to countries who might be using them for that purpose. Troy Air, of course, would sell

349

its machine to anyone prepared to pay a high enough price. Again, he had Fahad by the shorts.

Troy Air also made the sabots for the Supergun. These were the carbon-fibre bands that held the shell in place as it left the barrel, then fell away in mid-air. They were described as carbon-fibre drill casings in the company's catalogue, to confuse anyone who showed a little too much interest in them.

Amongst his other companies at the exhibition was Chesterfield Forgemasters who, along with other legitimate military articles, manufactured tank barrels. They had supposedly made a large number of sections for a special new type of high-pressure oil pipeline for use in Jordan, but in reality these sections of pipeline made up the barrel of the Supergun and incorporated special liners to reduce the wear caused by extensive firing.

John Winters Ltd, another of MacLeod's companies, had supplied the breech and the hydraulics for the weapon, shipped to Jordan as parts for an irrigation project.

MacLeod knew there was little chance of his ever being found out. All the financial transactions involved money laundered through IPBP to correspondent banks in other countries – the possibility of anybody making links was unlikely in the extreme.

Though competition in the armaments market was usually intense, among the private manufacturers MacLeod knew he led the field by an enormous margin. He was now in a position to sell Supergun technology to anyone who wanted it. The trick was to make the sale without being seen as the seller – to keep one's identity secret.

In every armaments deal he made, MacLeod remained in the background, paying a middle-man a hefty commission to take the credit for the deal. If there was war, and the intelligence agencies started investigations, it was the middle-man who would take the blame. MacLeod smiled at his choice for the Supergun deal – the British Prime Minister's son. He was quite certain that the truth would never come to light, it would be too embarrassing for all concerned. In fact, if the identity of the middle-man was exposed in the press, it could bring down the British government.

Still, Wayne was anxious to complete all his business with Iraq before war broke out. If the Americans and the Iraqis started battering it out, he knew that the CIA – amongst others – would conduct a secret war intent on eliminating Iraq's suppliers, a war in which the Israeli secret service, the Mossad, would play a key role.

Now that the Israelis had supposedly taken out Dr Torr, MacLeod was pretty sure that everyone in intelligence circles would consider the Supergun dead.

His main objective for the moment was to extract another billion dollars from President Hussein before handing him the nuclear shells. The managing director of Troy Air had just informed him that the nose-cone development program was complete, and that they had begun to manufacture components for the shells.

As for the nuclear warhead, he had facilities in South Africa to supply him with that. Ironically, this nuclear material came from the same installation that supplied the Israelis . . . Still, business was business.

Paul lay naked next to Anne in the darkness, listening to the sound of the crickets. He had returned to Klaw after his trip to Zambia, and she had been overjoyed to see him. Their love-making had been more intense than it had ever been, perhaps because she realised the danger he faced.

Her eyes opened. She held his hand tightly.

'Paul, you've got to do something. David and Charlotte are in Jerusalem. That'll be the target, for sure.'

'All the press reports are saying Saddam's Scuds aren't a threat. Everyone's talking about his arsenal of chemical weapons.'

'And you know he's got a gun that can lob nuclear warheads into Israel.'

'But I haven't got any hard evidence to back my story up. I can prove there's a Supergun in Namibia, but that's all.'

Anne sat up. 'You've got to prove they've got the Supergun in Iraq. And the only way you're going to do that is to get in there and find out what's going on.'

Anne gripped his hand. 'Paul, you know what they do to journalists they catch spying. There was that Iranian-born journalist they caught this year . . .'

'Farzad Bazoft – they hanged him.'

'You'll have to be very, very careful.' She stared into his eyes. 'There's more isn't there?'

'I saw Dr Torr with Wayne MacLeod in Namibia. MacLeod is involved . . .'

'Does he know you're onto him, Paul?'

'Fahad knows about me, but he may not have mentioned that to MacLeod.'

Anne got up and looked down at the bush in the moonlight. 'When I first met you on the reserve, in the Land Cruiser with me was an Iraqi – Hyde mentioned he was a guest of Wayne's. His name was Fahad.'

Paul felt his flesh creep. 'Dark hair, smooth skin, and a two-day stubble that he carefully cultivates?'

'Yes.'

'That's him – the guy who tried to have me killed in London.'

'So he'll be keeping an eye on you. Paul, how are you going to justify your presence in Iraq?'

'I'll say I want to film things from the Iraqi's perspective.'

She folded her arms. 'If you go, I'm coming with you.'

'No!' He paced around the room, gesturing with his hands. 'It's too dangerous.'

'Book the tickets . . . Go ahead of me if you want to – but I'm coming. That's all there is to it.'

Paul waited till Anne fell asleep and then got up very quietly. He searched the room, found her passport and stuffed it into his back pocket. Later he made his way silently through the bush to his plane.

He took off from Klaw in the first light of day, knowing that, without her passport, Anne would be unable to follow him.

Two days later Paul arrived on Harris.

It didn't take him long to find out that Peter Killick had been murdered, and that sent a chill through his bones, reinforcing him in the knowledge that he had to take every conceivable precaution.

Instead of booking into the Cabarfeidh hotel in Stornoway, he stayed at Scarista House – an exclusive country hotel on the west coast of Harris. That evening, in front of the peat fire in the lounge, he probed the proprietor on the details of Dr Torr's murder.

'Everyone was shocked,' the man said, 'but the police couldn't come up with anything. Anyway, if you're so interested you should take a look at Amhuinnsuidhe Castle in the morning – Wayne MacLeod's turning it back into a hunting-lodge. After Dr Torr's death the rest of his people left. Can't say I can blame them, can you?'

Paul sipped his whisky nervously. The proprietor leaned closer. 'Tell me, are you a reporter?'

Paul nodded.

'There were a lot of reporters snooping around here after the good doctor was murdered. That was when the rumours started, but I don't believe them. For me he was a holy man through and through.'

'How come?' Paul asked, taking another sip of his whisky.

'There isn't much money around the islands, but bless his soul, Dr Torr was helping the islanders. He put the local council onto a bank – IPBP – and our money's lent out at a very generous rate of interest. Not only that, though; the local people he employed were well paid.'

'Couldn't his followers have carried on after his death?'

'Ach, no. You should have seen Dr Fassbinder after the murder. In a terrible state, she was. There's a rumour she was raped.'

More guests arrived in the lounge and the proprietor served them while Paul bided his time. Eventually the man came back to him, and Paul continued the conversation. 'Tell me about the police investigation,' he said.

'Very strange. You know, normally when there's a murder on the island the police from the mainland come over to investigate. Well, this time they said it wasn't necessary. They left it to our local chaps – and it's still unsolved.'

Paul had the feeling that the whole situation was being controlled. But surely, if it was an intelligence operation they would have ransacked the castle? Unless the killing was merely to serve as a warning.

'Dr Fassbinder took it very, very bad,' the proprietor said.

'She was screaming at the local constable, demanding a full investigation. But he told her the mainland weren't interested.'

Paul drained his glass. 'Do you know where she's gone?'

'There's a rumour she went to Iraq . . .'

Everything was going as planned. Fahad had given Dr Fassbinder her own suite in the SAAD 16 complex, and she had a team of thirty scientists reporting directly to her. Since she'd arrived, forty-eight hours before, she'd worked without a break. He could see the anger etched on her face, and was pleased.

Her energy and intelligence were boundless. Already she was working on the installation of the nuclear warhead in the shell. It would be ready by the end of December.

Everything she ordered had to be sourced from Wayne MacLeod, who was charging insane rates. But MacLeod was their sole supplier. They had to pay, that was all there was to it.

Dr Fassbinder lit another Gaulois and started coughing. The model of the three-stage shell rested on her desk. Above it was a map of the Middle East. She'd demanded that she be the one to push the firing button. The Israelis had killed Vance and she was going to get her revenge.

She kept thinking about how they had raped her – humiliated her. The first shell would hit Jerusalem, unleashing a destructive force the holy city had never witnessed before.

She pressed the intercom button. 'Get me Fahad, I need him here now!'

She stubbed out her cigarette, quickly lighting another as Fahad came into her office. 'I need more computer power,' she said. 'The machines don't have the specification we insisted on.'

'These are the best machines in the world,' Fahad replied coldly. 'I can't get you more computing capacity.'

'Who is the expert here, ja? Me or you?'

Fahad was silent. He wanted to slap her around – but he needed her more than she needed him.

'Answer me. Or perhaps I should talk to the President?'

'You are the expert.'

'Very good. Now, you will please listen and get me what I need. Remember, the shell cannot be completed without it.'

Fahad fumed. How many more million would this cost? He would phone his contact in California. The equipment would have to be air-freighted in. The operation would be difficult as the US had denied Iraq all access to computers and military-related technology.

'I will organise what you have requested,' he said stiffly.

'Leave me alone, then, Fahad. I need to concentrate.'

Dr Fassbinder got up and went to the mirror. Her face looked terrible – there were black bags under her eyes and her skin was a ghostly white. She folded her arms and continued smoking, her eyes half-closed with exhaustion.

She remembered what had happened after they'd raped her . . . She had called the security men and they had swarmed over Vance. Then one staggered back, blood on the back of his hand where he'd tried to cradle Dr Torr's head. That was when she knew he was dead.

From that moment on, only one thought filled her mind – revenge. She had phoned Fahad that evening. He'd said he was certain it was the work of the Mossad. He ordered her to come directly to Iraq, to work in the SAAD 16 installation. She'd evacuated the castle that day, making sure no evidence of their work remained.

The local police investigation had been a farce – she guessed that British intelligence must have co-operated with the Israelis in the killing.

Well, now she would show them. The first firing would hit the Israelis where it hurt the most.

Part III

Paul arrived to find Baghdad in a state of tension. The naval blockade, the sanctions, the seizing of Iraqi and Kuwaiti assets abroad, and the massing of American and Allied forces in Saudi Arabia were sapping the people's morale, even though the local papers argued that the enormous army massed in Saudi Arabia was definitely for defence and not for attack.

Paul's excellent command of Arabic gave him the edge over the majority of Western journalists – in effect it was a passport enabling him to travel freely around the country instead of having to keep the company of a government interpreter. He met many Iraqi officials in his first few days in the capital and stressed that he wanted to get objective film coverage. He implied he was sympathetic to the Iraqi point of view. His reputation for objective film work in Vietnam stood him in good stead, and he was given plenty of assistance.

He based himself in the Baghdad Hilton but spent as little time there as possible – he kept on the move, constantly visiting new places and meeting new people. That way, he reckoned, he stood a better chance of catching sight of Dr Fassbinder.

At a military briefing he asked questions which showed his scepticism of Iraq's ability to fight off a sophisticated military giant like the United States. After this meeting he received a discreet phone call asking him if he would like to be taken on a guided tour of Iraqi weapons installations. Naturally, he replied in the affirmative. He was told that he must undertake to wear a blindfold while travelling, so that he should not know the location of the bases he was visiting. If he agreed to this, he would be picked up outside the Baghdad Hilton early the next morning. Paul realised he would be used as part of the Iraqi propaganda machine – to display their military capability to the

West. He figured it was worth the price – if he didn't do the report, someone else would, and he might miss a valuable lead in the process.

He didn't drink that night, and went to bed early. He wanted to be wide-awake for the next day's journey – his objective would be to film carefully, capturing the reality behind the façade the Iraqis would undoubtedly present to him. It would take all his skill.

Next morning at six he waited outside the main entrance of the Baghdad Hilton, dressed in a white shirt and trousers as instructed. He carried nothing on him except for his video camera and tapes. He'd been told that if anything else was found on him, it would be confiscated.

A battered Peugeot taxi drew up and the rear door swung open.

'Inside,' the driver barked in Arabic.

Paul jumped into the back seat and the taxi roared off. Just round the corner the taxi pulled up next to a van. Two men opened the back of the Peugeot, roughly manhandled him out of the taxi and blindfolded him.

'You try anything funny, you die,' one said very quietly.

They drove for a long time in the van, probably in wide circles to confuse him. Then he heard the sound of planes and guessed he'd been taken to a military airport. He felt the cold metal of a gun barrel pressed into the side of his skull.

'You will be the first Western journalist to see this installation,' a voice said in English with a guttural accent. 'Film only what you are ordered to, and keep your eyes where they belong. Now we take a plane journey.'

He was bustled out of the car and up some steps. He felt himself being strapped into an aircraft seat and heard the pilot conferring with the flight controller. He memorised the commands and the bearings given across the radio. It could all be a smokescreen, but he guessed that somewhere along the line, someone would give something important away.

He felt claustrophobic as the plane took off, the noise of its engines reverberating around the cabin. He guessed he was in a military jet, stripped to the bare essentials and probably used for ferrying personnel and equipment round the country.

The flight seemed to last for ever; wherever they were taking him, it was obviously far away from the capital. He tried to engage his captor in conversation but the man ordered him to remain silent.

After a while Paul asked if he could go to the toilet. Again the gun was pressed into his skull, but he continued to ask and the man finally agreed to take him.

He could smell that they had arrived at the right place. 'You may take the mask off once you are inside,' his captor said. 'Knock when you are finished. If the mask is off when I open the door, I will kill you.'

Paul went inside and started to gag. He pulled off the mask and stared down into the latrine pan – which had not been flushed by the last user. He operated the wall button, flushed the toilet clean and relieved himself. It was good to have the mask off. In the plastic and stainless-steel confines of the cubicle, he knew he wasn't going to find any clues about where he was going, but it gave him a chance to relax. After about five minutes he heard his guard bang against the door. Clearly he wasn't going to be given a chance to be on his own for long.

He carefully repositioned the mask so that he could see down from his left eye – he just hoped his captor wouldn't readjust it when he stepped out of the cubicle. Unlocking the door, he stepped outside and deliberately stumbled. He fell over, and heard his captor curse.

Paul dragged himself to his feet, and to his relief the man didn't check his blindfold. The plane was quite bright inside, with portholes running along its length. The only seats were at the front, near the pilot's cabin.

Paul sat down next to the window and stared down at the landscape. He drank in the details, remembering the position of the mountain ranges below him. They were heading north – but the choice of direction could also have been calculated to confuse him.

He was asked to buckle up his seat belt. At the same time his captor readjusted his blindfold, and to Paul's anguish the peephole he'd created for his left eye was covered up.

'We land soon.'

The whole cabin vibrated as the plane descended rapidly. For a few anxious minutes Paul wondered if the plane was going to make it. Then they landed hard, the whole plane shaking as they hit the runway. They taxied for a considerable time and then Paul heard the engines being shut down.

His captor asked him to unbuckle, then manhandled him out of his seat and down the aisle. He felt the searing heat as the door was opened.

The moment he was on the ground, the blindfold was taken off. He did a double-take. Fahad was standing in front of him, the dark eyes and the two-day stubble just as he remembered them.

'You look worried, Mr Norton. Are you a spy?'

Paul recovered his wits fast. 'The plane journey . . . I am not feeling well.'

Fahad leaned a little closer. 'We have met before?'

'I don't think so.' He smiled and extended his hand. 'Paul Norton.'

Fahad blinked. 'I know who you are, Mr Norton. Your reportage on Vietnam interested my President. Unbiased was the way it struck him. You are here because he ordered it. I believe, until recently, you were living in London, working on a feature film?'

Paul wondered if he was going to get out of this alive. Fahad clearly knew he'd filmed him coming out of the Rutland Gate house with Dr Torr. How much else did he know about him? Paul was anxious to defuse the situation.

'That's correct – a film on my father's lion rehabilitation work.'

Fahad straightened his uniform, his eyes never leaving Paul's. In the distance Paul caught sight of the buildings, almost identical to those he'd seen at the installation in Namibia. He was sure the same architect had been used.

'You know the punishment for spies in this country?' Fahad said softly.

'Execution,' Paul replied smoothly in Arabic. 'I know your laws and customs. I respect your culture, I don't despise it.'

'I like your attitude. You will please follow me.'

Paul walked across the hot tarmac into a reception building. He was shown into a large room which he guessed was the security centre. Video screens monitored areas inside and outside the buildings. Uniformed personnel maintained a constant vigil, ready to react at the first sign of trouble.

Fahad directed him through this area into a smaller room, and ordered him to sit in front of a video camera.

'This is a routine measure. My security people will briefly interview you, record the event on videotape and take your fingerprints. We keep a permanent record of every person who enters this installation.'

The interview was perfunctory, the questions simplistic, relating to his age, military service and education. Next he was stripped and searched, then given special clothes to wear inside the complex. His video camera and tapes were meticulously examined. These measures completed, Fahad escorted him to a lift that took them down into the underground bunkers.

'You are about to see one of the most sophisticated facilities of its kind in the world. We have computers that rival the most powerful in the United States. Some of the technology is American, some European, some Japanese and some Soviet. We have taken the best of everything.'

'Can I film this?'

'Certainly. In your commentary you can mention that we have seen three projects to completion here. The Badr-2000 with a range of two thousand kilometres and a payload of half a ton; another missile system, Uno, designed to put satellites into orbit; and a third that must remain classified.'

'If you're so confident, why the need for secrecy?'

'I leave you to draw your own conclusions. Iraq is determined to show the world that the Arab nations are capable of developing weapons at the highest level of sophistication and destructiveness.'

Paul waited for some mention of the Supergun but nothing was forthcoming.

Next Paul was shown a modified Scud B missile designated 'Al-Husayn'. This had an effective range of six hundred kilometres and could land within a kilometre of a sighted target. Paul knew the Al-Husayn had been used with great effectiveness on Iranian targets during the Iraq-Iran conflict in 1988. Another version, the Al-Abbas, had a five-hundred-metre accuracy but a shorter range of five hundred kilometres.

Paul guessed Fahad's intention was that his documentary should act as a further smokescreen to cover up the advanced stage of development of the Supergun.

His tour continued, and he felt a growing unease at the style and scope of the operation. As he was being guided through one of the design centres, he caught sight of Dr Fassbinder. She looked up at him, then returned to her work.

From that moment, Paul knew the work on the Supergun must be almost complete. He was certain that was what Dr Fassbinder was working on. And there was no doubt in his mind that the first target for the Supergun, should war break out, would be Israel.

A devastating attack against Israel would draw strong support in the Arab world – it would almost certainly result in many of the Arab states aligning themselves with President Saddam Hussein.

Paul knew it was vital that the US and British military commanders should know that the Iraqis had perfected the Supergun and would almost certainly use it to drop a nuclear shell on Israel.

He thought of Charlotte and David in Jerusalem. He had to get a message to them to leave the country, they were in terrible danger. Fahad squeezed his arm. 'I see uncertainty in your eyes, Mr Norton. But there is nothing to be concerned about. Our intentions are friendly. Our annexation of Kuwait was quite legitimate. Once the rest of the world accepts this fact, relations can return to normal.'

Paul nodded, swallowing hard. He wanted to get away from this place. Thank God he had made certain that Anne could not follow him to Baghdad.

Anne was furious. How dare Paul take her passport! But if he thought that was going to stop her from following him to Iraq, he had another think coming.

She'd never asked her father for a favour since she'd fallen out with him years before. He just hadn't been able to accept that, having completed her training, she didn't want to be a part of the CIA. But she had no qualms now about phoning him in

Washington. She'd never approved of what he did, but she saw no reason not to take advantage of his position.

'I need a new passport, Dad, and I need it today.'

'For God's sake, Anne, don't be crazy . . .'

'You can do it for your operatives, so why can't you do it for your daughter?'

'All right, damn you. But don't expect any more favours from me.'

By the time Anne arrived at Heathrow everything she read in the papers told her that Iraq was heading for war. She managed to get on a flight to the capital of Iraq that day, and her flight was uneventful save for her growing concern for Paul – she felt he was out of his depth. He might have had experience of war, but the world of intelligence, as she knew all too well, was a different thing altogether.

At Baghdad airport everything seemed calm and relaxed. Perhaps she'd been over-reacting. After all, Paul was in his element here, standing in the front line, getting unique footage that he could supply direct to the international television networks.

She collected her case from the baggage carousel and moved towards customs. The official scrutinised her passport and then checked a list cellotaped to the window of his booth.

'Dr Madison, would you please accompany me?'

'Why?'

'A routine check. This way.'

A security official fell in behind her. She turned and looked at the other passengers. Maybe she should make a break and run back to the plane? She took in a deep breath and told herself to relax.

She was shown into a windowless room with a table and two chairs.

'You will wait here.'

'Why? I want to get to my hotel.'

'Sit down. Do not make things difficult.'

'I'm an American citizen. I demand to speak to the Ambassador of the United States.'

'I will call the embassy. Now, sit down.'

Sweat ran down her cheeks. What the hell was going on?

She waited for half an hour and no one appeared. Frustrated, she got up and tried the door. It was locked. She remembered her CIA training; she remained calm. They had not given her her passport back. She should have held onto it.

An hour later the door opened and a smartly dressed man stepped into the room.

'Dr Madison, I apologise, there has been a mistake. You will please accompany me and I will take you to your hotel.'

'Can I have my passport back?'

'Most certainly. Now please, let me take your bags.'

She moved down a series of passages, flanked on either side by plain-clothes security guards. No one said anything to her and she focused on getting to the hotel. She went into a courtyard and was directed into the back of a waiting car. Security men got in on either side of her and they sped off towards the capital.

'Where's my case?' she asked.

Neither of the guards or the driver took any notice. She realised they probably didn't speak any English and had been most likely ordered to ignore her.

Eventually they pulled up outside a concrete building that looked more like a police headquarters than an hotel. As she was escorted inside, Anne realised they'd been lying to her. Finally, when she was thrown into a tiny concrete cell, she knew she was in serious trouble.

The cell had no windows – its only furnishings were a toilet bucket in one corner and a blanket on the concrete floor. Anne sat down on the blanket and tried to compose herself. Was Paul in the same predicament?

When he got back to the Baghdad Hilton, Paul phoned Klaw. He felt guilty about taking Anne's passport. To his horror, Mkhulu told him that Anne had obtained a new passport and was on her way to Baghdad. He contacted the airport, to discover that she'd arrived from London an hour before. Sweating profusely, he took a taxi to the airport, hoping like hell he hadn't missed her.

After two hours of searching round the airport complex, he knew she must have gone directly to a hotel. None of the officials could remember having seen her.

As he travelled back to the Hilton he began to feel uneasy. He asked at the reception to see if she'd checked in, but they hadn't heard from her. Next he phoned the airline to make sure that she'd been on the incoming flight.

'But she's not here, no one's seen her!' he shouted into the receiver.

'Sir, she was definitely on that flight. I suggest you speak to customs at Baghdad airport.'

He put the phone down and anxiously thumbed through the book next to his hotel bed. He spent another hour dialling numbers, asking questions and getting nowhere fast.

Where the hell was she?

Anne had been dozing when the screaming started. A man, she guessed, but as his cries become more desperate he sounded like a woman. Her flesh began to itch and she hugged her shoulders with her hands. Eventually the screaming stopped – but now she could not sleep as the fear began to take hold of her body. What were they going to do to her? She'd learned about places like this in her training.

The door to her cell opened and she looked up to see a man with his face covered by a stocking.

'Up.'

She rose compliantly and walked out of the door. He pushed her roughly forward and she stumbled down the passage

'Stop.'

She turned to face another door.

'In.'

The smell in the room made her want to vomit, a nauseous combination of blood and urine. The room was brightly lit, with red metal cabinets running along one wall.

'Please sit down, Dr Madison.'

She stared at the man sitting at the desk. He was dresesd in military uniform, his face also covered by a stocking. Round the area of his chin a light stubble perforated the thin nylon.

Fahad.

She felt his eyes running up and down her body, mentally undressing her.

She went over and sat down in front of his desk. He turned to the man who'd escorted her from the cell and barked a command. The man disappeared outside and closed the door.

'Fahad. I demand to see the US Ambassador immediately,' Anne said, summoning up all her courage.

Fahad pulled the stocking off his face, folded his hands behind his head and sat back in his chair.

'Anything else you'd like to demand, Dr Madison?'

'Why am I being held?'

He raised his hand and stifled a yawn. The silence became disconcerting. Eventually he opened a looseleaf file that lay on his desk and rifled through the pages not looking at her.

'The last time we met was in Botswana on Wayne MacLeod's reserve,' he said at last.

'That's correct.'

'Do not interrupt me. I am inclined to get irritated.'

Anne was tempted to say something sarcastic but restrained herself.

'You're an American,' Fahad went on. 'You come from a good family, you had an excellent education . . .' He leaned forward. 'Who can resist a pretty woman, especially when she works for such a noble cause?'

He began rolling a cigarette, and she watched his fine hands. There was a redness around the nails and she guessed it was blood.

'Now why would someone like you come here at a time like this?' The cold eyes bore into hers.

'Please, speak . . .'

''I've come to be with Paul Norton. Is he under arrest?'

'No. Do you know something about him I don't?'

Her mind went into overdrive. God, how much *did* they know about him.

Fahad opened the folder in front of him and took out her passport. 'Your passport is new . . .'

'I lost my old passport, I had to get a new one in a hurry.'

Fahad nodded. 'When did you apply for this new passport?'

She started sweating. 'A couple of weeks ago.'

'Don't lie to me, bitch. I always get the truth in the end.'

'All right, damn you. I applied for it two days ago.'

'Yes?'

'That's the truth.'

'How many people can get a new US passport delivered in less than forty-eight hours with no identification – especially when they're in a game reserve in Botswana?'

'The US government made a special effort to help me.'

He laughed. 'I know who your father is, my dear.'

Anne wished she could go back in time. How could she have been so stupid. She should have told her father where she wanted to go. But then he would have refused point-blank to organise the passport.

'I don't work for the CIA,' she said. 'My father and I are not on speaking terms.'

'But you phoned him for a passport. Anyway, the truth is unimportant. You are a very useful bargaining counter for us. You must admit, it is a little strange for the daughter of the head of the CIA to visit Baghdad at this time.

'You bastard!'

'And you were trained by the CIA, weren't you?'

Anne remained silent.

'Well, at least Paul Norton seems to like me. First he takes a film of me leaving my house in London and then he visits me in person – I had the pleasure of meeting him just the other day. He has a refreshing attitude – unbiased, unlike many of your fellow-countrymen.'

'So I'm your token American hostage?'

He rolled a cigarette, placed it between his lips and then reached for his lighter. He held the flame gently to the cigarette and inhaled slowly. The smell of tobacco filled the room, blanketing out the other unpleasant odours.

'It is my belief,' Fahad said, 'that you work for the Central Intelligence Agency and that you are here on an information-gathering exercise.'

Now the terror welled up inside her. 'That's not . . .' Her mind began to churn. She forced herself to concentrate. She could die . . .

He drew on his cigarette again, and she watched the glow at the end of it. The memories were coming back all the time now. She had been an only child, and her father had wanted a son. He had programmed her to be as close as possible to the son he'd wanted, and she had rebelled, quietly at first and then more openly, until she broke with him completely by not joining the CIA.

At last she managed: 'I do what I do today because I think it matters.'

'Gathering intelligence so your country can dominate the world, so your country can annihilate mine because we won't do as we're told? Because we don't believe in your God?'

'You're going to torture me, aren't you?'

She sensed him tense up as she confronted him.

'You're going to fuck me and reduce me to an animal.'

The cigarette dropped from his lips.

'You're going to humiliate me to make yourself feel powerful. This has got nothing to do with intelligence work.'

She forced herself on, God knew where she was going. Had they got Paul? She knew he wouldn't break. They'd have to kill him.

Fahad reached for the intercom and barked out a command in Arabic. Moments later, the guard who had brought her to him came into the room.

'He will take you back to your cell,' Fahad said. 'We will talk again later.'

When she had gone Fahad picked the cigarette up off the floor, relighting it with a shaking hand. She had touched something deep within him and he was afraid of it.

He had planned to have her beaten, then gang-raped in front of him. What was frightening was that she knew that – she expected it of him. His intelligence assessment was quite simple. She worked for the CIA and was probably a highly placed operative using an excellent cover. She had gone to MacLeod's reserve to spy on him; he wasn't surprised the CIA knew about MacLeod's operation.

Her love for Norton was probably genuine, but Fahad had no doubt that her loyalty to her country was absolute. He sensed she might be using Norton – she would know that Norton's neutral political stance, and his reputation as an unbiased combat cameraman, would ensure his access to the Iraqi military. Norton's credentials went without question.

It crossed his mind that they could be a team. She could feed information back to her controller that Norton would never use in his documentaries. It really was an ideal arrangement for the the CIA.

Fahad didn't want the United States using Dr Anne Madison as a martyr, either – another excuse for them to justify declaring war on Iraq. He decided that for the moment she would simply have to disappear.

He picked up the phone and dialled a number. A certain customs official would shortly have a fatal accident. After that, Dr Madison's disappearance would be watertight.

Paul put a call through to the US Embassy in Baghdad the next morning. After going through several tiers of officialdom, he reached someone of influence.

'Mr Norton, you say Dr Madison is an American national . . .?'

'Yes, she was coming here to visit me.'

'We issued a series of warnings to our citizens. I think her visit was a serious mistake.'

'For fuck's sake! I want to find her.'

'Mr Norton, do you know how many people go missing in Iraq every day? I know who you are and I know what you're here for. Why don't you ask your Iraqi friends where she is?'

He forced himself to remain calm. 'Look, I know it's difficult, but please, I'm very worred about her.'

'Sure. We'll help all we can. I just want you to be aware of the bigger picture. What's her first name?'

'Anne.'

'Where did she qualify?'

'Stanford.'

'Where was she born?'

'Washington.'

'Have you got her passport number?'

'Unfortunately not.'

'All right, I'll get back to you, Mr Norton.'

Dr Fassbinder ran her hands over the surface of the shell – all that was missing was the nuclear warhead. She thought of Vance.

Fahad had advised her that the nuclear warhead would arrive in the next few days. He anticipated that the first firing would be in early January. From the first of that month the Supergun would be on twenty-four hour alert. The order to fire would come directly from President Saddam Hussein. The target would be Jerusalem.

Dr Fassbinder clenched her fists. She must be patient now. The moment of revenge had almost arrived.

Paul lay on his bed, sweat pouring off his face. Where the hell was Anne?

He couldn't contact Sir Donald, he was sure all the phones were tapped, and by phoning the British scientist he'd be signing Anne's death warrant if she was in the hands of the Iraqis. Then he thought of David and Charlotte in Jerusalem. There was no way he could warn them either without blowing his cover and possibly giving the game away to Anne's captors.

Then he remembered there was a fellow-reporter staying at the hotel who worked for CNN. He had a satellite phone.

Paul took the lift up to the top floor, but unfortunately the fire-escape door that led onto the roof was locked. He put down the aluminium case that contained the satellite phone, picked up a nearby fire-extinguisher, bludgeoned the padlock off the door and went onto the roof.

It took about five minutes to unfold and set up the aluminium dish and plug in the phone. He had two vitally important calls to make.

Sir Donald Morgan turned over and pulled the pillow over his head. It took him some time to realise that the phone was ringing. He reached for the bedside light and knocked his alarm clock off the side-table.

'Hell and damnation!'

Wearily he picked up the phone and glanced at the time on the clock lying on the floor. Three in the morning. Jesus Christ!

'Morgan.'

'It's Norton. Paul Norton.'

This could be important. Sir Donald's mind was working

clearly now. 'Good God, Paul, where the hell are you? Is there something wrong?'

'I'm in Iraq. I may not be able to talk again.'

'What's going on?'

'I know they've got the Supergun.'

He groaned. 'Paul, they can't make a go of it. Torr's dead.'

'But Dr Fassbinder isn't.'

'Fassbinder?'

'Dr Maria Fassbinder, his number two. I saw her in the SAAD 16 complex. I think she's in the process of finalising the design of shells for the Supergun, and I'm almost certain the Iraqis have a nuclear warhead for those shells. I don't have to tell you the target.'

Sir Donald thought things over quickly. 'They'd need to do a test firing . . .'

'They've done that already, in Namibia, a month ago. I witnessed it.'

Shit! His agents had been trailing Norton, and they'd lost him. They'd reported that Norton was on safari in the desert. The incompetent fools! – he'd give them a roasting in the morning.

'How far did they fire?' he asked.

'Four hundred kilometres.'

'I need names . . .'

'Wayne MacLeod is behind the project. The Iraqi contact is a man called Fahad.'

'Where are you?'

'The Baghdad Hilton . . .'

The line went dead. Sir Donald stared at the receiver for a while and then put it down. He tapped another number into the phone.

'Operations, I hope you monitored that last call?'

'Yes, sir. Came from a CNN satellite phone, it'll take time to calculate its location, but we can do it very accurately.'

'Phone me when you know.'

Sir Donald lay back on his bed. Wayne MacLeod implicated? It didn't make sense. He'd make a few calls early in the morning and find out what exactly Paul Norton was up to.

*

373

Paul looked up to see the business end of a rifle barrel trained on his head. Slowly he replaced the phone and lifted his hands. The soldier gestured to him to move away from the satellite dish and indicated that Paul must lie face-down on the roof. Then he spoke quickly into a walkie-talkie.

Five minutes later the place was swarming with soldiers. Paul's hands were cuffed behind his back and he was taken down to the reception area. A high-ranking Iraqi officer was waiting for him. Paul breathed in deeply.

'You were using a satellite phone. You know the phone lines from this hotel are tapped. You must have been communicating with someone and transmitting classified information – details of your trip to our installation two days ago.'

Paul looked at the rifles pointed at his chest. The danger was very real, not just to him but also to Anne. He kept relaxed and forced a smile to his face, looking the officer directly in the eyes – dark, cold eyes that didn't have any trace of emotion in them.

'I borrowed it from CNN. I just wanted to learn how to use it.'

The officer nodded again, then gestured to his men to hand the silver case back to Paul.

'I accept your story. It is on record that your sentiments are pro-Iraq. But I must warn you that if you use the phone again without one of our censors present, you will be shot.'

The soldiers filed out of the hotel foyer, leaving Paul alone with the officer.

'You're pushing your luck, Mr Norton.'

'I have come here to cover your side of the conflict – if war breaks out I'll need to know how to use a satellite phone.

'Fahad has asked me to communicate a little something to you.'

Paul felt the tension building inside him. What now?

'Dr Madison,' the officer said. 'She is safe. But if you are found to be disclosing classified information . . .'

Paul gripped the officer by the lapels. 'You bastards, you've got her . . .'

The officer grinned. 'That is why I felt confident about releasing you. Fahad told me you love her.'

Paul released his grip, feeling sick to the core. He couldn't say anything. There was nothing he could do now – his hands were tied. One wrong move and Anne would die. '

'I will not disappoint you.'

'I hope not, for Dr Madison's sake.'

Anne felt a lot better after she'd had a bath and a change of clothes. Her new quarters consisted of three carpeted rooms. She guessed that her government must be putting pressure on the Iraqis to look after her.

She lay on her bed, wrapped in a white towel. She was worried sick about Paul. Was he alive? Were they torturing him? Her thoughts were soon interrupted. She heard voices in the passage, and then the door that kept her prisoner in this three-room suite was noisily unlocked.

The light came on in the main room and she got up off the bed, pulling on a tracksuit top and bottom. Two men came into her room, switching on the light.

She saw that they were officers, their uniforms dishevelled and their eyes bloodshot. They had been drinking. She backed into the corner.

The shorter of the two laughed loudly and moved towards her, while the taller one began taking off his clothes. She waited till the short one was close to her – so close that she could see the beads of sweat on his forehead and smell the liquor on his breath. She smiled and let her tongue caress her lips. He relaxed, and began to take off his jacket. Without warning she jabbed her right knee up hard between his legs. Then, as he fell back, she smashed the palm of her right hand onto his face and he collapsed to the floor.

The tall one moved in, brushing his moustache with the back of his left hand, then bunching his fists. He swore silently, his eyes resting on her body. Anne brought her right hand forward, as if to slap him in the face, and then gave a short, stabbing kick with her right foot that connected with his left knee-cap. He dropped, letting out a cry of pain and, his guard down, she chopped hard across the back of his neck with her open right hand, felling him cold.

Recovering her wits, she moved quickly towards the open door and let herself out. Outside, she realised she was being held captive in a suburban house. Moving past the kitchen, she saw a bottle and two glasses on the table – clearly this was where her assailants must have sat drinking.

She moved through the other rooms, rifling through the clothes in the cupboards to find an Arab head-dress and a white, flowing robe. Thus disguised, she moved outside into the darkness and hurried through the streets, anxious to put as much distance as possible between herself and the house.

By the time the sun rose, she was hot and exhausted. She was also completely lost in an alien environment. Her only hope was to make contact with the US embassy as quickly as possible, but she had no money for a phone call and could not speak the language.

In desperation she started knocking on doors. The first few were slammed in her face, then one opened to reveal a man in his mid-forties, dressed in a suit. Though he was obviously an Arab, he had an air of the European man about him, and his dress suggested that he was sophisticated.

'You speak English?' she asked desperately.

He grimaced. 'I think you'd better come inside.'

The door closed behind her and she found herself in a long white-tiled hall, the floor covered with Persian rugs. At the end of this hall was an atrium with a fountain.

'You look hungry. Can I offer you something to eat and drink?'

She nodded.

'Please follow me.' He led her into a lounge area, filled with large scatter cushions. 'Sit down and rest while I arrange something for you.'

Moments later a woman in a typical black Arab dress, her face partially covered, came into the room. She gestured to Anne to follow her and showed her to another room – on a table in the centre stood a carafe of water next to some fruit and cold cuts.

Anne thanked the woman, who closed the door, leaving her alone. Anne ate ravenously. Then she lay back on the leather couch next to the table. It was then that the tiredness overwhelmed her and she fell into a deep sleep.

*

Sir Donald looked at the report, wide-eyed. There was no doubt about it, Dr Maria Fassbinder was in the same league as her mentor, the late Dr Vance Torr.

He held his chin in his left hand and contemplated his course of action. The situation was dangerous because he had so little information.

His personal secretary came in and handed him another report. As he read the contents he opened and closed his hands. Then he reached for the phone.

'Chuck, I need to see you now, it's serious. No, it won't wait.'

Sir Donald put the phone down and tried to remain calm. He looked out of the window. It was dark already, and freezing cold. He saw lights on a Christmas tree in a window across the road. He felt detached from the festive mood, unable to relax, for the information he now possesed indicated that the Gulf Crisis could rapidly escalate into World War III.

His intercom sounded. 'Chuck Conroy to see you, sir.'

'Send him through.'

He lay back in this chair, the tips of his fingers pressed together.

'Donald, what's up?'

'Dr Anne Madison is being held by the Iraqis.'

Chuck scratched behind his right ear and sat down in front of the desk.

'She could have been one of our best operatives. It was her decision to leave the CIA. Hell, her pa was sore. Joe Colson, head of the CIA, and his daughter drops out after intensive training.'

'Please don't continue the charade, Chuck. I think the situation is extremely dangerous.'

Chuck got up and started to pace the room. 'You've got to believe me, Donald. I've always been open with you, you know that. She's not one of us. True, she leaned on her father to get her a passport in a hurry – but that was her only involvement with the agency.'

Sir Donald leaned back further in his chair and began to fill his pipe. 'She has disappeared. What if they torture her and she cracks? They could get her to make a statement that she's working for the CIA.'

'Jesus Christ!'

Sir Donald held a lighter to the wooden bowl of the pipe and sucked in the first smoke. 'How in God's name could Joe Colson let her go in there? I don't understand that.'

'It wasn't his decision – he didn't know what she wanted a passport for.'

'So, we now sit on the eve of war. The enemy has in its hands the daughter of the head of the CIA – a woman once trained to be a CIA agent. And her boyfriend Paul Norton knows that Britain and America allowed Iraq to obtain a satellite launching device that now turns out to be a nuclear weapon. It doesn't take much imagination to realise how the Iraqis will exploit the situation if we don't toe the line.'

'Aren't you at least grateful that we were keeping tabs on Norton?' Chuck countered.

'Norton has contacted me.'

Chuck moved back to the chair in front of the desk. 'And what did he say?'

'Why should I tell you anything, Chuck?'

'Listen, there's nothing to worry about. We know the truth.'

'Chuck, you know nothing. According to Norton, the Super-gun is operational and ready to fire a nuclear shell at Jerusalem.'

Chuck lifted his hands in a gesture of exasperation. 'Impossible. Torr is dead. They haven't got the ability to make those shells – he was the only person in the world who could design them.'

Sir Donald pushed the file on Dr Maria Fassbinder across the desk and Chuck Conroy read through it quickly.

'Bright lady, exceptionally bright. Where does she work?'

'She's an Iraqi spy. She was also Torr's mistress. For your information, she is working in the SAAD 16 complex at this moment – I don't think I have to tell you on what.'

Conroy was biting his nails, looking nervously towards the window.

'Yes, Chuck, it's very worrying. If they break Anne Madison and find out how much Norton knows, they'll fire that bloody Supergun of theirs immediately, no questions asked.'

'There's no way they can have obtained a nuclear warhead . . .'

'Are you one hundred per cent certain of that?'

'Oh my God.'

Mkhulu sat in the dark hut and watched the bones fall in front of the witch-doctor. The *sangoma* adjusted her animal skins, said nothing and scooped up the pieces. She threw the bones again. Lines of concentration creased her face as she gathered up the bones and threw them a third time.

'My friend, there is much trouble. You cannot avoid it.'

Mkhulu groaned. He wondered what would happen next to Klaw that could be worse than the calamities that had already befallen it.

'There is a man,' the *sangoma* said, 'a man to whom you are very close, a good friend. He is in terrible trouble. I see darkness for you. I have thrown the bones three times and the darkness is always there. I am sorry, but I have to tell you what the bones reveal.'

The woman was silent. 'What must I do?' Mkhulu said.

'There is no choice. You must find your friend, you must help him. There is a bond between you . . . I see it clearly in the bones.'

'This is craziness . . .'

The *sangoma's* eyes flashed in the darkness. 'Never consult the bones if you will not heed their warning. There is a reason for every man's life on this earth, and the reason for yours is more important than many others. Do not ignore what the bones say.'

Mkhulu fished in his pocket for money.

'Do not pay me. You must use all you have to help your friend.'

He staggered from the crude hut and out into the blazing sunlight. Wearily he pulled himself into the Land Rover, fired the engine and drove away from the kraal. The heat of the sun burned into his face and the smell of the sand road filled his nostrils – the raw essence of Africa.

Klaw seemed empty, almost soulless as Mkhulu returned to it. Johannes was out on an anti-poaching patrol. He unloaded the provisions he'd bought in the village, then opened the mail. In

379

among the bills he found an envelope addressed to him, written in Paul's hand. He did not open it.

After the sun had set, he cooked himelf dinner, then sat on the deck, eating and occasionally sipping at an ice-cold can of beer. When Paul returned with Anne, he promised himself, things would be all right again.

Later he reached for his saxophone. Perhaps he could find solace in his music. Adjusting the reed, he pursed his lips and caressed the mouthpiece. The image of the *sangoma* came before him – frightening in its clarity. He could not play. Shivering, he put down the sax and stared into the darkness.

Then he remembered that the letter from Paul lay behind him on the table, unopened. He dreaded that it would contain a message that fulfilled the *sangoma's* prophecy. Reluctantly he reached for the envelope and tore it open. Out fell two thin pages written in Paul's long, flowing hand. He read them quickly.

Paul wrote of the Supergun, of his discoveries, and his concern that a terrible war would erupt in the Gulf if the Iraqis fired their weapon. He wrote that he feared for David and Charlotte in Jerusalem, for he was certain that would be the Supergun's first target. The letter finished by reminding Mkhulu of the contents of Paul's will – that should he die, Klaw would belong to Mkhulu and Johannes in perpetuity.

Mkhulu went to the phone and dialled a London number Paul had given him – to be used if Mkhulu needed to contact him in a hurry. It rang for a long time before being answered by Paul's producer, Dave Emery.

'Yes, Mkhulu, he mentioned you might call. Look he's in Baghdad. Anne's there as well. Paul is staying at the Baghdad Hilton, here's the number.'

Mkhulu wrote it down carefully.

'Tell him from me, Mkhulu,' Emery went on, 'that I think he should get the hell out of there. I think his film will be a devastating success – he should concentrate on that and forget about what's happening in Iraq.'

Mkhulu put down the phone and walked back outside, suddenly acutely aware of the sights and sounds and smells, the bush. He finished his beer quickly. It was pointless, making phone calls . . .

Paul was in trouble, he was certain of it. There was no doubt that Paul was in Baghdad to try and stop the firing of the Supergun – everything else was just a front.

He wondered if Anne had made it to Iraq. She'd promised to phone him the moment she made contact with Paul, but he'd heard nothing.

Mkhulu picked up his saxophone and went to his bedroom. He pulled out his battered leather holdall from under the bed and threw a few clothes into it. The saxophone was carefully packed among them. He folded up the leather shaving-case, took the blackened combat knife from its sheath and hung it round his neck. Then, from a hiding-place under the floor, he took his credit card, passport, the Browning pistol Paul had given him, and ten thousand pula in cash.

It was another hour before Johannes returned. He didn't argue with his friend, he knew better than to object when Mkhulu had made up his mind.

Mkhulu left an hour later. He drove down the rough sand track, staring at the bush in the moonlight. Then in the road in front he spied three shapes, and slowed down. It was his lions – all three of them – lying across the track.

He got out and tried to shift them, but they refused to move out of the way. They just continued staring at him. Again the image of the *sangoma* appeared before Mkhulu's eyes.

'Damnit, I have to go!' he cried.

Then each of the lions in succession nuzzled him, turned and disappeared into the bush.

He felt he would never see them again.

The diesel-engined Landy couldn't manage more than eighty kilometres an hour, yet the air blasting on Mkhulu's face felt good. He watched the sun rising over the horizon and kept his foot flat on the accelerator.

He blotted the image of the *sangoma* and the lions from his mind, but the contents of Paul's letter played on his subconscious. He felt such an intense bond with this strange, tortured white man, and haunted by the violence of the events that had taken place in London. He was sure Paul was correct in his assumptions. But what could one man do against a nation intent on war?

The sun was high in the sky as Mkhulu pulled into the parking area at Gaborone airport, and it took him another hour to find the international departures desk.

'But, sir, there's no flight from Gaborone to Israel, you'll have to fly to Jan Smuts,' the air hostess at the counter said pleasantly.

He caught a Bop Air flight to Jan Smuts later that afternoon, and touched down in darkness. He approached the El Al counter for a return ticket to Israel.

'There's no point in trying to get on a flight till you've got a visa,' he was told.

'How do I get one?'

'It takes about a month. You apply to the embassy . . .'

'Well, can I get on the plane without a visa?'

'You'll never get through customs at the other end. They'll just make you come back on the next return flight.'

'I will persuade them to let me in.'

The air hostess was irritated with him. 'All right, go ahead, waste your money.'

He caught an El Al flight to Tel Aviv that Saturday evening. He slept for most of the journey, exhausted by his drive to Gaborone and his fight to get an air ticket.

The plane touched down at Ben Gurion airport at five past five on Sunday morning. He was the last one to leave the plane, avoiding the crush of passengers and hobbling down the steps with the assistance of one of the ground staff.

The arrivals hall was almost empty by the time he got there, his leather bag the only one travelling round and round on the baggage carousel. In the distance the customs area looked forbidding – Mkhulu hitched up his bag and headed slowly towards it.

The customs officer, a dark-skinned man with black curly hair, gave him an appraising stare, arching his eyebrows. Mkhulu smiled back at him, then handed him his passport. The officer thumbed through it quickly, his brow furrowing.

'No visa?'

'No one told me about a visa.'

'That's not my problem,' the man replied, shaking his head. 'You will return to Johannesburg on the next flight.'

'But I'm a musician, I've come to play in Jerusalem.'

'No visa, no entry.'

Mkhulu kept fighting. 'you have to let me in. I have an old friend who's waiting for me.'

'Does your friend live in Jerusalem?'

Mkhulu nodded quickly.

'All right, call him. Perhaps something can be arranged, but I can't guarantee it. There are pay phones next to the carousel.'

'I've only got South African money and a credit card – I haven't got any local coinage.'

The customs officer looked him up and down, noticing for the first time that Mkhulu had an artificial leg. 'Lost that in the army?' he asked.

'No, it was amputated when I was attacked by a lion.'

This seemed to impress the officer. 'One call, OK? Follow me.'

He showed Mkhulu sat to a glass-walled office and Mkhulu sat down at the desk and dialled David Katz, hoping like hell that he had the correct number.

The ringing seemed to go on interminably. Mkhulu felt the officer's eyes boring into his back. Eventually his call was answered – and, to his relief, in English.

'I need to speak to David Katz,' Mkhulu said.

For a moment he thought he'd been cut off, then he heard a familiar voice on the other end of the line.

'Katz.'

'David, it's Mkhulu . . . I'm at the airport . . . They want to send me back – I haven't got a visa. I'm sorry, but I think I'm going to miss the festival; you'll have to find another sax player.'

David caught on to the yarn that Mkhulu was spinning very quickly. After a short conversation, Mkhulu gestured to the customs officer to come to the phone. 'My friend wants to speak to you.'

The customs officer picked up the phone and spoke quickly in Hebrew, his eyes focused on Mkhulu. The conversation went on for some time and then he gestured for Mkhulu to come back to the phone.

'I think we can work something out. Your friend wants to talk to you again.'

Mkhulu grasped the receiver anxiously and listened to David's instructions. 'Keep your mouth shut, OK? For the record, you're a famous Kenyan jazz musician and I've paid for you to come out to play at the university. Stick to that story if they try to interrogate you. I'll sort this out as quickly as I can.'

Mkhulu was shown into another room, lined with chairs, and told to wait. He settled down, opened his case and took out his alto sax. The music flowed and gradually he began to relax, He saw the customs officer, through the glass partition, watching him play.

Anne woke in darkness, wondering for a few moments where she was. She felt strong. She switched on the bedside light and got up, pulling on her clothes.

Time, what was the time? She was running out of time. She had to get away before the Iraqis started an intensive search.

She opened the door and looked into the courtyard, listening to the water splashing in the fountain. Across the courtyard she saw a light in one of the rooms, and she walked barefoot around the tiled passage towards it. The door was half-open, and inside she could see the man who had let her in, hunched over an antique desk, writing. Behind him were shelves packed with books from floor to ceiling. She wondered if he was an author. He looked up and smiled at her.

'You slept a long time. Are you feeling better?'

'Yes, thank you. Now I must go.'

'You're afraid they'll conduct a house search?'

How much had she told him? Perhaps he had called the police already and they were waiting outside . . . Maybe this was a subtle form of interrogation . . . Anything was possible. She had to keep her wits about her.

'I don't know what you're talking about. I must be on my way.'

He rose, putting the top on his fountain pen. 'I don't think that would be such a good idea,' he said. 'For your information though, a house search has taken place already. Of course, I said I'd never seen you, but they had a recent photograph of you – a good likeness. So, though you are free to choose whether you leave or stay, I must advise you that I think you wouldn't last long outside these walls.'

He gestured to her to sit down on the couch opposite his desk. 'Your picture is on the television every hour,' he said. 'You are identified as a CIA agent, masquerading as a tourist.'

She raised her hands to her face. It was a disaster! What would Paul think? God, what would they do to Paul?

Then she looked again at the man opposite her. He was an Arab, in his mid-forties, cultured and handsome. Who was he? Why hadn't he turned her in? Did he work for the government?

He returned her stare. 'You want to know what will happen to me if they find you here?'

She got up quickly. 'You have been very good to me. And in spite of everything, I think I should go.'

He lay back in his chair and laughed. 'Where are you going to go?'

'I don't know.'

'They'll pick you up. You're the sole topic of conversation here – a symbol of the American oppressor.'

'But I can't stay here.'

'Do I look worried? They won't come here again. And I don't have any servant to gossip about you. So you have effectively disappeared.'

'You don't understand!' Anne said. 'I came here to find Paul Norton, a friend of mine. His life is in danger!'

The man shook his head. 'Paul Norton is highly regarded. He is a mouthpiece through which President Saddam Hussein hopes to address the West. I sense that the majority of people here feel you have betrayed him. I certainly believe he must think that.'

Desperation took hold of her. She'd never told Paul she had trained to be a CIA agent, had never thought it would come out. She'd always had the feeling that, if he ever found out she had trained to be an agent, he wouldn't understand.

She looked up at the thoughtful, handsome face opposite her. He had the self-confidence of a man who was successful at what he did.

'You've been very good to me,' she said.

'My dear, I think it would be difficult for any man to refuse to help you. Anyway, we are now bound together by circumstance – even by association I am implicated. You have incredible luck – it was a miracle you knocked on my door.'

Her eyes combed the room for clues as to this man's identity, but she was not rewarded. 'Are you an Iraqi?' she asked.

He shook his head. 'I am a Kurd, but I have lived much of my life in the West. My only loyalty is to myself, my only cause is my own survival. I had a flourishing import-export business here until President Saddam Hussein invaded Kuwait. Now I find myself grounded.'

There was something more, something he wasn't revealing to her. There must be a good reason why he hadn't turned her over to the police. Iraq was a police state – by hiding her he was risking his life. She decided to confront him.

'Why take a risk with me? If they find me here, you're as good as dead.'

He folded his arms and looked at her appraisingly. 'You're nobody's fool, are you?'

'You're an agent?' she pressed.

A glassy look came over his face.

'Don't hide from me. Which country do you spy for?'

He opened his mouth slightly, as if to protest, and then seemed to make a decision. He pulled out a packet of cigarettes, offered her one, which she declined, then took one himself. He lit it carefully, and sat back in his chair, blowing out a long stream of smoke.

'I was recruited during my years at Oxford. I suppose at that time I was a renegade. I didn't see much hope for the Middle East, I still don't – there's too much in-fighting amongst our people and not enough unity. If it wasn't for our oil, no one would pay much attention to us and perhaps that would be a good thing. All these petro-dollars have hardly bought us happiness.'

'You're with British Intelligence, then. But what can you hope to achieve?'

'Allied intelligence in Iraq is limited, almost non-existent. Your countrymen are somewhat nervous because they have little idea of Iraq's true military strength. I cannot blame them, the spectre of another Vietnam is frightening.'

386

Anne was disturbed. To this man war seemed inevitable. 'Surely it's better to try to find ways to avoid conflict,' she said, 'than to search for ways of winning the war if it starts?'

'Certainly. But Iraq is not going to give up Kuwait. The very fact that your friend Paul Norton is here indicates that war is about to break out. War draws men like him like a magnet. He was one of those who brought home the reality of Vietnam to ordinary people – perhaps he will do the same thing with this war.'

Anne wasn't sure how much she should tell this man. Perhaps he was a double agent – there were many in the Middle East. His eyes focused hers.

'I sense that you still don't trust me. I've told you enough to have me executed by a firing-squad. My name is Bandar, Lawrence Bandar.'

'All right, Lawrence, here's the bottom line. Paul is here because he believes that, with outside help, Iraq has developed a Supergun able to fire nuclear shells. He's convinced the target will be Jerusalem.'

Bandar gripped the edge of his desk tightly, his face drained of colour. 'Is this supposition?'

'He witnessed a successful test firing in Namibia.'

'But surely, after Dr Torr's assassination the project has ground to a halt?'

'Paul is convinced that Dr Torr's lover and former deputy-head of research, Dr Maria Fassbinder, will see the project to completion.'

Lawrence Bandar got up from his desk and began gathering up his papers. 'No one knows of this yet?' he asked.

'No. Except for someone Paul saw in London, a Sir Donald Morgan.'

Bandar stopped and stared at her. 'But surely Morgan was interested. He couldn't just have dismissed the matter. We've known for a long time that they were using Dr Torr.'

Anne began to realise that Paul hadn't been so crazy after all.

'Sir Donald said that the plans Norton found were at a very early stage of development,' Bandar said. 'He estimated the Supergun would take at least ten years to perfect. And the development was for satellite launching.'

'Well, he was wrong, Lawrence.'

Bandar nodded his head. 'He would have had Norton tailed, I'm certain of it. And he would have spoken to the CIA.'

'My father is Joe Colson,' Anne said quietly.

'So why didn't you use him to help Norton?'

'I was going to. I came here to find out what the hell he was up to.'

Lawrence continued to clear his desk as he spoke. 'This is serious. The UN deadline expires on January sixteenth only two-and-a-half weeks away. My guess is that they will use the Supergun the moment the Allied forces attack. A nuclear explosion in Jerusalem will have devastating effects on the Allied coalition.'

Anne realised time was running out. They had to do something. 'How can we find out where this Supergun is located?' she said.

Bandar's brow creased with worry. 'It's almost impossible. I don't have the contacts in the Iraqi military. Satellite location of the site will only be possible when the Supergun is fired, and by then it will be too late.'

'There has to be a way!'

'You must make contact with Norton. He's probably the one person in Iraq capable of finding the location. For the moment we must move to another place – if the Iraqis have any idea that you're looking for the Supergun, we shall both be in terrible danger. We will go to Baghdad, to a small apartment I have there.'

Lawrence hastily packed two suitcases with clothes for them both, then showed Anne the way into the garage. He opened the back door of his BMW.

'Lie down on the seat and hide under the blanket. If I'm stopped at a roadblock, keep quiet. I've never had my car searched before.'

The car roared out of the garage and Anne felt nauseous under the blanket. Lawrence had told her they were an hour's drive from Baghdad – she hoped she could last the journey without throwing up.

What was Paul thinking? Would he ever forgive her?

*

Paul sat in the bedroom, staring at the wallpaper. He had sat like that for the last twenty-four hours. He could scarcely believe what he had heard. Anne was a CIA agent.

It was the ultimate betrayal. He had felt he knew everything about her, yet he'd known nothing. Anne must have been playing a game with him, acting the innocent while constantly feeding whatever he found out about the development of the Supergun back to the Pentagon. But in that case, why hadn't they bloody well acted on the information.

She must have thought he was a naive fool, that was the only explanation. And now she had become the victim, pulling them both down. He had trusted her completely, trusted her without question. There had been no doubt in his mind that she loved him as much as he loved her.

In a way, it didn't quite make sense – all the sacrifices she'd made for him. There was no way she could have known that he would become involved in this, no way – it had all been a matter of chance. He had to find her, talk to her, try to find the truth.

The phone rang again, and this time he answered it.

'Mr Norton? I am President Hussein's personal assistant. He wants you to interview him tomorrow morning. You must be at the palace two hours beforehand at seven. You will be searched, and if anything suspicious is found you will be detained.'

He felt the old excitement, the knowledge that he had an exclusive.

'I accept your terms, I will be there.'

Hyde sat back in his Land Cruiser parked on the rise, holding the walkie-talkie close to his ear. He looked down across the bush below him.

'All-right, Johannes is out of the way,' he said into the receiver. 'Move in slowly.'

The sun was low on the western horizon, the bush quiet. Hyde pulled out his binoculars and combed the bush on the periphery of Bush Camp. He smiled. He could not see his men moving in – their camouflage was perfect.

His walkie-talkie crackled into life. 'We are at the base of Bush Camp.'

Hyde looked across to the setting sun. 'OK, proceed as agreed.'

Hyde pointed his binoculars at the wooden posts that supported Bush Camp. He saw the flames licking upwards. Gradually the blaze gained momentum and he heard the timbers start to crack in the heat.

He switched on the walkie-talkie. 'Get the hell out of there, Charles, she's going like a braai.'

In less than ten minutes the entire structure was a mass of flames. Hyde opened a beer, took a sip and belched with satisfaction. As he'd instructed, the sabotage work had been done quickly – they had no idea when Johnannes would return.

Hyde had decided on a new strategy. Now that Norton and Mkhulu were out of the way, he would ride Johannes till the man broke. Already, after the publicity surrounding the terrorist attack on Mkhulu, Klaw had lost its paying guests, and now, with the devastation of Bush Camp, he was sure the reserve would be close to bankruptcy. It was a war of attrition that Hyde knew he couldn't lose. After all, he had the unlimited resources of his father's international business empire behind him.

He picked up the walkie-talkie again. 'All right, Charles, fire the outbuildings.'

Hyde laughed with satisfaction. By the time Johannes came back, Bush Camp would be burned to the ground. And the man wouldn't have a clue how it had really happened.

Wayne Mcleod sucked on his cigar and perused the London skyline for a few brief seconds. Then he returned to his desk and looked again at the man standing in front of it.

'Josh, you will have to be patient,' he said.

'I don't want to leave it much longer. Fahad could soon be hard to terminate.'

MacLeod shook his head. 'Josh, stick to your orders. I need Fahad alive for the present.'

Josh picked at his nose – MacLeod knew he did it to irritate him. 'I need my second fifty per cent,' Josh said.

MacLeod remained impassive. He knew Josh gambled. That was why he always used him, because Josh was always desperate for money and would do anything to get his hands on it.

'You agreed to my terms,' he said. 'Payment of the final fifty per cent on termination.'

'But you didn't tell me this was going to go on for two years, you bastard!'

'Listen, Josh, certain financial deals I'm presently structuring depend on Fahad's being alive. Once these deals are through, then you can dispose of him.'

Josh eyed MacLeod with renewed respect. No one paid him as much for terminations as MacLeod did. 'I'll probably have to lure him out of Iraq,' he said consideringly.

'That should be simple enough. He trusts you, fool that he is.'

Josh shifted uneasily in his chair. It was obvious that MacLeod didn't trust him at all.

'You will help me to get him out of Iraq on some pretext?'

MacLeod held his cigar between his thumb and forefinger, an ugly smile on his face. 'Yes, I'm sure I can arrange that. But remember, there won't be much time. I want him out of the way soon after the Supergun is fired. The moment that war begins, my association with the Iraqis is over.'

Josh couldn't fault his logic. There would be an immediate hunt on to find out who had supplied Iraq with the technology to launch a nuclear weapon – but with Fahad out of the picture, it would get nowhere. MacLeod had nothing to worry about, as long as Fahad was dead. The other men he had involved in the deal would guarantee silence at British government level.

Josh said: 'You tell me when, all right?'

'Don't you worry, Josh. The way things are going in the Middle East at the moment, I think you'll get paid in February.'

Fahad looked at the faces of the men round the table, in the IPBP boardroom. This was his last chance to convince them that Iraq could honour the loan of a billion dollars.

'I am in a position to tell you,' he said, 'that our country cannot be defeated by the United States. We will retain our control of Kuwait.'

One of the Arabs closest to him took off his steel-framed glasses and rose. 'I cannot believe you will defeat the Allied Forces,' he said. 'There is no support for your cause. You are alone.'

He would have to tell them about the Supergun – they wouldn't be convinced otherwise. He took a deep breath.

'We have a weapon that the United States believed was impossible to develop. A cannon of such power that it can launch nuclear projectiles. The moment the US launches an attack, we will strike against Jerusalem with a nuclear warhead. I don't have to tell you what that will do to President Bush's support in the Middle East.'

The men around the table exchanged glances. Another rose, a tall, fat man with beads of sweat on his forehead.

'This could all be lies, Fahad! I do not believe that Iraq has such a weapon, or the nuclear warhead to fire from it.'

Reluctantly, Fahad raised his briefcase and laid it on the table. He opened the catches and took out the photographs. This was dangerous, but he was certain that no one at the table would betray him. They were greedy – they all wanted to back a winner.

'These photographs show the Supergun installation in Iraq. The others, taken at an earlier date, demonstrate the destructive capabilities of this weapon with a conventional warhead. The town in question, Kalabo, in Southern Africa, was totally devastated.'

The men round the table broke into fierce conversation, the photographs being rapidly handed back and forth. Eventually the tall Arab rose again.

'What collateral can you put forward?'

Fahad took another deep breath. In order to secure the loan he was going to have to do the thing he dreaded.

'My own assets,' he said, 'my shareholding in IPBP.'

The men round the table nodded. 'Your loan is granted. Pray that you have not lied to us, Fahad, because if you have, you will not only bankrupt us, you will also die.'

'I have not lied,' Fahad said. 'There will be many deaths in Jerusalem in the middle of January.'

The blindfold was removed and Paul ran his eyes carefully over the building before he was escorted inside. He had come alone – he would interview Saddam with an Iraqi technician operating the camera and doing the filming – this way he knew the Iraqis would be more likely to trust him.

Once inside, he was shown into a cubicle and ordered to strip, then his clothes were searched. When he'd dressed, he was taken to a lift which took him down to below ground level.

Paul could scarcely believe his eyes as the lift door opened – he had entered an underground palace. The entrance hall was enormous; priceless artwork decorated the walls and a huge Persian carpet covered most of the tiled floor. He was escorted down a corridor and shown into a comfortable lounge.

'The interview will be conducted here,' the commanding officer said icily. 'you have fifteen minutes to set up. Then the President, his interpreter and our film cameraman will be with you.'

It took Paul every available minute to get the lighting perfect, and set up the camera so he could view the monitor from where he was sitting on the couch. He went for a mid-shot, focused on both himself and President Hussein.

The officer came back into the room. 'The President will be with you in one minute. His personal guards will also be with him, though I assure you that they will remain silent. However, at the slightest sign that you might threaten the President's life, they will kill you.'

Paul broke into a cold sweat. He was now, so to speak, in the lion's den. He ran his eyes over the list of questions he wanted to ask Saddam, anxious that his reportage should remain neutral.

He waited and waited. The image of the valley at Halabje, of the dead woman and her child, haunted him, reminding him of why he had come this far and taken so many risks. Now his objective was to win the confidence of the Iraqis; only with that could he hope to get a lead on where the Supergun was located.

Without warning, the President was in front of him. Paul took in the dark eyes, the bushy black moustache and the full, dark-skinned cheeks. They shook hands.

President Hussein gestured to Paul to sit down opposite him. Paul knew better than to object to the interpreter; Saddam clearly wanted to make sure that the West got the correct version of what he was saying. In the background stood the guards, armed with assault-rifles.

The Iraqi film cameraman took up his place behind Paul's video camera – Paul hoped to hell he knew how to operate it.

The President was dressed smartly in a dark suit, with a white shirt and colourful tie. He would come across well on television, Paul realised. He was wise not to have come in his military uniform, which the majority of viewers would find intimidating.

'The President welcomes you, Mr Norton. He hopes you are relaxed and he is prepared to answer all your questions.'

Paul smiled at Saddam. 'I am honoured to be granted this interview. I want to hear the President's view on the UN deadline.'

Paul threw all his energy into the interview, looking into the face of the man who was about to confront the military might of the West. Was he scared? How did he possibly think he could win? Paul lost track of time, watching the eyes, the expressions of the face in front of him, trying to learn more about the man behind them.

Before he realised it, Saddam was rising, shaking his hand and bidding him goodbye. Then the room was empty, and he felt utterly drained. He was glad he'd done the interview, for now Saddam Hussein was no longer a photograph to him, but a real person. His own political stance did not matter: what mattered was relaying to the world the Iraqis' view of the events of the preceding months.

Paul got the cameraman to play the tape back, while the interpreter watched over his shoulder.

'Good, his humane qualities came across well,' the interpreter said.

Again Paul thought of Halabje, and wondered how any human being could have countenanced such a carnage.

Later that day the interview was carefully edited and then sent out by satellite across the world. It caused disquiet in many places, especially in intelligence circles. For the first time, the aggressor was shown in positive light – something that those who lobbied for war didn't like.

Paul had had to maintain his neutrality. He wanted to remain in Iraq if war broke out, to continue to broadcast the other side's point of view, and he would only be able to do that if they trusted his impartiality.

Most of all, he wanted to find out what was happening behind the scenes. How close was Dr Fassbinder to completion on the Supergun project?

*

Wayne MacLeod flew into Zurich to see his bankers. He felt elated when he heard that the IPBP had contacted them: there was every indication that the deal would go through. He had had no doubt that it would, it was all a question of tactics.

The Iraqis were probably wondering how he would get the nuclear warhead to them. Of course, they weren't to know that it was already in their country – he had always known the Iraqis would come to the party and had had no intention of risking non-delivery.

The bank's car was waiting for him as he walked out of the airport, and he was whisked away in a matter of seconds. Fifteen minutes later he was at the bank, being welcomed personally by the chairman, Mr Gohner.

'Please, Mr Macleod, you will join me in my office.'

They went up the stairs into a spacious room. The banker had a bald dome for a head and was at least a foot shorter than MacLeod.

'Please be seated.'

MacLeod eased himself into a chair and kept his eyes on Mr Gohner, who was clearly impressed by the amount that had just been deposited into his client's account.

'The money has arrived?' MacLeod said.

'All of it, in the manner you instructed. I must now move very fast, Mr MacLeod. I never ask my clients how they obtain their money – it would be indiscreet, and an answer might one day put me in a position that could prejudice their interests.'

MacLeod nodded; he guessed what was coming.

'I would advise you that we move this money almost immediately,' Mr Gohner went on smoothly, 'breaking it up into smaller units, spreading it over a wide web of investments.'

'My feelings exactly.'

'I can guarantee discretion. However, if the authorities become aware of the size of the deposit, there might be questions. I have thus taken the liberty of not even depositing the funds in your account but moving immediately to the next state. This – how shall I put it? – offers you a greater guarantee of invisibility.'

MacLeod gave him a thin smile. 'Very good. There may well

be investigations in the future, and I want a wall of silence to greet them.'

Mr Gohner put his hands on the table, and smiled too. 'Since the funds were never deposited with me, of course I do not have any recollection of their having existed. Now, there is the question of how the bank's fees will be met.'

'No doubt the standard percentage rate will apply? Then you will take it from my existing accounts.'

After a few more matter had been discussed, they shook hands. The Swiss held his client's hand a fraction too long and looked into his eyes.

'I think I should tell you that the bank has already been approached by the US, and certain accounts may be frozen. Yours is obviously not on the list and never will be. However, perhaps you should warn your friends in IPBP.'

'Of course. I thank you for the information.'

MacLeod walked out of the bank and down to the chauffeur-driven Mercedes. Of course, he would say nothing of what he had heard to Fahad. Once the nuclear warhead had been delivered, his association with Iraq would be over.

Darkness came, and with it a steady stream of passengers as one flight after another arrived at Ben Gurion airport. There was tension in the air because of the Gulf crisis. Mkhulu suddenly realised that it was Christmas Eve – he had lost track of time. He felt sad, remembering his childhood and how much Christmas had meant to him in those days. Now his family were gone and he was alone.

He felt a hand on his shoulder. 'Mkhulu. I'm sorry, it took a long time.'

He turned and was on his feet, smiling and shaking David's hand. 'All that matters is that you came. Am I free to go with you?' David nodded. 'Let's go. Charlotte's outside, we're taking you to dinner in the Old City.'

Charlotte stepped out of the battered car and hugged him hard. 'I don't know why you are here, but I'm so glad you came. It's good to see you.'

They loaded his case into the car and drove off into the darkness. Mkhulu decided he wouldn't talk about Paul till the morning, he didn't want to be the harbinger of bad news – they both seemed so happy. He turned to look at Charlotte sitting on the back seat, and saw that her skin had darkened, there was a radiant look about her. She flashed a glance across at David.

'Shall we tell him, darling? I feel terrible that Daddy will be the last to know.'

David concentrated on driving along the bustling street in front of him, but nodded his head.

'I'm pregnant, Mkhulu. And we know it's a boy.'

Mkhulu felt sick in his gut – they had to get out of Israel. He managed a smile.

'That is wonderful. I am so happy for you both, so very happy . . .'

He gripped the front dashboard and realised that there was no turning back, the *sangoma* had been right. Thank God he had come.

David pulled up at the side of a bustling pavement in the Old City. 'Here we are, prepare yourself for a culinary experience.'

The restaurant was packed with people who all seemed to be shouting rather than talking to each other. There was an amazing energy about the place. David ordered them two bottles of a local Israeli red wine called Carmel, and they tucked into a generous helping of kebabs. Mkhulu could not believe the enormous variety of people in the restaurant. Everyone was smoking.

Apart from his brief trip to London earlier that year, Mkhulu had never ventured abroad. He stared in fascination at these Israelis who seemed to have such a zest for living. He knew he spent too long in the bush, too much time alone. It felt good to be in a city packed with raw energy. The evening passed quickly and it was early the next morning when they finally drove home to David's flat on the outskirts of Jerusalem.

Mkhulu woke early, as he always did. He opened the shutters and stared out across the city. He heard curious cries in the distance and was awed by the thought that civilisation had existed in Jerusalem for over two thousand years. This was the centre of his own religion, of Judaism and of Islam; a crucible of war and conflict, the scene of man's finest achievements and his worst excesses.

He felt a curious emptiness. He had always been content with where he lived, but now travelling had revealed a new dimension of experience to him. He was hungry to see more places, to feel fresh emotions, to taste different foods and breathe in new smells.

A hand rested on his shoulder. He turned and looked into David's dark eyes.

'It's beautiful, isn't it, Mkhulu? It doesn't matter who you are or where you come from or what you believe, there's something special here in Jerusalem.'

'You want to live here forever?'

'No. But I always wanted to know what it would be like to live in this city. So much blood had been shed for our right to live here.'

'And more blood will be shed.'

He felt David's grip intensify. 'That is what's so terrible – the suffering and the savageness of this existence. I'm so glad you've come. Charlotte's very lonely, though she never complains. This isn't Africa . . .'

Mkhulu looked again across the skyline. 'But your child will be born here?'

'Yes, and that will change everything. It's one thing to face the possibility of war alone, quite another to do it when you have a child. With a child, you can't afford to die.'

Mkhulu knew the time had come. 'I did not come here for a holiday,' he said quietly.

David's face suddenly looked drawn. 'I guessed as much. Please, let's have some coffee in the kitchen. I don't have to work today, so there's plenty of time to talk.'

The dark, strong Turkish coffee gave Mkhulu the energy he'd been lacking earlier. He told David of his visit to the *sangoma*, of the letter from Paul, of Anne's departure to Iraq and of the call he'd made to Paul's producer.

'You see, Paul believes Iraq has this Supergun, that they intend to fire it, to pitch a nuclear shell into the heart of Jerusalem.'

He watched David's hand tighten round the coffee cup. 'But Mkhulu, what can we do?'

'I am going to Iraq. Paul is in terrible danger.'

David looked at him, his face filled with despair.

'I don't know. He's working with the Iraqi authorities and he's showing President Hussein's side of the story. My people hate him. You know Anne's been arrested? Evidently she's a CIA agent.'

Mkhulu shook his head. 'I don't believe that, David. I don't believe she'd have betrayed Paul. But you have to believe what I'm telling you about Paul: the real reason he's in Baghdad is to try to find the Supergun and stop them firing it.'

David poured some more coffee. 'It's just over two weeks to the UN deadline,' he said. 'I'm sure the Americans are going to act. They aren't going to tolerate Iraq's invasion of Kuwait.'

'But what about the rest of the Arab world, David? Don't they hate Israel? So when Iraq drops a nuclear warhead on Jerusalem, wouldn't Israel have to retaliate?'

David shook his head. 'They wouldn't do it. I don't believe they have the capability to build a nuclear warhead.'

'But what if they have?'

The battered car turned off the direct route from the Tel Aviv freeway to the beach, and into a wide street, the Rehov Shaul Hamalekh. Mkhulu stared at the soldiers armed with American M-16 rifles, and behind them, a high, bare wall topped with barbed wire. Behind that again, a huge concrete spire soared into the air, covered with what looked like sophisticated television aerials. He whistled through his teeth.

'You're looking at the headquarters of the Defence Forces – the Kirya,' David shouted above the banging and rattling of the old car. They pulled up some distance from the building and walked to the front entrance. Mkhulu looked up at the video camera above the door, and David followed his gaze.

'This is a high security area. They record everyone who goes in and out of the Kirya.'

The reception area was very basic, but the security was tight. David went straight up to the receptionist, a dark-haired woman in military uniform. 'I want to speak to Marc Golan.'

'You have an appointment?'

'Tell him it's David Katz.'

They waited while the woman spoke rapid-fire on the phone in Hebrew – Mkhulu couldn't understand a word. The conversation over, the woman looked up, clearly regarding David with a little more respect. 'Go through the door to the left, Mr Katz. Mr Golan will be there to meet you.'

She pushed a button, releasing an electronic lock, and as they passed through the metal door Mkhulu had the feeling he was entering a prison. David gripped his arm.

'Don't be intimidated. Remember, Israel is always fighting for survival. Marc has been in the army all his life – tension is running high because of the possibility of war.'

A short, bald, barrel-chested man with a nose like a hawk's strode forward. He pumped David's hand and embraced him.

'It is always good to see you. Please, who is your companion?'

'Mkhulu.'

Mkhulu shook Marc Golan's hand and felt the power of the man. The Israeli was dressed in a loose-fitting, short-sleeved shirt and cotton pants. Mkhulu could tell from the set expression on his face that he was a born fighter.

'Please, come through to my office.'

They were shown into a room strewn with papers, both on the desk and on the floor. There were two ashtrays, filled with butts, and in the corner a coffee percolator. Mkhulu took one of the chairs in front of the desk. Golan looked at his artificial leg.

'You lost that in the army?'

'No, a lion took me.'

'But you were in the army?'

'Yes . . . But I'd rather not talk about it.'

Golan nodded his approval. 'Action is what matters in this world, one can't take a back seat.'

Mkhulu told his story without embellishment, noting a scowl develop across Golan's hard face. When he had finished, Golan rose and strutted around the room.

'We are accused of having assassinated Dr Torr in Scotland a month ago,' he said. 'We didn't, and I don't know who did. So who killed Dr Torr is a mystery, but what is for certain is that now they cannot build that shell – so there's really nothing to worry about, my friend. But thank you for coming, for telling us. It confirms that the assassination of Dr Torr was in our interest.'

David looked at Mkhulu. 'Tell him the rest.'

'I do not think the assassination of Dr Torr stopped the programme,' Mkhulu said. 'Paul believes Torr's associate, Dr Maria Fassbinder, has continued with it.'

Golan moved back from the window and leaned over his desk, his biceps bulging under the short sleeves of his shirt. 'No one could do it except Torr,' he bristled.

'Paul Norton told me emphatically that Dr Fassbinder worked with Dr Torr, not for him – that Dr Torr was infatuated with her. There is no doubt that she would have been party to his final plans. Anyway, can you explain what happened to Torr's black case, which always contained the work he was currently engaged on? Why would someone kill him and not take the black case? Dr Fassbinder obviously has it, and all the vital documents inside it.' Mkhulu paused. 'Perhaps the whole point of the assassination was to make you *believe* that the project had been stopped,' he said.

A sweat broke out across Golan's face. He snatched up the phone and dialled furiously. When he spoke it was like a machine-gun firing – he was almost screaming. Eventually he slammed the phone down.

'We still don't have a clue who killed Torr,' he said. 'And no one knows what happened to his black case. Worse still, it is now known that the assassins raped Dr Fassbinder, and she thinks they were Israelis. So she has excellent reasons for seeing the Supergun programme through to completion – she'll want to fire that nuclear shell on us to get her revenge . . .'

'Please, I must ask you to assist me. I have to find out who this Dr Fassbinder is.'

He led them down a labyrinth of corridors and then into a lift. 'I trust both of you,' he said. 'Normally I should get clearance before taking you into our communications centre – the heart of the Kirya. From here we conduct our wars. We are going underground – the centre is in a bunker, built to withstand a nuclear, biological or chemical attack.'

As they stepped out of the lift, Mkhulu shivered. It was icy cold. 'Everything here is air-conditioned,' Golan said. 'The equipment, I'm told, functions better at this temperature. I'm not sure our people do.'

He led them into a long room filled with banks of computers, and with a control terminal directly in front of them. Mkhulu and David sat down behind two of the operators, while Golan remained standing.

'All right, now we find out about this Dr Fassbinder. Do you know her first name?' he asked Mkhulu.

'Maria.'

The operator to Golan's left typed in the name, pushed back his pebble-lensed glasses and stared into the screen.

'Innsbruck University. 1970, highest ever recorded marks for physics and mathmatics. She completed an MSc, then went to the Massachusetts Institue of Technology. Completed her doctorate in ballistics in just eleven months. Again, highest recorded marks, then . . . nothing.'

'What the fuck?'

'There's nothing more on her.'

'Call the CIA. Put me through to Chuck Conroy.'

Five minutes passed. Mkhulu noted that Golan was chewing his nails.

'He's on the line, sir.'

Golan snatched up the phone. 'Chuck, you told me the Supergun project was a dodo. Now I get word that the fuckers are ready to fire. Who's this bitch Dr Fassbinder, who's seeing the project through? Surely you guys know about her?'

Golan's face became drawn – clearly Conroy had bad news for him.

'She's an Iraqi spy? But why the fuck didn't you tell me earlier? Of course they'll use it! They hate us!'

Golan sank down into the chair next to the operator, his left eyebrow twitching. 'You can't tell us how to defend ourselves,' he said into the telephone. 'We have the right to retaliate. Anyway, who is this bitch?'

His face turned almost white. 'My God, and you say they may have a nuclear warhead?'

Golan stared at Mkhulu as the conversation continued. 'I don't give a fuck for diplomacy, Chuck!' he shouted. 'It's not you who's sitting here! It's not your children! Well then, speak to your President, but don't expect us to walk into another holocaust!'

He hurled the phone down. 'They know who she is now,' he

groaned. 'She's a genius. She worked for NASA on the space programme – she had affiliations with the Bader Meinhoff gang, she's rumoured to have made bombs for them. She hates Jews!'

David had never seen his friend so distraught. Mkhulu turned to them both.

'You have only one choice. You must go into Iraq, find this Supergun and destroy it. That is the law of the wild.'

Golan looked directly at Mkhulu, his face now covered with lines. 'Yes. Yes, that is what we should do. But life is not so simple. If we do that, then the accord President Bush has achieved with our Arab neighbours will crumble. But you know what is worse, the CIA already knew about this. They were thinking about it. Can you believe that? *Thinking* about it?'

David looked drawn. 'But we have to retaliate,' he said.

Golan stared at him. 'How?' he said. 'Where is this Supergun? We don't know. Do they have a nuclear warhead? We can't be sure. Don't you see, we don't have a target. Our only hope is your father-in-law. And right now, it appears he is supporting the Iraqis. And worse, they hold his girlfriend, a CIA operative. You know what they will do to her if he is suspected, even vaguely suspected, of spying?'

Mkhulu rose to his feet, towering over Golan.

'Paul Norton is a man of his word – he is not a traitor. You misjudge him. You forget that if it were not for Paul Norton, I would not be here and you would only know about that shell when it hit you.'

Golan looked at the crippled black man with renewed respect. There was a strength about him, a rare, rough-hewn honesty that few men he knew possessed.

'Sit down, please. I did not mean to offend your friend. I operate in Intelligence: we do not know the meaning of trust any longer. If those Iraqi bastards have a nuclear warhead they will use it on us, of that I'm quite sure.'

David looked across at Golan. 'But you have to do *something*.'

'No. We can do nothing. Our Prime Minister has struck an agreement with President Bush. Israel must not be seen as an aggressor, nor must the United States. It will have to be someone else who does something . . . And I know exactly who.'

*

Sir Donald Morgan left No. 10 feeling no better than when he had arrived. True, he had got the agreement he needed to proceed, but he had also received a stern warning from the Prime Minister.

On the face of it, the problem was simple enough. Iraq was in posession of a nuclear cannon and it had to be neutralised before war broke out. Very simple. The only problem was that it was New Year's Eve and he'd just been informed that the US and Allied forces would attack Iraq at midnight on the day the UN deadline expired. That gave him two weeks.

The operation would have to be achieved in total secrecy. The team would have to be British, because for the Americans or Israelis to be discovered with a hit-squad inside Iraq before the expiry of the deadline, would wreck any accord President Bush had achieved with the rest of the Arab world. So it would have to be the SAS, no doubt about that. But then came the next problem. They didn't know where the Supergun was, they hadn't a clue.

As soon as he got back to his office, Sir Donald reached for the special phone on his desk. First he must mobilise the SAS, then he had to make contact with Paul Norton.

There was a knock on the door. She froze. Then another two knocks, a pause, then five knocks in quick succession. It was Lawrence. Anne, who had been hidden away in this Baghdad apartment since Christmas, rushed to open the door and let him in. He looked tired and dishevelled.

'No luck?' she said.

'It is impossible to get near Paul's hotel,' Lawrence said, his face grim. The place is crawling with security people. If I so much as ask for Paul Norton they will be onto me. His phone is certainly tapped, so a call to him is out of the question too.'

Anne knew Lawrence had made every possible effort to contact Paul. She was going crazy, cooped up in the apartment, knowing that Iraq was moving closer and closer to war.

'I'll go back to my house, make contact with my controller in Britain. Perhaps they can contact Paul.'

'Can't I come?'

'Your photograph is everywhere. I'm sorry Anne, but for you

to step out of this apartment would be certain death. You know what they would do to you.'

She sat thinking for a few minutes. 'Get me the paper,' she said. 'I want to see the photograph they have of me.'

He went through to the kitchen and paged through the newspaper. 'Here . . .'

'All right. You've got a pair of scissors? Cut my hair.'

She hadn't had her hair short since she was a little girl, but it was a small price to pay for freedom of movement. Lawrence worked quickly and easily.

'You've done this before?' she asked.

'I had five sisters. I was the oldest and I always cut their hair.'

'You never told me you had a family.'

'I don't have a family. They're all dead.'

Anne was silent. There was always something that drove a person into Intelligence work, some trauma, some secret wound. 'I am sorry,' she said at last, knowing the words were trite.

'It wasn't something to be sorry about. I am a Kurd, though of course I have changed my name to avoid persecution. We have learned to live with death . . . and we have also learned to hate. No one cares about us. At least working for the SIS I have some chance of protecting my people from aggression.'

She felt the remaining hair on her head, and smiled. 'Now I know what it's like to be a man.'

He stood back and admired his handiwork. 'You are wrong. You are beautiful, very beautiful. All this does is reveal another aspect of your beauty. Here . . .'

He handed her a mirror and she stared at the foreign face she saw in it. She was surprised. She had thought she would look terrible, but instead she found herself looking at her face from an interesting new perspective.

'It makes me look . . . younger?'

'Well, yes. And certainly, I can hardly recognise you.'

He packed the scissors and comb into his shaving kit, and then got up. 'I must go.'

She looked at him desperately. 'You'll ask about Paul?'

'Of course. But Anne, you must promise to remain here till I return.'

She nodded, and a few minutes later he was gone.

It was as if she were in a prison. There was nothing she could do, no one she could speak to.

She walked into the bedroom and studied herself in the mirror. Yes, she did look very different, and if she dressed out of character, she was certain no one would recognise her. She opened the cupboard in front of her – it was full of women's clothes. They were probably the clothes of Lawrence's lover, she mused. One particular black dress caught her fancy. She slipped it on and found that it fitted almost perfectly.

Slowly a plan began to form in her head. She rifled through all the cupboards, finding a pair of shoes a handbag and some make-up.

Yes, she decided, it was time she took matters into her own hands.

Lawrence sat hunched over the transmitter, waiting to make contact. The house felt strange for some reason. He didn't feel in the least comfortable. Finally the signal came through and he gave his code.

'This is Canary. I still have the Humming-Bird.'

'Canary, this is Eagle. We have confirmation that the weapon is in operational condition. You have to establish contact, and fast.'

'I regret that may be impossible.'

'It is imperative.'

He leaned back and sighed. Then he felt the metal of a gun barrel pressed into his head. A sick feeling came over him. He wished he could die.

'End transmission. I am blown . . .'

The gun butt smashed into his skull and he toppled from the chair onto the floor. An Iraqi military officer stepped out of the shadows and sat down in front of the transmitter.

'Eagle. Eagle. This is Canary.'

There was no reply. The officer looked across at the man who had downed Lawrence Bandar.

'Sir, there will be no more contact. We should have got him before he used the transmitter.'

'No, I have learned all I need to. The British SIS know we have the Supergun, which means the Israelis know, and the

Americans. But they do not know where the Supergun is. And by the time they do, it will be too late.'

'What do we do with him?'

The officer looked down at Bandar, lying unconscious on the floor.

'Take off his clothes and work him over. You will then bring him to headquarters. I want him alive for questioning.'

Sir Donald Morgan looked at the radio transmitter for a while and then got up. He laid his hand on the operator's shoulder and sighed. The Iraqis had got Lawrence Bandar, he was certain of it. It didn't bear thinking about; he just hoped they wouldn't drag it out too long.

Thank God he hadn't mentioned Norton's name. But they'd find out who Humming-Bird was soon enough. Sir Donald had trained Lawrence himself; there was every likelihood he wouldn't break under torture, but there was no guarantee of it.

How long would it be before Lawrence died? It could be as little as twenty-four hours. In the meantime he had to make contact with Norton and find out just how much he knew.

Paul walked into the coffee shop and sat down at one of the tables closest to the window. He felt a growing pressure in Baghdad, people steeling themselves for war. He wondered what the hell Sir Donald was doing with the information he had passed on to him? There was no way he could make another illegal transmission without risking almost certain death.

God, what if Sir Donald wasn't taking him seriously? In that case he'd probably have a grandstand view of the beginning of World War III.

He ordered a coffee and considered his next course of action. In many ways he was trapped. If he left Baghdad, it would immediately arouse the suspicion of the Iraqis and lose him the trust he had established with them.

It was only after a few minutes that he became aware that someone was watching him. In the far corner of the room he caught sight of a woman wearing Ray-Ban sunglasses. She turned away as he stared at her, and he wondered who she was: close-cropped hair, tight-fitting dress, exquisite figure and very sensual lips.

He looked away and thought of Anne. Had she deserted him? Why had she never told him she worked for the CIA? She obviously felt she couldn't trust him. That hurt.

He tried to read another section of the morning paper, but it was useless. He was thinking of the woman in the corner of the room. Almost in spite of himself, he looked up – and sensed her look away. He got up and walked over to where she was sitting.

'Mind if I join you?'

She nodded, and he proffered his hand. 'Paul Norton.'

'You are here alone, Mr Norton?'

Anne. Good God, it was Anne! He fell, rather than sat, in the chair opposite her. A mixture of feelings welled up inside him. He knew how much nerve it must have taken her to come here. Maybe she had been tailed? Perhaps he was being watched? He wanted to squeeze her in his arms but he knew it might mean death for both of them.

She raised her dark glasses onto her forehead and looked deep into his eyes. 'Paul, there's a lot I have to explain . . .'

'How did you escape?'

'Not now. It is dangerous here. You have your room key?'

He nodded.

'Slide it out of your pocket and drop it on the floor. We will have one cup of coffee, discuss trivialities. I will get up, pick up your key and go to the room. After a few minutes you will follow me. Give three sharp knocks on the door and I'll let you in. You will say nothing to me. We will go into the bathroom, turn on the taps. Only then can we talk safely.'

Paul called a waiter and ordered coffee. Now, as he looked closer, he could see the tiredness and the strain on Anne's face.

'Your hair . . .'

Her eyes flickered, and he realised that he must follow her instructions. She knew far more about how to handle this sort of situation than he did.

'It is tense here, isn't it?' He posed the question as any man might, trying to engage an attractive woman in conversation.

'Yes, but I don't think the Americans will attack.'

'You can't tell, there's no guarantee either way.'

'You're a reporter . . .?'

He hated the whole charade, there were so many questions he wanted to ask her. Eventually she rose and said goodbye.

It seemed like an eternity while he waited, paid for the coffee and walked towards the hotel lobby. He had a constant vision of soldiers bursting into his room and dragging them both off.

Anne got into the lift and examined the room key. Paul's room was on the sixth floor. Just before the lift doors closed, a man stepped in and stood close to her. She could smell his exotic cologne and sensed his eyes on her dark-stockinged legs.

'You are available?' he asked quietly.

She pouted her lips and he pressed himself close to her.

'Let's go to your room.'

His hand drifted round to her backside and wormed its way between her buttocks. The lift stopped on the sixth floor, and she rammed her knee up hard between his legs. He collapsed, coughing, on the floor.

'Asshole,' she said softly as the doors closed.

She looked up and down the hall to see that it was empty, then moved quickly to Paul's room, opening the door as if she was entering her own room. Carefully she closed it behind her, then lay against it, praying.

In the coffee bar, sitting across from Paul, watching him, she had realised just how much she was in love with him. But there was no guarantee now that their relationship would continue. Why the hell hadn't she told him she'd trained to be a CIA agent? She wished she'd felt more confident with him, but there was always the anxiety that he might go away, leave her forever. And that was something she didn't know if she could live with.

There were three sharp knocks on the door, and she breathed in deeply and opened it. He came in. She moved towards the bathroom door but he grabbed her arm.

Please God, no! Was he going to hit her?

His lips locked over hers and they sank to the floor. She clawed at his clothes, tearing them off. Then they were naked, exploring each other's bodies like first-time lovers.

'Paul. Paul. Please, don't stop. Oh, don't . . .'

She wanted it to go on and on. No more questions, no more

409

deceit. If only they were far away from Iraq, back in Africa. Anne lost herself in the moment, everything dissolving into a vivid procession of erotic images as the waves of ecstasy broke through her body again and again.

Minutes melted into hours. Eventually, sated, she fell asleep in his arms, drifting away from the madness they were both swept up in.

Lawrence Bandar gritted his teeth as the steel manacles bit into the bones of his wrists. The bastards weren't going to show him any mercy, and he didn't want to think about what was going to happen next. They left him lying on the floor of the tiny, windowless concrete room in a mess of human excrement.

He had no conception of time. Often he stared at the weak light bulb in the ceiling. Every attempt to move brought shooting-pains from his wrists. In his mind he knew he would never get out alive, but his heart yearned for a miracle.

In the distance he heard animal-like screams – the begging voices of the tortured.

He was half-asleep when the door opened again and a guard dragged him to his feet. Lawrence walked down the concrete corridor, trying not to think. He was shown into a large room with red cabinets running down one side. Behind a desk, facing him, was a handsome Iraqi dressed only in white shorts. The man had a two-day stubble on his face and wore a cologne that broke through the stench that pervaded the room.

'Name?'

Lawrence remained silent. He would not cooperate. They would kill him anyway, he knew that, so why cooperate?

'Well, my silent friend, my name is Fahad.'

Lawrence felt his bowels move. He knew of Fahad and of his reputation as a torturer – the Butcher of Baghdad.

'I see fear in your eyes already. How much do I know? you ask yourself. Well, you'll have to keep guessing.'

Fahad got up from the desk and gestured to the guard to leave. He waited till the man had closed the door behind him.

'I like to work in private,' he said. 'I think you understand that.'

Lawrence stared at the concrete wall in front of him, trying to block out the voice of his inquisitor.

'I think it's time I got a reaction from you,' Fahad said. I'm feeling lonely.'

Lawrence felt him attach something to the manacles on his wrists. Then there was the noise of an electric motor, and a clanking as the chain behind his was drawn up.

His arms were swept upwards, jerking his back forward, and the manacles dug deep into the bone of his wrists as he was yanked up from the floor.

He screamed and screamed and screamed. The pain was unbearable. Fahad walked back behind his desk and sat down.

He must have blacked out, for he found himself lying on the floor, staring at Fahad's naked feet.

'Ready to talk?'

He said nothing. There was no point to this, they must just kill him. He thought of Anne laughing as he cut her hair. He thought of his five dead sisters. He could not allow Anne to be subjected to this, and if he gave her away they would find her, and this man would torture her.

'You are a hard man. But that in a way gives me greater pleasure.'

The noise of the electric hoist came again and he braced himself for the pain.

This time it was different, for Fahad had set the motor to a slower speed, lifting him very gradually so that the pain came in waves.

'No! Please God, no!' Lawrence screamed in spite of himself as his feet lost contact with the floor and his full weight came on his wrists.

'Adaptability is the hallmark of the human race,' Fahad said musingly. 'Look how you are already able to tolerate the pain. Of course, you will probably never have complete use of your hands again, they might even have to be amputated.'

Lawrence looked into Fahad's eyes and knew there would be no mercy. Fahad returned to his desk and started doing paperwork. Lawrence fought a losing battle against the pain that wracked his body.

'Oh God. Please let me down!'

411

Fahad looked up. 'What's your name?'

'Lawrence Bandar.'

'Very good. Very, very good.'

Fahad got up and went over to the control panel. Lawrence heard the sound of the motor and groaned as he was lowered to the floor. He heard Fahad summon the guard.

'Take him away.'

He was dragged back to his cell. On the concrete floor he screamed as the guard took the manacles off his wrists. Then the door slammed and he managed to bring his arms in front of him. He stared at his mangled wrists and cried like a child.

As well as pain, hunger and thirst racked his body. He screamed out for water till his throat was hoarse. He wished there was some way he could kill himself.

Without warning, close by he heard a woman screaming. Her voice echoed round his cell and he quivered with fear. What were they doing to her?

His cell door opened and he shrank back into the corner like an animal. The guard put a plate of food on the floor and a mug filled with water. Lawrence looked up into the guard's eyes.

The guard unzipped his fly and urinated over the food and the water. Then he turned and slammed the door behind him. Lawrence wept.

He couldn't use his hands so he fell to the floor and ate from the plate like a dog. Then he grasped the mug with his teeth and gulped down the fetid water.

At first he felt better, then his stomach seemed to burn and he cried out in pain. He started vomiting. The cell started to spin in front of him and he lost consciousness.

Marc Golan stared at the Israeli Prime Minister. He couldn't believe what he was hearing. He had already decided that he would defy orders if necessary.

'Golan, I understand your anger. But I have an assurance from the United States that as long as we do not attack, they will protect us. They have also made this plain to the Arab nations who have agreed to back them in the liberation of Kuwait.'

Golan rose to his feet and leaned over the desk. 'You know what will happen if Iraq drops a nuclear shell on Jerusalem?'

'It will not happen.'

Golan smashed his fist into the desk. 'You are mad! The Americans know that this Supergun exists, yet they are doing nothing, absolutely nothing, to find it!'

'They have given me their assurance . . .'

'Fuck their assurance! What about your people? Give me proof.' He waved his finger in the Prime Minister's face. 'Or I will take matters into my own hands.'

'You are stripped of command from this moment!'

Golan turned puce. 'I will make sure our people know of your weakness! Then, from the day that shell falls, you will live with the shame, the outrage, that you could have stopped it.'

The Prime Minister seemed to age before his eyes. 'Golan, you bastard,' he said. 'Of course this thing cannot be left alone. But it is imperative that neither we nor the Americans are seen to be involved in stopping it.'

Golan shook his head. The Prime Minister got up and stared at him.

'Action is being taken, but it is top secret. I will tell you the plan. But if you breathe a word of it to any man, then your career will be over.'

Golan sat down again in his chair and folded his arms. 'Let's hear it.'

'A crack team of the British SAS will infiltrate the Supergun installation and neutralise it. This will be a secret operation conducted before the UN deadline expires. You understand what will happen if word gets out about it?'

Golan stared at him. 'Did they tell you how they were going to find this Supergun?'

'No.'

'Then how can you trust them?'

A tense silence filled the room.

'All right,' the Prime Minister said, 'you have a point. But I don't know what the solution is.'

'Very simple. I have made contact with a man who has a lead. You tell the Americans you agree to follow their directive, but only on condition that I am involved in the operation to locate the Supergun.'

'All right, I will put it to them.'

413

Golan's eyes flashed. 'No. *Tell* them that's it . . . Otherwise you'll have to kill me to shut me up.'

The Prime Minister picked up the phone and quickly dialled a number.

'Yes, I need to set up a meeting with the American Secretary of State. Urgently.'

He replaced the receiver. 'You get your way, Golan.'

As he heard the cell door open, Lawrence's bowels exploded. Terror invaded his soul. Two guards came and dragged him to his feet.

'No! No! No!'

The manacles were slammed onto his wrists – but he dug his heels into the floor and fought the guards all the way.

They dragged his slowly down the passage. He saw the door to the torture chamber and managed to break loose, but his legs collapsed underneath him – he was too weak to run.

Then they were on him, kicking and punching him before they dragged him into the room. He was hitched onto the chain again and the door was slammed shut.

Sitting behind the desk was a person he guessed to be Fahad, with a stocking over his face. Fahad's hand actuated the motor switch and Lawrence was hoisted into the air, screaming.

Fahad got up and went across to the red cabinets. He took out a crocodile clip attached to a long length of electrical flex. He squeezed the clip open and clamped it onto Lawrence's penis.

'The routine is simple. To stop the pain you talk about yourself and give us the identities of those you are involved with.'

Fahad returned to the desk and pressed a button on the side. The voltage hit Lawrence like a bolt of lightning, tearing into his body and twisting it.

'No! Oh God, please . . .'

More voltage.

'Anne Madison. Dr Anne Madison.'

Fahad turned up the amperage and pushed the button. For a few seconds Lawrence blacked out, but another shock brought him quickly round.

'Please, please . . .'

'Talk.'

414

'She came to my house when she escaped. I did not know who she was. Then I saw the photographs on the television news . . .'

'You are an agent?' The hand moved towards the button.

'Yes! A British agent.'

The button was pushed down.

'Just a little shock that time, my friend. I like you to keep talking – you've wasted enough of my time already.'

'I took her to my flat in Baghdad.' Lawrence blurted out the address and Fahad snatched up the phone.

'Please don't hurt her,' Lawrence begged as he heard Fahad issuing instructions for Anne's arrest.

He hung from the ceiling for a long time, staring at the stockinged face.

'What else do you want to know?' he begged.

'The Supergun, who else knows about it?'

Lawrence knew that if he told them about Paul, it would be over. That then the Supergun would never be located before it was fired.

'I just heard about it from her . . .'

Lawrence blacked out as the current was switched on again. Fahad waited, drumming his fingers impatiently on the table. Then he looked at the amperage setting. It had been too high. Damn! He pulled off the stocking and went over to Lawrence. He slapped him hard across the face. No response. Damnation!

He went back to the desk and lowered Lawrence's body to the floor. Then he undid the manacles, laid the body out and pounded the area over the heart with his fist.

It was no good. Lawrence Bandar was dead.

It was dark when Anne finally woke up. The hotel room felt eerie. In the background was the vague hum of the air-conditioning unit. Something made her feel very uneasy.

In the bathroom she showered quickly, the cool water reviving her. She hadn't realised how desperate she had been for Paul. Now she was very scared. They both knew too much, far too much.

Alone, he was safe, but with her he might be killed.

She went back into the room and quickly penned a note to him. Then she eased out of the door, closing it very quietly. She looked up and down the passage but could see no one. Breathing in deeply, she moved towards the lift, but decided to take the stairs at least halfway, so it wouldn't look as though she had come from Paul's room on the sixth floor.

To her relief, the hotel foyer was crowded. She moved through the people towards the front entrance and asked the porter to call her a taxi.

She had to assume that she might be tailed, so she gave an address a block from where she was staying. By chance, the driver went past her apartment. Outside there were several cars, and her eyes went up to the balcony. All the lights were off in the apartment – and she'd deliberately left one on. Lawrence must have come back, or else someone had been snooping around.

The taxi dropped her off, and she started to walk towards her block. She had a strong sense something was wrong. Keeping her eyes in front of her, she walked through the entrance hall and took the lift. She pushed the button for a floor three floors below her own.

Leaving the lift and avoiding the open stairwell, she moved quickly along the carpeted corridor and tried the door that led out to the fire-escape. It was locked. Her eyes combed the wall and found the red, glass-fronted box containing the key. She slipped off her right shoe and broke the glass with the heel.

She had to work the key in the lock a little before the door finally opened. The fire-escape was metal, running up the side of the block of flats like a vine. Anne felt sick as she stared down at the street far below. She went back through the door and took the key out of the lock. Carefully she swept up the broken glass from the carpet and took it outside. The box looked as though it had always been broken.

Now she moved outside, locking the door behind her. Slowly she moved upwards. Perhaps she was being over-cautious, but she did feel uneasy.

Three flights of stairs later, she was on her floor. She tried the key in the lock, guessing that it would be a common fit for all the fire-escape doors. It was. She inched the door open very, very slowly.

She looked through the gap and felt a wave of nausea. Literally two metres from her, a man was standing, smoking a cigarette.

Lying on the floor next to him was a machine-gun. He turned and saw her.

She fought against the urge to slam the door and make a run for it. Instead she opened the door, made direct eye-contact with him and ran her tongue over her lip. She hitched her dress up slightly higher. Don't touch the gun, she silently ordered the man. Don't touch the gun.

He smiled.

Come closer, sucker, come closer.

He chucked the cigarette away.

That's my boy.

He began to drop.

No! Please, no!

She shot her right foot out, hitting him directly under the chin. He grabbed her leg and pulled her forward.

All the training was for this. She musn't panic. She forced herself to relax, falling backwards, letting her weight do the work. He came down on her and she rolled further back, tucking in her left leg and pressing the foot under the stomach.

'Come on, baby,' she purred, and felt his grip on her leg lessen.

She continued the backward movement, then pushed out hard with her left leg, sending him flying over her. He flew through the door and over the edge of the fire-escape. There was a muffled scream as he plunged into the blackness.

She picked up the machine-gun, lay flat down – and a man burst out of the flat, firing at her. She pressed the trigger and watched the bullets take him in the stomach and spin him round. Then she was on her feet, sprinting down the corridor, heading for the internal stairs.

Down, down, floor after floor, the breath bursting from her lungs.

On the first floor she cut back into the corridor and smashed open the door of one of the rear flats with her heel. It was dark inside, and she made her way towards the back.

A light came on and she stared at two men in the bed. She went past them, smashed the butt of the machine-gun through the glass balcony window and staggered out.

Her eyes took in the back of the flats. There was a parked car two metres below her. She went over the balcony and landed feet first on its roof. Shots exploded through the windows of the flat she'd left and she heard a man's scream.

She sprinted across the road and into a thoroughfare beyond. Then she kept moving in shadows, putting as much distance between her and the apartment block as possible.

She had to warn Paul. They must have got Lawrence. How much did they know?

Paul read Anne's note in the lamplight and felt a wave of nausea come over him. How the hell could she have been so stupid? Of course he knew that her presence put his life at great risk, the point was that she was in greater danger. He'd hoped to formulate a plan to get her out of the country, now he hadn't a clue where she was.

Time was running out. He had to get more information, but how? If he was seen to be asking too many leading questions, he'd be arrested. However, there was another angle he could always take, one that wouldn't arouse the suspicions of the Iraqis.

The phone next to his bed rang and he picked it up wearily. 'Yes?'

'Paul, it is me,' Mkhulu's voice whispered softly.

He felt his spirits rise. It was good to hear that voice, even if it was thousands of kilometres away.

'How are things at Klaw, my friend?'

'I don't know. I'm here at reception.'

'I'll be down now.'

He was on his feet, pulling on his clothes, a thousand questions running through his head. Why on earth had Mkhulu come to Baghdad? He ran down the hall and caught a lift to the ground floor.

The lift doors opened and he stared for some seconds at the immaculately groomed black man by the reception desk before realising it was his old friend. They embraced each other, then Paul led Mkhulu towards the lifts.

'Why the suit?'

'I am here negotiating a contract for the export of South African oranges,' Mkhulu said quietly.

'Ah. Of course, I should have guessed.'

The lift doors closed.

'I am . . .' Mkhulu began quickly.

Paul held his finger to his lips. Mkhulu understood that the lift was not safe, and remained silent. He followed Paul into his room, into the bathroom, and waited till he had turned on all the taps.

'It is safe now?'

'Yes, old friend. It is good, very good to see you. Why did you come?'

'A *sangoma* I consulted said you were in terrible danger. I read your last letter, then spoke to your producer in London.'

Mkhulu went on to talk about his trip to Israel, his meeting with Charlotte and David, and then with Golan.

'Mkhulu, you know what they will do to you if they know you're working with the Israelis?'

The black man nodded. 'Golan spoke to the British Intelligence. They got your call and they're sending in an SAS team. You have to guide them to the Supergun site.'

'Oh God, I don't know where it is. I'm still trying to locate it.'

'Perhaps Golan can help you. He is here too – disguised as an Arab businessman.'

There was no turning back now. They were all on a knife-edge. It was only a matter of time before the Iraqis realised what was happening.

'Where is Golan?'

'He will check into a room here tomorrow. At the moment he is supposedly having a business meeting.'

'And you?'

'I shall also be staying here, in the room next to his,' Mkhulu answered quickly. 'But Paul, where is Anne?'

'I don't know?'

Fahad drummed his fingers on the desk. He was losing his touch – if only he'd used a little less amperage on Bandar. The tension was getting to him.

He thought about the call he'd just received. It concerned the foreign journalist, Paul Norton. President Hussein liked Norton and enjoyed the publicity Norton was getting him in the US.

419

Evidently Norton was interested in knowing more about Iraq's military capability, and President Hussein felt that if Norton was given a few more tit-bits of information it might act as an extra deterrent to the US when the UN deadline expired.

President Hussein did not feel the US would attack. President Bush kept on making conciliatory offers. Perhaps if Norton had an interview with Dr Maria Fassbinder, that would persuade the US of the danger of a strike against Iraq. Naturally, Dr Fassbinder's identity would be kept secret, and Norton would be taken to the installation by a roundabout route again.

It was a good strategy, thought Fahad. But Norton was getting a little too close to President Hussein for his liking. Perhaps Norton could be found spying – these things could always be arranged.

Dr Fassbinder landed by helicopter and ran towards the buildings that marked the top of the installation. She was nearly two hundred kilometres from the SAAD 16 complex, in an isolated area that few people knew about, even in Iraqi high command. This was SAAD 20, run by another team of scientists and totally separate from the other programmes. This was close to the location of the Supergun and its arsenal of nuclear shells. Soon she would be installed here permanently, to complete her work.

President Hussein had just appointed her head of the entire weapons building programme. He was impressed with her extensive knowledge of nuclear technology.

Dr Aziz, the head of SAAD 20, was waiting for her. A short, fat, dark man, amply filling out a white laboratory coat of which the front buttons looked likely to explode at any minute.

'Dr Fassbinder, I must congratulate you on your appointment. It is a great honour.'

She nodded and shook his hand. 'You are ready to commence production?' she asked.

She was fully aware that Iraq could not afford to be dependent on foreign sources for nuclear material. Fahad had informed her of MacLeod's extortionate demands.

'We have just enough U-235 to make a bomb with twice the explosive power of the one the US dropped on Nagasaki.'

'When can I have it?'

420

'Delivery will take place today,' Dr Aziz said.

'And more U-235?'

'The centrifuges are working flat out. I think that before the UN deadline expires, you'll have enough for another three shells.'

'Very good. Now, take me on an inspection of the installation.'

They took a lift deep down into the ground and then donned special protective clothing. Dr Fassbinder could feel her excitement growing. Dr Aziz guided her into the huge, cathedral-like underground chamber whose vaulted arches seemed to stretch off into infinity. Line after line of giant centrifuges hummed away.

'How many are in operation now?' she asked.

'Over ten thousand. Enough to extract one hundred kilos of U-235 every year. The ring magnets and the high-tensile maraging steel you obtained for us ensure quality of supply.'

'I think that if the Americans saw this, they would be worried.'

He nodded. 'It was a good tactic to conceal the extent of the advances in our nuclear programme. Only when we have struck will the world take notice.'

She thought of the Israelis raping her. She dreamed of pushing the button, of firing the shell on Jerusalem.

'I am satisfied with your performance to date, Dr Aziz.'

The rest of her tour was spent in technical discussions with the other engineers in the plant. By the time she returned to SAAD 16 that evening, she was certain that in a few months Iraq would dominate the Middle East.

Paul stared at his shaking hand. Everything had been set up for him. There was nothing he had to do except take the trip and interview Dr Fassbinder.

Golan had assured him that the tracking device hidden in his camera equipment would never be located. Paul guessed he said that to all the spies who worked for him.

Once they had found the location of the base, Golan told him, they would be able to plan their attack. The whole operation would centre around kidnapping Dr Fassbinder. Having captured her, they would pressure her to lead them to the heart of the Supergun installation. A simple and logical plan, thought Paul, but full of holes.

'What if Dr Fassbinder refuses to co-operate?' he'd asked.

'She will co-operate. It's just a matter of technique.' Golan had replied.

Paul felt guilty about Mkhulu, but the black man had insisted on staying in the capital. If something happened to Paul, he said, he wanted to be there to help Anne – if she made contact.

Paul walked out of his hotel room, carrying his video camera and a playback monitor. The Iraqis wanted to be sure that sensitive information was not given away – they wanted to see everything he shot.

God, he hoped they didn't dismantle the camera and find Golan's tracking device.

The lift seemed to take an eternity to get down to the ground floor, then he was walking towards the entrance doors, seeing the Iraqi army car pull up.

Then, suddenly there she was. Anne. And there was nothing he could do. If he greeted her, the Iraqis would spot her in an instant. She was watching him from the other side of the road. What the hell was she doing here? She looked terrible. Why in God's name hadn't she contacted him?

Every survival instinct told him not to react – he was surrounded by Iraqi security officials. He wished there was some code he could use to communicate with her.

Then he was in the back of the big car, staring out of the rear window at her, crowds milling around her.

The car pulled off and he lost sight of her.

Anne slunk back into the seething mass of humanity. He hadn't even registered that he'd seen her. For the past few days she had lived on the street, and she felt desperate. It had taken all her courage to come to the outside of the hotel, she was so scared she might be spotted by Iraqi security agents.

Now she felt a hand on her shoulder and spun round, terrified that she'd been identified. She found herself looking into Mkhulu's cool dark eyes.

'Mkhulu, what are you doing here?'

His eyes darted around, then he took her hand and led her towards the foyer.

'Mkhulu, no! They'll recognise me!'

He kept moving, not releasing her hand, and she was forced to follow or risk making a scene. When they were alone in the lift she sank to the floor, exhausted.

'He didn't even wave to me,' she said, almost too low for him to hear.

'Anne, if he had, you would have been spotted. They're taking him . . .'

Mkhulu looked around the lift and realised that he'd been stupid to talk. He helped Anne to her feet and then walked her to his room. It was safe to talk there, he was certain. Golan had swept the whole place for bugs that morning – the Israeli wasn't taking any chances.

She lay face-down on the bed, sobbing. 'Please, run me a bath. I feel disgusting.'

He filled the bath with hot water, then guided her gently to it. 'There's no hurry, no hurry at all, Anne.'

He sat alone, listening to her in the bathroom, hearing the slosh of the water. Then she was standing in front of him, the towel wrapped tightly round her, looking like the old Anne except for the cropped hair.

He told her how he had come to be there, about the *sangoma* and about Golan.

'Golan is mad,' Anne said. 'If Iraqis capture him they'll torture him until he begs for death.'

'There's no choice, Anne. Either we find this Supergun or Jerusalem will be the centre of a holocaust that will probably trigger off World War Three.

She sat down on the bed next to him. 'But how will Paul find his way back there? He was blindfolded last time.'

Mkhulu thought for a few moments before replying. He couldn't lie to her. 'There's a transmitter hidden in his camera equipment,' he said. 'He knows about it.'

She held the sides of her face with her hands. 'My God, what happens if they run any kind of check on him?'

*

Paul stood in the hangar at Baghdad airport, the video camera and its support equipment laid out in front of him.

'You vouch that there is nothing hidden in this?' the Iraqi security officer asked for the second time.

'I have told you, there's nothing,' Paul said as calmly as possible.

'All right, we'll run it through the scanner.'

Paul felt nauseous. Golan should have warned him. Jesus Christ, what the hell was he going to do now?

There was a noise behind him and he turned to see a man in a pilot's uniform running towards them.

'What's taking you so long?' the pilot screamed.

'I have to search him,' the guard stammered.

'Look, we're late. If I don't go now, I'll be stuck here for another hour. Fahad will be furious.'

The guard flashed a look at Paul. 'You swear?'

'Look, I'm covering the war from your angle. I don't want to blow what I've got.'

The guard waved him on, and Paul breathed an enormous sigh of relief.

The flight was much the same as the previous one, with the same level of surveillance. Golan had told him that it was only once he was inside the complex that he'd have to concentrate. They'd need his guidance to find their way in and through it.

But this was a different installation from the one he had visited previously, and he guessed that it was the one that housed the Supergun. It was also slightly smaller, and its location appeared even more remote.

He entered it after following exactly the same security procedures as he had done the previous time, except that this time he was shown into a conference room to the side of the main entrance area. He left his video camera running the whole time, covering every section of his journey into the complex. It had become apparent that they weren't going to show him into the high-security area.

As they entered the conference room, Paul switched off the camera and deftly removed the video cassette, slipping it into his pocket. With the aid of an Iraqi technician, who clearly knew just what he was doing, Paul set up the camera on a tripod for the interview.

'How will the scientist be dressed?' Paul asked carefully.

'She will be wearing a mask over her face.'

'Fine. Then I'll also set the lights so that she always remains in the shadows. When she talks, you just pan across from me and focus on the outline of her body. It makes it look authentic without giving anything away.

The Iraqi nodded. 'Good. Keep talking – I'll check the sound levels for you.'

Once they'd set up, there was a long wait before the scientist arrived. Paul did not talk to the technician. Golan had told him to keep his mouth shut; the less you say, he'd advised, the less you're likely to give away.

At last there was a knock on the door Paul and the technician rose. Then Paul sucked in his breath as Fahad stepped into the room, his hand extended.

'Mr Norton, on behalf of President Hussein, I thank you. He asks me to tell you that he admires your courage – at least someone has the guts to show our side of the dispute.'

Paul nodded, then realised he couldn't just remain silent. 'I look forward to today's interview,' he said. 'I think this will put a new perspective on the conflict. The American public have a right to know what they're up against.'

Fahad grinned. 'I think that is a good idea. I'm sure the spectre of another Vietnam would appal them.'

Paul gestured at the two chairs in front of the camera. 'As you see, I have followed your wishes to the letter. The scientist will only be revealed as an anonymous shape in the shadows, and your technician will handle the filming.'

'Very good. Naturally, if I am not happy with your line of questioning I shall interrupt.'

'But you already have a typed a copy of my questions.'

'Ah, Mr Norton, I'm wise to the ways of the media. A subtle change could make all the difference to a certain line of argument. Our scientist is not skilled in interpreting such nuances.'

'Believe me, I'll stick to what I've promised.

Fahad raised his right arm and the scientist was led into the room. Paul was sure it was Dr Fassbinder, though her face was covered by a grotesque monster-mask. She sat down in the chair in the shadows. Paul moved into his own chair, straightened his open-necked shirt and indicated to the Iraqi cameraman that he should begin filming.

'I am sitting deep inside Iraq,' Paul began, 'in a secret military installation to which I have been brought blindfolded. Opposite me sits an unidentified member of Iraq's sophisticated military infrastructure whom I shall refer to as Dr Smith.'

The masked figure acknowledged this with a nod.

'Dr Smith, do you think the West underestimates Iraq's strike capability?'

He watched Dr Fassbinder's shapely legs cross and uncross. He was certain she had been carefully schooled in how to respond to each question.

'I think you must first understand that we have been able to choose from the best available technology,' she said. 'Though certain avenues may have been closed to us, others in the Eastern Block have been opened.'

Paul was taken by surprise at the bitterness in her voice. The death of Dr Torr must have affected her badly. 'But the United States has a formidable arsenal of sophisticated weaponry, including the recently developed Stealth bomber. Surely you are impotent against such firepower?'

Dr Fassbinder gave a dry laugh. 'Iraq has a huge land area, nearly half a million square kilometres. Does the United States think it can bomb the entire country? There are many secret installations such as this. We have the ability to retaliate, and retaliate hard, in seconds. In this complex there is a weapon that the West was unable to build – a weapon of devastating power.'

Paul allowed a second's pause before his next question. He wanted to calm Dr Fassbinder down, let a little more of her personality show through.

'There is concern,' he said, 'that there may be many American casualties. How do you feel about this?'

'Iraq has not looked for war, it has merely annexed territory that belonged to it originally. It reserves the right to defend its occupation of Kuwait.'

426

'Even resorting to chemical and biological weapons if necessary?'

He waited with bated breath for the reply. How much were they prepared to admit to?'

'If we had such weapons,' Dr Fassbinder said steadily, 'then maybe as a last resort we would use them. However, with our current arsenal there is no need for such primitive measures. I think I must state categorically, on behalf of President Hussein, that should the West strike, we will retaliate with maximum force.'

Paul thought carefully before posing his next question. 'Maximum force? That implies that you have a weapon the West does not expect you to have.'

'I will not be drawn by your line of questioning. It is enough for you to know we have the ability to retaliate, and retaliate hard.'

'Israel would be a logical target?'

'The Iraqi government has no quarrel with Israel, although it sympathises with the plight of the Palestinian people. So, no, Israel is not a logical target. Riydah is.'

Yes, thought Paul, it will be Israel. Everything now points to it. Your answer is merely an attempt to disguise the truth.

'You have obviously worked all over the world,' he said. 'How would you rate Iraq's current offensive capability?'

'In a word, awesome.'

'Thank you, Dr Smith, for a most illuminating discussion.'

'My pleasure,' she replied in her guttural English.

Paul got up and gestured to the cameraman to stop filming. Dr Fassbinder rose and came across to him.

'I am sure I recognise you from somewhere, Mr Norton.'

He sucked in his breath, a cold sweat breaking out on his forehead. 'Perhaps you went to one of my Vietnam lectures in London?' he said, as calmly as he could manage.

'No, it was somewhere else. Not that it matters. I hope you were pleased with the interview – naturally, you have to understand that secrecy is vital now.'

'Yes, I understand. But I wanted to give my audience an insight into this country's true retaliatory capabilities.'

'Why? Let them come, let them die,' she hissed, then turned and walked out of the room.

Outside in the corridor Dr Fassbinder met Fahad. 'You are pleased?' she asked him.

'Indeed. The interview was necessary – very, very important.'

She pulled off her mask and looked into his eyes. 'I do not trust Paul Norton. I think there is more to him than meets the eye. I do not think we should have brought him here to SAAD 20.'

'I have Norton worked out,' Fahad said with a thin smile. 'He's been spying on us, but basically he's impotent. No one has acted on his reports and he has done a lot to frighten the West into inaction.'

Dr Fassbinder shook her head. 'There's a very sharp mind at work there. A lot going on beneath the surface.'

'He's very useful to us. His reports could well persuade President Bush to avoid a war. There's already a lot of pressure in the US for him to back off and get out of the Middle East.'

'President Bush was head of the CIA. He doesn't strike me as a man who will back off.'

A scowl crossed Fahad's face. 'You'd better get back to work, Dr Fassbinder.'

'Ah, yes. The little surprise is almost ready for my Israeli friends.'

The Iraqi cameraman helped Paul load all the equipment into its aluminium cases. 'I wouldn't worry about that,' he said, as Paul began to fasten the locks. 'They'll scan the whole lot again when you get back to Baghdad. And nothing will be taken on the way.'

Paul felt his hands begin to shake again. This was an eventuality he hadn't bargained on. 'But why bother?' he stammered. 'What use would it be to check this stuff out again?'

'There are a lot of expensive things at this base – people are always trying to smuggle items out. Don't look so concerned, it'll be just a routine security check.'

Out on the tarmac runway, Paul did some quick thinking. He had to get rid of the camera. He was already blindfolded, but he'd insisted on helping to load the equipment into the transport – much to the amusement of the Iraqi air force personnel.

He heard the noise of hydraulics as the back of the plane opened, then he staggered forward with the camera case, tripped and fell.

The blindfold was removed. 'You can see now, just keep your eyes on the hold,' said the guard. 'I'll put the blindfold on again when you've finished loading.'

Paul picked up the camera case and staggered up the ramp into the hold. He turned. The others weren't watching him, they were lifting the other equipment. He slipped the video camera out of its carrying-case and then slammed the case shut, empty.

Quickly, quickly.

He rammed the camera in among some gear at the side of the hold – then moved on towards the back with the empty case. He just hoped no one had seen him.

A few minutes later everything was packed and the blindfold placed again across his eyes.

The flight was uneventful, but after landing at Baghdad he was thoroughly searched and his equipment stripped down before being scanned. But for the comments of the Iraqi cameraman he knew he would have been caught.

It was dark by the time he left the airport and took a taxi to his hotel. Now his thoughts turned to Anne. He hoped she had left him some clue as to her whereabouts. If the transmitter had worked, they'd all have to be ready to leave Baghdad at a moment's notice, ready to join the SAS team who would storm the Supergun complex.

In bed in his suite at SAAD 20, Fahad tossed and turned. Sleep would not come to him. Dr Fassbinder's face, hidden by the grotesque mask, flashed before his eyes again and again.

He got up and went to the bathroom for a glass of water. Something was bothering him. Perhaps it was what she'd said about Norton. Until that moment he'd felt he had Norton worked out, but now he wasn't so sure. Had he been right to allow Norton to visit SAAD 20 weapons complex? Maybe he was still in contact with Dr Anne Madison.

He reached for the phone and called security at Baghdad

airport. He wanted to check that they'd searched Norton carefully.

The official stammered. 'There wasn't time when he left, the plane was in a hurry. But everything was scanned when he returned. We found nothing.'

Fahad put the phone down and dressed quickly. He had a strong feeling they'd missed something. The instinct that had enabled him to survive for so long in Iraq warned him that all was not well.

He went straight to the base's centre and asked for the video recording of the morning's visitors. It was the equipment that interested him – all the different items.

The list complete, he phoned Baghdad airport again. The official who had searched Norton and his equipment had gone home, but Fahad screamed down the receiver that he was to be found and ordered to return to the airport immediately. Then he phoned his own headquarters in Baghdad – the central command of the security police.

'I want a permanent guard on the room of Paul Norton,' he said. 'I want the listening-devices and phone tap constantly monitored. I want a record of every single person he meets. Don't let him out of your sight. If he tries to leave the country, he must be stopped.'

He lay back in the chair, sweating. When the phone rang again he snatched it up angrily.

'Sir, I should have reported this to you earlier. Two days ago, Bandar's flat was hit. Two of our men were killed and the "attacker" got away.'

'We were waiting for her, but she surprised us.'

Fahad gripped the receiver tightly. How could they not have told him? 'She was armed?'

'She disarmed the guard at the fire-escape. Then she opened fire on us and got away.'

'You idiot! You bloody fool!' He slammed down the phone, then called the airport. 'This is Fahad. I want a complete list of all your passengers for the last week – arrivals and departures. I want their identities checked and rechecked. I want road-blocks up outside the airport now. All outgoing passengers must be stripped and searched. If anything suspicious catches your eye, call me. And let me tell you, if there's a mistake, if something is overlooked, it'll be the firing-squad for the man who fucked up.'

Golan pumped Paul's hand. 'You did it! The transmitter worked! We have the location and the layout of the base from satellite photographs. Now it is just a matter of planning our attack.'

Paul sat down wearily on a chair. 'I've got to find Anne . . .'

'Don't worry, she's safe with Mkhulu. They've left for the airport already.'

Paul brightened. At least something was going right. 'How long before we attack?' he asked.

'Soon. The SAS team is flying in now.'

'To where?'

'That I do not know. We must get out of here.'

Paul eyeballed Golan. 'If I vanish, they'll know what's going on and that base will be on full alert. And I don't think anyone will get near it unless they can take it by surprise.'

This appeared to throw Golan, who sat down again. 'I hadn't thought of that, but of course, you're right. There will be no chance for a small attacking team if the base is prepared for such an attack.' He stared at Paul. 'Yes, you must stay here and continue the charade till the last minute.'

He got up and shook Paul's hand. 'I shall keep communication to the minimum. Just try and stay within the vicinty of the hotel.'

Then Golan was gone, leaving Paul on his own, facing the prospect of another gruelling week in Baghdad.

The security guard came up to the taxi. 'Out,' he barked.

Mkhulu stared at Anne. They were trapped. There was nothing they could do except co-operate. They hadn't even entered the airport proper yet, and the road was flanked with military vehicles. To try to escape would be suicidal.

They got out of the taxi as orderd. Mkhulu realised that every vehicle going to the airport was being subjected to the same search – a long line of cars was strung out behind them.

Their cases were taken to a caravan and they were made to follow. 'Open them,' said an official, without looking up from his desk.

Anne felt secure. There was nothing in her or Mkhulu's cases to incriminate them.

'Passports,' the official ordered. He quickly thumbed through Anne's passport, then Mkhulu's 'You travel together, yet you arrived on separate dates?'

'So?' Anne repled, trying to sound relaxed, trying to forget that her passport was a forgery.

The official turned to Mkhulu. 'And you, I see you travelled to Israel before coming here. Why?'

'Business,' Mkhulu replied stiffly.

The official turned his chair and tapped some new commands into the computer.

'Miss Juliet Hanson, I see no record of your name on any of the incoming passenger lists.'

'It was a last-minute decision to come here,' Anne said. 'I got a cancellation.'

'Flight time, number and date?'

'I'll have to check my diary.'

The official pointed to a photograph on his desk and folded his arms. 'Good try, Dr Madison.'

Anne felt giddy. She shot a glance at Mkhulu. His face remained calm, hiding his true emotions.

'You are both under arrest,' the official said with satisfaction.

Fahad could hear the security officer breathing heavily as he read out the list of items he had searched and scanned.

'You have left nothing out, idiot?'

'No, sir.'

'You did the whole search and scan in front of the video camera?'

'Yes, sir.'

'Examine the video, see if you have left anything out. Then call me here.'

'Very good, sir.'

For the next half-hour the security officer studied the video footage intensely, looking to see if he'd left anything out. To his relief there was nothing he'd missed. He dialled Fahad's number at SAAD 20.

'Speak.'

'Sir, I have checked and rechecked every piece of information I have on Paul Norton's equipment. The list I gave you is accurate.

Fahad felt cold. In his gut he felt he had made a serious mistake by bringing Norton to the weapons base again. A knock on the door broke his train of thought.

'Sir, I wish to report that Dr Anne Madison has been recaptured, with a companion, outside Baghdad airport.'

'Very, very good. I want them flown here.'

This was excellent news – but he was still profoundly uneasy about Norton. His men had searched every room in the complex that Norton could have had access to, and had also covered the perimeter area of the runway. They had found nothing. Suddenly he had another idea. He picked up the phone.

'The plane that brought the British reporter, Paul Norton, to the base, and then took him back to Baghdad. I want it back here – immediately. You can use it to transport Dr Madison and her companion.'

The plane arrived at SAAD 20 in the morning, with Dr Anne Madison and her companion on board. Fahad went out in the first light of day to meet them.

Dr Anne Madison and a crippled black man were led out of the hold. Fahad smiled from ear to ear.

'Dr Madison, it is so good to see you again. Let me promise you that you will not escape from SAAD 20 – there is nowhere to escape to.'

He screamed an order to his bodyguards, and they moved in on the big black man, kicking his artificial leg from under him and then working him over with their fists.

'Stop it, you bastards! Stop it!'

'Of course, of course, Dr Madison.' Fahad raised his hand, and his bodyguards stopped at once. 'Just a subtle reminder, Dr Madison, that should you be so stupid as to try anything again, the cripple will suffer.'

Fahad saw the hatred reflected on the black man's bloody face as he issued this threat. 'Now,' he said. 'my men will show you to your cells. And, if you'll excuse me, I have work to do.'

He watched as Dr Madison and the black cripple were

marched into the base. The cripple interested him. He'd never tortured one before, and the thought excited him.

At his command his men now went up into the plane's hold and began their search. Within five minutes a soldier walked out carrying Norton's video camera.

'He must have left it behind, sir.'

'Keep your opinions to yourself.' Fahad snatched the camera from the soldier's hands and walked back into the base.

An hour later, he was looking at the pieces with Dr Fassbinder.

'Yes, a very sophisticated transmitter,' she said. 'It has Israeli components, amongst others, in its circuitry. Until I silenced it, it was giving a signal every thirty seconds. Whoever planted it knows the exact location of this base.'

Fahad felt sick. It was worse than he had imagined. Then he thought of Dr Madison and of the cripple. Perhaps, just perhaps, he could exert a little pressure on Paul Norton.

He called the Baghdad Hilton.

'Paul Norton? Ah yes, it is Fahad here. I must thank you for the interview . . . I found your video camera, by the way. You forgot it, of course; you left it behind in the plane . . . No. No, it is no problem at all. But I have removed the radio transmitter hidden in it, you understand why? Oh and by the way, I hold your Dr Anne Madison and a black cripple here . . . Yes . . . So if there should be any attack on this base, they will die very, very painfully.'

He put the phone down.

Now he would put a little more pressure on Norton. He took the lift down to the lowest basement and walked along the passage to the cells.

The black man was seated naked on the metal stool, as he'd ordered, his feet strapped to the floor, his thighs bound to the seat. Fahad looked at the metal leg that was still strapped to his right stump.

'What's your name?'

'Mkhulu.'

'Very good. And what do you do for a living?'

'I export oranges.'

'Very good, Mkhulu. Very good. I'm going to put a call through to the Baghdad Hilton. I want you to speak to someone.'

Five minutes later, he handed the phone to Mkhulu who gripped it nervously. 'Yes, Paul, I'm fine.'

Fahad watched the conversation develop, then his eyes shifted to the base of the stool and the spring-loaded device beneath it. In his hand he clutched the remote control unit that actuated a release switch on the spring. He pushed the button.

Mkhulu dropped the receiver as a metal shaft was driven up into his anus from the base of the stool.

'Oh God, please help me!'

Fahad stared at the blood on the floor, the excitement pumping through him. He snatched up the receiver.

'Don't worry, Mr Norton, he will live. But just remember how painful it will be for him, and for Dr Madison, if your friends should be so stupid as to try anything.'

Fahad watched as his men unstrapped Mkhulu from the stool and dragged him to the infirmary. He was quite sure Paul Norton would be totally compliant.

There was a sharp knock on the door, and Paul dragged himself off the bed and opened it. Golan stood in front of him, looking grim.

'I got your message. Paul, what the hell's wrong?'

'They found the transmitter. They've got Anne and Mkhulu. They're torturing Mkhulu. They let me hear the screams.'

Golan gripped Paul's shoulders. 'You must get away from here.'

'No. If I leave here they'll kill Mkhulu and Anne.'

'They'll kill them anyway,' Golan said.

'You have the location of the base. Continue your preparations. When you're ready to strike, I'll join you. That I promise.'

'I will do everything in my power to get them out – be sure of it.'

'Go.'

Paul watched the door close, and wept. What had he done? Everyone who was precious to him had been drawn into this horror, everyone who mattered to him could be destroyed in a matter of days. Charlotte and David in Jerusalem, Mkhulu and Anne at the Supergun base.

His only hope lay in the SAS team and Golan.

Inside SAAD 20 Dr Fassbinder looked with satisfaction at the four huge nuclear shells, their pointed tops gleaming in the cold light of the loading-room. Her calculations were finished, the exact trajectory of each shell had been carefully mapped out. They would be fired on Jerusalem at one-minute intervals, calculated to land in a pattern that would produce the most devastating nuclear strike in world history.

Other shells were already in stages of near-completion, though she doubted that a second salvo would be needed. With such an overwhelming display of power, Iraq would be in an unassailable position in the Middle East. Every one of her neighbours would rally to her side, the moment she had played her ace.

Fahad ran his eyes over the monitors in the SAAD 20 control centre. The compliment of troops guarding the base had been quadrupled, the air defences had been put on full alert, and on the runway stood ten MIG-29 Fulcrums – the most advanced Russian fighters. Around the perimeter of the base were surface-to-air missiles, anti-aircraft artillery linked to early-warning and fire-direction radars – a range of the best equipment from across the globe, controlled and integrated by systems from the French company, Thompson CST.

The base was impregnable. And if the Israelis attacked it, Fahad would fire the Supergun in retaliation. The accord President Bush had built up with the other Arab nations would collapse.

No one could stop President Hussein now.

Sir Donald Morgan eyed Lieutenant-General Sir Giles Roberts warily; he knew that the short, unassuming man sitting opposite him was one of the most powerful in the British Army. He had also commanded the SAS, the regiment whose men would now be utilised in this near-suicidal mission.

'This Supergun,' the Lieutenant-General said icily. 'Who supplied it to them?'

'That's what we're still trying to piece together,' Sir Donald lied smoothly.

'And, are you one hundred per cent certain this isn't a hoax?'

'Jesus, Sir Giles, I know what you're going to encounter. I wouldn't dream of asking you to authorise this unless I thought the danger was immediate.'

Sir Giles stared away from the intelligence man. He had been on such missions, he knew the danger and the chances of success. He, for one, did not underestimate the ability of the best Iraqi soldiers.

'All right,' he said. 'But I'll follow this thing through myself. You and the Prime Minister will be responsible for every one of those boys if anything goes wrong.'

'You've made your point.'

'And what about Norton? Will he co-operate? They've got his girlfriend. You know what they'll do to her?'

'Sir Giles, we're talking about the possibility of World War Three.'

'No, we're talking about people's lives. I'm not leading my men into that place unless I've got someone with me who knows the layout. Without Norton this mission is certain suicide.'

'Norton will co-operate. He was a soldier himself once. Evidently a good one.'

Sir Giles raised his eyebrows. 'He's been behaving more like President Hussein's best friend.'

'That's how he got to find out the location of the base.'

Sir Giles took the file from Sir Donald, his eyes moving quickly over the double-spaced lines.

'Yes, a fine soldier. Then something obviously happened to him in Vietnam . . . Does he have the stomach for killing? He knows the horror of war. Perhaps that's why he's trying to give the Iraqi point-of-view – to avoid bloodshed.'

'So what's your decision?'

'I'll take your word on Norton. We'll be ready in just over a week.'

'That's cutting it too fine.'

'It's four hours before the UN deadline – my men aren't going in earlier than that. They'll be working twenty-four hours a day on this. As I see it, they've got one chance. They've to get in and knock that Supergun out.'

'All right. But by God, you're cutting it fine.'

Paul felt the pressure closing him in, suffocating him. Every day dragged as he did interview after interview with the Iraqi military. But there were no hard facts that he could build into his reports – just invective.

The worse part was not knowing what was going on behind the scenes. And as the UN deadline came closer and closer, Paul wondered if anything was going to be done to knock out the Supergun.

He thought of Charlotte and David in Jerusalem – he knew that if the Supergun was fired, they'd most certainly die. And Anne and Mkhulu, what might be happening to them? It didn't bear thinking about.

Anne looked after Mkhulu as best she could. They'd hurt him badly. He was in continual pain and lapsed often into delirium.

She realised that once Fahad had fired the Supergun, their value would be at an end. They were only being kept alive to hold Paul in Baghdad and prevent retaliation.

For some reason, Fahad had left her alone. But in Mkhulu he'd found the most subtle instrument with which to torture her.

It was Tuesday, 15th January 1991. Paul was a nervous wreck. He'd given up smoking, but now, under the pressure, he found relief in the habit – in fact he was chain-smoking. He'd been allowed one call to Anne and she'd told him how bad Mkhulu was.

He'd never contemplated suicide, but now he wondered what he would do after the nuclear shells had struck Israel. He knew they would keep him in Baghdad, continue to use him until they tired of the international publicity.

As darkness fell, he considered using the CNN satellite phone to call Sir Donald Morgan. It would be almost certain suicide – he knew his every movement was being watched.

There was a knock on the door, and outside stood a waiter with his dinner. He ate in the room now, unable to sit in the crowded dining-room, preferring to be alone with his thoughts.

He tipped the waiter and took his food inside. As he lifted up the silver salver, he saw a note pinned to the top of the steak. He read it carefully.

Say out loud that you have a terrible headache. Leave your food, go out of your room and take a lift down to the lobby. Go to the counter, ask for headache pills. Then move towards the doors as if you want to get a breath of fresh air. Go outside, stretch, and look to your left. Then we will snatch you.

The note was unsigned but he knew who it was from: Golan. Paul folded it up and stuffed it into his pocket. Slowly he went through the routine he had been told to enact. He cursed silently in the foyer as he had to repeat again and again to the receptionist that he wanted headache pills.

'Ah, Mr Norton. Yes, the doctor left them for you.'

He took the packet.

'A glass of water?'

Shit! Act normal. 'Thanks,' he said.

He waited an eternity for the glass of water. The he opened the packet, took two pills and swallowed them quickly.

The receptionist leaned a little closer. 'I always read the instuctions before I take medicine.'

Paul looked into the man's eyes and got a vacant stare. He unfolded the instructions and saw Golan's handwriting. 'Black Mercedes will draw up. Rear door will open. Dive on back seat for cover.'

Hands shaking, he folded the note and walked towards the front entrance. He yawned, and went through the revolving doors. His tail was right behind him. Shit.

Outside on the pavement, seconds ticking by. Where the hell were they? It was taking too long. His tail was close by him now, hand resting on the gun inside his jacket.

A big car swept in front of him, gunfire erupting from the front window, lifting the tail into the air and pitching him back through the glass windows of the foyer. Paul leapt into the back, the glass of the car's windows exploding around him from retaliatory gunfire as they accelerated off. He heard the man with the machine-gun in the front passenger seat scream as the bullets took him.

The driver pushed the blood-soaked body off him. 'Damnation! The bastards were watching your every move.'

Paul was lying flat across the rear seat, thinking it was a miracle the driver hadn't been hit. 'Where are we going?' he shouted.

'Rendezvous-point just outside Baghdad. Your friend Golan wanted to come in with me, but it was too damned risky. He might have been recognised.'

The voice sounded vaguely familiar, a crisp blend of upper-crust English and Scottish brogue. There was a chilling edge to it.

Paul told him the worst: 'They'll be expecting you.'

'That's why I'm commanding this operation. It has the full sanction of the British Prime Minister and the American President. We have to succeed – whatever the cost.'

Paul raised his head above the level of the windows. They were moving incredibly fast.

'Who are you?'

'Ian Drummond, Brigadier Ian Drummond.'

Paul sank back onto the seat. The memories came flooding back. Those first few years in Vietnam, the years he'd tried to forget – spent a lifetime running away from.

'You would have made a fine commander, Paul.'

'And you, Ian, what have you made of your life?'

'I've always had what I need most – action.'

Paul looked across at the man who had been a close friend in Vietnam. At the long nose, the eyes that never rested and the thin blond hair that had now receded over the crown of his head.

'How come you took this command?' he asked. 'Surely this isn't your normal line of duty?' Paul knew that Ian was one of the most senior men in the British army.

'It's an SAS action – my regiment. We can't afford to fail. I wanted this command.

Paul shook his head. 'You're mad.'

'I read your file, Paul. You haven't changed – you want the same things I want – you've just gone after them in a different way.'

They were on an open highway now, the needle on the speedometer nudging over 210 kmh.

'Take the lad's gun. You'll need it.'

Paul prized the Browning out of the dead soldier's hand and slipped it into the waistband of his trousers.

'Now take off his watch and replace it with your Rolex.'

Paul did as he told him, sensing that Ian knew exactly what he was doing.

'There'll be a helicopter waiting for us. This is a combined operation with the SEALS and the US 101st Airborne Air Assault Division.'

A shiver went through Paul's body. They'd assessed the odds pretty well.

'We're going in tonight?' he said.

'No. Tomorrow, as the UN deadline expires . . .'

'Jesus Christ.'

'Paul, you are pivotal to this whole thing. And you're a walking wreck right now, so I want you rested. Then I'm giving you a thorough briefing. There'll be no time for bugger-ups.'

Ian swung the car hard off the tarmac and they screamed across the sand. Lights came on in front of them and Paul found himself looking at a UH-60A Black Hawk helicopter, its identification markings removed. Ian yanked up the handbrake and broadsided the car up next to the helicopter.

'Out! Keep running!'

Paul leaped out of the door and sprinted towards the hold, the breath bursting from him. A soldier leaned out and pulled him in. The chopper started to rise.

Ian jumped into the hold seconds later. The Black Hawk powered upwards as the car exploded into flames.

'You left the body behind?'

'Yes. It'll mislead the Iraqis – I'm hoping they'll think it's you. You don't leave a watch as expensive as a Rolex behind for nothing.'

Paul looked through into the cockpit, to the eerie glow of the instruments and above them, the pilot in his night-vision goggles. He felt Ian's hand on his shoulder.

'We'll get her out, Paul, that I promise.'

*

441

Charlotte looked around the flat again, heard the noises in the street and started crying. She touched her stomach where there was now quite a bulge. They already knew it would be a boy.

Now she was afraid.

David had been working very, very hard at the university – but it wasn't that that had frightened her. It was the man, Golan, who had come to see them. He'd asked her lots of questions about her father. Did Paul support the Arabs? Was he opposed to violence? Did she think he'd known Dr Madison was a CIA agent?

Charlotte hadn't liked Golan, but she'd answered the questions as best she could. She realised that what Mkhulu had been talking about must be true. And that meant Jerusalem would be the target for Iraq's nuclear warhead.

Every day she watched her father's televised transmissions from Baghdad. From the lines on his face and the grey bags under his eyes, she could tell he was under immense strain. Now she'd just heard on a newsflash that he'd been abducted at gunpoint from the Baghdad Hilton and that a nationwide search had been launched for him.

She was afraid her father was dead. She felt the baby move inside her. Africa was in her blood, and the continent had imbued her with a sense of fate, of the way life's events so often had a shape, a pattern: it would be symbolic for her to bear a child just as her father died . . .

She didn't hear David come in. His arms folded around her and he drew her close to him.

'Golan's gone,' he said quietly. I think he's in Iraq. I heard the news, Charlotte. They're going to try to knock out the Supergun.'

'And if they fail?'

'Don't think about it, Charlotte, just don't think about it.'

Wayne MacLeod chewed with satisfaction on his cigar. His newspapers were taking an anti-Iraqi, pro-Israeli stance.

He got up and stared out across the grey London skyline. Every record of his dealings with Iraq had been destroyed. It was the perfect way to conclude a very profitable business relationship with a government now labelled 'the enemy'.

He was now poised to make several very large US acquisitions. And he had the wholesale approval of the British government, who were clearly delighted that a London-based company should become one of the world's media giants.

Naturally, his range of holding companies would continue, behind the scenes, to trade in sophisticated weaponry, but only once the tension in the Gulf had dissipated. If the Iraqis won, then he would have a customer for life. If they lost, well there'd be plenty of other customers for his products.

He picked up the morning edition of the *Daily News*, his flagship paper. The lead was a story on Paul Norton's abduction from the Baghdad Hilton.

He pushed the intercom button. 'Stephanie, get me Hyde.'

Norton had really overstepped the limit in his Baghdad reports – far too biased in Iraq's favour.

The phone rang. 'Hyde. How's the reserve . . . ? Very good. You've seen the papers . . . I think Norton's finally bought it. You burned Bush Camp down? What next?

'You've moved in squatters. Good. We'll wait till we hear official confirmation that Norton's dead, then we'll get Klaw for nothing . . . No, no, his daughter isn't going to want the place. And you say Mkhulu's disappeared? Even better. That just leaves Johannes. He's easy meat.'

He put the phone down. Norton's reserve would be the icing on the cake. Everything was working our brilliantly.

Now he must prepare for the interview with *Time*. They wanted to do a cover on him. It would be perfect if it coincided with the start of the Gulf War. Quite fitting.

Paul's head was spinning. For the past four hours, sitting in a large hangar, he'd been through debriefing after debriefing. Photographs of Fahad and Dr Fassbinder had been flashed up on a large television screen in front of him, plus satellite pictures of the SAAD 20 complex. He'd been exposed to the whole plan of attack – daring and horrifyingly dangerous.

Golan walked out of the shadows and sat next to him.

'What do you think, Paul?'

'I think, what if you fail?'

'We, Paul, we. You are coming in with us. You will guide us through the base.

He felt a hand on his shoulder and looked up to see Ian standing close. 'It's time you got some sleep. The doctor will give you something to knock you out – something that won't affect your judgement when you come round.'

Paul rose wearily. 'I don't need it. I'll fall asleep quickly enough after what you've put me through.'

Ian guided him out of the hangar towards a group of large tents, looking strangely black against the desert sand, highlighted by the moonlight. Paul sensed that there was something his old friend wanted to say.

'Paul, you're perhaps the only one who understands just how insanely dangerous this operation is. You know the layout of SAAD 20, the sophisticated nature of the installation. That's why I want you with me. It's not that I want to push you somewhere you don't want to go; it's that a lot of my men are going to die, but having you along may save a few lives.'

Paul dug his hands into his pockets, and stared across the empty sands. 'I love the Middle East,' he said. 'I respect these people. It's the bloody petro-dollars that have destroyed them. If there wasn't any oil here, there wouldn't be a war.'

Ian let out a dry laugh. 'You haven't changed . . . Wars are inevitable – human greed creates wars.'

'What did Vietnam achieve?'

'It convinced the United States that if they fight this war, they have to win it and win it quickly.'

'But this isn't your war, Ian. Do you really care about the fate of Kuwait? What are you really doing here?'

'I'm a soldier. I follow orders. And I find nothing in the scope of this operation that makes me question it. Anyway, why are you so high-and-mighty? It was you who brought about this action.'

'If only the intelligence people had acted faster on my information, this would never have been necessary.'

'Paul, stop asking questions. Always it's bloody questions with you. Isn't doing enough?'

Paul stared hard at Ian's profile in the darkness. That was the difference between them: Paul asked questions first, then acted;

Ian performed the action and dismissed the doubts that came later. But perhaps I'm deceiving myself, Paul thought. He hadn't thought about shooting Cilliers, had he – he'd just done it.

'Goodnight, Ian,' he said.

Ian pressed something into his hand and walked away.

Paul watched the soldier move off into the darkness, then went into the tent and collapsed on the makeshift bed. There was no choice, he knew that – he had to go in with them. God alone knew what Fahad was doing to Anne.

He pulled out his lighter and flicked it on. In the dancing flame he looked at what Ian had given him – a razor-thin combat knife.

He drew it out, examined the blade, and then replaced it in its scabbard. Then he strapped it to his calf muscle, above his right ankle.

The time for thinking was over.

Anne sat next to Mkhulu's bed, bathing his head with cold water. He was dying and there was nothing she could do about it.

She looked at her watch. Outside it would be burning hot. It was midday, and only twelve hours to the expiry of the UN deadline. There was no doubt in her mind that Fahad would fire the nuclear shells on Jerusalem. She felt totally powerless. All she could do was wait.

Charlotte watched the clock ticking on the kitchen table. Darkness had fallen over Jerusalem, and the UN deadline for Iraq's withdrawal from Kuwait would expire at midnight.

At the first sign of US aggression she had no doubt that Iraq would attack Israel. And she and David would die in the ensuing holocaust. What in God's name had happened to her father?

The noise of the chopper blades beat hard against the night air. Paul adjusted his camouflage jacket, then tied the cravat around his neck. He was covered in equipment, and had night-vision goggles pulled up against his forehead. On either side of the Black Hawk in which he was sitting stood Apache AH-64s, ready to escort them deep into enemy territory.

Ian leapt into the hold and barked the order to take off. The

445

noise of the fleet of choppers rising into the night air was deafening.

They flew low across the sands from the secret base, heading towards SAAD 20. Ian had told him that the journey would take three hours, bringing them to their destination just before midnight.

Radar jamming would commence as they converged on the base. Once they were in, they would be on their own. None of them wore uniforms, none of them had identity papers, and all were equipped with cyanide pills – to be swallowed in the event of capture and torture. Their chances of getting in undetected were minimal. As for the odds against their knocking out the Supergun – no one wanted to calculate them.

If they failed, they would die. It was as simple as that.

Fahad felt the tension rising. His personal preference would have been for firing the Supergun the moment the deadline expired, but President Hussein would have none of it. The President still believed that the US was calling his bluff and that nothing would happen after the expiry of the deadline. He wanted to keep his ace up his sleeve.

Hussein expected a new deadline to be set, along with continued threats from the US. But for Fahad this was irrelevant. As far as he was concerned, someone knew about the location of SAAD 20 and it was only a matter of time before it was attacked. He had already decided what he would do in that eventuality – push the firing button of the Supergun.

Anne could hardly keep her eyes open. She hadn't slept for the past forty-eight hours and she kept dropping off. It was then she noticed that Mkhulu's eyes were closed. She felt for his pulse.

'Oh no, please not this!' she cried, knowing it was useless, knowing he was dead.

The rage hit her without warning and she smashed her fists against the locked door of the room.

'Let me out, you fucking bastards! Let me out!'

Nothing happened. No one reacted.

She staggered back over to the bed and started hitting Mkhulu's body.

'Don't die! Oh God, how could you die?'

Then she collapsed on the floor, sobbing, wondering what the hell was happening to her, blaming herself for his death.

'Closing fast,' came the US pilot's voice over the headphones. Paul checked his pistol and his rifle, and pulled the night-vision goggles down over his eyes.

The ropes were thrown down out of the chopper to the ground below. He heard the explosions start almost immediately – the sky was lit up with anti-aircraft fire. Over the headphones came a scream of commands. In front he saw one Apache suffer a direct hit and burst into flames. He felt sick to his gut.

Then the anger came over him and he was scrambling forward, jumping out of the hold and swinging down the line towards the ground below.

Everywhere there was fire. He heard the screams as some of the men from the other choppers were hit on their way to the ground. He lifted his machine-gun and sprayed the area immediately in front of him. He knew exactly where he was – the entrance to SAAD 20.

His legs pushed hard against the tarmac, bullets sang around his head. In the night-sight he picked up a gunman on the roof; he dropped, pivoted and fired. The man sagged forward, gripping his stomach.

Paul made it to the doors, ripped the charges from his waistband, clamped them around the locks and jumped away, activating the remote detonator.

The explosion was blinding. He called out through his radio for the rest of the team to move in.

Without waiting, he burst in through the doors, raking the interior with his machine-gun. Ian came up alongside him, and Paul indicated the next door to be blown. In seconds Ian had the charges in place and danced back across the floor. Paul threw himself flat down as the explosives ripped open the lock.

Retaliatory fire came from the next section and they both lobbed in grenades, the flash following almost instantaneously. Now they were at the lift doors and Ian was screaming for the next team to follow up.

The men came in, dragging their equipment. Immediately,

they set to work, attacking the lift doors with blow-torches. This cutting team worked fast, placing more charges through the holes they'd made in the metalwork.

A couple of muffled thuds and lift doors were blown back. Ropes were thrown down the shaft and Paul followed Ian, abseiling downwards. He felt sick with fear as he descended. It was absolutely suicidal, going down into that black hole. But before he realised it his feet were hitting the top of the lift. Ian attached charges to the cable and they lay back against the sides of the shaft. Two sharp blasts severed the cable.

Spotlights now illuminated the shaft, shining down onto them as they examined the top of the lift. Ian yanked open a central inspection door and stared into the empty cage. He screamed into his radio for the next team to come down the shaft, and the men abseiled down the ropes as he spoke, joining Paul and Ian inside the metal lift-cage. They attacked the lift exit doors here just as they'd done at the top of the shaft, cutting holes in the metal and placing charges. Then they all climbed out through the inspection cover and Ian pushed the button on the remote detonator.

The explosion shook the cage, then Ian leaped down inside it and started to force the doors open. Paul came down after him, positioning himself to the side.

As the doors slid open, Ian opened fire, raking the hall in front of him. But a blast of retaliatory fire hit him straight in the gut.

Paul opened fire, screaming as he did so, hitting the man who had shot Ian. The rest of the team cannoned down through the roof of the lift and fanned out into the hall.

Ian dragged himself to his feet, his mouth bloody. He gripped Paul by the lapels.

'Keep them going. Don't stop. Maintain pressure!'

'Who's in command now?'

'You are.'

Paul was about to object, but Ian's grip intensified.

'Do it!'

Then his friend collapsed, dead in his own blood.

*

Fahad ran from the control room, shouting commands. 'Don't let them get any further! Seal off all sections!'

He sprinted down the corridor as sirens screamed and soldiers thundered towards the upper level of the underground complex.

Fahad came to the door of Dr Fassbinder's private suite and banged on it hard. She opened it, bleary-eyed, and stared at him.

'What is the meaning of this?'

'We're under attack. We must fire the Supergun immediately!'

She darted back into her room and he caught a glimpse of naked flesh as she dressed quickly in a jump-suit. Then she was next to him, running down the stairs to the main control room. She threw switches, and Fahad watched the firing-chamber on the video monitors.

Outside, in the darkness, giant metal covers slid back across the desert sand to reveal the Supergun enclosure – like a gigantic funnel with the huge gun upright in the centre. The black metal barrel began to tilt downwards, so that it pointed to the north-west.

Back in the control centre, Dr Fassbinder leaned towards the microphone which was linked to the ammunition bunker next to the firing-chamber. Fahad looked on, relieved that the Supergun had not been positioned within the complex but several kilometres away – another security measure.

'Load shell one.'

On the monitor Fahad watched the operation of the elaborate hydraulics system as it lifted and transported the shell towards the breech of the Supergun.

'Prepare shell two for immediate reloading.'

Dr Fassbinder looked across at the control screens. 'I shall go for a conventional firing. The shells will take a direct trajectory.'

'Your first target?'

'A densely populated civilian area of Jerusalem – the Old City. I want to kill as many of them as possible.'

Fahad smiled. This was the moment he had been waiting for.

Paul felt sick. He and his men couldn't find their way down to the lower level – there must be other lifts and stairwells. In the distance, down the corridor, the firing intensified – more and more Iraqi soldiers were being moved in against them.

His group had been cornered in a dead-end. One after the other they fell in a withering hail of bullets. There was no way they could win. Already the sacrifice had been horrific. He had to make a decision fast. If he fought to maintain this position, he would certainly die. At least, alive, he might still have a chance.

He ordered his men to lay down their weapons and surrender.

The guns clattered to the floor as they threw them down. Then there was a long silence.

'Rise and place your hands on your heads,' came the icy command in Arabic.

Paul translated, and his men obeyed the command. He heard the noise of the Iraqi troops approaching.

An Iraqi officer ordered them to line up, facing the wall. The shooting started seconds later – a bullet in the back of the head for each of them. Paul wanted to scream with rage.

Next to him there was a dull thud, the splash of blood against the wall and the sigh as the soldier crumpled in a heap on the ground. He felt the pistol barrel against his own neck.

Oh God. Oh God. Did it have to end this way?

There was a dull click as the hammer came down, but no explosion.

Paul cried out, and hated himself for the weakness. There was laughter behind him.

'Mr Norton. You are a fortunate man. Our commander requests your presence at a unique event,' a voice behind him said in good English, and he was pushed along the corridor, past the trail of bloody bodies.

It had all been for nothing.

Another five minutes and he reached his destination.

'Inside,' the officer barked.

He stepped into the huge control centre and saw Anne strapped to a chair, a man behind her holding a gun to her head. Her mouth was covered in adhesive tape. She looked at Paul desperately.

Fahad turned away from the screens and smiled.

'Ah. Mr Norton. How good of you to come. Naturally, this

will be an excellent scoop for you. How many journalists can claim to have witnessed a turning-point in world history?'

Paul took in the situation quickly. One wrong move on his part and Anne would be dead. He wondered what had happened to Mkhulu.

'You're a madman,' he said softly.

'No, but I think you are, Paul Norton. Who else would have been crazy enough to think they could storm this base? After all, it was designed by some of Europe's top military advisers. For your information, you never even came close to the nerve-centre. You didn't even make the second level. And anyway, the Supergun isn't located here.'

Dr Fassbinder continued punching commands in to the computer.

'Five minutes to detonation,' came an icy report over the intercom.

'Very good,' she replied. 'Prepare for immediate reloading after detonation.' She leaned back from the keyboard.

'Dr Fassbinder, would you care to explain to Mr Norton what he is about to witness?' Fahad asked graciously.

She turned and looked into Paul's eyes. 'The first explosion will be twice the size of the Nagasaki bomb. However, that is only the first of four. By the time we have finished, the city of Jerusalem will be a wasteland.'

Paul couldn't believe the callousness of it. 'Why not one shell? Surely that would be enough.'

Dr Fassbinder gave a thin smile. 'There are no ethics in war, Mr Norton. There is only one issue for me – to annihilate as many Israelis as possible.'

In the monitor directly in front of him Paul watched the barrel of the Supergun lining up. He glanced to the other monitors, saw the breech team completing the loading of the giant shell. He thought back to the drawings he'd shown Sir Donald Morgan and remembered the man's scepticism. Then his thoughts turned to Charlotte and David in Jerusalem. He felt sick – there was nothing he could do. This strangely beautiful woman with the raven-black hair was the only person who could stop what was about to happen. Her long fingers worked the keyboard, expertly controlling the operation.

He started to talk, searching for something.

'You were in love with Dr Torr, Dr Fassbinder – it must have been hard for you when he died.'

He saw her fingers falter. 'How do you know about this?'

'You mean, how do I know about Amhuinnsuidhe Castle? The testing in Namibia? The meetings with Wayne MacLeod?

He saw how Fahad sucked in his breath at these disclosures. There was more, Paul knew there was more. He just had to try and convince Dr Fassbinder that he knew more of the truth than he actually did. For her, the motive behind firing the Supergun was pure revenge. And he had guessed enough of the truth to know that the Iraqis were exploiting her – had been exploiting her for a long time.

'So, the Israelis found your hide-away. And they killed Dr Torr.'

She almost snarled as she turned. 'You were the one – you were the one who told them!'

'I should have been – but someone beat me to it.'

'It was Mossad,' she hissed, and turned back to the controls.

'But how could Mossad have found out about your work?'

She shook out her hair. The timer above her indicated that it was just over four minutes to firing time.

'I think you should shut up, Mr Norton,' she said. You're making me even more determined to kill as many Israelis as I can.'

Paul racked his brains, looking for something to unhinge her.

'The Israelis didn't get a tip-off,' he said, but they were aware that Iraq was developing a nuclear warhead. Naturally, when they heard of Dr Torr's assassination they were pleased. They automatically assumed that marked the end of Iraq's plans to develop their own nuclear weapon.

'I was the one who told British intelligence about your design facility at Amhuinnsuidhe Castle, and they did nothing about it. The Americans were aware of the programme as well – but experts in both those countries believed the Supergun to be a white elephant.

'But all that is now largely irrelevant. The question you have to ask yourself, Dr Fassbinder, is, if the Israelis didn't kill Dr

452

Torr, who did? His death was very convenient for Iraq, it immediately smokescreened the whole intelligence world.

'With Dr Torr out of the way, everyone thought the Supergun programme was finished. No one knew about you – except for the Iraqis, who knew you would continue the programme through to completion. So don't you see – it could well have been Iraqi intelligence who murdered Dr Torr and had you raped. What better way, after all, to make you finish the work on the Supergun?'

He noticed that Fahad's face was darkening. It was only then that he realised how clever the Iraqi had been. It must have been Fahad who'd ordered the death of Dr Torr. Of course – brilliant – the ultimate deception.

'You are crazy,' Dr Fassbinder said slowly, turning and looking into Paul's eyes. Paul could see the uncertainty was building in her mind. He followed his line of speculation further.

'Someone wanted Dr Torr out of the way. He wasn't co-operative. He had dreams . . . dreams of launching satellites with his Supergun. He was difficult to control. So once the design had been completed, what better way to turn the others off than to have him killed off by the Israelis – knowing, of course, that you were around to complete the work? No one in intelligence knows about you.'

Her hands were moving more slowly. 'How do you know about these things? Do you work for MacLeod?

He watched the seconds ticking away and thought of Charlotte and David in Jerusalem, of Mkhulu, of Johannes – and then of the lions. What was this madness?

He said: 'It took a lot of money and a lot of influence to manufacture the parts for this weapon, to raise the money to finance its development. Money that's all gone to MacLeod. And now, whose newspapers are canvassing for war with Iraq?'

Dr Fassbinder continued flicking the switches on the command panel and shouting orders.

He pictured in his mind the lonely castle, Dr Torr asleep, the men bursting through the curtains, killing him as he lay next to her. Then taking her and raping her. He realised that if they had been Israelis they would have killed her – inevitably. He knew,

453

he had seen it again and again: in war the law of the jungle applied.

'The men who killed Dr Torr, who were they?' he said.

'Israelis.' She spat the word out.

'They hated him, didn't they? But then, having raped you, why didn't they kill you? It would have made far more sense to have you dead, wouldn't it? I mean, you could have recognised them. The only logical thing for them to do was kill you.'

Fahad was on his feet, moving towards him. Paul had only seconds left. He broke into Arabic, imagining the words the men would have used when they raped her.

'Fuck the bitch, fuck the bitch.'

She turned and looked at him. 'You were one of them!'

'No, my language is English.'

'That was Hebrew. It was what I heard when they assaulted me . . .'

He repeated the words again slowly. 'Fuck the bitch, fuck the bitch.'

'Shut up you bastard!' she screamed.

'Dr Fassbinder, I'm talking to you in Arabic, not Hebrew. And, as you know, Israelis do not like to talk in Arabic . . .'

The blow caught him hard across the head and sent him sprawling across the floor. He saw Fahad above him, the butt of his pistol raised to strike again.

Paul looked into Fahad's eyes. He remembered the child and the woman in Halabje, and the hatred burned in his soul. He pointed his finger at Fahad.

'They were his men. They wanted Dr Torr dead. Don't you bloody understand?'

As Fahad advanced on him, he saw the expression on Dr Fassbinder's face. It was one of total desperation. Her hands hammered away at the keyboard, and Fahad looked over to her.

'What are you doing?'

'The barrel is slightly out of alignment,' she said coldly.

Fahad chuckled. 'I'm glad you are concentrating on your work and not on the words of this madman.'

Dr Fassbinder stared down at Paul.

'Fire!' she screamed.

Paul felt sick to his gut. He had failed. And now there was no

454

way he was going to get out of this alive. He looked across at Anne, bound to the chair, and he knew in an instant what Fahad would do to her.

The timer progressed another minute.

'Fire,' Dr Fassbinder said quietly.

Another two minutes, and all four shells had been fired. Fahad looked down at Paul.

'It is over, my friend. Now the entire might of the Arab world will descend on Israel. The United States and Britain will be powerless to stop the tide. We have won already.'

There was the noise of doors closing around the control room. Fahad backed away from Paul and spun round. Dr Fassbinder drew out a Glock pistol and centred it on Fahad's chest.

'Bastard.'

Fahad started to raise his gun.

'Drop it!'

To Paul's surprise, Dr Fassbinder moved behind Anne and started to untie her hands.

'He was lying!' Fahad said deperately. 'The Israeli's were speaking in our language to confuse you!'

The bandage came off Anne's mouth, and she launched forward, sinking her nails into Fahad's face.

'You killed him! You killed him!'

It was then Paul realised that she was talking about Mkhulu. He pulled himself up and looked into Dr Fassbinder's eyes.

'Who are you, Mr Norton?' she said. 'What is your interest in this affair?'

'Do you know how many people will die when those shells land?' Paul asked coldly.

Anne pulled away from Fahad, crying. Dr Fassbinder moved forward and pointed the Glock at him.

'Fahad, you will escort us out of here.'

'You will never make it out alive.'

'Then you die.'

Her finger closed around the trigger, a calm smile on her face. Paul could see Fahad knew that this was the way you cocked the Glock for firing.

'No!' Fahad cried. 'Please! I will get you out. But you must hand me my gun.'

She bent down and expertly unloaded Fahad's pistol. 'You take this unloaded pistol and escort Mr Norton and Dr Madison. I will walk behind you, my weapon concealed under this clip-board. You try anything, I will put a bullet through your spinal column.'

She kicked the unloaded Colt across the floor to Fahad. 'Move!'

Grudgingly Fahad picked up the weapon. Dr Fassbinder flicked another switch and the security doors opened. Fahad's men were waiting outside.

'It's all right,' Fahad said quickly, glancing at Paul, who he knew understood their language perfectly. Paul nodded to Dr Fassbinder.

'To the helipad,' she said quickly to Fahad.

To Paul's surprise, it took them only a few minutes to reach a lift that carried them straight to ground level. He realised then that there was another way into the complex he hadn't known about. It was sickening to think how many lives had been wasted trying to get in through the main entrance.

The ground shook beneath them, and Paul dropped down, as did Fahad and Anne. Dr Fassbinder remained standing.

'Final detonation,' she said calmly.

Paul sobbed with despair.

'Mr Norton,' Dr Fassbinder said, 'Jerusalem is four hundred kilometres from here. What you just heard was the final destruc-tion of the Supergun complex and Iraq's refining facility for nuclear material.'

Fahad looked at her aghast. 'But how?'

'Vance never trusted you,' she said calmly. 'There was always a second option in the firing programme. Vance believed in ballistics, not in killing. You said that the Supergun was to be a deterrent, and President Hussein promised us that. You broke that promise. But worse, far worse . . . I know you killed Vance.'

Fahad dragged himself to his feet and started running for the lift entrance.

Her first shot took him in the centre of the back, the second in the centre of the head. His blood showered against the alumin-ium lift doors as he died with a sigh. She turned to Paul.

'You can fly the helicopter?'

He nodded.

'Come, then. We have no time to lose. You must head north towards Jordan and pray to God the Allied air attack hasn't started.'

Paul pulled the cyclic lever slowly back and eased the chopper off the ground. In the distance he saw the huge mushroom cloud rising from the desert floor.

He headed north, maintaining cruising speed.

'You cannot go any faster?' Dr Fassbinder asked nervously.

'Yes, but then we'll use up our fuel too quickly.'

'Go faster. We have no time to lose.'

He accelerated, not questioning her reasoning. He couldn't believe what she had done earlier. His faith in human nature was restored.

But then he thought of the four shells that would soon land on Jerusalem.

'Mr Norton, I hope you are not holding back. I do not have to tell you that if we run into the Allied air attack we shall die.'

A cold sweat broke off his brow as he willed the machine to go faster. He looked round to see Anne staring coldly ahead.

It was over, but at a terrible price. He had failed.

The helicopter ran out of fuel an hour later and Paul drifted it down next to the road that ran northwards. He knew that to land in the desert would be suicidal.

It was very cold as they watched the breaking dawn. He held Anne close to him and felt her warmth against his chest. Dr Fassbinder drifted off behind the helicopter, leaving them alone with each other.

Neither of them spoke. Words seemed inadequate at that moment. Paul watched his breath condense in the cold air. He felt very, very tired.

The first rays of sunlight caught the glass of the helicopter cockpit. Then the stillness of the dawn was broken by the sound of a pistol shot.

Paul pulled away from Anne and ran behind the chopper. Dr Fassbinder lay in the sand, the still-smoking pistol lying next to her, the alabaster skin of her face splattered with blood. Anne came up behind him, pulled off her jacket and placed it behind Dr Fassbinder's head.

'Why?' Paul croaked.

'Shhh. She's still alive.'

Anne took her hand and held it. The dark eyes rested on her.

'Don't you understand?' Dr Fassbinder whispered. 'I loved him. Even though I was working for the Iraqis I loved him more than I have loved anyone. Why did they kill him? He gave them so much.'

Paul stared into the rising sun. 'They knew he wouldn't do it,' he said. 'They knew he'd never allow the Supergun to fire nuclear shells.'

'He was playing a game with them, bleeding them dry. But he wanted to launch that satellite. It was his dream.'

She gripped Paul's hand. 'You don't have to worry. The shells . . . I achieved his dream, I fired them into space. No one will die . . .'

He felt her grip lessening. Her eyes burned with a feverish intensity. 'Let the world know the truth,' she said. He could barely hear her. 'Then he will get the recognition he deserves.'

She sank back, let out a vague murmur, and then her eyes closed forever.

They had been waiting for an hour in the shadow of the helicopter when Paul heard the noise of a car approaching in the distance. He and Anne had already worked out a plan of action: he would approach the road and she would remain hidden behind the chopper, covering him with her gun.

Following the plan, he walked out into the centre of the road that stretched off across the sand, travelling in a straight line to the south, into Iraq. The silver image of the car came closer and closer.

The car swept past him and he gesticulated wildly for it to stop. There was the screech of tyres and a smell of burning rubber, then the Jaguar pulled up a hundred metres further on. The silence of the desert was all-pervasive. A man dressed in a white robe got out of the car and walked towards him. There was a machine-gun cradled in the man's hands.

'I am not with the army. I need a lift out of Iraq,' Paul said quickly in Arabic.

'Then why are you flying a military helicopter?' the man asked, stopping in his tracks and levelling the muzzle of his weapon at Paul.

'It's a long story. My girlfriend . . .' Paul gestured to Anne to come out of her hiding-place and she stepped out into the open. Now they were both exposed. It was a gamble, but then they didn't know that the next vehicle to come down the road mightn't be an Iraqi army truck.

'Where do you want to go?' the man asked.

'We want to get out of Iraq. It doesn't matter where.'

'There was a long silence. A baby screamed from inside the car.

'Your baby sounds sick,' Anne said in English.

'She is sick . . .' the man faltered, also in English.

'I am a doctor, perhaps I can help.'

The man dropped the muzzle of his weapon. 'Please come then. My wife is very worried.'

In a few moments Anne and Paul were at the car. Then Anne was holding the baby in her hands, examining her. She looked up at the father.

'We need to get her to a hospital. She has a viral infection.'

'But will she be all right?' the mother asked desperately.

'Yes. Don't worry. We must just give her plenty of fluids.' Anne replied calmly.

Paul climbed into the front of the car with the man, and Anne got into the back with his wife and the baby. They moved fast towards the border. The man told Paul of the previous night's bombing of Baghdad.

Paul breathed a sigh of relief. It was over.

Epilogue

Sir Donald Morgan shifted in his chair again, looking first at Anne, then at Paul.

'Of course, none of this must come out,' he said.

Paul held the side of his chair tensely. 'But what about all the men who died . . . ?'

'They'll be decorated. But that'll be behind closed doors.'

Anne got up and walked along Sir Donald's bookshelves, looking up at the rows of books that reached to the ceiling.

'So you're not going to do anything?' she said bitterly.

Sir Donald cleaned out his pipe and worked some more tobacco into it. Then he lit up and inhaled. A pleasant smell of pipe tobacco filled the room.

'You know,' he said, 'Vance Torr was the greatest designer of artillery this century. There's no doubt about it. But the man rejected authority, defied control. Perhaps there may be some truth in what Dr Fassbinder told you, but by God, he was playing a dangerous game. It could easily have backfired, and then it would have been World War Three.'

Paul looked across at Anne, then out of the window, towards the park and the grey London skyline beyond.

'And that other bastard . . .' he said. 'Wayne MacLeod.'

'Paul, his involvement is pure supposition on your part. And MacLeod is an influential and powerful man. He carries a lot of clout . . . how can I put this to you? . . . it would not be politic for enquiries to be pursued any further.'

'The man's a cold-blooded murderer!'

Anne came up behind Paul and rested her hand on his arm. 'Sir Donald's right, Paul, leave it alone.'

Paul thought back to a time long ago, on Klaw. He remembered his father holding his hand as they watched the sunset. He remembered his father's words: 'Paul, it will all pass, but this will remain. Stay close and remember this – it is easy to own a part of Africa, but it is almost impossible to possess it in your soul.'

He thought of Mkhulu, and he realised there had been enough killing.

'Paul . . .' Anne's voice intruded on his thoughts.

'Yes,' he said with a sigh. 'You're right. It's enough. It's over.'

Sir Donald stared at the television screen and watched the Prime Minister's resignation speech. Of course, the general public and the majority of people within the government would never know the real reason why he was going.

He looked at the Prime Minister's tired face. The man had done what any other would have done to protect his son. The young man could never have suspected what an elaborate trap Fahad was luring him into; then, when Fahad applied the pressure, he in turn had pressured his father. That the Prime Minister had ignored certain security warnings, thus enabling the Iraqis to continue their Supergun programme, was only known to a few – but the price of their silence was his resignation.

The next item on the news was the folding of IPBP. The shareholders were bankrupt, and one of the victims was the council of the Islands of Harris and Lewis. Fortunately, media tycoon Wayne MacLeod had come to bail them out, on certain conditions. Really, Sir Donald thought, MacLeod was a pretty good chap, one way and another. A pity Norton had such a bee in his bonnet about him.

Sir Donald changed channels and watched the continuing bombardment of Baghdad. God, how many people would ever realise what a close shave it had been? Now it was just a matter of slowly but surely battering the Iraqis into submission – they didn't have a hope in hell against the forces mustered against them.

In the cold light of dawn they moved out on foot. The smell of the bush was in Paul's nostrils again – how he loved it. He squeezed Anne's hand and then led the way forward.

They were both unarmed. It was the way he liked to be in the bush – brought him closer to it, let him feel the fear and the intensity of it.

This was the place he always came to. It was close to where the lions would rest. He loved to watch them in the first light of the day.

The clearing felt strange when they came to it, and Paul couldn't see his lions. He moved into the centre of the open patch of ground with Anne. He felt sick to his gut. Two of his lions were stretched out on the ground, dead, flies buzzing around them.

'Oh God, Paul. Oh God.'

Then he heard the noise of a rifle bolt, and Wayne MacLeod emerged from the edge of the clearing, an Oberndorf Mauser rifle in his hands, pointing at them.

'Don't try anything. As you can see, I'm a very good shot.'

'You bastard, MacLeod.'

Anne stared at the tall, white-haired man, then moved closer to Paul. The air was still around them.

'You mutilated my son,' MacLeod said.

Paul felt very cold. 'Hyde deserved it.'

'I'll get my revenge on you – you bastard!'

'You're a sick man, MacLeod,' Anne said softly. 'You're the one who built that nuclear cannon for the Iraqis.'

MacLeod's eyes widened. 'What's this rubbish?'

'You dealt with Fahad in London, you leased your castle on Harris to Dr Torr, your holding companies in Europe and Africa made the parts to build the Supergun. You were the one who paid Dr Vance Torr to develop it. And we know that there's an identical cannon to the one that was destroyed in Iraq located at your weapons testing base in Namibia. We also know you have the contract, via your French companies, to build a new military air base for the Botswanan government. We also know that you used the IPBP Bank as a front to extract money from your clients. It was a clever move to send it into liquidation, wasn't it – it gave you control of the island of Harris.'

MacLeod grinned. 'Ah. Then you won't be surprised to know that what's about to happen next will be disguised as a hunting accident by the Botswanan authorities.'

MacLeod raised the rifle to his shoulder and centred the bead on Paul's head. 'I am an honourable man,' he said coldly. 'Your wife dies last.'

Anne watched his finger on the trigger. It was then that she heard the call of the lion. She knew by heart the different calls of each of the three lions who had once been Shiva's cubs, and this was the last of the three.

MacLeod pivoted as the lion burst from the bush and leaped towards him. Anne screamed.

One shot. Then a second.

The lion was on him, crushing him down, sinking his claws into him. Then there was silence.

Wayne MacLeod staggered to his feet, his long silver hair soaked in blood. The lion lay dead at his feet.

Paul stared at the lion, then snatched up the Mauser.

'That's it, Norton,' MacLeod said with a deathly grin. 'Kill me. But this time you'll get the death sentence for sure.'

Paul lowered the rifle slowly and watched Wayne MacLeod walk off into the bush. Then he started towards the dead lion. Instinctively the lion had acted to protect them and avenge the killing of his brothers.

Paul leaned over the lion's body and gripped the cat's fur desperately. The he looked up at Anne.

'Paul,' she said, 'you must never lose faith. He died for you. Don't you understand? Everything you gave, everything your father gave, has been vindicated.'

He drew himself up, took Anne's hand, and they walked back into the bush. She was right. It was a sign that he had to make the film. He must go on.

He must answer the call of the lion.

CHRISTOPHER SHERLOCK

Hyena Dawn

**A FIGHT TO THE DEATH –
THE FUTURE OF A CONTINENT
War-torn Mozambique, 1978.**

A story of war fought under the merciless African sun. A war with Rayne Gallagher, a mercenary leader, fighting other men's wars; his lover Samantha, a beautiful American photographer, caught in the crossfire, and Tongogora, committed to the fight for what he sees as freedom. This is an utterly believable story as the Soviets and the West struggle for surpremacy in the battlefield that is Southern Africa.

CHRISTOPHER SHERLOCK

Eye of the Cobra

Wyatt Chase lives hard, drives fast – a Formula One driver with the nerve and talent to win the world championship. But on the verge of victory, his past turns against him. Just as he thinks he's got the top spot at Calibre Shensu, the leading Formula One team, his world implodes. Some-one is using the team as a cover for highly secretive business dealings that are plainly worth killing for – someone who wants Wyatt Chase out of the picture.

Racing from the drama of the track to the intrigue of the boardroom, from Rio to Monaco, from New York to Mount Fuji to the fiefdoms of Colombian drug lords, *Eye of the Cobra* is rubber-burning action from start to finish.

CHRISTOPHER SHERLOCK

Night of the Predator

**A LAND ON THE BRINK
OF APOCALYPSE –
A family fighting for survival**

MAX LOTION has one obsession – to save one of the most sacred areas of Africa from certain destruction at the hands of an unscrupulous mining company . . .

DAVID LOXTON, Max's father and deadly adversary, is a zealous politician and arms manufacturer who is set on building his country to a position of new wealth and power . . .

VICTORIA, Max's sister and a successful lawyer, is involved with George Zwane, a colleague-turned-terrorist who has vowed to avenge his father's death . . .

Never has one family been so bitterly divided over a world which can only survive through brutality and terror.

'Christopher Sherlock is set to take the reins . . . as the quick talking, quick thinking adventure writer of the 90s'

Sunday Star

BRYCE COURTENAY

The Power of One

Five-year-old Peekay, no stranger to the injustice of racial hatred, learns the hard way the first secret of survival and self-preservation.

A spellbinding story of cruelty, sadness, love and faith filled with unforgettable characters, and told with great compassion and humour by an explosive new force in international writing.

'The ultimate international bestseller!'
The New York Times

'Bryce Courtenay's first novel is a triumph'
The Sunday Times

'Grippingly told'
Today

A Selected List of Thrillers available from Mandarin

While every effort is made to keep prices low, it is sometimes necessary to increase prices at short notice. Mandarin Paperbacks reserves the right to show new retail prices on covers which may differ from those previously advertised in the text or elsewhere.

The prices shown below were correct at the time of going to press.

All these books are available at your bookshop or newsagent, or can be ordered direct from the address below. Just tick the titles you want and fill in the form below.

Cash Sales Department, PO Box 5, Rushden, Northants NN10 6YX.
Fax: 0933 410321 : Phone 0933 410511.

Please send cheque, payable to 'Reed Book Services Ltd.', or postal order for purchase price quoted and allow the following for postage and packing:

£1.00 for the first book, 50p for the second; **FREE POSTAGE AND PACKING FOR THREE BOOKS OR MORE PER ORDER.**

NAME (Block letters) ....

ADDRESS ....

....

☐ I enclose my remittance for ....

☐ I wish to pay by Access/Visa Card Number ⬚⬚⬚⬚⬚⬚⬚⬚⬚⬚⬚⬚⬚⬚⬚⬚

Expiry Date ⬚⬚⬚⬚

Signature ....

Please quote our reference: MAND